Spatial Echoes

Spatial Echoes

Jayanti M Dalal

Translated by Narendra Upadhyaya

PARTRIDGE
A Penguin Random House Company

First Edition: 2008 Second Edition: 2014 Soft copy Rs.699.00 E-book Rs.169.00

To order additional copies of this book, contact
Partridge India
000 800 10062 62
orders.india@partridgepublishing.com

www.partridgepublishing.com/india

Dedication

DEDICATED
TO
PROMINENT INDUSTRIALIST,
EDUCATIONALIST, WRITER,
PHILANTHROPIST, SOCIAL WORKER
AND
EX-SHERIFF OF MUMBAI,
DR. MOHANBHAI PATEL.

I am grateful to:

Mr. Thomas Finn (Ireland)
Mr. Narendra Upadhyaya
Mr. Kumarpal Desai
Mr. Dion Fernandez
Dr. Mohanbhai Patel
Mrs. & Mr. Harish Nagrecha
Mr. Navnit Shah (U.S.A.)
Mr. Jay Gajjar (Canada)
Mr. Girish Joshi (BARC)

Foreword

PRESENT DAY SENSITIVITY AND THE SEARCH FOR WORLD PEACE

Like the nuclear explosions there are also explosions in the literary creativity of a writer which are to be found within his mind and his heart. The Gujarati novel entitled 'Shoonyavakashmaa Padgha' written by Jayanti M. Dalal named 'Spatial Echoes' is a similar explosion that must have occurred in his thought process.

It is true that quite a few novels have been written in the past in the Gujarati language depicting the social, religious and psychological ethos of the community. Nevertheless, there are very few novels that have been written in the context of and with a background of the present day sensitivity of the Gujarati community, particularly in the recent past. It is true, Jayanti M. Dalal has been a long time contributor in the sphere of Gujarati novels and Gujarati short-stories; but in this particular creative work he has successfully developed an altogether new subject for the Gujarati reader which no one else had ever dealt with earlier.

He has tried to focus on a large variety of subjects in this single creative piece, which on the one hand, touches the sensitive problem of communal amity, and on the other, the battle for world peace. The writer has also succeeded in creating a new world out of his rich imaginative power through the medium of the different characters he has incorporated in this novel. In doing so, he has created an altogether new world out of his own imagination.

In this novel, the author has covered a very wide spectrum which includes Umreth of Gujarat on one hand and Geneva of Switzerland on the other, with a view to engulf all the ideologies and approaches which he considered relevant. Through the medium of the three main characters incorporated in the novel, namely, Sanatan, Iqbal and Ivan along with the description of the modern and latest laboratories established in Malaysia, the writer has highlighted the dangers involved in terrorism on one hand, and the imperative need of world peace, on the other, with the help of the theme and the various events associated with it.

The novel describes, in detail, the efforts that were made by a scientist named Dr. Sanatan who, although he was strong, yet appeared to be a weakling who was making constant and unrelenting efforts for world peace to save it from complete annihilation. At the end the President, while appreciating his efforts said, "Well done my friend. I heartily congratulate you for spreading in all directions the rays of peace emanating from the Sun. The 'Spatial Echoes' of peace that reverberates from the vacuum will become immortal and will be heard by humanity for centuries to come".

Thus the novel presents two diagonally opposite situations the world is experiencing today. One, which focuses on the hard and tragic reality in which the stock-piling of atomic weapons is dragging the world towards a third world war and two, which shows that science is also trying to use its inventions for ensuring permanent peace on this earth. The real achievement of the author in writing this novel is that he has been able to echo the peace efforts not only more strongly than the race for armaments but he did it in a very touching way all throughout the pages of the novel.

Date : 10-10-2007   **-Dr. Kumarpal Desai**
Ahmedabad   (President, Gujarati Sahitya Parishad)

Preface

The world scenario arising out of religious fundamentalism, irreligious strife, attrition, hegemonistic ambitions and growing communalism have given rise to terrorism, which has shaken the world.

On 11th September 2001, the twin towers of the World Trade Centre, which were 1368 and 1362 feet high and 110 stories tall, considered to be the pride of America, were reduced to rubble after terrorists crashed two planes into them, in a blatant act of terrorism. That heinous act took the lives of 2823 innocent people. The Americans still have not been able to forget this terrorist act by Islamic extremists.

On 26th November 2008, there was an eighth terrorist strike against Mumbai. The attacks began on 26th November 2008 and ended on 29th November 2008 when Indian security forces, in Operation Black Tornado, regained control of all attack sites. A group of ten terrorists opened firing at Chatrapati Shivaji Terminus station and thereafter they attacked on the Oberoi Trident, the Taj Mahal Palace & Tower, the Orthodox Jewish-owned Nariman House and other various sites where about 200 innocent people were killed.

How shall we ever forget these horrible and frightening terrorist attacks? Where will the story end? The terrorists do not belong to any religion, community, country or creed. The time has come to crush these terrorists, who shed blood in the name of religion, region or country.

In the last two decades, terrorism has spread its tentacles rapidly in the Indian subcontinent. The terrorists spread chaos in the Jammu and Kashmir valleys, and have rendered lacs of Kashmiri Pandits homeless and destroyed their lives. Today the trend of terrorism has spread to most countries. If the nations, who have suffered due to such terrorism, come together as one, will they be able to uproot the evil of terrorism? Let us pray to God, that He may give the terrorists the wisdom to stop their acts of terrorism.

I have always imagined that there was life on the planet Mars millions of years ago. But the life was destroyed due to the inhospitable environmental conditions prevalent on Mars. Then after ages elapsed, life evolved on our Earth.

The problems facing us in these current times have been in my conscience for the past two decades. I have humbly tried to give some perspective to the current burning issues like Environmental Decay, Nuclear Proliferation, Hindu-Muslim unity, Terrorism and World Peace.

I would like to caution the nations who are blindly running in a race for earthly comforts, that to disregard the laws of nature, to destroy the environment or to indulge in a nuclear war will surely bring about the downfall of mankind. If all the nations of the world want to live in peace and harmony, they should address the issues of the environment, the destruction of nuclear weapons and the way to world peace. These should be the prime goals. The increasing race for nuclear arms and the ever deteriorating environment will lead the Earth to its destruction. There are strong indications that such a horrifying and scary future awaits us.

My heartfelt thanks goes to Mr.Narendra Upadhyaya in shaping the destiny of my novel. Along with this I would also take this opportunity to thank another good writer friend, Ashit Hyderabadi, for his useful suggestions after reviewing this novel.

I sincerely thankful to Ms. Antoniet Saints & Ms. Ann Minoza of Partridge, U.S.A. for publishing my novel. The characters in this novel, Sanatan, Radha, Iqbal, Karim Abdullah, Aziz Maqbool, William, Ivan and Dr. Homi Bhabha, along with the other characters have emotionally tested me.

To date all these characters have played out their lives in my mind. Today they are in front of you. If you can welcome these characters into your hearts, and in doing so, do not miss the opportunity to give a loving salute to those soldiers and scientists who are striving for world peace.

I would like to request you to give me your feedback on how you liked this novel; indeed, I would be grateful if you did so.

JAYANTI M. DALAL
E-mail: jmdalal@rediffmail.com
Website: www.jayantimdalal.com

Chapter 1

Vidyacharan Sharma was taking a science class. He cast a serious look over the students and asked, "Can anyone tell me when and how life evolved on the planet Earth?"

Adjusting his spectacles, Vidyacharan gravely stared at the students. A hush fell over the class. For a long time when nobody replied, he thought of replying to his own question. At that moment a student sitting on the second bench raised his right hand and stood up.

"I believe that life evolved on the earth many thousands of years ago." Sanatan said.

"What about my other part of the question?"

Before Sanatan could reply, another student eagerly said, "May I reply, Sir?" It was Iqbal. After a pause, he said, "Life evolved out of water on this planet, but I am not sure how that happened."

Vidyacharan said, "Only two clever students have tried to answer such a serious question. Let me congratulate them on their attempts! Now, I will reply to my own question."

"In order to understand the evolvement of water, let us consider how the Earth came into existence. Millions of years ago, this planet was a blazing ball of fire. Liquids and gaseous substances were burning on its surface. With the passage of time, the fireball cooled down. A cloud of steam surrounded the Earth, which eventually descended on the Earth in the form of torrential rains. The rains further cooled the Earth. On the surface of the Earth, which was like a boiling pot, the liquids began to cool down slowly and began taking solid shape in the form of rocks, mountains and craters. When the planet Earth was flooded with water, rivers, streams, and oceans came into existence."

Having spoken so much, Vidyacharan paused for a moment. Sanatan and Iqbal were listening to their teacher with rapt attention. All the other students, too, were listening to their teacher with great interest. The teacher, Vidyacharan continued the lecture, "Millions of years elapsed after the creation of the Earth. With the passage of time, heat conducive to the birth of living elements became possible. Initially, algae grew in water and that was followed by the growth of more and more vegetation. Step by step, different kinds of creatures and animals came into existence. Thus, we can say, without doubt, that life evolved out of water. Does anyone know about the quantum of water on the Earth? Three quarters of the Earth is submerged under the waters of the oceans, whereas, only a quarter of the Earth is *terra firma*! Gradually, the human race came into existence. Archaeologists have revealed that man lived in caves around twenty thousand years ago."

Before Vidyacharan could continue any further, the school-bell rang announcing the closing time of the school. Still, summing up his lecture, he hurriedly said, "Today, we have learnt in brief about the creation of the Earth and life. Tomorrow, we shall learn more about the most essential thing necessary for the existence of living beings, water. Mull over what I taught you today, and tomorrow you may ask me any questions cropping up in your minds."

As soon as Vidyacharan Sharma left the class, the students began murmuring. Slowly, one by one, students came out of the class, carrying their school bags.

"Hey, Sanatan, what are you thinking about?" Iqbal asked, patting Sanatan on the back.

"Well, I was thinking, how wonderful this subject of science is. Isn't it great! And, how wonderfully and lucidly our teacher explains the secrets of this universe to us!"

"In fact, I also was thinking just that." Iqbal said, supporting Sanatan's viewpoint.

Although both of them were walking towards their homes, innumerable thoughts were chasing each other in their minds. Usually, when they walked towards their homes, they talked about many things other than their studies. But today, listening about the Earth and the creation of life, their minds were busy thinking. They walked in silence. As they reached a crossing of the lane a cyclist accidentally bumped into Iqbal. Saving himself from falling off, the cyclist rebuked, "Hey, why don't you guys watch, where you are walking?"

"I am sorry!" muttered Iqbal.

The collision with the cyclist brought them out of their reverie. Then Iqbal turned into the lane to his home and Sanatan continued walking straight towards his home located in *Vada Bazar*.

"So you have arrived, son!" Sanatan's mother, Kusum said as she cleaned wheat. "Go and freshen up. Meanwhile, I will take this wheat to the mill for grinding."

Placing his schoolbag on a nearby barrel Sanatan entered the bathroom to wash his hands and feet. He washed his hands and feet and then his face. Wiping his hands and feet dry, he went up to his room on the first floor and sat on a swing. As he was nudging his right foot to accelerate the pace, his mind was also rocking with thoughts.

After a while he heard his mother calling out to him. For a moment, he didn't react. At last, Kusum came up and saw Sanatan was lost in deep thought.

"Don't you want to eat something?" Kusum asked.

"Oh no, Mom."

Kusum was perplexed.

"How strange! Everyday when you return from school you demand something to eat. What's happened to you today? What are you thinking of? Do you know I've been calling you for so long?'

Sanatan smiled at her, stopped swinging and stepped on to the staircase.

"Today our teacher talked about some wonders of science." He said.

"I see! What did he say?"

"He said many interesting things about how life evolved on this Earth."

"Well . . . well . . . ! Think of what your teacher taught you some other time. Come down now. I've baked your favourite cookies."

Popping a cookie in his mouth Sanatan asked, "When will papa return, Mom?"

"You know, your father comes home at seven in the evening after closing his shop. Don't you want to go out with your friends today?"

"No Mom; I don't feel like going anywhere today."

"Well then, better you do not go. Read something peacefully at home."

"Throughout the day I have studied in school, and now you are asking me to read again!"

"Did you not say that you don't feel like going out? That's why I asked you to read and that does not mean your text books. Anyway, you are a clever student! If you don't want to read your study books, read anything."

"Mom, today a great many thoughts are surging through my mind. Many questions are cropping up, which only Papa can answer. That's why I asked when he will come."

"You know well that a lot of customers flock to the shop during evening time! That's why your Papa may get home late. Do whatever you like. Let me get on with cooking."

Sanatan remained lost in thought for sometime. Then having changed his clothes Sanatan called out to his mother.

"Mom, I am going to Iqbal's house."

"All right son, but, if uncle Yakub is busy reading his medical books or attending to his patients, don't disturb him."

"Oh, no." Sanatan said and went out of the house. "Come in son . . ." Aunt Saira welcomed Sanatan.

"What's Iqbal doing, aunty?"

"Iqbal has gone to get some milk from the dairy." Saira replied.

"Where is Yakub chacha?"

"He must be busy with his medicines and his patients."

"Well, if Iqbal isn't home, I will go." Sanatan said.

"Oh, you have just come and you talk of leaving? Iqbal should be coming anytime now. How are you faring at your studies?"

"Quite well . . ."

"Both of you are not only clever at studies, but you both are wise and good natured. I will pray Allah to grace you both with all sorts of happiness and success in life."

As they were talking, Iqbal came in.

"Hey pal, what stories have you been telling to my Mom?"

"Why do you want to know what was I talking to her about? It's between us." Sanatan chuckled when uncle Yakub came into the room looking for something.

He heard Sanatan's last words. He said, "My dear Sanatan, if Iqbal is the right eye of your aunt, you are her left eye. Looking at your friendship I pray Allah to strengthen your friendship that it should never break."

"Well Chacha! Just bless us!"

While they were talking Saira went to the kitchen and returned with a plate of biscuits, savories and potato wafers. Picking up some Sanatan asked Yakub, "Chacha, we all worship God. Has God created human beings?"

For a moment Yakub stared at Sanatan; after a while he began to speak in a slow mild tone.

"Dear son, after thinking about a lot of things, a man's mind cannot transcend beyond a limit. The religious scriptures say that God created this world."

"If that's true, what is the origin of the human race?" Iqbal, sitting near his friend, quizzed.

"Well, according to Charles Darwin's viewpoint, after the Earth was formed, vegetation came into existence for the first time in the form of algae. The plants and trees that you see have life within them. The great Indian scientist, Jagdishchandra Bose, has proved this fact. After the growth of vegetation, minute creatures, and later apes among other animals, evolved. Gradually over a period of many thousands of years modern man evolved from apes. They satiated their hunger by killing other animals and creatures. Then Man gradually urbanized. He left the caves, became civilised and civilizations followed. This is the way human evolution took place."

Suddenly Yakub said, "*Lahaul-bila-Qoowat*! I forgot that a patient was waiting for me in the clinic."

Leaving everybody, uncle Yakub rushed to his clinic.

"Listening to your uncle, I too forgot, I had kept milk boiling on the stove."

Saira said rushing towards the kitchen, "Oh, it's spilling!" she exclaimed.

Taking down the vessel from the stove Saira began to cook. Iqbal laughed lightly. "So this is the day of science for us, eh!" "Hmmm . . . You are right." Sanatan remarked, "The story of this universe is certainly wonderful. And what can I say about the seven wonders of this world!"

"Very true, Sanatan! Can I tell you something; I have seen the Taj Mahal—one of the seven wonders. When we visited Agra, my *Abbajan* took me to see the wonder that is the Taj Mahal."

"*Yaar*, Iqbal, the world of science seems quite wonderful. When I saw the pictures of the pyramids of Cairo and the Eiffel Tower of Paris, I felt that man has made great progress."

"That's correct; the invention of trains and airplanes bring people and other countries so much closer!"

"Yes; our ancestors wouldn't have thought that, through scientific inventions, man would be able to create so many things for comfort and happiness. Yes, our town doesn't have electricity but the city folks enjoy the comfort of electricity." Saying this Sanatan laughed aloud.

Sanatan looked at the wall clock. As it was turning dark, he couldn't see clearly. He picked up a lamp and saw by its light that it was seven o'clock.

He exclaimed, "Oh! So much time has passed!"

Peering out of the window he said, "I must go now."

"Supper is ready. Why don't you and Iqbal have it together?" Saira asked, coming out of the kitchen.

"Oh no, aunty! Not today. My mom must be waiting for me. It's already turning cold. I should go now."

After having said that, Sanatan left. When he reached home, his father Kanaiyalal had already arrived. Seeing Sanatan, "Well, you have come home. What was Yakub doing?"

"He was busy, as usual, in his clinic."

"Yakub is, in fact, an angel. And his wife Saira is certainly a gentle and kind lady."

"Papa, for how long have you been a friend of Yakub chacha?" "Son, our friendship is of more than twenty-five years standing!"

"He had many patients today." Sanatan said.

"It is natural. He is an accomplished doctor. Merely by feeling the pulse, he can diagnose the disease of a sick person. Precisely for this reason he is popular in Umreth as *Unani Hakim*."

"Papa, what is the meaning of *Unani*?"

"Well, it is a branch of medical science which originated in ancient Greece. Yakub has studied the *Unani* system of medicine in Ahmedabad. Many people, besides the Muslims, prefer *Unani* treatment to *Ayurvedic* or Allopathic treatment."

Kanaiyalal paused for a while, then, suddenly, remembering something once again resumed. "Besides being a pious Muslim, Yakub is an angel. What I like about Yakub is, whenever somebody needs his services, even at odd times, he doesn't refuse and reaches the patient's place in no time. I have never seen an able doctor like him who can diagnose an illness just by examining a patient's pulse."

"If you are finished talking, come down for dinner." Kusum called out from the kitchen.

"Both the son and the father settled down for dinner and, during the course of the meal, Kanaiyalal spoke about many things, which enlightened the ever-curious Sanatan.

———————◈———————

Chapter 2

In the morning, when Sanatan and Iqbal set out for school, the clock tower struck ten. Both friends walked briskly towards their school. Crossing over Vhorwad, they reached the *Muleshwar Mahadev* temple. Their school was near the railway station. When they reached Jubilee School, the children had gathered in the school compound for mass prayers. The duo joined the other students for prayers. After the prayers were over, the students left for their respective classes. The routine of the school rolled on with the teachers, teaching their subjects hour after hour. As Vidyacharan Sharma entered the class at four in the afternoon, Sanatan and Iqbal were elated. Sanatan and Iqbal enjoyed learning Mathematics and science; but were rather average to learning Geography and History. These two subjects were drudgery for them. Sharma sir resumed his lecture, which he had left incomplete the previous day.

"Yesterday, I had spoken to you about water having great significance in the evolvement of the life on this planet. Now, let's move on. Water has three states—solid, liquid and gaseous. In solid sate it is ice, as a liquid it is called water and in the gaseous state it is steam. Due to various combinations of molecules, water is available in three different states. Because of this, it changes into three different forms dynamically. This means, despite change in its physical properties, its basic formulation never changes. It means that water, ice and steam—are one and the same. Their names are different. When ice melts we get water. When we heat water it turns into steam. When steam is cooled, it again turns into water and when water is frozen it turns into ice. Moreover, when water is boiled, distance between two atoms increases. Gradually, all these atoms move about freely in the empty space and these moving atoms collide with each other. We cannot see this process with our eyes . . ."

Having spoken so much, Vidyacharan paused for while. Like a maestro on the stage, he had a unique way of teaching difficult science lessons in a very lucid manner. Looking at his students he resumed speaking.

"The scientists of the entire world have been conducting various experiments to understand the composition of water, but nobody except Nature knows its specific secret. When we shall acquire complete scientific data, its significance will increase manifold, which is a concrete fact. Similar to sunlight, water too is a natural source of energy. Extensive scientific research work is in progress to find ways to harness these natural sources of energies." Vidyacharan had a knack of straying from the main subject to reduce the boredom and return to the main subject in an effortless manner.

"When we freeze water, the distance between two atoms decreases and even their dynamism gets reduced. As water is cooled down further, atoms come so close that ultimately water takes the form of ice. All this seems difficult to understand; correct?" he interjected with sparkling eyes, smiling mockingly behind his glasses.

Iqbal stood up and asked, "Sir, these days the issue of heavy water is being discussed in the newspapers; what is it about? How is heavy water separated from the normal water?

"Today, the scientists are striving to fathom those secrets. During the Second World War II, heavy water was produced in a factory in Norway, which was used to manufacture atom bombs. The scientists of the world are doing research on water for developing atomic energy. How far they will succeed, the future can only reveal."

"Sir, were the Hydrogen bombs, which were dropped on Nagasaki and Hiroshima two years ago in 1945, also made using heavy water?" Sanatan asked anxiously.

"No doubt about it" Sharma sir said.

"You must all be aware that the after-effects of an atom bomb explosion were quite severe. Many people lost their lives. Thousands of houses were turned into ruins. Thousands of people were maimed. A large number of people suffered from blood—cancer due to the adverse effect of radiation. For many years to come, the Japanese will not only suffer various grave ailments but newer diseases of finer strains will be generated."

"Sir, can the scientific invention of atomic energy be put to use for the benefit of mankind?" Iqbal quickly asked.

"Of course it can be. As a matter of fact, such inventions should be accelerated for the benefit of mankind." Sharma sir paused, and smiling suggestively said, "When the universe was created, the Supreme Divinity endowed every human being with two kinds of inherent qualities—Divine and Evil! The good people always think of ways to spread peace and happiness in the world. But, on the other hand, the wicked remain engrossed in usurping other's properties through vengefulness and oppression. They have no repentance even if thousands are annihilated in the achievement of their evil aspirations." The voice of Sharma sir grew heavy. He wiped his face with the palm of his right hand. He was sweating profusely, perhaps out of suppressed anger.

"We read daily in the newspapers, of how people in Japan are spending their days in severe pain and anguish! When will the diseases, lameness, and the days and nights of heartrending cries subside?" Sharma sir spoke in a husky voice as if sounding a prophecy, "The day is not too far off when the end of this Earth will come because of the dangerous intentions of wicked minds. However, the real need is to develop science for the benefit of mankind, to ensure lasting peace and not plan for mass destruction.

"Sir, is it possible that the atomic invention could be put to peaceful means?"

"Certainly! A sharp knife could be used to cut vegetables, and the same knife could be used to stab someone to death. Statesmen and scientists must devise a mechanism for world peace, and not for the destruction of the universe."

As Sharma sir concluded his sentence, the school bell rang as if it was a sign of approval of a universal hope. He picked up his books and left the class. The school was over for the day and the children rushed out of the school compound towards their homes.

On his way home, Sanatan placed his arm around Iqbal's shoulders. They always walked that way. Suddenly Sanatan stopped and spoke with disgust, "These British rulers are real Barbarians!"

Iqbal was taken aback at this sudden outburst. He asked, "What is biting you, Sanatan?"

Sanatan said, "Remember what Sharma sir just said?"

He fell silent. Then replying to his own question, Sanatan continued,

"There are two kinds of people in this world—good and bad. The British are bad. Against their oppression, the Mahatma Gandhi has started his peaceful satyagrah which means the soul force of truth against brutal violence. It is high time that the British should be compelled to quit India."

"You are right, Sanatan. But, the other day, my father was saying that, Nehru, Jinnah, Sardar Patel, the Viceroy and Gandhi were discussing the division of our country on the basis of religion. My father was deeply shocked. He was saying that we were born, raised and have spent our entire lives here, so how could we think of going to Pakistan just because we are Muslims? Don't you think our leaders in Delhi are committing grave injustice to the people of India?"

"Perhaps, there is truth in what uncle Yakub said. The other day, when I was at my father's shop, he was telling a customer that the division of the nation on the basis of religion could spell tragedy for the people. He was saying that, if Jinnah was demanding a separate nation for the Muslims, and the Muslims find it unjustified, why don't they object to his suggestion with one voice?"

"Maybe, my father does not approve of the idea of carving out a separate country for the Muslims. Just think, despite our different communities, religions, customs we have been living peacefully and happily like good brethren since the time of our ancestors."

"I feel the way the entire Indian populace is fighting against the British regime with fervour, sense of unity and a deep sense of patriotism, without bringing in religious or class discrimination is praiseworthy."

"Certainly, but I fear that a seriously dangerous situation is developing in our country. Our neighbour Ambalal was saying that, separate nations for Hindus and Muslims would be very desirable. This way peace for the people of both communities could be guaranteed".

"But, haven't the Muslims and Hindus fought battles in the past and yet lived together? Then, why should India be partitioned?" Iqbal's voice was strained.

"Don't you think this is a political ploy by the British to avoid granting independence to India?" Doubt crept into Sanatan's voice.

"I have no doubt that independence would certainly be achieved anyhow. The Satyagrah Movement initiated by Mahatma Gandhi seems quite effective. My *Abbajan* was telling that, in the last five years since 1942, despite the severely oppressive and tyrannical British regime, the chivalrous spirit of the Indians has not been dented.

"If our country becomes partitioned, will your family and you go to Pakistan?" Sanatan asked with a quivering heart. The fear of losing his friend was reflected in his question.

"Do you remember uncle Rahim, who came from Lahore last year? Many times he has tried to convince *Abbajan* to leave Umreth once and for all and go settle in Lahore. But *Abbajan* had told him that, until I pass my matriculation examination, we shall not leave Umreth. You are aware that my sister Zubeida lives with uncle Rahim and is studying in Lahore for the past ten years".

"Your family has a house in Lahore, correct?"

"Yes, Sanatan, we have a large family mansion in Lahore. Once a year my *Abbajan* visits Lahore, because our whole family and all our relatives live there."

"Iqbal, don't you think there is a big difference between villages and big cities?"

"Of course, life is entirely different in big cities like Lahore". "I shudder to think that, by the year-end after passing our matriculation we shall be separated. My Papa is anxious to send me to Bombay. Last year, my maternal uncle Jitendraprasad came to our home. Since I am a good student he had stressed the need of my studying at Bombay. I also have two other uncles living in Bombay."

"This means, from the next academic year onwards, you will go to Bombay to study?"

"What else can I do, Iqbal? Our town doesn't have a college and that's why we'll have to go to a big city for higher studies".

"Sanatan, our childhood has been spent in this town. We grew up together. That's why I wish to study further in your company. But my uncle living in Lahore insists that I should go to Lahore and study there. In his last letter he wrote that after the marriage of his two daughters, he feels lonely. He doesn't have a son. If I go, his loneliness will vanish and he will get my support. Even *Ammijan*, too, desires that I study further at Lahore. Under such circumstances, I feel that I may have no choice but agree". Iqbal said with dejection.

The days were flying fast. The days of the examinations were nearing. Because of this, Sanatan remained engrossed in his studies as he was aiming to score the highest number of marks possible.

That evening, when the school closed for the day, the students filed out of the school. When Sanatan and his friends reached the temple of *Muleshwar Mahadev* he saw that a juggler was performing some magical tricks. He was wearing a colourful loincloth and a cap on his head. He was calling the spectators, playing a tambourine, to watch the monkeys' games. Sanatan also joined the crowd.

Two monkeys were dancing and jumping in response to the gestures of the juggler. One of the two monkeys removed his cap and holding it in his two hands, went around begging the people standing in a semicircle to throw some coins in the cap.

After the monkeys' tricks ended, the magician brought out a large cane basket with a lid on it. He placed the basket on a makeshift platform erected on the road. A small girl was accompanying him.

Playing the tambourine he bellowed simultaneously, "Where are you now?"

"On the ground," the little girl replied shrilly.

"Climb up on the platform and sit in the basket", ordered the juggler.

Quickly the girl climbed up on the platform and sat in the basket.

The juggler closed the lid on the basket with the girl inside.

Again he shouted, "Where are you now?"

"In the basket," the shrill voice answered back, again.

"Tell me the truth; where are you now—are you on the ground or in the sky?"

This time the shrill voice replied, "In the sky".

Heavy silence spread among the spectators. The juggler picked up another identical cane basket. He placed it on the ground and closed its lid. Then, he picked up a Been (a musical instrument) and began playing it by blowing into it. After playing the Been for some time he put it away and picked up the tambourine to play.

After a while he shouted, "Hey, girl, where are you now?" "In the sky . . . ," the shrill voice replied.

A short time later, when the juggler opened the lid of the second basket near him, the girl emerged from it. She folded her hands greeting the spectators. All around, the people clapped happily and praised the juggler.

During this time the monkeys went around the spectators collecting money.

Again the juggler called out, "Look here, my benefactors! Now I am going to show you a thrilling act. It's the final item of my show. So, don't move."

Continually playing the tambourine, he again picked up a large cane basket and showed it to the people. He jumped into the basket to show that it was empty. He placed the basket up on the platform. Again, he ordered the girl to sit in the basket. Following his order the girl climbed up on the platform and sat in the basket.

The juggler called out, "Hey girl, where are you now?"

"In the air . . ."

"Want to come on the ground?"

"Yes . . . no . . . no . . . yes . . ."

For a while he continued playing the tambourine and chanted a Mantra loudly. He showed the empty cane basket placed alongside him. Both the monkeys clapped vigorously.

Iqbal, Sanatan, Kisan, Bansi and their other friends were enjoying watching the juggler's show.

After some time the juggler called out, "Hey girl, come back on the ground and sit in this basket."

"No, I am afraid." The shrill voice replied from the basket placed on the makeshift platform.

"Are you getting down or not? Shall I have to force you to come down?" asked the juggler in mock anger.

"Ok . . . I am coming."

A few more moments elapsed. The spectators were watching with bated breath. Meanwhile, the juggler pulled out a large dagger and said,

"The girl has come back into the basket."

He gingerly opened the lid and pushed his hand holding the dagger inside the basket. As he pulled his hand out, the girl also emerged with him. She stood up; but the dagger was stuck into her neck and she was bleeding profusely. Although that was the juggler's trick, the spectators felt that the girl was really bleeding. He took the girl around giving them a closer look. The spectators showered the juggler with money.

When Sanatan came home, he was not able to forget the image of that small bleeding girl with a dagger pierced through her neck.

When he sat down for dinner he didn't feel like eating. Somehow he forced a couple of morsels down his throat and then gave up.

❧

Chapter 3

The examinations were nearing. Sanatan and Iqbal were making herculean efforts to score the highest number of marks possible in the examination. It was decided that Sanatan was to go to Ahmedabad for the exam because Bansi's elder brother was staying at Ahmedabad. Bansi had insisted on taking Sanatan along to Ahmedabad with him. This way, proper arrangements of boarding and lodging were made for Sanatan at Ahmedabad. After the examinations were completed, Sanatan and Bansi returned to Umreth. Sanatan had done well in his exams, and so, everyone in the family was very happy.

On the following evening, some friends living in the locality and a few school mates decided to congregate at *Bhadrakali Vav* (*Vav* is a large step-well with steps leading to its water level). At around three in the afternoon, Sanatan reached Iqbal's home. They talked a lot about how they had fared in their examinations and then both of them walked to Bhadrakali Vav. Their other friends Bansi, Kanu, Kishan, Fakhruddin, Bipin, Dhimant and Rehman had already arrived.

It is generally believed that *Bhadrakali Vav* was built by the benevolent king, Siddharaj Jaising at the behest of his mother Minaldevi in 1097 A.D. This seven floor step-well is an excellent example of ancient architecture. Initially, Minaldevi had <u>*Malav*</u> Lake built in Umreth. From a historical viewpoint Malav Lake and *Bhadrakali Vav* hold great significance. Today, *Bhadrakali Vav* has fallen into ruins. Despite that, water jets could still be seen springing up from its depths.

When Sanatan and Iqbal reached the spot, Kishan was chopping raw mangoes, and Bansi was busy chopping onions.

Bipin said, "I went with a couple of friends to Dakor and got fresh new mangoes from the tree by rielting them with stones."

It was not as if the boys didn't get mangoes to eat at their homes. In fact, there were mounds of mangoes at their homes; but felling mangoes from the trees and eating them fresh, was a unique fun experience altogether. The boys used to hoodwink the orchard guards and enter the orchard. Whenever the guards would see the miscreants, they would give chase. Bipin and his companions had thus collected the mangoes through mischief and an element of danger for if caught they would be thrashed.

"Well done, Bipin!" Sanatan chuckled as the others joined in laughing aloud.

After a short while when the salad of onions and green mangoes was ready, the boys sat down in a circle. They discussed many topics. Also, they relished the snack along with their talks.

The boys were very happy. For a long time they chatted noisily about their school, other students and the teachers.

When there was a little lull in the conversation, Bansi said with a tinge of sadness in his voice, "In a few days many of us will leave this town and go to cities for higher studies."

Then rubbing his palms Bipin got up and said, "Oh yes friends, after that, we shall have to spend the rest of our lives cherishing sweet memories of our childhood days. It's my suggestion that, till then, we all should meet at least once every week. What do you say, Iqbal?

Everybody agreed in chorus and welcomed Bipin's suggestion.

"Will you be going to Lahore, Iqbal Miyan, for further studies? Hope you won't forget us *yaar*?" Dhimant said.

"I have developed so much affection for this place that I don't feel like going to Lahore. It is easy to forget that we have been raised from the soil of this town?" Iqbal's voice turned heavy with emotion.

"I think that Sanatan and Iqbal will have a tough competition as to who secures the highest number of marks in the examination." Rehman said changing the subject.

"I bet Sanatan will top the class," said Fakhruddin clapping. "No, no, I think Iqbal will make it to the top this year."

Dhimant and Kanu echoed their opinion loudly.

"Now . . . , now . . . don't quarrel on that. Whether Iqbal gets to the top or anybody else for that matter; we shall remain friends" Sanatan said stopping them both.

"It is immaterial who gets to the top. What is necessary is we should all prove to be excellent students and bring honor to our school and town." Iqbal voiced his support for Sanatan.

"Why not, Iqbal . . . ! More than our town, we should bring pride to our country."

All the friends happily cheered the duo.

As the daylight waned, the friends, climbed up the steps of the step-well. The sun had already set. The lake waters were shimmering in the fading light. When

Sanatan reached his house, Shammi, the barber was climbing up a pole to light a street lamp.

It was the early morning of 6th June 1947.

The result of the Matriculation examination was announced. Sanatan's father, Kanaiyalal came rushing home with a newspaper. As soon as he entered, he shouted happily, "Kusum . . . ! Where are you? Listen; our Sanatan has passed with the highest marks"

"Really . . . ! What great news you have brought!"

Sanatan came rushing down from his room upstairs. Tears of happiness and parental pride were rolling down the eyes of his parents. He took the newspaper from Kanaiyalal. He peered down at the fine print of the newspaper and jumped in ecstasy. He had stood at first place in the merit list. Iqbal had stood at second place.

Kusum rushed into the kitchen and returned with a box of sweets.

"I knew that Sanatan would pass with flying colors. I had already brought the sweets last evening." She found it hard to hold back her joy.

"Here, eat this, my son. You have made your parents proud today." Kanaiyalal put a piece of a sweet into Sanatan's mouth.

Sanatan touched their feet with reverence, joy and filial love.

He said, "I must go and congratulate Iqbal."

"Sure, go. And also, convey our congratulations and blessings to Iqbal."

Sanatan rushed out eagerly to meet his best friend. Walking fast he reached Iqbal's house. Iqbal's home had a festive look. Everybody greeted him joyously. Iqbal met him at the doorstep. He embraced him and took him inside the house. Iqbal and Sanatan gave each other sweets. Iqbal's father, Yakub, suggested that both should go to their teacher and seek his blessings.

"Yes *Chacha*, we will go soon."

"Now that you have passed your Matriculation, when are you planning to go to Bombay to seek admission to a college?" Yakub asked.

"Maybe my father and I will go to Bombay in a day or two."

"Where will you stay in Bombay? You have many relatives over there."

"We haven't given it much thought as yet. But, I would prefer to study by staying in a hostel. What about Iqbal? Why don't you allow him to come to Bombay with me for the continuation of our studies?"

"I have no problem with that. But my brother, Rahim, has written from Lahore that there are excellent colleges there. He has been insisting that Iqbal go to Lahore for further studies."

For a while nobody said anything. Then Yakub said, "Why don't you go to meet your teachers? Go and offer them sweets and take their blessings."

Iqbal and Sanatan left the house with packets of sweets tucked under their arms. They met their teacher Vidyacharan Sharma and took his blessings. Later they met the other teachers. After about an hour Sanatan returned home. Kanaiyalal said, "I think that we should leave within a day or two for Bombay. Since you have secured a place in the merit list, we shall have no difficulty in gaining admission to a good college."

"Yes Papa, our teacher was recommending Ramnarayan Ruia College at Matunga. Besides the college has a hostel at Sion-Koliwada."

"That would be the right choice. Alright, let us leave tomorrow."

On the next day, Sanatan and Kanaiyalal set out for Bombay. Sanatan easily secured admission in Ruia College. Congratulating him, the principal said, "Arrangements for your stay in the hostel will be made when the College re-opens in a month's time."

During the next four days, they visited many of their relatives. Sanatan's paternal uncles and also his maternal uncle insisted that Sanatan stay with them. But Kanaiyalal politely declined their offer as Sanatan's studies demanded scholarly surroundings.

Sanatan and Kanaiyalal returned to Umreth after a week. When they reached home it was already dusk. Hurricane lamps were lit in all the rooms of the house. Sanatan's mother was waiting for them. The three of them talked for a long time.

On the following evening, Sanatan returned home after meeting his friends. His mother was lighting the hearth to cook meals for the dinner. He went upstairs to his room and sat on a swing. It was time for his father's arrival. Suddenly he heard someone talking down below. He went up to the railings to see and heard his mother's words,

"Today Lakshmi had come. We chatted a lot. Your friend Vasudev and Lakshmi like our son, Sanatan. They want their daughter Radha to get married to Sanatan. They want us to give our decision."

"Oh really! Lakshmi came! They are in town for some time now to spend the summer vacation. So, what are you saying? They liked Sanatan?" said Kanaiyalal.

"They want to betroth their daughter Radha to our Sanatan. Lakshmi wanted to know if we approve of this proposal."

"Where is the question of disapproval? Vasudev is my intimate friend. But we should first ask Sanatan. Kusum, we should find out the boy's wish. It is his life."

"To be frank, I like Radha very much. Our Sanatan won't refuse. Although, the girl is from Bombay, she is wise and matured and also good looking."

"Well, well, but before you let your imagination run wild, just ask your son. Though he is an obedient son, it will nevertheless be better to let the boy and girl meet."

Listening to his parents, Sanatan smiled inwardly and returned to his room upstairs. After some time Kusum called Sanatan to come down for dinner. Sanatan came and while eating Kusum broached the marriage proposal.

"Sanatan, what do you think of Radha, uncle Vasudev's daughter? Her parents want you to get married to her at the earliest possible time."

"Oh! Mom! Why so much hurry? You know well that I propose to study further at the college in Bombay. I don't want to get married until I complete my studies."

"But, uncle Vasudev and aunty Lakshmi trust us and have faith in you. She insists that you get engaged to Radha and your marriage could be solemnized after your graduation."

"But what's wrong in thinking about the whole affair after I complete my graduation?"

"Well, your viewpoint is not wrong. But they wish that, if their daughter is engaged then both of them could heave a sigh of relief. Lakshmi even said that, they were prepared to wait for marriage until we were ready."

"But, I have not attained a marriageable age yet."

"That's what you think. When I was your age, you were born," Kusum laughed.

"Have you spoken to Papa about all this?"

"I am speaking to you only after discussing this with him."

"Sunday is just two days away. Papa will be at home. Then we'll discuss it peacefully."

"What should I tell Lakshmi?"

"Tell her we'll reply on Monday. What's the problem in waiting for two more days?"

"Son, I only wanted to point out that it is hard to find a good girl like Radha. Moreover, you are well aware of how noble her family is! Besides, they are all good people. Thus, we should take hold of such a good opportunity. When opportunity knocks, it is wise to open the door!" With that, Kusum left her son. There was not much point in discussing the issue any longer.

Then two mornings later, Kanaiyalal said, "Look, Sanatan, after you two meet formally, say 'Yes' you will like Radha but if you say 'No', it will damage our reputation."

"Papa, I will always agree with the girl that you might choose as my wife. What parents wouldn't wish the best for their children? Do whatever you think is best for me."

"I have deep faith in you, my son. I am confident that you will never do anything that might tarnish our name. In accordance with our custom, the parents decide in matters of marriage; but I wish that you should talk to Radha."

"Well, but I don't think that is necessary."

"Oh! But, even uncle Vasudev is of the opinion that, before you choose Radha as your wife, you should first talk to her. That is informal."

"Alright, whatever you say."

Kanaiyalal was very happy to see that Sanatan agreed with him. Sanatan was keen on his studies. Sitting on the swing in his room he used to read books on various subjects of interest. He would pick up anything to read if it was related to science.

The next day uncle Vasudev, aunty Lakshmi and their daughter, Radha came to Kanaiyalal's house. Leaving the shop before his manager came, Kanaiyalal went home early. When Kusum went upstairs, Sanatan was reading a book, seated in his swing.

"I am sending Radha up to you. Put your book aside for a while. When she comes here, talk to her and try to understand each other so that you can live together happily." With these words of advice she went downstairs.

After a while Radha tiptoed to Sanatan's room. Sanatan smiled and offered her a seat on the swing.

For a while neither uttered a word. At last Sanatan broke the silence.

"Look, if you remain silent in this manner, we won't be able to decide anything."

"Yes, I know. Ask me whatever you would like," Radha said, adjusting her sari.

"But if you continue to feel shy, I won't be able to talk to you. Please, look at me."

Shyly but mustering courage Radha glanced at him. She lowered her eyes and instantaneously a smile lit up her face.

Looking at Radha, Sanatan said, "I like you very much. Do you also approve of me? Look, I am meeting you for the first time but you don't have to feel shy. We both are faced with the most important decision of our lives. That has brought us together today."

"What do you want to know about me?"

"You have been living in Bombay and have studied there.

I am a person from this small town. Would you like to spend your life with me?"

"Yes . . . why not?" Radha said, looking into Sanatan's eyes.

"There is something else."

"What's that . . . ?"

"Well, it's nothing serious." Sanatan smiled and added, "I intend to continue my studies after graduation, even if we get married. I hope you won't disapprove of it."

"I have no objection to your further studies. Why should I create any obstacle to your studies? Honestly, I won't bother you," Radha's smile was bewitching.

Although, Radha was very young, her thinking seemed mature. At dinnertime, Sanatan declared his decision and agreed to the betrothal.

The betrothal ceremony was scheduled in seven days. The ceremony went quite happily.

A day before Vasudev and his family were due to leave for Bombay, Kanaiyalal invited them over for lunch.

Vasudev's son, Shalin who was taking care of the business at Bombay, arrived with his wife Madhavi. Pulin, the second son of Vasudev, who was studying in the second year of college, had already come to Umreth.

Radha was the youngest child of Vasudev. She was studying in sixth standard and had a very friendly and cheerful disposition.

It was Lakshmi, who had broached the idea of getting her daughter married to Sanatan while they were at Bombay. As Radha was betrothed to Sanatan, she was very happy today. It was like her dream come true. After lunch, members of both the families were seated. Vasudev and Kanaiyalal were talking.

From now on, Sanatan also, is our son. When he comes to Bombay we will take care of him. You don't have to worry about his comfort."

"Well, initially he will stay with his maternal uncle. But later he will move to a hostel and study."

"Why a hostel, Kanu? You know well that I have a four-bedroom apartment. I'll allot a separate room to him."

"Sorry to interrupt you, Papa; but I would prefer to stay at the hostel and study. And I, certainly won't study staying at uncle Vasudev's apartment," Sanatan said.

Vasudev and Kanaiyalal were happy with Sanatan's mature thinking.

Chapter 4

At the end of June, Sanatan prepared to leave for Bombay. His parents, his other friends and Iqbal had come to the railway station to bid farewell to Sanatan. Iqbal went all the way to Anand to bid him farewell. Next morning, Sanatan reached Bombay at his maternal uncle Jitendraprasad's residence. His college was scheduled to open in the first week of July. But the colleges in Ahmedabad were to open in the month of August.

Iqbal's father had been thinking of sending his son to either Lahore or to Ahmedabad for further studies. He had been waiting for a letter from his brother in Lahore. Bansi, Fakhruddin, Bipin and Sanatan's other friends decided to pursue their studies in different colleges of Ahmedabad.

Jitendraprasad asked his nephew, "Why did you decide come to the Ruia College?"

"It's because this college has an excellent reputation for science. Moreover, from the first term itself I will have the facility of staying in the hostel."

Suddenly, Jitendraprasad was reminded of his days in college. Having acquired higher education while living in Bombay, Jitendraprasad had become a Civil Engineer. He had suffered great hardships and troubles as a student. Despite being financially poor, he did not lose courage nor was he disappointed. He used to stay at a boarding house while studying and used to make some money by giving tuitions. Eight years previously he had married Madhuri. After his marriage he got a job in a construction company with a high salary. Madhuri had proved lucky for him. Jitendraprasad, who had progressed in life through perseverance, insisted that the clever Sanatan stay with them and pursue his studies. Many times, while talking, Sanatan used to say, "Uncle, having learnt about your life, you are an excellent example for me. You are my inspiration. Your ideals are everything to me."

"Remember, Sanatan, nothing is impossible in this world. The one thing we should know is how to make our way though difficulties and complexities."

"Uncle, I forgot to mention that a couple of days ago I went to meet uncle Rasik living in Matunga and uncle Poonamchand living in Andheri. Both uncles remembered you well."

"Have you met your fiancé, yet?"

"Where would I get time to meet her?" Sanatan replied with embarrassment.

"What do you think of your nephew? He is shrewd." Madhuri chuckled as she commented, "He will go and meet Radha and would never let you know of it."

"Come on aunty, how can you tease me in such a way?" "Look son, we just feel like saying what we feel is true."

Sanatan's college opened in the first week of July 1947 and Sanatan moved to the hostel. Although the professors came to classes for lectures, most of the time they would drift from the main subject and begin discussing political events taking place in India. Everywhere in the college, campus grounds, canteen and classes or buses and trains, discussion on matters of the impending attainment of Independence was going on. While one group was against the division of India, the other group was praising the leaders of the independence struggle. In such a scenario studies generally took a backseat.

Despite that, Sanatan used to concentrate on his studies until late at night. Physics was his favourite subject. He could instantly memorise the equations in chemistry. In class if a professor asked a question, Sanatan could answer without hesitation. This way, gradually Sanatan became a favourite student of the professors.

One auspicious day, the betrothal of Prachi and Ashwin was solemnized at the residence of uncle Poonamchand. Aunty Vishakha, in high sprits, was welcoming the guests. Vinod, who was studying in Bhavan's College, was also seen happily doing work in the house.

When uncle Rasik and aunty Manjula arrived at the house, everyone was delighted. Their daughter, Purvi, was studying in Khalsa College and their son, Atul, was working in a bank. Uncle Rasik said, "Atul's bank is working today, but I asked him to put in a request for leave for today."

"That's better." Uncle Poonamchand said, "Our Sanatan too, has come directly from college."

The event was celebrated with much joy and happiness. Sanatan stayed with the family members for a long time. He was glad to have met all of them. Putting on his shoes, as Sanatan was preparing to leave for the hostel, uncle Poonamchand said,

"Sanatan, it's already late at night. Be careful."

When Sanatan boarded a train at Andheri railway station, the dense darkness of night had enveloped the place. When he reached the hostel, he was totally exhausted. Very soon he fell asleep.

At last, at midnight on August 15th 1947, India was declared Independent. Pandit Jawaharalal Nehru addressed the nation and his speech was broadcast live by the All India Radio. He exhorted the people to work to rebuild the newly independent nation. The people of India looked at the new dawn with great hopes and aspirations. Mahatma Gandhi led the country to independence from the yoke of slavery of the British rule and he was one national leader who not only promoted Khadi, but at whose call thousands did not hesitate to accept martyrdom. As the struggle for the Independence came to an end on that day, festivities broke out all over the country. These festivities were celebrated with banners of victory and processions. Mammoth crowds thronged the streets.

Within four months of the attainment of the Indian Independence, *Diwali* festival began. But there was not much joy in the hearts of the people. Important public places were floodlit. During the holidays, taking leave of his maternal uncle and aunt, Sanatan left Bombay to visit Umreth. He had done well in his examinations. Sanatan hardly realized how much time had passed since talking to his parents.

The next day, Sanatan woke up early. Seeing a newspaper stuck in the letterbox Sanatan picked it up. He looked out of the window. Except for a solitary milkman, the street was deserted. Winter had set in and the air had turned chilly.

Sanatan squatted and scaned the headlines of the newspaper. It was dated 16th December 1947.

"Owing to the stubborn attitude of the Muslim leaders under the leadership of Mohamed Ali Jinnah, the so-called saviour of the Muslims, India was partitioned into two separate nations. Communal violence broke out. Hindus and Muslims became blood-thirsty. The sense of fraternity and respect for each other nurtured over centuries suddenly vanished. Communal violence broke out initially in the cities. The people of India, who had fought the British together, were overwhelmed by the demon of communal madness."

When the proclamation of the existence of Pakistan was made, the Pakistani government compelled the Hindus to leave Pakistan. Tortured by the blood-thirsty Muslim community the Hindus left for India, leaving behind their households, properties and many other things. Similarly violence broke out in India, too. The Hindus became enemies of the Muslims and the Muslims became the enemies of the Hindus. An age old sense of fraternity and friendships and togetherness were forgotten in a moment. The sudden onslaught of the venom spread. It became endemic.

The British observed the events with suppressed laughter. The seeds of communal hatred were sown so firmly that the people of the Hindu and Muslim communities were thrown into the deadly jaws of communal violence. The people of both communities struck at each other with vengeance. Hatred and vengeance overtook friendships. Nobody trusted anyone anymore. Communal violence had engulfed both the countries. India and Pakistan has turned to slaughter houses and shambles.

With the outbreak of bloody violence in the towns and cities, Independence and festivities were marred. However, the heat of the communal violence had not yet touched the lives of the people of Umreth. The schools and market places were bustling as usual.

Then one day "Ahmedabad caught in whirlpool of Communal Hatred: Violence Spreading in Gujarat" '— the newspaper headlines screamed, 'The days to follow were full of misery.' Sanatan peered over the news in fine print. '79 people were reportedly killed and 112 were grievously injured in Ahmedabad city during the daylong carnage between the Hindus and the Muslims.' Reports of violent massacres of ordinary people on either side of the borders were reported. '*Loads of dead bodies are reportedly being brought by vehicles and trains plying in the border regions between India and Pakistan. Mahatma Gandhi has announced a fast unto death to quell the communal violence.*'

Young Sanatan believed that either the climate was making him feel cold or the fear was shaking him from within! After a while, after his father finished his prayers, he handed over the newspaper to him.

Kanaiyalal asked, "So, what's in the news?"

Sanatan burst out, "Father, violence has gripped the nation. Even the newly created Pakistan is not free from the violence that has spread in Lahore, Karachi and Hyderabad. Also, a terrible situation prevails in Ahmedabad following the outbreak of violence in the city."

Kanaiyalal exclaimed, "What! Riots have broken out in Ahmedabad?" He could not believe his ears.

"Oh . . . God!" Kanaiyalal expressed his shock. He didn't have words to express how he felt. He spread the newspaper on the floor sitting down.

Sanatan repeated, "Yes father, around 80 people were reportedly killed in the riots just yesterday. Indefinite curfew has been imposed in the city."

"Oh my God, what's going to happen to this country?"

"Iqbal was admitted to a college in Ahmedabad. I hope he is safe there."

"Iqbal came to town just last night. Yakub met me last night on my way home. He told me about Iqbal. As you were tired from the journey and went to sleep early, I could not tell you last night." Kanaiyalal said.

Sanatan got up and said, "Papa, I want to meet my teacher, Vidyacharan Sharma. Let me go to the school where I can meet him. He will be glad to meet me after such a long time."

Without looking up from the newspaper spread before him Kanaiyalal said, "Alright, go and meet him. But why don't you take a bath first?"

"Sure, Papa; but I might want to meet Iqbal and some of my friends too. Since Iqbal is here these days I must meet him."

"I will wait for you at lunch."

Kanaiyalal's entire attention was caught by the news-reports on the situation in Ahmedabad.

An atmosphere of uneasiness had spread in the streets of Umreth, but it was business as usual in the market. However, small groups of people were seen discussing the latest outbreak of riots and political events in hushed tones in the streets. The atmosphere in the streets of Umreth seemed unusually quiet to Sanatan.

Sanatan went to the school to meet his teacher, Vidyacharan. When he reached the school, he saw that the activities carried on as usual. Suddenly, the headmaster appeared and asked all the students to assemble in the school playground.

He announced, "I have received instructions from the Police Superintendent to close the school early today as law and orders gone out of control. I want all the students to go home safely. It is better that you all go in groups with your friends. Before you come to school tomorrow tell your parents to send you to school only if the situation is normal."

The students then dispersed for the day picking up their schoolbags and rushing towards their homes. Sanatan talked to his teacher, Vidyacharan, for a few more minutes and then, he too, left for his home.

Since that day Umreth town, too, was engulfed in the violent fire of communal hatred and violence. The people of both the communities—Hindus and Muslims—had been living together with love and affection for years. But suddenly, a spark of communal hatred was ignited by mischievous rumours and a chapter of the devastation of humanity was created. If a Hindu was found walking alone on road, he would be stabbed by a Muslim and if a Muslim was found by a Hindu, he would be hacked to death by a sickle. The Hindus and the Muslims were divided into two groups. Whatever weapon like a stick, iron rod, axe, sickle or dagger that came into the hands of the miscreants, was used against the enemies.

After walking a few yards, Sanatan looked behind him. The road was deserted. Suddenly a group of people appeared coming from the side of the railway station.

Suddenly he heard cries, "Catch him . . . Kill him . . . Cut him down . . ."

The sudden, violent cries from behind him made Sanatan shudder with panic. He did not stop to think and ran as fast as his legs could take him. He did not pause to look where he was heading. As he turned the corner of a street, he glanced back over his shoulders and saw a small group of Muslims chasing him. All the people of the group were armed with daggers, sticks or swords. He clenched his fists and ran towards the main post office with all his strength and stamina.

As Sanatan ran swiftly, he saw a door of a house adjacent to the post office slightly ajar. Without much thought, he pushed the door of the house open and entered its courtyard. Somebody slammed the doors behind him. Panic gripped him as he turned around to face an old man facing him. Sanatan was trembling with uncontrollable fear!

"My dear son," said the old man in hushed tone, "Don't be afraid. *Insa Allah* you are safe here."

Instantly Sanatan recognized the old *Maulvi*. Trembling, Sanatan embraced the *Maulvi* as he patted him affectionately.

"Were you going to your home, son?"

"Yes, *Maulvi Sahib*." Sanatan was still trembling with fear.

"Alright, follow me. I will hide you from those hoodlums."

Exactly at that moment, as if echoing his words, there were noises outside his house. A group of Muslim youths passed by, shouting.

The Maulvi Sahib guided Sanatan to the inside of the house. He asked him to sit on a mat and not to worry any more.

The old *Maulvi* affectionately asked him in a hushed tone, "What is your name?"

"Sanatan," he replied.

"Where do you live? Who is your father?"

"I live in *Raghunathjini Pole* in *Vada Bazar*. My father, Kanaiyalal Motilal Shah owns a clothes-shop in *Panchvati*."

"Oh! So, you are a son of Kanaiyalal? I know your father well."

"*Yes,* Maulvi Sahib. *My parents would be worried about me, if I don't reach my house on time under these circumstances. I had told my father that I would arrive home by lunch time.*"

"Yes son, I can understand that. But your father will be pleased when he would learn that you were protected by Suleman *Maulvi*."

Sanatan listened to him in silence.

Peering at Sanatan carefully, the old man asked, "If I am not mistaken, aren't you a friend of my nephew Iqbal?"

"Oh yes," Sanatan replied, "Iqbal is my close friend and his *Abbajan,* uncle Yakub, loves me like his son."

The Maulvi *called out his wife from within the house, then turned towards Sanatan and said,* "Look, it is dangerous to venture out immediately. Those goons must be looking for you and wondering where you went!"

Sanatan preferred to remain silent. He was thinking of the mess he had landed in!

"Today the people have become fiendish. They have forgotten to discriminate between the good and the bad; right and wrong. How costly this achievement of the Independence is for us! That too, at the cost of the blood of our own people! Only *Allah* knows when these killings will end," Suleman was saying with a tinge of sadness in his voice.

Sanatan glanced at his wrist watch. He showed his anxiety. The *Maulvi* chuckled, "I hope now your fear has subsided. Won't you eat something?"

"*Maulvi Sahib*, I have lost all desire to eat."

The *Maulvi* turned to his wife, who had meanwhile appeared from the inside of the house. "Will you bring something for this boy to eat?"

"Sure . . . sure . . ." Maulvi's wife, Mehrunnisa, smiled affectionately.

In a short time Mehrunnisa brought some dry fruits and fresh fruits for Sanatan to eat.

Sanatan said, "Will you give me some water please. My throat is parched."

Mehrunissa rushed inside and appeared with a glass of water in her hand. Sanatan quickly gulped down the water. He asked for some more water. Mehrunnisa brought him some more water and turned to the *Maulvi*,

"You've done a good job. Now, how will he reach his house? His mother will be worried stiff about him."

"How's your health now?" The *Maulvi* asked his wife. "I have a fever and am feeling a bit under the weather."

"How will you reach his house? There is a lot of disturbance in the town." Mehrunnisa commented on the situation in the town.

"Don't worry. Sanatan and Iqbal are close friends. When Yakub is here, we'll find some way to enable him to reach his house safely."

"Alright, but be careful. It is a bad time. If you see any danger on your way, return to our home immediately."

"What would they gain by harming a *Maulvi*? *Allah* is the protector of all. He will look after me." Saying this *Maulvi* Suleman began descending the stairs.

He paused and said "Don't open the door until I return. All the Hindus and Muslims of the town know me and respect me.

Don't worry about my safety."

"When you return, knock thrice indicating that you have arrived safely. After looking out of the window, I will open the door."

Quickly Suleman left his home. The road seemed deserted and eerie. It was four o'clock in the evening. Uneasy gloom had spread in the town. Only stray dogs were seen roaming or running helter-skelter in the streets. The *Maulvi* walked through Vhorwad and reached *Kansara Bazaar*. He paused to think, 'should I go and cross *Gandhi Street* to reach *Kazi Wad*a or take a circuitous route via the Court?' He felt that the road by the court should be safer. He walked ahead towards the court on Bhadrakali Road silently chanting the name of *Allah*. He reached the intersection of three roads in *Vada Bazaar*. He glanced to his left. At some distance a large group of people stood. It was a Hindu locality.

When he reached *Hakim* Yakub's house, he heaved a sigh of relief. He knocked at the door. *Hakim* Yakub peeped from a window from the upper floor. Seeing the *Maulvi* at the door, he rushed down to open the door.

"*Salam Alekum*, Yakub." The *Maulvi* uttered lightly.

"*Valeikum Assalam, Maulvi Sahib*! Why are you on your own at such times?" *Hakim* Yakub blurted out the question in a single breath. "Please come in . . . come in."

Suleman entered the house quickly, as Yakub immediately bolted the door from the inside. Both went upstairs and sat on a swing.

Yakub asked, "Where have you come from? At such times! Is everything alright?"

"I have come from my house. There is a little trouble. I need your help."

"Tell me."

"Iqbal's good friend, Sanatan has taken shelter in my house. Now, I need your help to enable him to reach his house."

Yakub was startled. He asked, "Is he alright? How did he come to your house? Don't worry! I will come with you. I know that boy."

He called out to Iqbal. Iqbal came rushing up. Suleman explained the circumstances under which Sanatan had taken shelter in his house.

Yakub said, "Your friend Sanatan is held up in *Maulvi Sahib*'s house. I am going out with him to enable your friend to reach his house safely."

"Shall I come with you?" Iqbal asked. "No." Yakub said.

"If you feel that the road to his house is not safe, bring him here. Don't take any unnecessary risks." Sairabano cautioned, handing over a glass of water to the *Maulvi*.

Pushing his hands through the sleeves of his *Sherwani,* Yakub asked, "How is your wife's fever today?"

"Her fever has subsided, but she is feeling weak."

Yakub took time to prepare small packets of herbal powders, which he placed in his pocket. Then both of them set out from the house, asking Iqbal to shut the door behind them. On the way, they planned ways and means to escort Sanatan to his house.

"What do you propose to do?" Yakub asked in a hushed tone.

"Well, we'll make Sanatan wear a cap and dress him like a Muslim. This way the others would think that he is one of us. I hope *Allah* will have mercy on us."

"Just think how worried Kanaiyalal would be about his son.

May *Allah* make our way safe!"

"Amen!" intoned Suleman.

Having arrived at Suleman's home, Yakub checked Mehrunnisa's pulse and gave her the medicine. Seeing uncle Yakub, Sanatan ran and embraced him.

"How are you, Sanatan?" Yakub smiled at him.

"Uncle, *Maulvi Sahib* is an angel. He has saved me from the hoodlums. What would have happened to me if he had not given me shelter?"

"Oh, just don't think of that," said Yakub. "We need to hurry. Before it turns dark you must reach your home. Sanatan, put on this cap and *sherwani*. In this disguise nobody will recognize you."

Sanatan donned the *sherwani* and placed the cap on his head. Sanatan thanked *Maulvi* Sahib and Mehrunnisa for their care.

Soon, Sanatan and Yakub descended the steps and came out onto the road together.

Before they reached Bhadrakali Road from the court, an armed group of Hindu hoodlums was seen passing in the distance. Soon afterwards, they reached the intersection of the three roads near *Vada Bazaar*. Another group of the Muslim fanatics were standing at some distance. Somebody from the Muslim group recognized Sanatan. He whispered in the ears of the gang-leader.

The leader of the group shouted, "That is a Hindu boy. Hand him over to us at once!"

Hakim Yakub responded in a loud voice, "So what, if he is a Hindu? He is a human being. Don't you dare touch him!"

A voice warned, "What'll you do?"

Yakub challenged, "If anyone comes forward to touch him, he will be sorry he was born. I will protect this boy whatever the cost." Silence prevailed for a moment. He turned to Sanatan,

"Run home son, I'll hold them!"

Before Sanatan could begin running for his home listening to uncle Yakub's instructions, a Muslim youth threw a dagger at Sanatan. But unfortunately the dagger pierced deeply into the chest of Yakub who was shielding Sanatan. Blood spattered out.

"*Ya Allah* . . . !" the words escaped faintly from the lips of *Hakim* Yakub as his lifeless body crashed to the ground as Sanatan escaped from the jaws of certain death.

Chapter 5

The sun had almost set. Although Sanatan had said that he would return by lunch time, there was no sight of him until evening. As a result, Kanaiyalal was terribly upset. Every now and then he would go to the window and look out. Suddenly, as he looked down the road, he saw Sanatan and rushed down to let him in. Sanatan was sweating profusely. He was bewildered and trembling with fear. Sanatan's mother Kusum came out from inside the house. Seeing that Sanatan had arrived safely, tears rolled down her cheeks. Sanatan collapsed in her arms.

Clasping her son to her bosom she asked, "My son, where were you all this time?"

In jerking sentences, Sanatan described the course of events after he had left school. He narrated how he took shelter in the *Maulvi*'s house and later how Yakub tried to bring him home. At last, he said, "Thank the Almighty, mother, that I have returned alive. I didn't have any hope of survival. Thank god, *Maulvi* uncle sheltered me in his house. But what is shocking is that uncle Yakub was stabbed."

"Oh, no . . ." wailed Kusum.

"I think he died. As I was escaping from the place, I turned and saw that he had fallen on the ground, there was blood and mud all around."

"Were you not afraid to shelter in a Muslim's house?"

"No Mother, uncle *Maulvi* had already won my heart with his affectionate words. Sometime later when

I met Aunty, my fear had absolutely vanished. Talking to them I felt that both the elders were like angels for me."

"Do you know how risky it was to come all the way from their house to our home?"

"Uncle Maulvi had taken this decision after a lot of thought. He knew that unless I reached our home, you both would be very anxious and tortured."

"That's very true. Several of our neighbours were at our home and they left a while ago, after consoling your mother." Kanaiyalal interrupted the conversation.

"Someone informed us that police has found dead bodies of two boys, brutally killed, in a gutter near the school. Having heard that, I was deeply shocked. I wept bitterly". Even while talking about it Kusum seemed to be in severe anguish.

"Mother, please don't cry now. I am hale and hearty and standing before you." Sanatan wiped his mother's tears.

She said, "You just said that Yakub was stabbed. How did that happen?"

"On seeing a man pull out a dagger, uncle Yakub asked me to run and escape. I mustered courage and I ran towards the house with all my might. Meanwhile, I think the dagger thrown by that man struck uncle Yakub. As I looked back on hearing the cry of *"Ya Allah!"* I saw the stout body of uncle Yakub slump to the ground."

Kanaiyalal was so shocked that he found it difficult to find words to speak. Sanatan was still trembling with fear. He too, sat down on the floor with a thud.

"Oh God, You saved our son, but took away Yakub, who was like our brother!" Kusum wailed, looking skyward.

"Sanatan, uncle Yakub has sacrificed his life for you! What gloom would have engulfed Sairabanu and Iqbal when they heard this news! It is necessary to visit and console them at their house, which is only a few minutes away, but how helpless I am that I cannot go!" Kanaiyalal felt breathless saying this. Sitting in a chair he banged his fist on the nearby wall, and wailed aloud.

Kanaiyalal and Yakub had been good friends since childhood. Despite their different religions— Hindu and Muslim—they never nurtured any kind of emotional differences. Both loved each other like brothers.

Kanaiyalal was inconsolable. Kusum brought a glass of water for him. She said,

"Have courage. If you become weak, how shall we survive? Think of Saira. She must be absolutely stunned today. Their lives have suddenly been devastated. Just look at our predicament, we cannot go and console her in her hour of need."

Gulping down some water Kanaiyalal handed over the glass to Kusum and stared at the ceiling blankly.

He then blurted out suddenly, "I don't know how this night will pass. Everyone is thirsty for blood."

Sanatan sat huddled near his father. Gloom had suddenly descended on the family. They didn't even get up to light the lamps. They sat huddled in the darkness together. Resting his head on his bent knees Kanaiyalal was glumly thinking about the past events.

A neighbour came to remind him that a meeting of the residents of adjoining localities was convened at eight in the evening in Kachhiya Pole. In the cold darkness he peered at the clock. It was almost eight. They were preparing to face the eventualities that could occur during the night. The residents of the community mostly comprised of Hindu Banias—a trader community. They didn't believe in bloodshed. Hence, instead of planning to attack the Muslims, they discussed ways and means of self-protection, in case the Muslim fanatics attacked them. Women were asked to keep buckets of water mixed with chili powder. Young boys and girls were assigned to collect and pile up soda-water bottles. In case a street fight broke out, these could be used as missiles to beat back the hoodlums. Whoever had hockey sticks, knives, daggers and swords, were asked to keep them handy. The residents divided themselves into small groups of four to five persons for patrolling at night.

After the meeting ended Kanaiyalal came home. Sanatan and Kusum were talking in whispers.

"What happened?" Kusum asked anxiously.

"Well, the ways and means to protect our locality throughout the day and night was discussed. We have to keep something ready to retaliate if we are attacked."

"Oh!"

"It is my turn to do the patrolling tonight."

"Where do you think the attackers would strike from, father?" "They might attack only through the area inhabited by Muslims living in *Kazi Wada*. However, they will not have the courage to reach our locality as they will have to pass through a large area of Hindus."

Around midnight noises from adjacent colonies were heard. Suddenly, firing of rifles could also be heard. The patrols alerted the people to meet any untoward incident. Each person was out and about and picked up any weapon at hand, ready to strike.

The dark sky was suddenly lit up with light from flames as some shops and houses were set ablaze at a distance in *Od bazar*. Shattering the peace of the night, the cries of people were heard, 'Kill them all . . . cut them all.' One could see that the residents of *Raghunathjini Pole* come out in large numbers carrying sticks. At the same time, a large crowd had gathered at the entrance of *Kachhiya Pole*. Even the residents of *Dalal Pole* were out in the streets. Rage and anxiety were written clearly on their faces.

After an hour or so, the people began to disperse. Dawn was breaking. Arvind, living in Kachhiya Pole, was a close friend of Kanaiyalal. Both of them sat on a wooden bench in a shop.

"Arvind, do you think mankind will always remain barbaric? Will they never be civilised?"

"On what basis can you say that mankind will never improve on this earth?

"Isn't there an invisible power that has created this universe?"

"Yes, there is."

"Now, if that invisible power has to run the affairs of this universe, it will have to create the people of two kinds of elements—good and evil. The Creator of this universe has quite thoughtfully created man. Mankind has been divided into two segments—divine and demonic. If only the divine are left, who would bow down before the Creator of the universe? Thus, you need to think from the angle of the Creator that mankind can never improve." Arvind expressed his philosophy of life.

For a while both of them fell silent. Suddenly, Arvind said, "I've heard that, while trying to protect your son, Sanatan, *Unani* Hakim, Yakub sacrificed his life. Is it true?"

"Yes, my friend. It is true. Yakub was certainly an angel. He laid down his life to protect my son. This unusual event of a Muslim sacrificing his life for a Hindu boy will be written on the pages of the history of mankind."

Another twenty-four hours elapsed. The news of communal violence spreading all over the country was circulating among the people in hushed tones. Hundreds and thousands of people of both Hindus and Muslim communities were being slaughtered. Once, these same people who were close friends for years, are now out to spill each other's blood. There was a look of grave distrust in their eyes. When the heavens had fallen on humanity, who could protect whom? Until the hatred and slaughter stopped, the people had to live with tension.

The Pakistani government had compelled the people of the minority Hindu community to leave their country. Throngs of Hindus left, taking whatever they could along with them and wearing whatever they could, leaving behind their households, trying to save their lives by entering India. The Indian government, through a nationwide broadcast, announced that, '*the government will provide opportunities for self-employment to the Muslims. Not only that, the government will ensure that, the Muslims can continue to live happily, peacefully and prosper in India. We will create such a Constitution that there shall be no discrimination between Hindus and*

Muslims. In spite of that if any Muslim wishes to migrate to Pakistan, they may leave India of their free will.'

In Kazi Wada, in a house, a mother and her son were talking in hushed tones. They were worried by the grim incident that had taken place late that evening. They were Iqbal and his mother Saira.

"Iqbal . . ." A voice wailed bitterly.

"Yes Ammijan, control yourself!" Iqbal said.

"What shall we do now? Your *Abbajan* has left us for his heavenly abode. All hell has broken loose on us."

"Oh Ammijan, be patience. There is no use crying. *Abbajan* was an angel. He was always a propagator of peace. He lived the highest form of life as a man." Iqbal's tone became heavy with emotion.

"Whatever was destined to happen; has happened. In order to protect the life of Sanatan, he sacrificed his own life and provided a shining example of Hindu-Muslim unity and fraternity. He was keenly interested in moulding your career. But now, all his wishes have turned futile. His heavenly journey is untimely.'

"Ammijan, I don't know how to calm you." Saying this Iqbal fell silent for some time. In fact, Iqbal too was crying silently. The only thing was that his mother could not see the tears gushing out of her dear son's eyes in the darkness.

"Shall I light a lamp?" Iqbal asked.

"Oh *Allah*! What's the use of lighting a lamp? Now, no lamp on the earth can bring light into our life." She was inconsolable.

Iqbal didn't reply. He knew there was no use.

After a while he said in a measured tone, "Ammijan, many from our locality are planning to go to Pakistan.

They have asked me if we shall join them. What do you say?"

"Oh Iqbal, we have been living in this town ever since I can remember. What happiness can we ever gain in Pakistan? We have all our contacts and acquaintances here. And this communal violence will be quelled in a few days time. We don't have to go anywhere leaving our country, our native place."

"*Ammijan*, even I don't feel like leaving our native place and our country. Don't you think my heart too suffers anguish on thinking of leaving all our dear ones and my friend Sanatan? But, Ammijan, these days Hindus and Muslims seem to have lost their reason. Nowadays nobody is thinking of the loved ones of others, but only of their own community. They are engaged in massacring the people of the other communities. Under the circumstances, I don't think it is advisable to continue to live here. We should be leaving for Pakistan as soon as possible."

Having heard Iqbal his mother fell silent for a long time. At last she said, "My mind has turned numb. How about leaving for Lahore for four to five days until the peace returns?"

"Ammijan, people say that the situation will worsen with each passing day. They also said that, later it might be very difficult to even venture out of our house."

"In that case, Iqbal, do whatever suits you."

"Some people are preparing to leave in about two to three days. We should accompany them. That is the best possible recourse. Pack up whatever we can carry in our hands and on our head. Leave everything behind that cannot be carried. We shall buy whatever we need once we reach Lahore."

"Why don't you find out when we shall leave?"

"Very well." Saying this, Iqbal descended the steps of his house. Remembering something Sairabanu asked, "Oh Iqbal, have you met Sanatan?"

"Ammijan, I don't think it is possible to meet Sanatan. I tried, but in vain."

Iqbal cautiously walked ahead in the darkness of the night. For her part, Saira began packing her belongings. Iqbal returned late at night.

The next night, a young bearded man knocked on the door of Iqbal's house. Iqbal opened the front door slightly and peered in the darkness outside. A shadowy figure appeared from the nearby wall and came into the house.

He said in hushed tones, "Can you get ready within the next hour? We're preparing to leave. A truck has been arranged to ferry us safely out of this village."

"Sure, where are we to go?"

"You and your mother, right? Only two; come to my house as fast as you can."

"Sure, we'll reach your house soon." Iqbal replied.

The bearded young man vanished in the darkness outside. Sairabanu had already packed the luggage to be taken along with them. In twenty minutes they were prepared to leave. Hesitatingly she lengthened the wick of the lamp. She went around the rooms of the house where her family had lived for over sixty years. Every wall, every corner and every mark on the walls had a story to tell. She looked around frantically as if she wanted to retain the image of the house in her mind.

Iqbal called out softly, "Ammijan, shall we leave now? The time is short."

Silently, as the mother and the son bade a silent farewell to their ancestral house, tears welled in their eyes. Wiping his tears with his sleeves Iqbal hoisted the load on his head and carried another bundle in his hand leading his mother through the narrow lanes of the locality—the route of escape to freedom in Pakistan.

Chapter 6

Another twenty-four hours passed. Gradually the disturbed atmosphere began to quieten down.

The next day, when the curfew was relaxed, Kanaiyalal decided to go to visit Yakub's house. Kanaiyalal began walking on Bhadrakali Road. He saw *Maulvi Sahib* coming from the opposite direction.

As their eyes met, the *Maulvi* asked, "How are you Kanu?"

"Quite well . . . , *Maulvi Sahib*!"

"Where are you going . . . ?"

"I'm going to Yakub's house. I wanted to see Iqbal and Sairabanu."

"Oh! But don't you know that the mother and the son left for Lahore last night?"

"What did you say?" Expressing his amazement Kanaiyalal said, "We could not meet them before they left."

"Look, Kanaiyalal, we are all helpless before the wish of *Allah*. Well, I'm late going to the *Dargah*."

"Very well *Maulvi Sahib*, now it is useless to go to Yakub's house. I'll go back home."

Maulvi walked towards the *Dargah* and Kanaiyalal walked back towards his home.

Across the borders separating India and Pakistan, along Rajasthan and Punjab, interminably long caravans of people were seen traversing the treacherous path. Their path was perilous. The women folk of the Hindus transiting out of Pakistan were raped and then killed mercilessly on the way to India. In a tit for tat, the trains and vehicles entering Pakistan carried loads of dead and mutilated bodies of men, women and children. If the men entering India tried to intervene and protect their womenfolk, they were stabbed to death instantly. Their possessions were plundered. In a similar manner inhuman attacks were committed on the Muslims wanting to cross over to Pakistan. Their wives, sisters and mothers were pulled away and raped and then stabbed to death. The men were not left alone either. They were either mutilated or left to die with broken limbs. This way, it seemed as if inhumanity, hatred and mass massacre had been let loose. Thousands of young men and women were left dead and mutilated on roadsides. Never before was such a ghastly, shameful and hideous face of human nature seen. The demon of communal violence was let loose on innocent people.

Week after week the daily newspapers brought the news of widespread communal violence spreading in the country. If Gujarat was reeling under the heat of the violent riots Punjab, Uttar Pradesh, Bihar and Bengal were not free from its horrendous impact. Mahatma Gandhi undertook a fast unto death in Calcutta to quell the violence of communal hatred. The newspapers reported that Gandhi visited Noakhali and had managed to bring peace between the two communities. Peace prevailed in Calcutta too. At last, Mahatma Gandhi ended his fast unto death. The top political leaders in Delhi heaved a sigh of relief.

On the following day, the newspaper headlines screamed that the Indian borders were afire. The newly carved out nation, Pakistan had staked claim on Kashmir on the basis of higher density of Muslim population in the Hindu state ruled by Maharaja Hari

Singh. The *Razakars* had invaded Kashmir. They had moved closer to Srinagar. Timely action initiated by the Indian Military and accession of Maharaja Hari Singh to the Indian Union saved Srinagar from falling into the hands of the Pakistani invaders.

Despite the tension on the national borders, some sort of normality was returning to Umreth town. Routine activities were resumed. Schools reopened and business began as usual in the market place. Kanaiyalal had begun going to his shop regularly now.

It was the 30th of January 1948. Sanatan met his friend Bansi coming from the opposite direction. They inquired about each others welfare, entered a tea-shop and ordered two cups of tea. A radio, blaring film songs was placed over the counter. A shabby waiter placed two earthen pots containing tea before the two friends. Bansi began humming the film song being broadcast on the radio. Sanatan smiled at Bansi and picked up the earthen pot to sip. All of a sudden the radio went off the air. Bansi cursed under his breath and looked with irritation at the counter.

After a moment's silence the radio came to life again. A male announcer announced in a grim voice, *"We have just received the news that Mahatma Gandhi is no more. The father of the nation is not alive."*

The announcer was solemnly saying, ". . . . *as Mahatma Gandhi came walking towards the place of prayer at Birla House this morning, an assassin, identified as one, Nathuram Godse, came forward and shot Mahatma Gandhi in the chest three times with a pistol. The assassin, Nathuram Godse was immediately taken into custody. The Union Home Minister, Sardar Vallabhbhai Patel rushed to the spot immediately who, incidentally was with the Mahatma, a few minutes before in the Birla House. The Prime Minister Jawaharlal Nehru has appealed the people to maintain calm in these moments of great sorrow . . . ."*

The announcer continued giving more information on the event. Sanatan and Bansi left their tea unfinished. They got up and came out of the tea shop. Suddenly the atmosphere of the town turned gloomy. Shops on both the sides of the roads were immediately shut. People thronged at restaurants, tea-shops or cigarette stalls where radio sets gave news of Gandhi's assassination in Delhi. Sanatan took leave of Bansi and turned towards his home. In a short while Sanatan reached *Vada Bazaar*. He crossed the spot, where uncle Yakub had shielded him from an attacker's dagger and while saving Sanatan was killed. Sanatan's throat was choked with the sorrowful memories. Quickly he moved towards his house.

His father had already arrived home after closing the shop. The entire country was shocked and tormented at the sudden death of Mahatma Gandhi. Schools, colleges, all the government and private offices and business houses of the entire nation were closed. It was as if with the death of Mahatma Gandhi, the life of the entire nation had come to a standstill!

Reaching home, he hoarsely shouted, "Mummy! Daddy! Gandhji has been shot, he is no more!"

Kusum and Kanaiyalal were seated on a swing on the veranda and were talking animatedly in hushed tones.

Sanatan turned pale as he sat down on the floor.

Kanaiyalal's voice was choked as he said, "It is the greatest tragedy that has struck our nation today. Is this the price we have to pay for attaining freedom?"

On 31st January 1948 Mahatma Gandhi was cremated in Delhi. The entire nation was plunged into a sea of sorrow. The people mourning the death of Mahatma Gandhi were seen gathering at the roadside tea-stalls, cigarette shops and restaurants. A running commentary of the cremation of the Mahatma was being aired live from *Rajghat* at Delhi. A similar scenario was repeated in all Indian villages, towns and cities. There was not a single person in the crowds listening to the radio commentary who was not silently weeping in memory of the greatest martyr. On that fateful day nobody had their meals. Most Indians mourned the death of Gandhi as if someone from their own family had died.

Although, the exodus of the refugees was still going on from place to place, people were coming to terms with the changing scenario. The severity of winter was fast receding in the western parts of India. Life went back to normal for the Indians.

Ten days after the death of Mahatma Gandhi, Sanatan decided to return to Bombay. One night he told his mother,

"Mother, tomorrow I shall leave both of you and go to Bombay to continue my studies."

"Dear son, our blessings are always with you. May you succeed well in all spheres of life. We only hope that you progress in your studies. By the way, will you go straight to your hostel after reaching Bombay?"

"No, I will stay at my maternal uncle's place for a couple of days and then go to the hostel."

The next day, bowing down to his parents Sanatan said, "Please, look after yourselves. I will always be worried about you."

"Don't think like that. God is our protector. Why should you be worried? Don't worry about us. You should concentrate on your studies only." Saying this Kusum's throat was choked by a surge of emotion.

Picking up his suitcase Sanatan went on to the road. He had no courage to look back at his parents bidding him farewell.

He reached Bombay early the next day. After staying at his maternal uncle's house he reached the hostel of Ruia College that was located close to *Koliwada* railway station. His room-mate,

Ravindra Shah from Uganda, was also his classmate. Wherever they went, whether it was to their classrooms or to the laboratory; they were always together. They would return to the hostel for lunch. After a siesta they would concentrate on their studies.

Ravindra used to say, "I don't know, somehow I find physics a bit confusing and tougher than Chemistry. At times I have to struggle hard to understand some of its topics."

"Well, interest in a particular subject differs from person to person. In fact, I cannot express how happy I am to study physics and chemistry"

"As a matter of fact, I specifically requested the hostel warden to make you my room partner, so that I could get proper guidance and these subjects could be better understood by me."

Sanatan smiled, "My dear friend, by helping others in educational pursuits, one doesn't really lose anything;

rather one's knowledge gets strengthened. Don't you worry! Ask me anything any time you wish."

The next day, an experiment related with reflection of concave and convex lenses was conducted in the laboratory. Sanatan was very quick to set up the gadgets in a perfect manner and noted the readings. He asked his instructor to check it.

The instructor examined his readings with respect to different positions of the lenses. He was pleased to find that even the minutest notations were perfect. Patting Sanatan on his back the instructor said, "Well done, Sanatan. It is a matter of pleasure for me that you have been able to complete this experiment, calling for so much accuracy, in such a short time."

Sanatan also loved chemistry experiments. He exercised extreme caution while handling different kinds of chemicals and while mixing them in test tubes or heating them on a gas burner. Steadily and gradually he achieved perfection and progress in his studies.

The schedule for the final exams was announced in the colleges. Sanatan began studying with very deep concentration for the examinations. At this time, suddenly, he received a telegram from Umreth.

The message read—'*MOTHER SERIOUS—COME SOON.*' The sender of the telegram was his father, Kanaiyalal.

Immediately, that night he informed his maternal uncle, and his other two uncles. Having received the news, his maternal uncle and aunt as well as both his uncles and aunts accompanied Sanatan to go to Umreth by the night train.

Chapter 7

When the train reached Anand railway station early the next morning, the weather was cool. Everybody alighted from the train carrying their baggage and boarded the Godhra Local train. The train chugged out of the station on time and arrived at 6 o'clock. Bipin had come to the railway station. Everybody came out of the station in a highly-strung mood. They were all worried. Bipin, Sanatan and his maternal uncle as well as his aunt sat in a *tonga*. Both uncles occupied another *tonga*. The silence of the streets of the sleepy town was rhythmically broken by steady 'tap . . . tap . . .' sounds from the hooves of the horses.

As they passed Jubilee School, Sanatan inadvertently glanced in that direction. The fond memories of the days of his childhood spent in the playground of the school were in the air. His mind was flooded with the memories of learning in the classrooms of the school. As he passed Muleshwar Mahadev's temple, he looked at the house of *Maulvi Sahib* in the distance. He was reminded of the day he had taken shelter in *Maulvi Sahib*'s house. The memories of ghastly communal violence that had rocked the town came rushing to his mind.

Reaching *Raghunathjini Pole* the *tonga*s stopped.

As soon as they entered the *pole* they realized that an ill-fated incident had happened. Some men were engaged in the preparation of a cremation and talked in hushed tones.

Kanaiyalal was standing and lamenting. Seeing Sanatan and the other relatives, he could not control himself and sobbed bitterly. He hugged his sobbing son, saying with grief, "Sanatan, your mother has departed for heaven leaving us both behind."

Sanatan's throat was choked with emotion. He couldn't say a word. He fell on his mother's breast and cried hysterically.

"Oh my mother . . . my dearest mother . . . ! Oh my mother, why didn't you wait for me? How shall I be able to live without you . . . ?"

After a while, uncle Poonamchand very tenderly made Sanatan get up and took him away from the dead body of his mother.

"Sanatan, if you have an emotional breakdown, what will happen to your father? Have courage, my son!" uncle Rasik said placing his hand on Sanatan's shoulder,

But Sanatan cried inconsolably. He wailed, "Why was it not in my destiny to meet my mother for the last time?"

As the others began preparations to carry the body for the last rites, once again the painful memories that flooded Sanatan's mind made him sob uncontrollably.

Kanaiyalal stood watching and crying silently. Tears filled up in his eyes. Kusum had never complained of any discomfort throughout her life. As far as Kanaiyalal remembered she had never complained of even fever or graver illness. That is why Kanaiyalal was terribly shocked.

An elderly relative lit up a sunbaked cow-dung cake and put it in an earthen pot. Some other relatives tied the dead body of Kusum on a bier. After some time, the chant of 'Sri Rama . . . Sri Rama . . .' filled the air and the relatives lifted the bier. Kanaiyalal and three other relatives shouldered the last remains.

Sanatan walked ahead of the funeral procession. Bipin placed his right hand lightly on Sanatan's shoulder.

At the burning ground the dead body of Kusum was untied and placed on the pyre. Sanatan touched the right toe of his mother with a burning piece of wood.

Staring at the burning pyre Sanatan's throat was choked with grief. He placed his head on his folded knees and sat huddled under a tree and silently wept remembering his mother.

Surrounded by relatives Kanaiyalal was staring at the lifeless body being consumed by the flames. Sanatan slowly turned his head towards his father sitting beside him. Tears seemed to have dried up in Kanaiyalal's sorrowful eyes as he stared at the leaping flames.

As they were returning from the crematorium, Kanaiyalal's heart cried out in anguish. When he thought of the future, he was becoming increasingly upset. During the whole day, neighbours and relatives paid visits to sympathize. Kanaiyalal sat surrounded by his brothers at his right side and Sanatan and his brother-inlaw, Jitendraprasad at his left side. He would silently nod his head and fold his hands whenever somebody entered the house or left, but did not lift his head to look at anybody. He was constantly thinking of Kusum. He wondered how he could live the rest of his life without her support.

Towards evening when the father and son were alone, Kanaiyalal asked, "I believe your final examinations are scheduled towards the end of the month. And as far as I know, you should stay until the last rites are over on the twelfth and thirteenth days after the death of your mother. I'm worried about your studies and your forthcoming exam. How cruel nature is; that such a tragedy has happened, when your exams are impending!"

"Papa, whatever was destined to happen couldn't be stopped from occurring. Don't worry about my exam. I will go to Bombay after all the rites are complete. After going there, I shall put in a bit more effort. In any case, I have already completed my preparations for the exams. But yes, I don't feel like going and leaving you all alone here. I shall be worried about you." Sanatan replied.

Right at that moment someone knocked on the door. Sanatan opened it. Uncle Arvind entered the house followed by his wife Madhu. Going to the kitchen, Madhu said, "I have brought some supper for you."

Kanaiyalal lamely protested, "Oh, but . . ."

"No 'buts'. I know that you have not eaten since morning. How can you remain without food? Let me know, should you need anything." With these words, aunty Madhu and uncle Arvind went to the kitchen.

Madhuri returned from the kitchen, and served food to everybody.

Kanaiyalal said, "I don't feel like eating anything."

"Look brother, whatever was in our destiny has happened. Who wouldn't be sad after losing one's dear one? The dead is not going to return if you don't eat. We have to sustain our life. Have something to eat." Madhuri insisted.

After initial refusal, but later succumbing to the insistence of both brothers and Jitendraprasad, the son and the father agreed to take a little bit of food. Then all of them ate together.

Making small talk, Jitendraprasad said, "I am planning to go to Bombay. Your aunt shall stay here. I'll return for the rites on the twelfth and the thirteenth day."

"Alright" Sanatan said nodding his head, "I'm going to remain here."

"Sanatan has to stay here until all his mother's last rites are accomplished. From tomorrow onwards the recitation of *Garudpuran* will begin. Besides, Sanatan's presence will be required for the last rites on the thirteenth day." Madhuri spoke of the socio religious customs.

The days flew by. One night, Sanatan asked his father,

"Papa, what will you do here alone? It's better that you come along with me to Bombay."

"No Sanatan, how could I keep the shop closed for long? Somehow, I will have to look after our shop."

"Yes; that's right, but if you come along to Bombay, your anguish would be mitigated." Sanatan said like a mature man.

"Oh, don't worry about that. Anyhow, I will have to learn to live alone from now on." Kanaiyalal said with a deep sigh.

"What about cooking arrangements for you?"

"I will cook for myself. Don't worry about me on that count." Saying this Kanaiyalal's throat was choked. He found it hard to suppress his anguish.

On the twelfth and thirteenth day ceremonies Radha's parents as well as Jitendraprasad arrived from Bombay. All the relatives offered their condolences to

Sanatan and his father. Arvind and Madhu took control of the household affairs. The services of a female cook were also arranged. The thirteen days had passed by swiftly.

Then all the relatives left. Sanatan decided to delay his departure by a day. Leaving his father alone he had to go to Bombay for his studies. He didn't like it, but at that moment there was no other recourse. As they were leaving, Vasudev offered to leave Lakshmi and Radha behind, but Kanaiyalal declined the offer.

That night Sanatan and Kanaiyalal were all alone. Sanatan could see that his father had difficulty sleeping properly. At times, he would wake up in the middle of the night and stand near a window weeping silently. Sanatan would get up and try to soothe his father.

Sanatan was reminded, how his mother used to narrate to him legends and stories from the *Mahabharata, Ramayana, Vedas and Upanishads* and also read chapters from the *Geeta*.

Once, while making a point in her talks, his mother had told him of the legend of the unbroken friendship of Krishna and Sudama. He was delighted to listen to the legend. He asked, "Mom, you said that taking pity on his poor friend Sudama, Krishna had miraculously turned his hut into a palatial building. Even the other ordinary houses of Sudama's town also looked glorious painted afresh! Not only that, but the people of the town were dancing with joy and also wore new garments and jewellery. Tell me Mom; is it true that the God can really change our life like that?"

"Oh yes son, when a true devotee of God seeks His refuge, he can have such an experience."

"Does that mean that God controls this universe?"

"Of course son; I can recall many more such incidents of the grace of God. Nevertheless, it is difficult to fathom His secrets."

"Mom, the other day, weren't you telling me about an aircraft called *Pushpak*? Now, such aircrafts have been invented. And a man can travel from one country to the other using such aeroplanes."

"How can I explain to you that a great many secrets of the universe will be revealed making use of the ancient religious scriptures? Our country is a land of accomplished and enlightened sages. If the ancient scriptures are studied in a proper manner, a lot more secrets will be revealed."

"Mom, the other day you were talking about Tansen, the great singer in the court of the emperor Akbar. He had ignited the lamps of the court merely by singing Deepak Rag. How was that possible?"

"Son, for such accomplishments, one needs to perform deep penance and meditation. Our body has *Kundalini* power within us. Some sort of waves spring up from this power and they collide with some form of waves in the air. Only then such a thing becomes possible."

"Mom, although I am of a much younger age, I learn a lot from such legends."

"Look Sanatan, there is nothing impossible in this world. The day will come when the secrets of the universe will gradually open up. My grandfather was a scholar of Vedas and Vedant. He was engrossed round the clock in the pursuit of finding out the secrets of Nature. My father too, was a great scholar and a religious man. He was a voracious reader. I have been nurtured amid great and accomplished scholars."

Kusum had explained at length to satiate Sanatan's spirit of inquiry.

"But Mom, the creator of the universe must have taken such great care of the minutest details!" Sanatan had asked.

"I've told you that it is difficult to understand the wizardry of the Creator of the Universe. The Supreme Creator has produced intelligent people and alongside, He has also produced insects. As He created the flowers and vegetables, He also created the birds and animals. Thus, He has created equilibrium in the universe." For a while she had fallen silent. Kusum had laughed lightly and said,

"Sanatan, it is already ten at night. Now, go to sleep. You will find the answers to your questions when you grow up."

Sanatan was reminded of his talks with his mother. His heart was filled with grief. How wonderfully his mother had nurtured him! How inspired thinking had cultivated his mind! He felt as if he had been left in mid-sea by the death of his mother.

His father's life was devoid of such interesting thoughts. He was hardly interested in such discussions. Perhaps, due to this, Sanatan always pestered his mother instead with queries and a spirit of inquiry.

Be it the legend of King Harishcahndra or the legend of the devotee, Prahlad or Narsinh Mehta, Sanatan used to become emotionally charged listening to the legends of great saints. And especially when she used to narrate the enchanting events of those great sages his small mind used to fly across the skies in search of secrets of the universe. Since childhood he had treasured colourful dreams within himself.

When Sanatan went to school, his mother used to advise him, "You must study well in order to accomplish the greatest achievements. You should contemplate on whatever you have studied. The collective strength of noble thoughts helps us to attain great success."

On the following day, he left for Bombay. He was not willing to leave his father alone, but he was helpless.

"Papa, look after your health. Please call me whenever you need me. I will come back instantly."

"Don't worry about me, my dear son. Arvind and Madhu are taking good care of me. When your examinations are over, come home for your vacation."

Having reached Bombay, Sanatan went straight to his hostel. He was disturbed to find that his room-mate Ravindra was not there. Suddenly, he saw the hostel warden Dr. Kulkarni, coming down the stairs.

Seeing Sanatan, he said, "Oh Sanatan! It's good that you have come back. Ravindra has been admitted to hospital following injuries he sustained when an explosion took place in the laboratory yesterday. His face was injured when the test tube burst during an experiment."

Hearing the warden's words, Sanatan became deeply distressed.

Chapter 8

The days of the examination were nearing. Both friends, Sanatan and Ravindra, had resumed studying with vigor and began reading their books until late at night or after waking up in the early morning. One day, Sanatan had been away at Umreth when the Chemistry practical examination was held in the laboratory. Ravindra, was busy doing the experiment alone. Different kinds of hazardous chemicals were stored in bottles in the laboratory. Equipment such as glass tubes, conical flasks, pipettes, burettes, and burners were laid on the table used for performing the tests. Ravindra began to conduct tests of chemical formulations in accordance with the equations.

After mixing two chemicals he placed them on a burner and settled down to wait for fifteen minutes to get a third kind of a chemical. Suddenly, he saw a piece of sodium stored in kerosene. He picked up a tube and placed the tube on a wooden stand. After that he washed the surrounding place on the table using water. As he bent forward to wash his hands in a washbasin, drops of water splashed into the test-tube. It exploded suddenly and glass-splinters lodged in his face. Luckily his eyes were saved. Immediately he was taken to a hospital for treatment. With immediate medical care Ravindra recovered but he had to live with a couple of scars caused by the injury.

When Sanatan learnt of the entire episode, he was filled with anxiety. He asked, "Ravindra, don't you know that the contact of water with sodium could cause an explosion? You should have exercised greater caution."

"I was aware of that but, while washing my hands, perhaps I was a little careless as some water splashed around which caused the explosion."

"Thank God that the explosion didn't cause any serious injury to you. Sometimes the chances of grave damage are great."

"Sanatan, my friend, this incident has taught me to realize that haste is dangerous. Concentration is very necessary. A small error could cause a serious accident. I will act with extreme caution in future."

"By the way, which chemicals were you using? What did the professor teach you?"

"I took one part of ferrous chloride and mixed it with silver nitrate and placed it on the burner to heat; which resulted in a new chemical of whitish sediment-like precipitate."

"Look Ravindra, we have very little time. Only a few days are left until the examinations begin. Although, we have studied all the subjects so far, we need to revise and grasp them."

"I faced many difficulties while you weren't here. You help me to understand science better. You can easily memorise chemical equations, whereas, I have to cram them. In fact, at times I am jealous of your memory."

"Ravindra, each of us has a different way of studying. I might be good at physics and chemistry but you excel in your command of languages. Well, let's go to bed and get up at four in the morning. What do you say?"

"Sure, as you say."

Switching off the light they went to sleep. Thoughts about their studies were swarming in their minds. In the morning, at precisely four o'clock, they woke up and continued to read throughout the day. At around five in the evening both friends strolled towards the King's Circle garden. For a long time they sat on a bench. They discussed many different issues about their studies. Later, they decided to meet Abhijeet, their friend. They strolled to Abhijeet's home in Shantiniketan building and picked up Ravindra's physics guidebook. Abhijeet's mother insisted that they have lemon juice, which they relished.

Later, both walked down Vincent Road towards King's Circle. Dark shadows of the late evening were fast enveloping the city streets as they entered a café adjacent to the Aurora Cinema. Ravindra ordered coffee for them and said, "After a few days I will go to Uganda and you will go to Umreth, correct?"

"Of course; after my mother passed away, my Papa has become lonely. I'm worried about him."

"If you have brothers or sisters like I do, you would not have to worry."

"Well, Ravindra we're all born with our share of pangs and difficulties written by destiny. Tell me who is entirely happy? Each person has varying problems and that causes anguish and pain. Nevertheless, we must not lose heart, but face the challenges posed by life with a smile on our face."

"I am reminded of a family in Uganda. Out of that large family, six of them are doctors and some of them are specialists. Despite that destiny has played a cruel trick on them which has a tenyear old boy in the family suffering from cerebral palsy. The illness is incurable. In spite of having so many doctors in the family, the boy's ailment cannot be cured. It is unbearable to see the painful and difficult life of that boy. They have a large palatial house and abundant wealth but none of them have either the time or the enthusiasm to enjoy life." Ravindra narrated the woes of that family.

"It is precisely for this reason that I am telling you to live the life the way it is gifted to us and try to make the most of it by paving our way to develop our minds for such a purpose."

"Hey, let's stop there. It's already seven. We must rush to the hostel!" Ravindra said, standing up.

After a few days, Sanatan asked Ravindra,

"Ravindra, we've studied all our lessons diligently but what about you? Are you prepared?"

"All of us have a habit of reading our books until we reach the examination hall which we cannot give up."

"Well, I used to do so in my school-days also. But now that I have studied with concentration I won't have to do it this time round."

After the long stroll both friends returned to the hostel. Dinner was ready. They took their seats in the dining hall. Sanatan was reminded of his mother while eating and his throat was nearly choked. When he was at Umreth he used to frequently quarrel with his mother on the recipes she cooked, as he didn't relish something or the other. Having completed their practical examinations in the laboratory, whenever they reached the dining hall the food used to be usually cold. Despite that, quietly he ate, whatever was served, without complaint. He could not find fault with the cook as he used to do with his mother.

After dinner they stepped out of the dining hall and went to the railway platform of Matunga station and sat on a bench. The night sky was filled with innumerable shining stars and the bright moon. Curiosity gave rise to many questions in Sanatan's mind.

"Ravindra, you are aware that the light from the stars located billions of miles from us takes an eternity to reach."

"Sanatan, although the moon resembles a planet; in reality it is a sub-planet of the earth. Besides, our religious scriptures have described it as one of the nine planets affecting our lives. Look at the moon. Do you know what that shadowy figure is, resembling a deer?"

"Well, I don't know anything about it. Do you?"

"Although the sun and the moon are billions of miles away, our earth is affected by their light waves. The scientists are trying to probe the secrets of the nature hidden for ages. Many a time they succeed but at times they fail in their pursuits. It is certainly very difficult to explore and understand the secrets of nature."

"But that has encouraged scientists to put more effort into their research."

"Right you are! The earth, on which we are standing, also revolves around the sun."

"Yes, I remember. Our teacher taught us in school that due to the earth revolving on its axis, when one part of the earth faces the sun, the other half turns dark. We call this day and night." Ravindra was reminded of his school days.

"At times, I am lost in thought about various natural phenomena. But after a while I lose all sense of direction. The idea of light waves and sound waves traversing long distances fascinates me."

"It is good that you reminded me about it, Sanatan. Is it possible to exercise control over the light and sound waves at our will? Is it not possible to harmonise them with the radioactive waves emitted by our physical bodies?"

Sanatan chuckled, "We are too young friend, to think on that level. Perhaps the great scientists of the world are already busy unravelling the secrets of the waves."

"As a matter of fact, long distances between far off places have been reduced thanks to the inventions of the steam engine and aeroplane which have been developed by the enterprising scientists. I have heard that the sages in the ancient past had done great research in this area. The secrets of the Universe have been exposed in various religious scriptures. If somebody studies the ancient scriptures, a great many secrets of the Universe could be brought to light, and I have no doubt about that. The Germans, British and American scientists took away scriptures to their countries and they are very busy in their research. Since our country was reeling under the British rule, such pilfering was made possible." Ravindra was in a talkative mood.

When he was studying at school in Uganda, his teachers found it difficult at times to give satisfactory answers to the mindboggling questions of young Ravindra.

"Ravindra, are you aware of the Pushpak aeroplane referred to in our ancient epic Ramayan. One could reach heaven by boarding a Pushpak aeroplane. But our parents or forefather could never have dreamt of reaching a distant country by flying in an aeroplane. However, this has been made possible by the inventions of the great scientists."

"Sanatan, I remember that you told me about that. It seems that one day you will grow up to be a great scientist." Saying this, Ravindra jokingly winked at Sanatan.

Sanatan smiled at the joke but replied, "I don't believe in soothsayers or prophecies. I believe in striving to attain a goal. Nevertheless, I believe that science has brought a great amount of welfare to the people at large, but has also given birth to such inventions which have brought about the massive destruction of humanity." After pausing for a moment Sanatan continued, "You know, Ravindra, my school-friend Iqbal in Umreth used to ask me a lot of questions like you are asking. He had to leave Umreth with his family and settle down in Lahore following communal violence. I don't know where he is today."

"When a man is born in this world he does not have either a friend or a foe. But later, with the passage of time, why do so many have enmity for the same man?" Ravindra asked.

"Man, because of his nature, usually acts in a dastardly manner like a born-rival. But I fail to understand what pleasure he gets by acting in such a manner. The spirit of humanity has been forsaken by almost all the countries today for their selfish motives. Out of their selfish motives, the religious Gurus have devastated the religious philosophies. As a result man has become cruel, satanic and irreligious." Sanatan said with deep anguish in his voice.

Getting up from the bench, Sanatan glanced at his wrist watch and said,

"Shall we go to the hostel, now?"

"Why not!"

"Let's go then!"

"Not now."

"What do you mean?"

"I am reminded of a dream I had early this morning. I remember that the dream had something to do with science, I was thrilled. Unless I tell you about that dream, I won't be able to rest."

"Well, in that case tell me about your dream." Sanatan settled down on the bench.

"Listen, once I set out on a voyage accompanied by my family, that is, my wife and children, and reached an island. As the island was very large, we brought out our car from the ship to roam about. As there was no place for parking, we parked it on a slope nearby. I was looking at the splendorous natural beauty all over the island. Slowly I gazed up at the sky where there was another island. And what I saw awed me. It was full of wonder and surprise. Suddenly, the words slipped off my lips, '*Oh god, having brought me to this wonderful land, if you had not enabled me to see the enchanting natural splendour, my life would have remained incomplete. Milions of thanks . . .*'

"Now tell me quickly without lingering. Say clearly what you have seen." Sanatan requested inquisitively.

"I saw that, the water level was six feet below the above island. A plastic sheet was stretched out to prevent the water from falling down onto the lower island. Many helicopters could be seen flying from the lower island to the island above. Many tourists were going that way. Having gone up to the island, they were splashing in the water wearing colourful swimming costumes. Seeing such an enchanting scene from below, I was awed by this supernatural creation of God and I prayed in appreciation of His wonders.

"Then?"

"For almost an hour my wife, children and I watched this splendorous natural beauty. Suddenly darkness descended. The helicopters flew down from the upper island to the lower island. The People swimming in the water were also gradually vanishing. Darkness was making the island eerie. Having realised that, all of us immediately entered the car which was parked on the slope. Turning the ignition key I started the engine. Suddenly we felt a jerk. I was not able to apply the brakes. I shouted out. "Pray God; or we'll soon sink in the sea, in a few minutes."

Sanatan was engrossed in listening to Ravindra's tale. His mind was agitated. He was very anxious to listen further. He asked Ravindra,

"Tell me quickly, what happened next?"

Chapter 9

"To my utter surprise the heavy car, instead of sinking, began to float on the surface of the water and was gradually moving towards the coast." Ravindra paused for a moment and then resumed.

"When we reached the coast, the car stopped. Brightness had spread everywhere. Hundreds of robust and well-built hermits clad in saffron colored robes, almost double our height, had gathered to receive us. The chief a priest-like hermit came forward and asked,

"Were you driving the car?"

I replied in the affirmative. On hearing me he bellowed, "In that case, get ready for your punishment."

Out of fear I cried out, "Swamiji, although I was driving the car, I didn't know that the car's brakes had failed. Despite that, I'm ready to bear whatever punishment you give me; because, you have played a significant role in saving our lives."

"Do you know, to stop your car from sinking and pull you up to the coast, how much magnetic pulling power we all had to use? Do you know what price we have paid to save your lives?" The chief priest asked sternly.

"Swamiji, we're sorry. We are ready for whatever punishment you wish to inflict on us."

"In that case, come with me."

We followed the chief priest. We entered a large cavern. After we entered it, we emerged before another large cavern. That was a magnificent cave. Several saffron-clad hermits were going about.

Traversing several such caverns we emerged into large open ground. A large cave was on the opposite side. Thousands of hermits were looking ahead. A large-framed person of about thirty feet in height was seated on a ten feet high stone platform. His face was almost four feet long and his eyes were one foot each. There was a benign flow of light streaming down on the hermits standing before him. Watching his magnanimous personality I was filled with joy. On seeing the magnificent idol of the lord Buddha my eyes were blinded by its bright luminance. I prostrated with reverence and said,

"Oh! Almighty God! I had heard so much about your omnipotence. But today, the mission of my life has been fulfilled as you have conferred me with this blessing to appear before you."

Sudha, my wife and my two children, Megha and Vedant stood before the magnificent idol of the lord with folded hands. Suddenly, the ear-splitting tolling of bells could be heard. Musical notes added to the resounding notes coupled with devotional songs, sung in heavy tonal voices. A few hermits were singing in an unknown language. The entire atmosphere was charged with divine and devotional music.

All of us sat down. The chief priest-like hermit whispered in my ears,

"Your punishment is to sit through this devotional singing. Once this service is over, you will be freed from your guilt."

"But, what will happen to our car, Maharshi?"

"Arrangements have been made for it. After the devotional singing is over, your car will be sent safely to the island, where you landed from the ship."

'We silently concentrated on the devotional singing. We were glad to perceive God before us. Tears rolled down our cheeks. With the conclusion of the last devotional song, the sound of the Tabla, Mridang and other musical instruments gradually doubled, trebled and all of a sudden the crescendo stopped. The echoes subsided. When my eyes opened, I found myself sleeping in my room'!

Having spoken at length Ravindra fell silent. Suddenly a local train entered Matunga railway station. Though it was ten at night the train was packed with commuters. Some alighted and a few boarded. The train then moved out of the station. Immediately, both the friends also got up from the bench and walked towards their hostel. Sanatan was not able to forget the dream that Ravindra had narrated. After taking a few steps, Sanatan said, "Ravindra, you are fortunate that you had a vision of God."

"Whatever you may make of it is up to you. But I feel sure that the thoughts that have been swarming within my mind for many years will come true someday."

"What are you thinking of?"

"I am thinking that life exists on other planets."

Hearing Ravindra's words, Sanatan immediately said, "Even if I believe your dream to be true, I feel sure that several secrets of science are connected to your dream."

After some time they reached their room. They became immersed in their studies. The annual examinations were over. Both of them performed well in their examinations. As soon as the vacation began,

Sanatan left for his home in Umreth and Ravindra went to Uganda.

One day, sitting on the swing in the house, Sanatan observed,

"Papa, you seem to have lost a lot of weight. You have become weak."

"Oh, that's your opinion. I don't have any problem."

After some time he saw his father cooking in the kitchen. He felt sad.

"Papa, don't your meals come from uncle Arvind's house?"

"No, I cook at home."

"Why?"

"Actually, Arvind insisted on sending me meals regularly. Even when I tried to dissuade them from sending food, his wife insisted on sending meals until . . ." Kanaiyalal's voice seemed to grow heavy with grief as he stopped short.

"Why, what happened . . . , what happened to them?" Sanatan asked.

"It's about their daughter, Shobha . . ."

"What about Shobha? Didn't she marry Navnit, that son of the oil-merchant, Harkishan Gandhi living in Odbazaar? I know them all."

"How did you feel about them?"

"I thought that they are very wealthy, and hence could be proud of themselves."

"Well, Shobha's mother-in-law is terribly inconsiderate and unbearable. Right from the beginning she was not in good terms with Shobha and she made her life miserable by frequently quarrelling with her on trivial issues. Shobha, the poor girl! She had to wake up very early in the morning and had to go to the well to fetch water for the house and then slog for the whole day doing household chores."

"But they are quite wealthy. Shouldn't they have found a servant?"

"Yes, servants are available aplenty, but why would they want to spend money when Shobha was available to slog for them. None of the family members had any compassion for her. Even Navnit proved to be a Mama's boy. He blindly agreed with his mother's rebukes and thrashed his wife frequently. At last, Shobha found it impossible to endure the torture inflicted by Navnit and his mother. About a fortnight ago . . ." Kanaiyalal could not complete the sentence, as he found it difficult to say anything more.

Sanatan anxiously asked, "What happened then?"

"Early one morning she went to the well as usual, but she jumped in and committed suicide. Her suicide sent shockwaves through the entire town. Whoever heard of it hated and castigated Harkishan Gandhi's family! The incident shocked Arvind. His wife Madhu and he didn't eat for almost four days."

"How are they now?"

"They are alright, presently. Only time can heal such wounds."

Listening to his father, Sanatan was deeply shocked. His heart was filled with abhorrence for such so-called wealthy leaders of the society and community.

Sanatan's summer vacation was being spent usefully. The clothes shop owned by his father was also running well. Sanatan used to remain at home until his father returned in the late evening after closing the shop. While his father was at work, Sanatan occupied himself by reading various books on science at home.

Sometimes he would cook and then father and son would eat together. At times, they would ask a widowed woman living near the court to prepare them something for lunch.

After Shobna's untimely death, Arvind and Madhu were feeling deep anguish. Although outwardly they presented a tranquil appearance there was severe turmoil within their hearts, they were in agony. Gradually they had accepted the death of Shobha as a bitter part of their lives. Navnit and his parents were arrested by the police for driving Shobha to commit suicide. Almost every day Kanaiyalal used to visit Arvind's house without fail and express a few words of sympathy.

Shobha had been born into severe poverty. After Shobha's birth, Arvind was promoted where he worked. Temperamentally Arvind was a hard working, frank, honest and god-fearing man. Whatever work was entrusted to him by his boss, he would do diligently and with sheer dedication. He was always ready to be as helpful as possible. His daily routine would begin only after completing his daily religious rituals.

The days passed and a day arrived when the clouds shrouding the fate of Arvind were removed. Madhu was the only child of her parents. At some unfortunate moment her parents went on a pilgrimage to Shrinathji. Their bus collided with a speeding truck coming from the opposite direction. Seven people died in the accident including Madhu's parents and seven others were injured. They had left a good amount of money for their only daughter. This way, unexpectedly, Arvind became a wealthy person.

Almost a month had passed since Shobha's death. Late one evening, Sanatan went to Arvind's house, accompanied by his father. Madhu was singing a devotional song of Meerabai in an emotion-filled voice sitting on a swing. She was unaware that the darkness of the night had already enveloped her house. Arvind also hadn't yet come down from upstairs. As soon as she had finished singing the devotional song, Kanaiyalal and Sanatan entered the house.

Raising the wick of the hurricane lamp, Madhu smiled and said, "How lovely! Today, both the father and son have graced my house!"

"Today, we had an early dinner. The trader of my neighboring shop, Nandlal, died all of a sudden, so everybody in the market closed their shops early. Sanatan insisted on coming early and listening to you singing devotional songs," Kanaiyalal offered an explanation, entering the house.

"It was our good fortune to listen to you singing a devotional song of Meerabai in your melodious voice!" Sanatan endorsed his father's compliment. By that time, Arvind came downstairs.

"Sanatan is planning to return to Bombay next week." Kanaiyalal's voice trembled as he spoke.

"Uncle, I am trying to convince my Papa to accompany me to Bombay and wind up the business here. Even my two uncles living in Bombay were insisting that he should settle down in Bombay with them. But he wouldn't listen to anybody." Sanatan lamented.

"Look, Sanatan, perhaps you are not aware of my affection for this town. You have spent only your childhood here, but I've lived here, my whole life." Kanaiyalal spoke emotionally.

"It is true that my brothers insisted on me leaving the town, but now the memories of your mother wouldn't allow me to go away anywhere. I just cannot think of leaving Umreth now."

"But what's the problem now, Papa? Uncle, why don't you explain it to my father?"

"I am sure while he can work, your Papa won't leave the town. I feel Sanatan, that it is better for you to complete your studies and then get married. After that you can take your father along with you."

"That's all foolish talk, Uncle. I've three more years to study for my graduation. Who will look after my father here?"

"Aren't we here? You won't have to worry about anything while we are alive. Who do we have to live for now? We three will live together for the rest of our lives, supporting each other and reminiscing about our past." Reminded of Shobha, Arvind's tone grew heavy with grief.

"No, Uncle, why should you say so? Who do I call mine in Bombay?"

"Well, don't you have Radha there? You've many relatives, your uncles and even your in-laws are there to turn to, if the need ever arises!"

Sanatan blushed listening to the words of Arvind, but he said, "Would you believe, Uncle; that in the last twelve months I have barely met Radha, twice or thrice? I have a different set of priorities for my studies. I cannot forget that my Papa slogs here to enable me to study at Bombay."

"Arvind, I have flatly refused to go," Kanaiyalal said emphatically.

"Look, Sanatan, don't ask your father to accompany you to Bombay against his wishes."

"But uncle, he is alone here."

Arvind cut him short, "Do you think we both are dead? Our dear daughter, Shobha is no more. Perhaps, you cannot understand how painfully we are enduring each passing day. If your father remains here, we shall have his support in the time of our grief."

"Oh uncle, I understand your pain but . . ."

"Look son, now that's final. Let us live our remaining life in each other's company."

For a long time nobody uttered a single word.

Suddenly Sanatan asked, "Is it not possible that, all three of you come to Bombay and settle there?"

"Oh yes, that might be possible. But for that you need to complete your studies, get married, and then call us to live with you," Madhu said cheerfully.

After that Sanatan gave up insisting that he would take his father to Bombay. Despite the persistence of Arvind and Madhu, Kanaiyalal didn't agree to the idea of re-marriage.

After two days, Sanatan went to Bombay, taking leave of everybody. Two years had elapsed. Time seemed to fly swiftly. Sanatan always maintained first place in his studies. He was the favourite student of all the professors. Whenever possible he would sit in the library for long hours and ponder over books. He loved physics and chemistry. While doing practical tests, he did them with such intense concentration, as if he was going to invent something new.

Only a month was left until the final examinations when Radha insisted on going to the Regal Theatre.

After the show, they went and sat on the promenade of the Gateway of India.

"Sanatan, I always find it difficult to keep thoughts of you from flooding my mind. Do you think of me, too?" Radha rolled her eyes mischievously.

"Yes, I think of you sometimes." said Sanatan.

"Oh! Sometimes, eh! It is hard for me to spend these days of separation from you; but memories of the days we meet add to my joy." Radha was in a talkative mood.

"Yeah Radha, I realize that. But, do you know that I propose to pursue my Master's degree after my graduation?" Sanatan was serious.

"Well . . . well! Who is stopping you from studying further?" Radha's voice was heavy.

"No, you are not stopping me; but it seems to me, that for some reason I am making you unhappy."

"I will always pray for your success, Sanatan; but living away from you is equally soul-destroying."

"I don't know what destiny has in store for us, Radha; but don't worry; time will fly. One day we both shall have reasons to be happy and all the sadness at parting that we are enduring will be a forgotten thought."

Radha rested her head on Sanatan's shoulder. After remaining silent for a long time she said,

"Your happiness, success and achievements are all mine too. I know we need to endure the separation for our better future. Don't worry. I'll never disturb you while you are studying."

"It's late now. Shall I escort you home?" Sanatan enquired.

"Sure," Saying this Radha got up and walked hand in hand, with Sanatan.

Leaving Radha at her home, Sanatan returned to the hostel. After a month when his examinations were over, Sanatan left for Umreth.

After about twenty days, a letter was received by Kanaiyalal, informing him that Lakshmi was seriously ill due to blood cancer. Because of this she did not want Radha and Sanatan to delay getting married.

———◈———

Chapter 10

On reading the letter, Sanatan was shocked. He was jolted out of his belief that he wouldn't have to worry about anything but his studies for the next two years. But the news of the sudden illness of Lakshmi and her insistence for early marriage disturbed Sanatan. He thought of the fact that just a month ago he had been talking to Radha about his dreams. He read the letter once again and with that he saw his dreams evaporating. He was alone at home since his father was away at the shop.

Towards late evening when Kanaiyalal returned from his shop, Sanatan handed the letter over to him. Kanaiyalal read the letter and looked up at Sanatan to see any tell tale signs of Sanatan's feelings in the matter. He saw that his son was not happy, and indeed showed clear signs of distress.

Sanatan said, "Papa, I am confused. What shall we do now? As you know already, I intended getting married only after I finished my studies. Even Radha's parents had agreed to that, and now I have received this letter!"

"Yes, I have just been thinking about that. Without doubt, blood cancer, is certainly a very serious illness. It is up to you to decide if you would like to marry now or later."

"Papa, I have been thinking about that since this letter came this morning. I intended to study for my Master's degree and then perhaps go for my doctorate." A lost look showed on Sanatan's face.

"Is it not possible to pursue your studies after your marriage? I have seen many people pursue their studies even after their marriage. And they have attained great success in their lives." Kanaiyalal tried to assure Sanatan.

"But Papa . . . !"

"Just listen to me. Try to place yourself in their situation. Just think what you could have done. Basically to achieve excellence in your studies what you need is concentration. And I am sure that nobody can find fault with you on that count. You possess the necessary zeal and passion for studies. My dear son, I know that you are capable enough to fight against all odds and excel."

"You mean that I should be prepared for an early marriage?"

"That's it, Sanatan, that's it. You are a wise person."

The following day was Sunday. In the morning Kanaiyalal suggested, "Let's seek the advice of Arvind and Madhu with regard to your marriage."

They reached Arvind's house. After the death of Kusum, Kanaiyalal used to meet Arvind every Sunday morning and they would have breakfast together.

At the breakfast table Kanaiyalal broached the subject of the marriage while informing them of Lakshmi's illness.

Having discussed it at length, Madhu said "Kanubhai, you have wisely taken the decision." Then looking at Sanatan she said, "It is also a matter of pleasure that you have agreed to the marriage. Being a mother I can very well understand the pains of a mother. I will pray God to grant a long life to Lakshmi. If you don't get married now, and if anything untoward happens later, you will never be able to forgive yourself. I think arranging an early marriage is in the interest of all. Whatever you have decided in this regard is justified."

Sanatan listened silently.

Within two days all of them firmly resolved on settling their children. They consulted Ramprasad Shastri for the most auspicious time for marriage. Shastriji suggested two auspicious dates a month later.

On the fifth day, a reply from Bombay was received selecting one of the two dates and the marriage date was finalised.

Despite her illness, Lakshmi became emotional on hearing the good news. As Kanaiyalal had accepted their proposal, everyone in the family was filled with a sense of appreciation and pleasure. As he had agreed to the marriage, respect and affection welled up in everybody's hearts.

One evening, Lakshmi told her daughter, Radha, "Dear child, we had promised you that until Sanatan completes his studies, we won't force your marriage with him. But my sickness has compelled me to breach my promise. I don't know how long I will live for."

Hearing her mother's words, Radha's eyes filled with tears.

"Mom, don't say such things."

"Radha, you know very well that I will not be able to live long due to my terminal disease. I will get eternal peace, if you get married while I am still alive."

Radha listened in silence. Tears were flowing from her eyes. On one hand, she had the pleasure to know that she wouldn't have to endure separation with

Sanatan and on the other hand, her mother's sickness worried her.

When the date of the marriage was fixed, Kanaiyalal and Sanatan began the preparations. Arvind and Madhu too, extended full support and help.

In the following week, Vasudev, his son Shalin and daughterin-law, Madhavi reached Umreth for the marriage arrangements. They discussed the venue of the wedding in Bombay, a place for the guests to stay and such other details. The next day Vasudev, accompanied by Shalin and Madhavi, returned to Bombay.

After Vasudev reached Bombay, hectic activities started in his house. The necessary purchases of the bridal trousseau wedding outfits, ornaments and other paraphernalia began. Having completed his graduation, Pulin had decided to join his brother Shalin in their family business. Vasudev had been planning to free himself from the day-to-day business activities, as his two sons Shalin and Pulin took good care of the business. Lakshmi wasn't very old; but as she was afflicted, everybody in the family was deeply concerned about her health. Her daughter-in-law Madhavi took charge of the wedding preparations besides the daily chores of the household while following her mother-in-law's advice. Within a few days gold jewellery and saris were bought. Also new outfits for the men folk and the children of the family were bought. The purchasing tasks stopped a week prior to the wedding date. Radha was brought up with great affection and all kinds of material comforts. Despite that, she was a simple, modest and a family-loving girl. She was a good-natured person who empathized with all in the family. She made sure that she did not offend anybody and that nobody was displeased by her talk. Moreover from the beginning, she could cook well and take care of the other household work. She engaged herself in work and never tired of doing it.

One evening Vasudev arrived home early from the office. Madhavi had gone to her parents' house and was to return late that evening. Lakshmi was lighting a lamp before the idol of Lord Krishna. Radha was busy cooking supper in the kitchen. He sat on a swing placed on the balcony. Radha emerged carrying a glass of water for her father.

"Come dear daughter, come here. Sit with me." He moved aside to make room for her.

"Wait; I'll join you in a few minutes. I have put the vegetables to cook on the gas burner. Just wait until I bring some tea for you. That will refresh you, Dad."

Radha picked up the empty glass and went to the kitchen. After a while she returned to the balcony with a plate of snacks.

"Oh my child! You really take great care of this old man." Vasudev laughed.

"I know how hungry you are when you return home. These snacks are your favorites."

For a while Vasudev stared at Radha's face. Lively and innocent Radha used to enliven their home, merely by her presence. Whenever Radha smiled the dimples on her cheeks made her look all the more beautiful.

"Why are you looking at my face, Papa?"

"Looking at your face, I am recalling when you were an innocent child. When you were a small girl you looked so enchantingly beautiful and lovely that, after bathing you, your mother used to apply a black mark on your forehead to avoid the malevolence of the evil eye."

Radha smiled. For a moment she remained silent, as if lost in some thought. She laughed lightly and asked,

"What do I look like now, after I have grown up?"

"Today you look even more beautiful and lovely. It is a fact that the parents always like their children no matter what they look like. On Sunday you will get married and go to your husband's house. After you leave, to whom will I talk about such silly things?" Saying this Vasudev's voice turned sad.

"You should not subject your heart to anguish with such frivolous thoughts. How shall I be able to forget all these days spent with you? Shall I ever get to see these beautiful moments of sunrise and sunsets again?"

"I am sure of one thing, and that is you shall live very happily after you get married at your in-laws' house. Your father-in-law, Kanaiyalal has been stricken with deep sadness after the death of his wife, Kusum! After your marriage, you will have to shoulder the responsibility of taking care of Sanatan as well as Kanaiyalal. I pray God that you will always remain very happy."

Radha asked, "What did Dr. Parikh say about Mom's health?"

"Well, Radha, the doctor said that the results of the tests on your mother aren't very good. Research is going on around the world to find a remedy to cure leukemia; but the scientists haven't achieved a breakthrough yet. He has changed the medicines. Now, let's see how she responds to the change in medication. Hmmm. where is your Mom?"

"She is reciting her prayers in her room."

"Radha, have you noticed; despite so much physical pain she is hardly showing any signs of her suffering on her face? Her willpower is very strong."

"I've been seeing that she has qualities of patience and forbearance. In the time of sickness, if a person doesn't lose selfcontrol, half the illness vanishes."

At that moment the doorbell rang. Radha opened the door. Madhavi was standing outside. Seeing Radha she smiled sweetly.

"Oh, hello, *Bhabhi*! You are so early!" Radha said.

"Your brother was scheduled to meet someone at Churchgate. He gave me a lift up to our home. Have you already cooked dinner, Radha?"

"Yes. When my brothers arrive, we shall all sit down for dinner."

"Did mom take her medicines at noon?"

"Yes."

"How is she feeling now?"

"She seems normal now. But when she has a severe ache in her stomach, she feels as if she might die." Radha said.

"That's why we should never let her alone." With these words Madhavi turned to the bedroom where her mother-in-law was praying.

An hour later, both of Radha's brothers arrived. Later, the entire family made their way to the dining table for dinner. Lakshmi disagreed when a suggestion was made to serve dinner in her room. Lakshmi too, joined the others at the dining table. Looking at Madhavi, Lakshmi said,

"Why don't you and Radha join everybody else at the table?"

"No, Mom, you may finish your meals comfortably. Madhavi and I will eat later after you finish yours." Radha said softly on behalf of Madhavi and herself.

Shalin briefed his father and brother about the business meetings he had during the day. When a momentary silence prevailed, Lakshmi said,

"Why don't you leave your business affairs in the office? It is better for you to have your dinner in peace. The food cannot give you proper nourishment if you eat with your mind agitated."

Vasudev agreed and ate silently. He knew that Lakshmi disliked business talks in the house. But the silence was short lived as Madhavi talked about the preparations for Radha's imminent wedding.

Lakshmi said, "Look Shalin, nothing should be lacking in the wedding celebrations. And yes, nobody should worry about my illness. I'll be all right. Spare no expenses and see to it that, there should be no reason for Radha to feel bad."

"Mom, how many times have I told you to stop worrying about me? How hard Daddy and my brothers are striving for the wedding preparations! You are becoming unnecessarily worried for no reason."

"I am not worried. Your Dad doesn't know much about our customs."

Lakshmi waited for a moment before asking, "Shalin, have you taken possession of the two empty flats from your friends at Walkeshwar?"

Shalin said, "Oh yes, mom; I have already received the keys to those flats."

"Who will go to the railway station to receive Kanaiyalal?"

"Pulin and I will go and receive them." Shalin replied.

"That's good."

Everybody finished their dinner. Lakshmi went to her room. When all of them got up from the dining table the clock struck nine.

On Thursday Vasudev got up early and came out of his room. He found Radha out on the balcony staring at the dancing waves of the sea. She looked up beyond the buildings as the sky gradually changed colors from silver grey to bright white and ruddy gold. After many days she had a desire to watch the rising sun. The first rays of the rising sun peered from behind the tall buildings. A few patches of clouds added glamour to the dawn. She gave a start as she felt a soft touch on her shoulder. She looked back and saw her father gently smiling at her.

"Hey dad, why have you woken up so early?" She leaned her head on her father's shoulder.

"Oh, I just woke up for no reason. Both your brothers were preparing to go to Bombay Central Station, and that woke me up. Your Mom is fast asleep. I tried to catch some more sleep and found it hard to get it. At last, I came out here."

"Really! How nice you are! Tell me, what have you been thinking about me? After they left, I came out here to enjoy the reddening sunrise."

"Look Radha, how wonderfully God has created this universe, to enable us to watch such enchanting scenes! Here, there is no discrimination between the wealthy and the poor. See there, how many people are enjoying the splendor of nature!"

"Dad, sit in the easy chair. I'll get tea for you."

Radha knew that as soon as her father woke up he needed a cup of hot steaming tea. Up until now, Lakshmi took care of Vasudev's needs. Despite sleeping deeply, Lakshmi used to wake up as soon as Vasudev woke up.

Handing over a cup of tea to her father, Radha sat opposite to him in a chair.

"Did Mom sleep well at night?"

"No, she found it difficult to sleep due to pain until midnight. But when I woke up, I found her sleeping soundly."

After sometimes Shalin and Pulin came home.

"Was the train on time?"

"Yes Dad, we've taken them to the flats in Walkeshwar and made them comfortable. We also made excellent arrangements for cooking there. When we arrived there, the cook was already there." Shalin said, looking at his father's face.

At about ten in the morning, Vasudev and Lakshmi went to meet the groom's party at Walkeshwar.

Welcoming them Kanaiyalal looked at Lakshmi and said, "Lakshmiben, I didn't approve of one thing."

"Why, what has happened? Is there something making you uncomfortable?"

"Oh no, it is nothing like that . . . , the arrangements you have made to make our stay comfortable are absolutely superb. But you shouldn't have come here when you are so ill. I didn't approve of your coming here when you are already very sick." Kanaiyalal expressed his anxiety.

"What nonsense, Kanu! How can you say such childish things? I am getting Radha married into your family to strengthen our friendship. Whatever you need, just send instructions. Don't hesitate."

While they were talking, Sanatan emerged from the bathroom. He dressed and went to the drawing room. He bowed down to Vasudev and then, Lakshmi, respectfully. Both of them blessed Sanatan by touching his head.

Suddenly the telephone bell rang. Vasudev picked up the receiver. Shalin was on the other end. He said,

"Daddy, Madhavi's father has suffered a heart attack, and has been taken to Harkisondas Hospital. Madhavi and I are going to the hospital."

Listening to this, Vasudev was stunned.

———◈———

Chapter 11

Twilight had set in a long time ago. "The Queen's necklace" concave, as the seaface from Walkeshwar to Nariman Point is called, glittered beautifully. The pulsating waves were sparkling in the moonlight and the multicolored neon lights and streetlights gave it the look of a fantastical land.

Sitting on the sandy beach of Chowpatty, Sanatan and Radha were looking at people walking about and enjoying the happiness of being together.

For sometime they sat in silence. At last, breaking the silence Radha said,

"Sanatan, what are you thinking about? Why don't you say something?"

"Tomorrow we shall be married. I have been wondering if I shall be able to make you happy." Sanatan replied seriously.

"Discard such thinking. Next week our days of separation will be over. I hope you are not repenting your decision to get married to me?" Radha asked mischievously.

"Radha, I love you intensely. There is no question of my repenting." Explaining the reason behind his anxiety Sanatan added, "I will have to remain engrossed in my studies after our wedding. Would you approve of this?"

"Why do you ask that, Sanatan? Well, I shall never come in the way of your studies." Radha said emotionally. She paused and then added, "I believe that one day you will be a great man."

"Oh! Do you have faith in me?"

"If I had no faith, I would have chosen some other man. What was there to stop me?" Radha laughed naughtily. "In fact, Sanatan, when I saw you for the first time, I liked you. For me, it was love at first sight." Radha placed her head on Sanatan's chest.

"You have been brought up amid so much affluence and prosperity in Bombay. Would you like to live in a small town like Umreth?"

"Why not? I have always liked the people of Umreth and their innocent and frank disposition. I have to visit Umreth once a year accompanied by my mom."

Listening to Radha's words, Sanatan's love for Radha knew no bounds. He placed his hand on Radha's waist and pulled her close to him. After pausing for a moment Sanatan said,

"Next Sunday at this time, photographs of our union will be taken, and we will be married."

"Yes, Sanatan . . . ." writing the word '*Sanatan*' on the sand with her index finger Radha said, "They will be the most treasured and memorable moments of our life."

Looking at the pulsating sea-waves Sanatan said,

"Shall we get up now? Shall we go home? It is already quite late at night. Your folks must be awaiting you."

"Uhhh . . . everybody at my home knows that I am with you, so nobody will be worried about me."

"But on Sunday you will become my wife, and so I shall have to worry then", Sanatan smiled, looking at Radha's face.

"There's no need to worry about me. You will have no reason to worry about me." Saying this Radha held

Sanatan's extended hand and got up. Both of them began walking. Radha asked,

"Now your annual exams are over. What do you propose to do now?"

"I want to study further for my M. Sc. And then I wish to undertake research study for my Ph. D. I will have to come back to Bombay and study in a college.'

"I just hope that all your dreams will be fulfilled. Why would there be sadness when you love me so much? I will look after your household in Umreth, look after your father and take care of all your comforts. I shall be pleased if you become a man of integrity as much as a man of idealism."

"Radha, I have forgotten to tell you something. After the wedding, on the following day, we'll leave on a tour of Agra and Simla. Our tickets have already been arranged," after pausing for a moment Sanatan added, "for our honeymoon!"

While uttering the word '*honeymoon*' Sanatan looked at Radha's face in such a manner that her face turned red.

Leaving Radha, Sanatan reached the house at Walkeshwar. Meanwhile, his room-mate, Ravindra, had already arrived from Uganda.

"Ravindra, when did you come, friend?"

"I arrived an hour ago. As soon as I received your letter, I decided to attend your wedding. But, dear friend, you have turned out to be a smart Aleck! You were betrothed so quickly and now you are getting married so soon!"

"Everything has been decided due to an exigency." Then he explained at length how he had agreed to get married to Radha and how the marriage ceremony was planned in such a hurry.

"Now, tell me what should I be doing?"

"Presently, there is nothing much to do. I have sent wedding cards to some of our college-friends and also talked to a few on the phone. It will be your responsibility to look after them when they all arrive. Now, will you be staying here until the college reopens?"

"No, dear pal, I will return to Uganda after the results are announced next Wednesday."

"But why when you can still enjoy the facility of the hostel?"

"My father is an old man. He is not keeping well. Under these circumstances, my father wants that I should take the reins of the business in my hands. So, looking at the situation, I have decided not to return to Bombay for my studies, whether I pass my B.Sc. or not, but I have decided to get involved in the family business."

Listening to Ravindra, Sanatan said, "I feel bad that your studies shall remain incomplete. However, considering the reason that you have cited, I feel that your decision is justified. I won't insult our friendship by expressing my thanks to you for taking the trouble to come all the way from Uganda to attend my wedding, but I am sincerely pleased."

"Sanatan, tomorrow you will get married and on Wednesday, the results of our exams will be announced and I will return to Uganda. I hope you will not forget me."

"What nonsense! Do you think we shall ever be able to forge each other? No, friend, no!"

As they were talking, Kanaiyalal came up to them. Looking at Sanatan he spoke up, "Both of you friends, go and sit down for dinner now. You may go on talking while having your meals."

Both of them got up. After washing their hands and face, they sat at the dining table for dinner. While having their meals they talked a great deal about their college days.

It was almost midnight. The marriage ceremonies were to begin early the next morning so everybody would have to wake up early in the morning. Kanaiyalal left to go to sleep after instructing Sanatan to wake up early. Both aunts went to sleep in another room after imparting a few instructions to Sanatan.

The next morning Sanatan woke up early. When Sanatan came out of the drawing room after changing, his father was talking to his two brothers. Soon his two aunts appeared wearing beautiful silk saris. Looking at the clock, aunt Vishakha said,

"Now, all of you must get ready quickly. Sanatan, you must go and have a bath. The ceremonies of Mandap Muhurt will start at seven o'clock sharp."

On hearing his aunt, Sanatan picked up his toothbrush. Uncle Rasik went to one of the bathrooms. Poonamchand asked his elder brother, Kanaiyalal,

"Yesterday you were to Harkison Hospital with Vasudev to see Biharilal; how is his health?"

"He is better. He will be allowed to go home in about four days."

As uncle Rasik came out of the bathroom, uncle Poonamchand entered. Kanaiyalal got up and went to the balcony facing the sea. He saw that specks of clouds were scattered in the sky. Those were the signs of the onset of the monsoon. Suddenly uncle Rasik placed his hand on his shoulder and said,

"Hello, brother; now you are a *Sasurji*, a father-in-law! Eh! Great!"

Kanaiyalal turned and smiled broadly, "God has been merciful. The only thing I am feeling is the absence of Kusum on such a happy occasion." And with those words gloom crept into his voice.

"Oh yes, Kanu, I can understand how you feel at such times. But what can we mortals do against God's will?"

"Now, my only desire is to see Sanatan live a happy life."

"Surely your prayers will be answered by Him. Oh, I just forgot to tell you something that I had intended to say, when I came here."

Kanaiyalal looked at him quizzically.

Uncle Rasik continued, "Before you return to Umreth, you must stay with us for a few days. When shall we have an opportunity to spend a few days with you again, in Bombay?"

"Oh yes, I will surely come to your house once Radha's father and mother give us a send-off. Tomorrow evening Sanatan and Radha will proceed for Agra. After that I am at your disposal."

At seven o'clock exactly a priest began the rituals. Other relatives too had arrived. The daughter-in-law of Poonamchand, Prachi and uncle Rasik's daughter Purvi, were present, wearing new saris known as *Sela*. Sanatan's maternal uncle, Jitendraprasad and aunt Madhuri also arrived on time. They were extremely pleased to give a special gift (*Mosalu*) to the happy couple. Arvind and

Madhu too, arrived from Umreth, as if this event was happening in their own family.

The ritual of Mandap Muhurt was initiated. Everybody was happily enjoying the event.

Vasudev and all of his family members were awaiting the arrival of Sanatan's marriage procession to reach the Natraj hotel. The marriage procession started from Bhuleshwar. The lilting melodious sounds of the *Shehnai* were adding romance to the atmosphere. Overjoyed, Lakshmi had totally forgotten about her illness. She came forward to receive the groom with enthusiasm wearing a headgear, known as a *Mod*. At 12.50 in the afternoon, Radha's hand was placed in the open hand of Sanatan. Many people sat in rows partaking of the feast.

The bride's farewell, known as *Kanya Viday*, was scheduled for four in the evening. The time to send Radha to her in-laws' place had come. This event of bidding farewell to the newly wedded bride is always very emotional. The eyes of everyone present were moist. Radha came forward and embraced Lakshmi. The flood of tears Radha had held in control until now flowed freely as she clung to her mother. Radha began sobbing bitterly. Regaining her composure she turned to her father. Sobbing uncontrollably she clung to her father and laid her jeweled head on his chest. Vasudev affectionately moved his hand on her head as he uttered the words of blessing—"*May you remain happy always!*" Thus, the marriage ceremony was celebrated with grandeur and joy but mixed with a tinge of sorrow at the parting.

The reception stage glittering brightly in the dark night looked transformed. It was as if the palace of

Indra—the god of heaven—was suddenly on earth. Vasudev had spent lavishly. Besides plenty of relatives, several industrialists and two ministers also attended the function.

At ten o'clock in the evening, the newlyweds sat for dinner along with other intimate relatives. When the families of Vasudev and Kanaiyalal dispersed at midnight, everybody was exhausted.

On Monday night, at eight o'clock a small group of relatives gathered on platform number one of Victoria Terminus railway station to bid farewell to the newlyweds—Sanatan and Radha—proceeding on their honeymoon to Agra. The relatives garlanded the bridal couple. When the time of the departure of the train neared, Radha clung to her mother, Lakshmi.

Precisely at 8.40 p.m. the engine of the Punjab Mail gave a long shrieking whistle followed by a shorter whistle and slowly chugged out of the grandiosely built Victoria Terminus railway station. The relatives gathered on the platform waved their hands and handkerchiefs to wish the newly married couple a happy journey into the future.

At around six in the evening the train reached Agra. A compartment attendant helped them take out their bags and bedding. Ten minutes later they reached the foyer of the Hotel Clarke. A bellboy carried their baggage to room number 201. Meanwhile Sanatan completed the formalities of checking in.

Bolting the door from the inside Sanatan turned around, and saw Radha peering at herself in the full length mirror. He reached behind her and looked at himself. He took her in his arms in an emotional embrace.

Lovingly trying to free herself from his embrace, Radha looked up at his face and said, "Hey, what are you doing?"

Sanatan chuckled, "Tell me what should a young husband do with his bride when they are alone in a hotel room?"

Again he took her in a fond embrace and planted a kiss on her ruby red lips.

Radha's face turned red. She blushed and warmly pressed Sanatan's head to her bosom. Reading the changing lines of emotions on Sanatan's face she asked emotionally,

"Won't you wait until the night comes?"

"Oh, Radha! No, I can't resist my passion!" Saying this Sanatan pulled Radha to the double-bed. And soon the two lovers were bound in bliss.

When they went down for the dinner at night, Sanatan booked two seats on Agra City Tour Bus at the reception counter. They spent the whole night in giving vent to effusions of love and passion.

In the morning, Radha woke up early and entered the bathroom. Sanatan was still asleep. Radha emerged from the bathroom after a hot shower. Wet hair clung to her forehead and bare shoulders, as she appeared wrapped in an oversized towel. Sanatan watched her sinuous and seductive gait and moved forward to take her in his arms.

"Oh, for God's sake, not now!" Radha pleaded but could not extricate herself from Sanatan's embrace.

"Your beautiful face looks all the more lovely and fresh like a flower in full bloom after your shower. I just feel like staring at your fresh flower-like face!"

"Now, stop being a poet. Otherwise the bus will go away and leave us behind."

Having dressed they came to the foyer. It was a little before nine.

The guide welcomed the tourists on board. There were six couples from France, and also a few middle-aged tourists from South India besides Sanatan and Radha. In all there were eighteen tourists in the mini-bus.

The guide picked up the microphone of a portable PA system. His voice came through clearly over the noise of the bus engine. He began, "Welcome, ladies and gentlemen, to Agra—the city of the world famous Taj Mahal! We'll take a sightseeing tour of this great city during the first half of the day. In the evening we'll visit the Taj Mahal. You'll be pleased to learn that today there is a full moon and luckily the sky is clear. It is a great experience to watch the beautiful Taj Mahal in the moonlight." He took a deep breath as he surveyed the eager faces of the tourists.

"Ladies and Gentlemen, it is said that this great city of Agra was formally established in 1475 by Badal Singh. Incidentally, Agra is mentioned in the Mahabharat as Agraban. This city in those days was considered to be the sister city of Mathura, which was more prominent than Agraban. Agra came into its own when the Lodhi Nawabs chose this place on the banks of the river Yamuna to be their capital city. Sikander Lodhi made Agra his capital but Babar defeated the Lodhis to capture not only Agra but also laid the foundation of the Mughal Empire." He stopped to glance outside the bus at the passing areas of the city.

"Babar heralded a new era for Agra. However, in the mid 16th century, and earlier years of the 17th century, during the reign of Akbar, Jehangir and Shah Jahan, Agra reached its zenith. It was during Akbar's period that Agra became the centre of art, culture commerce and learning. This trend reached its peak when Shah Jahan became the ruler. During this time the symbol of love—Taj Mahal was built. The buildings constructed during this era were purely in the contemporary Mughal style and of very high quality, which is still reflected in whatever monuments remain in Agra."

Waving his right hand towards the road as they passed by he continued, "I will take you through the historically important places of the city and the main shopping areas like the Taj Mahal complex, Kinari Bazaar, Raja Mandi and Sadar Bazaar." The guide spoke in a clear rich voice. With his pleasant smile and excellent manners he won the tourists over.

The bus came to halt in the parking lot. The tourists alighted and walked towards the massive 2.5 km long Red Fort. Radha clasped Sanatan's hand. The guide took them around to see Diwane-Aam, Diwan-e-Khas, the Octagonal Tower, the Palace of Jehangir, one after the other. Situated to the right of Diwan-e-Aam is Moti Masjid. Later, they walked down to Diwan-e-Khas and opposite that to Machi Bhavan and Sheesh Mahal. They had a whirlwind tour of many tourist attractions in Agra city. Befoe leaving the guide informed them to be ready for a pick-up at six in the evening for a visit to the Taj Mahal.

After a sumptuous lunch some of the tourists retired to their rooms while the others headed for the market places. Sanatan and Radha decided to take some rest before getting ready for the evening tour. Sanatan went to the reception desk to collect the room-keys. The clerk at the reception desk handed over the keys and an envelope to Sanatan.

"Sir, this message was received after you left for the tour of the city."

"Thanks. Where did the message come from?"

"Bombay, Sir."

Radha snatched the envelope from Sanatan's fingers. Sanatan thanked the clerk again and walked towards the stairs following Radha. Reaching the room Sanatan unlocked the door. Radha tore open the envelope to find a message and reading the brief message gave a shriek of jubilation. Sanatan looked quizzically at her.

"What is it that is making you delirious with joy?"

"Sanatan, it is because of the news I have just received. But first you must promise me."

"Promise you what?"

"You must promise to give me whatever I ask in exchange for the news I share with you."

"Agreed!" Sanatan shook Radha's hand.

"My dear husband, you have topped the university list in B.Sc. Besides, you have topped this list with the highest marks in Mathematics and Physics too."

She rushed and clung to Sanatan and kissed him passionately.

"Oh Sanatan, I can't tell you how I am happy today!"

Sanatan smiled happily, "Who has sent the message?"

Radha placed the sheaf of paper in his hand.

"Oh, it's from your father! Great! My father must have received the news. Let me call uncle Rasik."

After talking to his father Sanatan replaced the receiver in the cradle.

"This evening, my father is organising a big party at which your family members shall be present."

On hearing this, Radha's face brightened with joy.

———◈———

Chapter 12

That evening Radha and Sanatan were sitting on a marble bench facing the Taj Mahal which was bathed in white moonlight. Both of them went around the beautiful monument of love. Several tourists were roaming here and there and in the garden enjoying the beauty of Taj Mahal.

After sometime, sitting on the lush green lawns opposite the Taj Mahal, Sanatan and Radha were silently watching the great monument of love. Sanatan held Radha's arm and lifted her palm to his lips and kissed it. Smiling pleasantly Radha looked at Sanatan and said,

"Seeing this grandiose structure made of marble, the Taj Mahal, we can see how much Shahjehan loved Mumtaz."

"What else do you know about this epic-like structure and the only symbol of love in the world—the Taj Mahal?" Sanatan asked.

"Listen; almost twenty thousand labourers and craftsmen toiled for eighteen and half years to build this beautiful structure of exquisite artistry, the Taj Mahal. The construction of the Taj was completed in 1653 A.D. After the death of Mumtaz, Shahjehan must have been totally anguished and sad! Despite that, he created this grandiose monument in the memory of his loving wife. Tha shows how much he cared for his wife."

"You have said the truth." Sanatan said, "True dedication and integrity can melt rocks, or can instill life within an idol of stone. This Taj is an excellent example of this fact."

Cool wisps of breeze tousled the long tresses of hair over Radha's face. Looking into Sanatan's eyes, Radha asked,

"Will we remain engrossed in love as Shahjehan and Mumtaz used to remain engrossed in each other's love?"

"Yes, we will," Sanatan added, "In the presence of Taj, I once again reiterate my promise that I made to you today afternoon."

Radha was touched by his gesture. She held his face between her palms and kissed him first on his forehead and then on his lips. She slowly said,

"I believe you, my dear. I know you will never disappoint my faith in you." She paused for a moment and continued, "Shahjehan created this artistic monument of love, but I expect from you . . ." Radha stopped short and lowered her eyes.

"Arrey, why did you stop? Tell me further; what is it that you expect from me?"

"I need a child playing in my lap as a token of our love. Will you give that to me or not?" Lowering her eyes, bashful Radha asked him.

Sanatan laughed, "We haven't completed a week of our marriage and you want a child?" Sanatan replied, pressing Radha's head to his chest.

"There is a reason for that" Radha said. "Whenever we talk, our talks centre around the topic that you are ardently desirous of studying further and you are aspiring to become a scientist. I too, wish that you should become a great scientist and I should be privileged to be recognised as the wife of a great scientist."

Sanatan was enthralled in listening to her. He pulled Radha closer to him and held her in a tight embrace.

Continuing Radha said, "You will be busy with your studies and if our child shall be playing in my lap, my life will become full. I have complete trust in you that you will achieve success I fulfilling your dreams."

Looking into Radha's eyes, Sanatan said, "With God's grace your, wishes too, shall be realised."

It was almost midnight. The atmosphere was turning a little bit cooler. Looking at Radha slightly shivering in the cold, Sanatan said,

"Radha, are you feeling cold? Come on, get up. We will go to the hotel. Tomorrow morning, we have to go to Fatehpur Sikri."

Holding Sanatan's hand, Radha stood up. After coming into the hotel they warmly embraced each other. Changing their clothes they stretched out on the bed. They were eager to get involved with each other as soon as they stretched out on the bed. They were lost in the sublime joy of love as if there would be no tomorrow.

The next morning they left for Fatehpur Sikri. They were awed to see the different archaeological splendours like Bulund Darwaza, Diwan-e-Aam, Diwan-e-Khaas, Panch Mahal. Seeing all those monuments Radha said,

"Looking around these palaces and forts, we get to know the splendour of the Mughal Emperor's way of life.

"Despite that, they were not able to live in peace and happiness."

"Why?"

"It was because of the obsession for the throne. In order to snatch the reins of the empire, sometimes a son would fight his father or sometimes a brother would get his brother killed. It was common in those days. The first half of the Mughal dynasty was that of massacres and killings. Since the British began ruling over India, the Hindus and Muslims lived together like peaceful brethren. The country became a slave, but that put an end to the in-fighting." After pausing for a moment Sanatan added,

"During the British rule a great man, Mohandas Karamchand Gandhi was born in Gujarat. The cycle of time continued to revolve. The World War II came to an end. During this period, oppression by the British was increasing for the Indians. Mahatma Gandhi firmly resolved to throw off the British yoke and make India independent under his leadership, swaraj was declared the goal. Due to the efforts of several great men like Mahatma Gandhi, Jawaharlal Nehru, Sardar Patel and the martyrdom of innumerable brave people India received Independence. But what is saddening is that India was partitioned into two separate nations. Violence broke out between The Hindu and Muslim communities. The Muslims separated and got Pakistan. The blood of innocent people flowed. The honour of countless women was defiled. Whole townships were plundered and destroyed. This was how Pakistan was created."

While talking, Sanatan became serious. He was reminded of his school-days. Looking at Radha he said,

"Do you know, Radha; during the communal violence, I too, was completely trapped. In order to protect my life Hakim Yakub Chacha shielded me against a dagger wielding attacker and in the process became a martyr." He narrated the incident in great detail. After a pause he added,

"Due to this communal violence the dearest friend of my childhood, Iqbal, had to escape to Lahore. Who knows how and under what conditions he is living?"

Tears welled up in Sanatan's eyes. For sometime, both were silent. In order to lighten the atmosphere Radha changed the subject of their conversation.

"Shall we return to the hotel? We can talk on our way"

Both of them reached the hotel. They sat in their room taking tea and snacks. At night, they dined in the dining-room and returned to their room.

Before settling to sleep Sanatan switched off the lights and said,

"In two days' time, we shall be in Simla." With these words he pulled Radha towards him in a tight embrace.

On the evening of the third day when they reached Simla the climate was unbearably cold. Snow was falling like rainfall. The atmosphere looked cold and enchanting. The beauty of the natural splendour spread everywhere. Sanatan and Radha were fascinated by the snow-capped mountain peaks, tall green trees, and the greenery as far as they could see. When they reached Hotel Everest, they experienced the warmth of the room. They switched on a heater and the room became even hotter. They enjoyed watching the snowflakes that resembled cotton fluff.

"What a pleasure it would be to permanently live here in such a cold atmosphere!" Sanatan said suddenly.

"That's what you feel." Radha said immediately. "Go and ask the local people here, what trouble they face in such a season? During winter when layers of snowfall cover their courtyards and roads, what trouble would fate bring them?"

"Come, Radha, let's go to the dining room for dinner." Sanatan changed the topic rubbing his palms together.

"Oh no, no; I don't feel like going out in such chilly weather in the freezing cold. Let's get our meals here."

"Radha, you need not be afraid of the cold. A heater will be on in the dining room. Put on your sweater and tie a scarf around your ears to prevent them from freezing. We should enjoy our trip to such a hill-station."

Standing before a dressing-mirror Radha began dressing up. Watching Radha's lovely face in the mirror, Sanatan was filled with a surge of passion. He took her in his arms and kissed her passionately. Radha too, entwined herself around Sanatan like a vine.

After a while disengaging herself she said,

"We have a whole night for love making. Sanatan, have you come here before?"

Sanatan shook his head. "No" he said and then asked,.

"Have you come here before?"

"Yes, I have come here twice with my father." Radha replied.

"In that case, you must be aware of the topography of Simla." Sanatan asked walking towards the dining hall.

"We'll talk after dinner." Radha said with a smile.

After dinner both of them returned to their room.

Sanatan reminded her, "Radha, do you remember, you must talk to me about Simla's topography and share more information about it with me."

"Yes, I remember very well." Radha said, changing her clothes.

"You change your clothes too. We'll talk in bed."

After some time both of them stretched out on the bed. Radha began narrating.

"Around one hundred and fifty years ago, Simla was a small and obscure village surrounded by impenetrable forests. It is said to have derived its name from the goddess Shyamladevi. An English Army officer, Major Kennedy's sight fell on this unknown and enchanting village and in 1822 AD he built his first residence. Gradually, more Englishmen came here and developed the village. In 1870, the Viceregal Lodge was built as the summer residence of the Viceroy of India, Lord Mayo. Since the British found it difficult to pronounce the word 'Shyamla' the original name was distorted and became 'Simla'." Radha told the history of Simla in a perfect manner.

"Radha, what subject did you choose for your B.A.?"

"Economics, why do you ask?" Radha smiled and asked.

"I have seen that you have a good command of history, so I thought, history could have been your main subject for graduation."

"Why, can one not talk about history unless one has chosen history as a main subject for their studies? When you become a scientist, will you talk about any other subject than science?"

After a momentary silence Radha resumed talking.

"The natural, scenic beauty of the Shivalik hills that we saw while coming from Kalka by the Toy Train, cannot be forgotten." Pausing for a moment Radha said,

"This land has something unique about it. The 96 kilometre long narrow gauge railway line is the longest hilly railway line of India. When the Toy Train chugs on the railway track surrounded by high mountain peaks, tall oak, fir, pine and spruce trees through 103 tunnels, 919 curves and 889 bridges, a traveller never gets tired of watching the splendour of nature's raw beauty and experiences heavenly joy."

"Radha, are there any tourist spots of interest?"

"The Mall Road in Simla is well-known as a fashionable area. A church is located here, which is over a hundred years old. Exotic artifacts made out of woodcarvings are available in abundance at Lashkar Bazar. The other important places of tourist interest are Shedvik Fall, Summer Hill and Prospect Hill."

"You seem to know Simla like the back of your hand." Sanatan said happily.

"Out of all the hill-stations of India, this is my favourite place. Even Daddy too, loves to come here frequently."

Sanatan pulled Radha who was lying beside him, in his arms to kiss her and then said,

"Radha, I am feeling sleepy."

Entwined in Sanatan's arms, Radha spoke in a seductive voice,

"Sanatan, this brightly lit tube-light is watching us!"

Lying on the bed, Sanatan switched on the table lamp and switched off the tube-light.

"Is it ok now, Radha? I shall only be able to see you now."

And both them plunged into passionate joy.

In the morning at seven they opened their eyes. Looking out of the windows they saw that the weather was clear. The snowcapped mountains in the distance were glistering as the sun was rising in the East. Watching the tall lush green trees, unique feelings were evoked in their hearts. Natural beauty was also spread over the mountains and the valleys. During breakfast in the dining hall Radha bumped into her college friends Naina and Sudhendu. They were glad to have their company. After a while all the four left the hotel in a cab on a tour of Simla town.

"That is Scandal Point." As soon as the cab stopped, Radha spoke up.

Looking at Radha, Sanatan asked mischievously, "Does this have a history too?" Sudhendu and Naina too, laughed at the humour.

"Yes, it does have a history" Radha said. "The late Maharaja of Patiala, Bupendra Singh, was an accomplished horse-rider. He used to come frequently to Simla. Watching his deft horse-riding the lovely daughter of the Viceroy fell in love for Bhupendra Singh. When the Viceroy heard of this, he forbade Bhupendra Singh to enter Simla. It is said that Bhupendra Singh and the daughter of the Viceroy vanished one day from this spot. The incident created a furore in the English community. After that incident this place has come to be known as Scandal Point."

"Wonderful, you have been a very nice guide!" The three were listening to her with rapt attention; Naina clapped her appreciation.

"Naina, Radha knows very well the geography and history of Simla. Had I known this fact earlier, I would have kidnapped Radha from Scandal Point." Saying this Sanatan laughed aloud.

Radha too, smiled pleasantly.

"Now, where are you taking us, Radha?"

"There is a spot about 82 kilometres from here, known as 'Honeymoon Point', a favourite spot for newly-weds. If everybody wants, we can go there."

Everybody agreed. The cab travelled towards Mall Road and reached Jakhu Hills. Getting out of the cab, Radha said,

"Here's an ancient temple of Hanuman. During the battle of Ramayan, when Lakshman fainted, Hanuman rested here, while he was carrying the Dron Hill with the Sanjivani herb growing on it."

After visiting the temple Sudhendu exclaimed,

"Wonderful . . . wonderful . . ."

After that, they visited the 'Honeymoon Spot'. They enjoyed watching the scenic beauty of nature. When the cab brought them back to the hotel, they were famished. All four of them had lunch together. Then they sat in the hotel lobby and talked a lot.

Having spent three days amid the heavenly beauty of the nature of Simla, Sanatan and Radha returned to Umreth, via Baroda by Frontier Mail.

Kanaiyalal opened the door for them. He said,

"Come in, come in, children."

He went to the garlanded photograph of Kusum and said in an emotionally choked voice, "Look who has come to your house, Kusum. Your son, Sanatan has brought his bride home." He turned to look at Sanatan and Radha standing behind him, as tears rolled down his cheeks.

Bowing down before Kanaiyalal, Radha said, "Papa, don't worry about anything now. You should be happy that, your son has achieved the first success towards his cherished goal."

"Dear child, I am proud of you both. All right, now go and take your rest. You both must be tired from the long journey. Aunt Madhu has invited us for the lunch at her house."

Sanatan carried the pieces of baggage one by one to his room on the upper storey of the house.

After two hours, uncle Arvind's voice was heard. Immediately Sanatan went down.

"How are you, uncle?" Sanatan bowed down respectfully to Arvind.

"I am well. So, you have been to Agra and Simla?"

"Yes, uncle."

"How was the climate there?"

"It was very pleasant, uncle." Radha who had come down in the meantime replied modestly.

"Now, all of you get ready. Your aunt is waiting for you at home."

Sanatan said, "But, uncle, why did you take so much trouble? Now that Radha is here, she could have cooked."

"Oh! Look Kanu, your son has grown up. He thinks by cooking food for you all, Madhu is troubled. What do you say?"

"We have been each other's strength." He turned to Sanatan, "Beta, they enjoy being helpful to us. They are not separate from us."

Radha quickly entered the kitchen and emerged after ten minutes with steaming hot tea for everyone. Arvind sipped the tea and exclaimed, "Arre wah! Kanu yaar, I envy you. Henceforth, every morning you'll get such delicious tea."

Radha blushed, but said with a smile, "Uncle, promise to come here for tea daily. Then you won't have any reason to envy papa."

"Very clever, Radha! Very clever! Kanu, you are lucky to have such a nice daughter-in-law."

After some time all of them set out for Arvind's house. Madhu received Sanatan and Radha in the traditional manner and with due ceremony.

During lunch, the discussion ensued about Sanatan's plans for further studies. Sanatan declared his intention of taking up a room in a hostel while Radha was to live in Umreth. He would come to Umreth whenever he could manage during his holidays.

After about a week after their return from their honeymoontrip, Sanatan left for Bombay. Without any difficulty he gained admission to Elphinstone College to study for his M. Sc. He also got a room in a hostel without any difficulty.

Radha and Sanatan wrote letters regularly to each other.

Once, Radha was seated on a swing in her room. She must have read his letter three times. Suddenly, she felt a wave of nausea. She had to go to wash her mouth. After some time aunt Madhu arrived to take her along to a temple. Radha told her that she was not feeling well. The experienced aunt took her to a gynecologist's clinic.

Having examined Radha, he said, "You are pregnant, my child. Take good care of your health from now on."

Madhu and Radha were ecstatic to hear the doctor's prognosis. She advised Radha not to lift heavy things in the house and to eat well. Later that evening she wrote a letter to Radha's mother informing her of Radha's pregnancy.

During the month of August there were four holidays in succession owing to religious festivals. Shalin and Madhavi decided to accompany Sanatan to Umreth. Madhavi asked about Radha's health. They were all happy that she enjoyed good health. At night, when Sanatan found Radha alone in their room, he pressed her to his chest. She lightly pushed him away saying,

"Sanatan, we should be careful now. You are going to be a father soon."

"What!" Sanatan became very happy. "What did you say; I'm going to be a father? Are you sure?"

"You were to come here for these holidays, so I thought I would give you a surprise."

"Oh, I do declare! This is indeed a pleasant surprise."

"My brother Shalin and Madhavi have not come here just to meet me. They have come here to enquire about my health."

For the next two days everybody in the house was very excited.

The days flew like the wind. In the seventh month of pregnancy, Shalin and Madhavi once again came to Umreth to take Radha with them for her first delivery at her parents' home.

It was March. Spring had already set in. Colourful flowers bloomed on the slopes of Malabar Hill. Pink, orange and white Bougainvillea covered the walls of the buildings. But Sanatan was engrossed in his studies.

It was the last day of the examinations. He glanced at his wristwatch.

After coming out of the college, Sanatan called Radha's home. Everybody from the house had gone to Dr. O. J. Shah's Maternity home at Opera House. He hailed a cab and ordered the driver to take him to Opera House. Within minutes he arrived there. Radha's mother Lakshmi and Madhavi were sitting near Radha in the ward, while Vasudev, Shalin and Pulin were waiting outside the ward.

Greeting Sanatan with a broad smile Shalin happily echoed the traditional wish,

"My heartiest congratulations on being blessed with a son!"

Sanatan beamed with joy.

———◈———

Chapter 13

Sanatan and Radha were alone in the hospital. The baby had arrived.

"Radha, how good God has been to us. He has fulfilled your wish!"

"Shall I tell you something, Sanatan; my heart hungers to see my baby. Whenever I will see him sleeping beside me, I will feel, as if you are sleeping beside me. Truly, we are the ones blessed by our elders and graced by God. Really, this child has given me heavenly bliss."

"Since when did this child become yours only? Say, our child. This child is a symbol of our love." Saying this Sanatan's face glowed with pleasure.

Sanatan wrote a letter to his father informing him of the birth of his and Radha's son. Kanaiyalal wrote back. Everybody was very happy.

Radha stayed at her home for two full months. The other family members wanted her to stay for a further two months, but somehow Radha had been increasingly wanting with each passing day to go to Umreth and be in Umreth during the Diwali festivities. Within a week Kanaiyalal, Arvind and Madhu arrived from Umreth to Bombay to play with Sanatan's son.

After four days, at a suitable time Sanatan, Radha, the baby, Kanaiyalal, Arvind and Madhu left for Umreth. Waves of happiness were pulsating through Sanatan's life.

Days flew like the whirlwind. Once again the time arrived for Sanatan to leave for Bombay to attend college for his final year of studies for his M.Sc. in Nuclear Physics at Elphinstone College. Sanatan found it somewhat hard to concentrate on his studies with Radha and his son back in Umreth. Nevertheless, he passed the final examinations with distinction. After the exams were over, he returned to Umreth.

The results of the M.Sc. exam were announced. Sanatan had passed with the highest marks.

One evening, with happiness and joy radiating on his face, Sanatan said,

"Radha, the government of India is opening an Atomic Research Centre in Bombay. I have applied for a post of junior scientist. I have received a call-letter for an interview. I will be leaving for Bombay the day after tomorrow."

"Sanatan, I pray God to enable you to achieve greater success in your studies and in the field of science. You may happily leave for Bombay. Don't worry about us."

Sanatan stayed at his father-in-law's house. Having appeared for the interview at the Atomic Research Centre he returned to Umreth. After a fortnight, he was once again called for the second round of interviews and was selected to join the Atomic Research Centre (ARC) as a junior scientist in the nuclear reactor plant.

After returning from Bombay, Sanatan told his father and Radha about the job-offer he had received.

"Sanatan, I think now you should rent a house in Bombay and take Radha and Tapan with you." Kanaiyalal said.

"Papa, what will you do alone in this town?"

"Sanatan, don't worry about me. What can an old man like me want?"

"No papa, just remember what you had said, when I asked you to come with me to Bombay following my mother's death."

"Oh yes, I had said, I would stay with you after you get married and settle down."

"Then, what's the problem now, Papa? Your son has a job now." Radha said.

That evening Arvind and Madhu had come to meet them. Kanaiyalal informed him that Sanatan had obtained a job as a junior scientist in the ARC at Bombay. They expressed their happiness.

Then Sanatan said, "Uncle Arvind, my Papa has advised me to acquire a rented house in Bombay and take Radha and Tapan with me. I have asked my papa to accompany us to Bombay."

"That's not a bad idea." Madhu replied.

"Now that your son is ready to look after you, there is no reason why you shouldn't go with him." Arvind said.

Within four days, Sanatan convinced his father and sold the shop. Sanatan wrote to Pulin to arrange for a rented house somewhere in Chembur. Before their departure for Bombay, Pulin wrote to inform him that an annexe in a bungalow in Chembur had been rented.

Finally, Sanatan and Radha, accompanied by Tapan and Kanaiyalal, reached Chembur and settled down in their new house.

Sanatan was as good at his work as he was in his studies. He believed in doing his work with dexterity and integrity. His superiors took note of his intelligence, dedication and deftness. Impressed by his modesty and good manners Dr. Swaminathan assigned important research work to him. Gradually, his coworkers began to take note of Sanatan as a well-mannered, amiable and earnest person. Sanatan used to work very hard. He would always remain eager to read magazines and books on atomic research and related articles from all over the world. He read detailed accounts of researches carried out in Sweden, Germany, England, America and Russia. They had pioneered and done significant work in the field of nuclear technology. As he had access to all this literature, Sanatan took deep interest in the subject. Whenever he needed any book or a magazine, Dr. Swaminathan would use his influence and get the required publication for Sanatan. Dr. Swaminathan was deeply impressed by Sanatan's intelligence.

Many times, Dr. Swaminathan told Sanatan,

"I am proud to see that you are always anxious to learn more and more about atoms. And that is why I am trying to provide you with as much information as possible about atomic science."

Sometimes Sanatan would laugh and ask Dr. Swaminathan,

"Sir, the research that has been done to date or whatever is being carried out is taking place in America and Russia. Is my conclusion correct?"

"In a way, what you say is half correct. In fact, the scientists of Sweden, Germany and England began the research on the atom. After that, the superpowers of America and Russia plunged into atomic research for establishing their supremacy over other nations. The scientists of these two countries are carrying out noteworthy research not only in atom or atomic weapons, but also in other fields of science. Besides, I must say that the scientists of other nations also remain engrossed in carrying out in-depth research work on the secrets of nature."

"What is the position of India in all this?" Sanatan asked eagerly.

"It cannot be considered significant. But as an Indian, I am proud of our nation that Sir Jagdishchandra Bose proved to the world that vegetation has life within it. For the progress of India, it was of the utmost importance to produce energy from nuclear power. When this fact was realized, the Tata Institute of Fundamental Research, also known as TIFR, was established under the chairmanship of Dr. Homi Jehangir Bhabha, in 1945. In the year 1948, the Atomic Energy Act was passed. By 1950, the research reactor 'Cyrus' and in 1953, 'Dhruv' atomic reactors had been established at Trombay. In 1954, the Indian Atomic Energy Commission was established, which set up the Atomic Energy Establishment at Trombay. On 3rd August, 1954, the Department of Atomic Energy, also known as the DAE, where you are working, was established. Dr. Bhabha was appointed as its Secretary. Dr. Bhabha dreams of ushering in a green revolution in India through nuclear power. The scientists are deploying their mental wealth in several fields. For so many years our country has reeled under the British regime, hence we haven't been able to get proper direction and facilities. Owing to this we have not been able to take a large leap in the scientific field. But now that our country has attained independence, I am pleased to say that we have hundreds of scientists who could find their place at the forefront."

Having said this much, Dr. Swaminathan felt that his throat was parched and sipped some water from a glass. Explaining his viewpoint on science and scientists, Dr. Swaminathan continued,

"You know that an atom has two kinds of power within it. On the destructive side, there are nuclear weapons and atom bombs; whereas, on the peaceful and useful side are energy, medicine, agriculture and industry which are most important. When energy will be produced out of nuclear power, Indian experts won't have to look pleadingly at foreign lands, and for that purpose Dr. Bhabha has trained a team of expert scientists in India."

"Sir, I consider it my privilege to be working with such a great and modest personality of our nation."

"Dr. Bhabha is working without consideration of heat or cold, day or night to take this atomic centre of Trombay to greater heights. I have heard that he avoided getting married so that he could sacrifice his life for scientific research. Sanatan, you have within you such qualities befitting a scientist. You have truly imbibed the qualities of basically a German scientist who carried out invaluable research work while living in America. I will not be surprised if you achieve the nearly impossible and unique achievements in the field of science in the future. India will always prosper and shine due to scientific gems such as you."

Sanatan listened to Dr. Swaminathan in silence. After sharing a cup of tea with him, he took his leave. Dr. Swaminathan's words were echoing in Sanatan's ears.

After about a year, Dr. Swaminathan escorted Sanatan to introduce him to Dr. Homi Bhabha. Dr. Bhabha welcomed them with a smile.

"Sanatan, I am very pleased with your style of working. Your spirit of inquiry to find out the secrets of atomic and nuclear fields calls for appreciation. In future, you may have to play a very significant role in the Atomic Research Centre at Trombay. I want you to go to America for three years to carry out research in the atomic and nuclear fields."

Sanatan was thrilled. Instructing Dr. Swaminathan Dr. Bhabha said,

"Dr. Swaminathan, kindly explain to Sanatan matters relating to research work in detail.'

"Please give me a week, Sir. By that time, I will have finalized everything and I will report to you."

Sanatan came home that evening and informed Radha about it. She was excited to learn that Sanatan was handpicked to go to the US, but the next moment the thought of having to live without him for three long years saddened her. Nevertheless, she agreed to live in India and wait for Sanatan to come back.

After a fortnight, Sanatan left for the US leaving behind his father, the year-old-Tapan and Radha. In America, Sanatan excelled in his research studies. He worked on a unique theory of energy propulsion and harnessing synergy within electro-magnetic waves and other natural energy sources. After three years he was awarded the MS in Nuclear Physics by the University of Pennsylvania.

On completion of his time in America, a jubilant Sanatan returned home to India. Now, he was promoted to the role of a senior research scientist in the ARC. He was also allotted a spacious house in the campus.

One evening, Sanatan went to the Taj Mahal Hotel in Bombay. Representatives of scientifically and technologically advanced nations were participating in an International Seminar. Sanatan was scheduled to present a paper at the Seminar. Mr. Jefferson, representing the National Aeronautics And Space Administration, also known as NASA, was also a participant at the Seminar. Various dissertations on the 'Development of Newer Energy Sources' were presented. Sanatan's speech, delivered to a packed auditorium, on 'Alternative Energy Resources' evoked great interest among the participants. After the session was over, as he shook hands with Sanatan, Mr. Jefferson said,

"Sanatan, I am impressed by the paper on 'Alternative Energy Sources' you presented in the Seminar. Congratulations, young man!"

"Thank you Mr. Jefferson, for your compliments."

"I believe India can become a leader in the power sector if your theory is put to use."

"But Mr. Jefferson, I have merely expressed my thoughts before the seminar. Moreover, this subject still needs extensive research and then practical application."

"Do you have any doubt about its viability, Mr. Sanatan?"

"I think it would be premature to pass any judgment on my research, Mr. Jefferson. Anyway, it was my pleasure meeting you. We will keep in touch."

"Sure Mr. Sanatan, may I have your calling card? I am looking forward to an opportunity to meet and discuss the subject of your interest at length with you."

They exchanged their visiting cards; shook hands and then Sanatan emerged from the Hotel. He sat in his car waiting for him in the porch. The car sped towards Chembur. When Sanatan reached his office in the ARC, his secretary, Ms. D'Souza, told him that Dr. Homi J.

Bhabha, the commission's secretary was awaiting him. Sanatan knew that Dr. Bhabha wanted to make use of nuclear energy for peaceful purposes like agriculture, electricity generation and space research. Sanatan entered Dr. Bhabha's cabin.

"Welcome Sanatan, I hope, I have not caused you inconvenience by asking you to meet me immediately," said Dr. Bhabha.

"Not at all, Sir."

Sanatan waited patiently for the chairman to speak. He was intrigued as to why he was called with such urgency. It was most unusual for the chairman who was known for his cool temperament.

"So, how was the Seminar? I learnt, the gathering highly appreciated the paper on 'Alternative Energy Sources' presented by you today."

"Yes sir, the audience was appreciative."

"But, I'm interested in that remark you made about harnessing the attributes of solar radiation for evolving power generation."

"But Sir, that was a passing remark or perhaps an observation made towards such a possibility."

"Exactly, that's what I am hinting at—a possibility. A possibility that could change the future of the world!"

"Sir, I merely referred to that as a remote possibility and after mentioning it during my lecture, I thought, I shouldn't have done so."

"Perhaps, you don't know that you are on the right track."

"Sir, I'll try to see what made me think about such a possibility in the first place" said Sanatan.

"Yes my son, I want you to ponder more deeply on it. And yes, from now on don't mention it to anybody other than me."

"Yes, Sir."

"My congratulations once again, on the highly scholarly paper that you presented at the Seminar today. Alright, you may go now."

"Thank you Sir, thank you for your compliments. Good night Sir."

Sanatan left the Chairman's cabin and headed towards his office. As he walked, he was wondering who had reported his speech to the Chairman. Suddenly he was reminded of a reporter from the "Times of India" who was frantically jotting down every word he spoke in shorthand. He had even tried to ask if the TIFR or ARC were working on exploring possibilities of harnessing solar power for generating power. He remembered that he said absently, "Only the chairman of Atomic Energy Commission can decide on that."

It is possible the reporter had tried to speak with the chairman to find out the details and in that effort he had read out the part of his lecture delivered at the Seminar to the chairman. What intrigued him most that after the delivery of his speech not only a correspondent and his chairman, but someone else was interested in his passing thoughts. And that was Mr. Jefferson of NASA.

He entered his office and removed his jacket and loosened his tie. Placing his bag on the side table he stretched back in his swivel chair and closed his eyes in deep concentration. As if awakening from sleep after a while he pressed a bell to summon his secretary.

He ordered tea for himself and asked for his associate Mathur to be sent in.

Mathur had acquired his MS in nuclear physics from the University of Illinois only the previous year. An Alumnus of Delhi University, Mathur was a witty but serious scientist. He had an excellent rapport with Sanatan. Mathur was present at the Seminar.

They discussed the day's events. At last, Mathur said,

"It looks like you have placed your finger on some unknown switch, Sanatan, which has lit bulbs in alien brains."

"But, I can't understand why there is such undue interest?"

"Perhaps, you unconsciously said what was developing in the depths of your mind. Such things happen at times." Mathur explained.

"Let's begin checking various theories on alternative energy sources. Perhaps we shall be able to find an answer." Sanatan said finally.

For the next ten days or so, the two explored and analysed various theories. But there was no answer to the question baffling them.

One evening Sanatan returned home after his work. Radha was waiting for him on the balcony. After drinking a refreshing tea, Sanatan and Radha came out on the lush green lawns to take a stroll. The sun was setting behind the tall tamarind trees growing on the periphery of the sports grounds. Sanatan was intently looking at the setting sun, as if to find an answer from its rays, which were changing colours every minute.

He turned to Radha, "I think I've got an answer. I'll have to speak with the chairman."

Radha gave a perplexed look at Sanatan. Immediately Sanatan returned to his study and frantically made some notes. The next day morning he asked his secretary, Ms. D'Souza, to make an appointment with the chairman.

At around eleven Sanatan was ushered into the chairman's office. Dr. Bhabha asked his secretary to close the door and not to pass any calls on to him until Sanatan left.

———◈———

Chapter 14

"I'm sure you've checked your theories." Dr. Bhabha said, as he looked at Sanatan's papers.

"Yes Sir, I had been working on this until yesterday. The scientific hypothesis works out in this manner." Sanatan brought out his diary. Sanatan explained the theory at length to his boss with the help of the notes he had made the previous night in his study. Constantly for half an hour Dr. Bhabha kept his eyes closed in deep concentration, listening intently to each word spoken by Sanatan. Then he opened his eyes and looked intently at Sanatan in silence. But Sanatan was oblivious to the look of his chairman. He was summing up his discussion looking at the last of the notes in his papers. At last, when he concluded, Dr. Bhabha came around the desk and shook hands with him.

"In my career, I never met such a promising scientist as you!" Then he pressed a bell and his secretary appeared. "Bring us some tea, dear. And don't forget the cookies."

He turned to Sanatan, "Do you know young man, that, you have stumbled upon a great invention. I think your invention could change the future of the world and humanity. I'm sure you've realised that."

"Oh, yes, Sir."

"But you may have to go to the US to give final shape to your research,. We don't have the facilities in our labs. Even if we want to develop the facilities, the cost will be too high and the government might not support us at this stage to organise the facilities in our establishment."

Dr. Bhabha paused to hear Sanatan's reaction. But when Sanatan didn't offer any comment, he continued,

"You have been an excellent scientist all through your career. I will request the government of India to sponsor your research studies in the University of Illinois. I want you to consolidate your knowledge and make use of the modern laboratory facilities there."

"Yes Sir."

"I'll get you enrolled at the University from the next academic year onwards. Your salaries will remain unchanged. Besides, you'll be paid the necessary expenses that you may have to incur matching the American lifestyle. The Indian consulate will know of your affiliations with the ARC. Other than that, you don't have to reveal your contacts with this institution to anybody. I hope you understand. How old are you?"

"I am twenty-nine, Sir."

"That's good. I think you can begin preparations to go to America. Check on the validity of your passport. Attend to all your family matters. In the next three months you may have to leave."

"Thank you, Sir, for choosing me for this study."

"You deserve it, son. Go ahead, the country needs bright people like you." Dr. Bhabha moved forward to shake hands with him again and saw him to the door. It was already five in the evening. Sanatan walked to his office at the other end of the building. Having arrived there, he concentrated his attention on the unfinished tasks at hand. When he reached home at night, his wife Radha was waiting for him.

"Congratulations, Sanatan! The editorials of the leading national dailies have appreciated your lecture on energy. Whatever you are doing is beyond my ability to understand, but let me say, whatever you are doing is something great and wonderful."

"You won't believe it, Radha, but Dr. Bhabha invited me to his office. He told me that in about three months I will have to go to the University of Illinois at Chicago to do research. I understand that I may have to stay in the US for a period of three years. I shall have to go alone initially, but when the arrangements are made, I will organise to call you there." Sanatan replied sombrely.

"That's unnecessary. Tapan is studying in a school and your father too, is here. You may study with concentration and dedication."

"Will you be able to stay without me?"

"I won't like it, but somehow I will spend my days with your memories. By the way, what are you going to research?"

"The research is about harnessing energy from solar power." Sanatan gave a short reply. After some time all of them sat around the dining table. Kanaiyalal asked,

"What about your job here?"

"Papa, my tour of America has been sponsored by the Indian government. My services will not be discontinued. Dr. Bhabha has assured me that my job will be waiting for me on my return from America."

Time flew by. The day of Sanatan's departure for America arrived. Kanaiyalal, Radha and little Tapan went to Santa Cruz airport to bid farewell to Sanatan. He boarded the newly acquired aircraft L-1049— Lockheed Constellation.

When Sanatan reached O'Hare International airport, the grandeur and vastness of the airport impressed Sanatan's scientist mind. When he stood near the conveyer belt to collect his baggage, for a moment he was reminded of Radha, Tapan and his father. He was alone, in a huge and prosperous country. Moments later, remembering his mission he steadied his emotions. He picked up his bags from the conveyer belt, slung his bag over his shoulder, placed his two suitcases on a trolley, and walked towards the customs hall. Soon after completing the customs formalities he emerged from the airport. He had read and heard a lot about America, and this day he had another opportunity to experience life in America. It was the same America that wanted to show her superiority over other countries on her financial prowess. The lesser countries swallow the words of America as Gospel while tolerating their arrogant attitude and adhere to the code of conduct written by them. America was the only such country, whose financial fortunes grew by the arrangement policy of the Pentagon, which sold arms to other countries. From the O'Hare airport Sanatan reached the loop station through a subway. Making enquiries, he learnt that he had to take a cab or a bus to reach the campus of the University of Illinois. He had heavy baggage, so Sanatan came out of the railway station and hailed a cab.

When he reached the university campus he was filled with joy. He was given boarding in a hostel set amid tall trees and lush green lawns. He had a single occupancy room. He was happy to enter the well-furnished room. From it Sanatan could see Chicago city spread out in the distant horizon. His journey lasted over thirty-six hours. He was extremely tired. He stretched out on the bed and soon was fast asleep.

After a couple of hours he heard someone knocking at the door. It was the hostel supervisor wanting to check if he was comfortable. He looked at the clock on the bedside table. He had slept for almost three hours. Looking out of the windows he saw that it was already dusk. He thanked the supervisor and assured him that he was comfortable. He switched on the light. Thousands of miles away from his hometown, Umreth, he had come here for higher studies. He had left his dear ones and his favourite city for that purpose. He changed and went to the dining hall for dinner. After many years, he was sitting down for dinner all alone. All around many students from different countries were busy chatting and partaking of meals. But Sanatan was reminded of his mentor Dr. Homi Bhabha. He was lucky that, Dr. Bhabha had especially chosen him to pursue a specialised course in this university. He resolved mentally to be worthy of Dr. Bhabha's trust, which he had placed in him.

His thoughts were interrupted as someone gently tapped the table opposite him and asked, "May I sit here, if it's not a bother to you?"

He looked up, "No bother at all. Please sit by all means." He smiled at a bright young man of his age looking down at him. He seemed to be of East Asian origin.

"I'm Ivan. I'm Malaysian."

"It is a pleasure meeting you, Ivan; I'm Sanatan from India."

"Your appearance betrays this fact. Indeed I'm pleased to meet you too. I'm impressed by the richness in your voice."

Sanatan laughed, "You seem to be a wonderful man. You certainly know how to flatter others in the first meeting."

"No, I'm not flattering you. I'm serious. Your voice is certainly very rich."

"Thanks, Ivan. But I love your nice manners to put the other at ease. That reflects your rich culture. Who is in your family, Ivan?"

"Only my father; my father is the richest man in our country. We own an island—Sohali, southwest of Malaysia. We have business interest in pearls, coral and fishery."

"That's great! My father is a trader in a small town in India. I've been working in a private firm and the owner was kind enough to sponsor my studies here." He intentionally didn't reveal his employment with the Atomic Research Establishment.

"That's very nice."

"It seems you aren't married. But I'm married and have a son too."

"Oh! Really! How come you got married so early?"

"Well, in India as soon as a boy completes his graduation, the elders in the family want him to get married. This happened to me." Sanatan replied briefly.

"In which room do you stay?"

"Don't you know that I don't stay in this hostel? But I come here often for dinner and meet my friends. My father has bought a penthouse for me in Carbon Dale. There are six bedrooms, a dining hall and a drawing room. And I live all alone in it."

"You must be finding it lonely at times."

"Yes, you are right. That's why I invite my good friends at times. I've two servants to take care of our penthouse and a cook to take care of my culinary needs."

After dinner they came out of the dining hall. Sanatan promised Ivan that he would visit his house over the weekend. Sanatan went up to his room and sat down to write a letter back home to Radha and his father. After writing two long letters he carefully folded them, placed them in an envelope and pasted it. Putting them under the table clock he changed into his pyjamas and stretched out on the bed. He was to report to the administrative office the next day and complete his formalities for admission.

Sanatan dreamt he was in his home at Chembur. Dr. Bhabha was visiting him. He was grateful that an illustrious personality like Dr. Homi Bhabha was visiting his house. Radha was telling him that she wanted him to bless their son, Tapan. Dr. Bhabha took Tapan on his lap and kissed him on his cheeks. Sanatan was telling his son, "Do you know, Tapan, on whose lap you are sitting? He is the greatest scientist of this century."

Sanatan woke up in the morning. He dressed, had breakfast and prepared his briefcase with the necessary papers for completing the formalities for admission. He had also carried the banker's cheque for the specified amount to be paid. The official told him his tuitions were to begin after four days. Sanatan spent those four days going around the city in a bus. He also toured the sprawling campus.

Almost every alternate day Sanatan wrote letters to Radha in India and similarly received her letters. Tapan was growing fast and was enquiring about him. Kanaiyalal's health did not pose any worry. On the other side, Sanatan was maintaining regular contact with his mentor, Dr. Homi Bhabha. He used to update him about his progress in his studies. At times, Dr. Bhabha would make useful suggestions to him. The first year went by uneventfully. Sanatan was anxious about successfully completing his research studies. Dr. Bhabha assured him, not to worry, as he was confident of his passing with flying colours.

Time passed quickly. One day, Sanatan and Ivan were sittin in a coffee shop when Ivan said,

"So, our results will be announced next week."

"Yes, I'm anxiously waiting for it."

"But, you don't have to worry about your passing the tests. Your track record through the year has been quite exemplary."

"Hey, don't glorify me." Sanatan laughed. "Why don't you talk about yourself? You have been a pet student of our research director, Dr. Ronaldo."

Ivan smiled pleasantly and said,

"Actually the whole credit goes to you. Why do you forget that you used to solve a number of questions, which baffled me? Besides, you have an excellent memory and sharp mind. How did you become so clever?"

"I don't think I'm as clever as you are making out. However, since my childhood, I've been taught the virtue of developing concentration in whatever I do. My parents have brought me up with great care. How could I waste their money and efforts by failing to succeed?"

"I'm impressed, Sanatan. My father would be very happy to meet you. He is expected to visit me next weekend."

"That's nice. I'd love to meet him." Sanatan added, "Shall we go; I have to write a few letters to India and after that be on time for dinner."

"In fact, I was about to invite you to have dinner with me at my house. Why don't you put off your letter-writing until tomorrow?"

"Well, if that's your wish, I succumb to thee, Sultan of Sohali!" Sanatan got up and bowed.

Ivan slapped him on the back and exclaimed,

"Hey, don't tease me; I might be a powerful man in Sohali, but here, as students, we're equal. By the way, aren't all the men equal in God's eye? Then, why discriminate, friend?"

"I am not discriminating, I was joking."

"I knew that."

Sanatan paid off their bill for coffee and came out on the road. Ivan's car was parked a little away. Ivan opened the passenger side and invited Sanatan to get in. He drove the car towards his house. Within fifteen minutes he was parking his car in the underground car parking lot. They took an elevator to reach his penthouse. A uniformed servant opened the door and let them in. They handed over their overcoats to him and walked into the drawing room. The room had a small bar. Ivan went around the bar and asked,

"What would you prefer? I'm sure you won't say 'no' to a little drink."

"Sure, I'll have cognac. Besides, I'm already cold."

"That's better."

Ivan poured cognac into two glasses and came over to Sanatan. Handing over one to him, he asked,

"Have you ever tasted genuine Malaysian food?"

"No, never. But are there vegetarian recipes in Malaysian menus?"

"Of course there are. I'll ask Larsen to cook some vegetarian Malaysian dishes today. I too will eat veggie food with you." He clapped and a stoutly built cook appeared.

Ivan reeled out a long list of dishes to him.

Sanatan exclaimed, "Oh, so much heavy food!"

Ivan laughed, "It's not heavy. Malaysian dishes are lighter to digest, less spicy than your Indian dishes and less salty. Moreover the ingredients like asparagus, mushrooms, tender bamboo, dill and soy make it highly nutritious."

As Larsen left, Ivan sipped cognac and said,

"My mother used to be an excellent cook."

"You must be missing her cooking living here."

"I've never had an opportunity to taste her cooking."

"Why, what happened?" Sanatan asked quickly.

Ivan took a gulp of the remaining cognac from his glass. He looked up with a hint of tears in his eyes and said slowly,

"She is no more."

"Oh! I'm sorry." Sanatan got up from his chair and walked towards Ivan standing near the bar.

"How did she die?"

"I was very young when she died."

"Was she ill or something . . . ?"

"No, she wasn't ill. In fact, my father and mother were dockworkers at a port in Kyushu. I think, you know where Kyushu is." Then he added, "It's a seaport on the West coast of Nagasaki in Japan."

Sanatan just said, "Hmmmmm . . ."

"The Americans bombed the port on 9th August 1945. My mother was working in a shed near the Japanese naval stores when the Americans attacked. My father and I were saved because at that moment my father had taken me to the doctor of the labour camp as I had severe flu. She died in the bombardment." Ivan said heavily.

"I am extremely sorry to learn of her tragic end, Ivan." Sanatan compassionately patted him on his shoulder.

Chapter 15

For one long minute both fell silent.

"That incident shook my father. When I grew up and studied well, my father, now a business tycoon decided that I should acquire enough knowledge in nuclear physics and put my knowledge for the development of the good of society at large, unlike what the Americans did."

"That's wonderful."

"My father is totally against the atrocities and injustice imposed by the so-called developed countries on the hapless and poor people of the undeveloped countries. He aims at establishing such world-order where the existence of the poor is not threatened and they have equal rights to live as they choose without the dictates of the wealthy nations." After a pause, Ivan added in a resolute tone, "And I've decided to fulfill the wish of my father."

"I am fully appreciative of your father who has witnessed and indeed been a victim of the wrath of the barbaric American bombardment of Hiroshima and Nagasaki, where lakhs either lost their lives or were maimed for life."

"My father's mission in life is realising some means to achieve peace and prosperity for the people all over the world."

"But, that cannot be achieved unless the world is freed from the dangers of the armament race." Sanatan supported his viewpoint.

"My father abhors the armaments race of the Super Powers. Unless a full stop is put to the production of lethal weapons of mass-annihilation, world-peace can never be achieved." Ivan observed.

"Certainly, we the young generation must strive to work for world-peace."

"I really wonder if world-peace that we dream of and desire could ever be achieved."

"Why not, Ivan, why not?" Sanatan asked passionately. "When right-minded people come together and work in unison, it could certainly be achieved."

"But, to me, today, it looks like a distant dream."

The two friends continued to discuss the future of world-peace, and a short time later Larsen entered with a respectful bow.

"Sir, dinner is ready. When you are ready, just call me."

"We've almost finished our drinks. Lay the table, Larsen. We're coming."

"Right, Sir . . . ." Larsen left.

Sanatan enjoyed the Malaysian food and asked for the recipe of each item from Larsen who obliged him. Ivan was pleased to observe that Sanatan was genuinely enjoying the Malaysian dishes.

After the sumptuous dinner, both friends returned to Ivan's study. Larsen brought them hot chocolate with vanilla ice cream and some pastries that Ivan ordered later.

Half an hour later, Sanatan collected his overcoat from the Valet. Ivan followed him to the elevator. He said, "Let me drop you to the hostel in my car."

"No, no; I'll take a cab, Ivan. Thanks. Don't bother."

"What bother? I won't drive this time. I'll ask my driver to chauffeur the car and we'll continue our conversation."

When they emerged from the house it was already snowing heavily and there was a cold wind blowing. But inside the car it was warm, as the driver had thoughtfully switched on the heater, long before the duo had arrived.

"When we arrived at your place, it wasn't quite as cold as this, was it?" Sanatan observed.

"Well, it is difficult to predict the climate of this windy city of Chicago. There is bright sunlight one moment that could soon be changed to snowfall or rain within a moment." Ivan chuckled.

Reaching the hostel the driver stopped the car near the gate of the hostel. Sanatan shook hands with Ivan, opened the door and stepped out. Ivan left and Sanatan reached his room. He switched on the room-heater and lights simultaneously. He took off the overcoat and placed it on a heavy clothes-hanger and sat on a chair near the table. Several books were placed systematically in a bookcase. He pulled out a voluminous book on nuclear research written by an American. He had received the book that very morning from the library through a friend.

He made notes of minute details in his diary and read until midnight. Tired he got up and stretched out on the bed.

A fortnight passed. Sanatan was reading in the library. Ivan tiptoed to where Sanatan was sitting in a far corner. Sanatan saw him as he neared him. Ivan asked him to come out of the library. Sanatan collected his books and notes and followed him to the cafeteria.

Once in the noisy atmosphere of the cafeteria Sanatan enquired,

"Yes, what's the matter?"

"Sorry, if I've disturbed you, pal. But I couldn't wait to share my news with you."

"What is the news?"

"My father is coming here tomorrow on a business tour. He will be staying with me for at least a week."

"That's wonderful!"

"By the way, he is also looking forward to meet you. I have written to him about you. My father always used to say, a man is recognised by his speech. You, certainly, are a thorough gentleman."

"Well, well; thanks for being so charitable with your compliments."

"So, what's the news from India? How are your wife and son?"

"They are very well. The little sonny is anxious to see me."

"And your wife?" Ivan winked and laughed at his own joke.

"Well, she must be anxious to meet me, too."

"Then why don't you get them here?"

"And where will I lodge them; in my hostel?" Sanatan asked mockingly. Then he added, "Anyway, just ten months are remaining until the completion of my research studies, and then I'll be with them again!"

"If you wish, you can be with them now."

"And how?" Sanatan was slightly irritated.

"Get them here. They can stay at my house."

"Your house?"

"Yes, why not? It's large enough to accommodate a whole army unit."

"Pal, you don't understand."

"I understand; that's why I am suggesting this. If they come here and stay in my house, the loneliness you are enduring will end. Moreover, I can see that you are always thinking of your family back home in India. Let me enjoy the company of your son while you are in America."

"Thank you, Ivan. Indeed you are very kind. But, I'm sure that it would be an unnecessary bother to you."

"What nonsense! I have already spoken with to father about it. On the contrary, he was very happy about my idea. Now, without delay write a letter and arrange for the necessary travel documents and get them here."

"Sure, thanks again. I'll write to them today."

"If you thank me one more time I will punch you." Ivan laughed happily.

That evening Sanatan wrote three letters—one to Radha, the second one to his father and the third letter to Dr. Homi Bhabha narrating the offer made by Ivan. Dr. Bhabha gladly assured him of official assistance to make the necessary arrangements for his family to travel to America.

Sanatan and Ivan were waiting at the airport. A British Airways Boeing 707 came to halt in the departure area. Gradually, the passengers alighted and emerged into the vast lounge of the airport after security and customs checks. As soon his eyes fell on him, Ivan's father, William, waved at his son from a distance. William was short and wore a light coloured suit of costly material with a flowing overcoat draped over his shoulders. He came forward pushing a baggage trolley. Ivan quickly moved forward and embraced him warmly. He took charge of the trolley. Indicating Sanatan, he introduced him to his father.

"Dad, this is Sanatan, my course mate."

"Oh! Hello Sanatan. How do you do!" He extended his podgy hand.

Sanatan took his hand and said, "I'm honoured to have met you, Sir. It's a rare privilege for me to be with you today."

William said with a chortle, "Why do you say so, son? Don't be formal. I'm a business tycoon for my business associates, not for my dear ones. And you are among the dear ones."

"I'm touched, Mr. William." Sanatan said with feeling.

"Where is the car, Ivan?"

"It's outside waiting for you, Dad."

Soon they emerged from the sprawling airport lounge to the kerb. The driver of a Rolls Royce limousine saluted smartly as he opened the kerbside door for William to enter. William beckoned Sanatan to join him on the rear seat. Ivan took the seat next to the driver and Sanatan went round the car and occupied the seat beside William.

"Dad, how's the business back home?"

"No complaint, son."

And then he continued talking about his business affairs in Malaysia until their car came to a halt in the porch of their penthouse. The driver alighted and opened the door for him. A valet in a black suit appeared in the doorway and opened the door for Sanatan. William welcomed Sanatan,

"Come in, young man, come in."

Ivan and Sanatan followed him to the drawing room. The vale prepared a large glass of bourbon and handed it to William. He sipped and approved of the taste and placed it to one side. The valet politely asked

Sanatan which drink he preferred. Sanatan ordered a small peg of whisky on the rocks. Ivan too followed suit.

They sat across from William who took the large swivel chair. Taking a sip from his glass William said to Sanatan,

"I've learnt that you've topped your class, Sanatan! Excellent, young man, excellent! Keep it up."

"Dad, Sanatan is one of the most brilliant students of this University."

"So, what do you propose to do after your doctorate?"

"Sir, I'll return to India."

"Do you have any employment in India?"

Sanatan hesitated. He didn't feel like lying to this amiable man that he was unemployed. He said,

"Sir, I'm a scientist employed with an organisation of the Indian Government."

"Oh! That's great! I thought that you couldn't be an ordinary person." Ivan exclaimed.

"Look, Sanatan, I'm glad that you are in a government service. However, a scientist doesn't always have a free hand in conducting research and putting his inventions to use when he is employed in a government service."

"That's true, Sir."

"Therefore at this point of time in your life, should you find it necessary to seek my help in achieving your legitimate goal, do let me know. I'll be glad to place my resources at your disposal. But, Sanatan, please bear in mind that such research must be useful for the overall good of humanity. That's my major concern."

"I understand that, Sir. I'm highly appreciative of your kind gesture."

"Oh! By the way, when are your wife and son arriving? I was glad that you accepted Ivan's offer."

"I can't thank both of you enough for your kind gesture and generosity. My wife, son and also my father are expected here within a couple of months."

"That's great. Just remember, the life woven with noble and ideal qualities is never wasted. The fragrance of the good work of a man always spreads after his death. I will pray God to help you always in completing your life in a noble manner. You have my blessings. You will never get peace anywhere in the world such as that obtained on Sohali Island. I will be pleased if you accept my invitation to visit Sohali."

William asked him to remain for dinner. When dinner was served he made him sit beside him at the right side of the table.

"I hope you will like our Malaysian food."

"I've already relished it once as a guest of Ivan, Sir."

"Oh, really!" William was very happy that day.

After dinner Sanatan took his leave. Ivan arranged for a car to drop him at the hostel.

That night Sanatan wrote a letter to Radha and narrated all he had discussed with William and Ivan. He also wrote how anxious he was to meet them all after almost a year and a half.

That night, Sanatan enjoyed the soundest sleep ever since his arrival in America.

After about a month Radha's letter arrived.

On March 15th Radha, Tapan and Kanaiyalal were to arrive by an Air India flight to New York.

Chapter 16

Having cleared the customs check, Radha and Tapan, followed by Kanaiyalal, emerged from the customs hall and suddenly Radha spotted Sanatan standing at a distance. Instantly their eyes met and Sanatan's face lit up. Radha's eyes twinkled. They put their baggage on a trolley. Sanatan inclined his head forward to his father, Kanaiyalal, with respect.

While walking with Ivan on one side and Radha on the other, Sanatan introduced Ivan to Radha.

Radha folded her hands and greeted him, "Hello, I am very glad to meet you in person. However, I would have recognized you, even if you had met me alone, thanks to Sanatan's letters."

Ivan chuckled, "Sanatan is very good at drawing up a precise description of his friends' personalities through his words. I would also have recognised you, if you had come alone."

"Oh! Is that so?" Radha murmured.

Then Ivan turned to Kanaiyalal," How was your flight?"

Kanaiyalal didn't understand English but he understood what Ivan had asked. He gave a monosyllabic reply, "Fine." Then he said something to Sanatan.

Sanatan smiled in understanding and interpreted what Kanaiyalal had said, "He says that it was the first time he had flown on an aircraft. Frankly, he was very excited at the prospects of leaving the shores of India and travelling thousands of miles to America. For him the experience was fascinating.'"

"And how about you, Bhabhiji?" Ivan asked Radha.

"Oh, you called me 'Bhabhiji'! Where did you learn this word?"

"Well," Ivan said, pointing to Sanatan, "He taught me that. I asked him how an Indian addresses the wife of another, and he explained it to me."

"I'm glad you've begun learning about our Indian culture!"

Sanatan remarked humorously.

All of them laughed.

Radha and Kanaiyalal were amazed at the enormous size of the John F. Kennedy Airport. They all walked and sat in the visitor's lounge and discussed what was occurring in their lives.

Eventually they hailed a cab to LaGuardia Airport. The flight to Chicago was about to leave. When they landed at Chicago Airport, night had fallen and it was pitch dark. They emerged from the airport and headed towards the parking lot. Ivan's two cars awaited them. They arranged their baggage and seated themselves in the cars. They drove alongside the Michigan Lake for a while and then entered the South University. A short while later, both the cars entered the underground parking of a huge building at Carbondale.

Ivan gave the necessary instructions to his drivers and escorted Kanaiyalal, Radha, Tapan and Sanatan to the elevator. Quick as a flash, the elevator brought them to his top floor penthouse. A uniformed Valet opened the door for them. He seated them comfortably in the drawing room. Soon fresh fruit-juices were served. After exchanging pleasantries, Ivan asked his Valet to show them to their rooms.

The large spacious halls and luxurious bedrooms impressed them greatly. The floor was covered with thick Mongolian carpet. Their feet sank into it as they walked on it. Since the penthouse was centrally heated, they were protected from the impact of the severe cold outside. The glittering Italian crystal chandeliers highlighted the splendour of the elegant furniture displayed in the main hall and the dining rooms. Heavy dark velvet curtains with a backdrop of silky net curtains created a dreamlike effect. Radha and Kanaiyalal felt as if they had been ushered into some royal palace.

When they were alone, Radha could not help but appreciate the grandeur of the house, "I must confess, Sanatan; I've never seen anything so grand before. It looks like your friend is very wealthy."

"Yes, Radha, he is literally sitting on a goldmine. But he also has a heart of gold. In spite of having so much wealth at his disposal, he is not one to be pompous and proud. In fact, Ivan believes in the absolute simplicity of life, which is reflected by his demeanour."

"I'm glad you have found such a person as a friend," said Kanaiyalal to Sanatan in the Gujarati dialect.

"You're right, Daddy. As well as that, his father is a very kind and loving person. He is very hard working. His life story is a legend of rags to riches."

"Is that so? What is he doing?"

"Well, he began as a dock worker back in 1945 and has risen to this level through his sheer determination and Herculean efforts. He owns the Sohali Island and he is one of the richest people in Malaysia."

The cook, Larsen, came into the drawing room and said, "Will you all come for dinner please."

The dining table and chairs were very artistic. They were made out of transparent acrylic plastic and added beauty to the already magnificent surroundings. They all feared that just by touching them they would ruin their splendour.

After partaking of their meals, all arose. Radha and Kanaiyalal were extremely tired because of their long journey. All the dishes were tasty.

Radha said, "From tomorrow onwards I will cook Gujarati dishes and you will be very happy to taste them."

In reply Ivan said, "Bhabhiji, give instructions to Larsen and he will cook your favourite recipes, which you all will like.

After the dinner, Sanatan and Ivan entered the study room. They began to read and discuss their study topics.

"Please tell me Sanatan, is it true that the intensity of Cosmic rays changes with different positions of the sun during the day?"

"You see, we have been conducting research on that aspect. Basically, in order to understand the phenomena you must realize that every planet including our Earth possess definite magnetic properties and gravitational pull."

"But, I've learnt that some kind of research has been taking place in this direction in your country." Ivan said.

"Maybe your information is correct. Likewise, research is being conducted in many other countries of the world. But, as you know, it's like a marathon. It is the ultimate winner who matters."

"That's true. But, I think you have substantial knowledge of the research in the nature of cosmic rays and its application."

"In fact, I was curious to learn about the magnetic and gravitational properties of the sun and its solar power for evolving some kind of energy waves. While studying that aspect, I came across the phenomena of cosmic rays. During my studies, I've noticed that the intensity of cosmic rays was not constant all the time. I can't definitely pinpoint its cause at this moment."

"How do you think solar power could be used for energy evolvement?"

"It's like this. I'm sure you are aware of the fact that the Sun revolves around the Earth and how the days and nights are caused."

"Yes, ... Hmmmm"

"Well, even during the night on one portion of the Earth, the Solar Rays don't die down on such parts of the Earth."

"Is that true?"

"It's true. The wavelength and the frequency of the Solar Rays nevertheless get weakened, but it never totally dies down. My intention is to replenish such weaknesses of the solar rays by using the magnetic properties of the Earth and making them equally strong everywhere."

"Oh, that sounds like an impossible task."

"It's difficult; but not impossible. Many impossible things have been made possible through the sheer diligence and conscientious efforts of the scientists."

"How long do you think you would take to complete your research?"

"I can't say. It could take anything from a few months to many years. I'm currently studying towards achieving that."

Late that night Ivan showed Sanatan into his bedroom and said,

"Goodnight, Sanatan. We will all take breakfast tomorrow morning."

When Sanatan entered the room Tapan was fast asleep and Radha was waiting for him.

"After so many months, we will be lonely no more" Radha said, blinking. "When you are in front of me, how shall I be able to sleep? Unless you hold me in your arms, I will not sleep at all."

Sanatan switched off the light. He embraced Radha forcefully and then he said,

"In your absence I did not feel well. But what could I have done?"

Both slept the night through in each other's arms.

In the morning Radha opened her eyes. She stood and looked through the window. Away in the distance, the sun was rising in the sky with rays of many colours. To go out into the balcony she opened the handle of the door.

All of a sudden the cold breeze came inside. Radha closed the door immediately but the cold breeze woke Sanatan up. Radha was standing some distance away. He asked,

"Hey Radha, what are you doing standing there?"

"The Almighty has created such a wonderful universe. I was enjoying the beauty of nature. Like Bombay there are a large number of trees, tall skyscraper buildings, and best of all, my favourite sight which is the sunrise. Even though we are thousands miles away from Bombay the creator is still the same in this unknown country." Sitting near Sanatan, Radha spoke.

"You are right. But in constructing the different minds of a human being the Almighty has made a very diverse universe. Don't you feel the creator has made such a wonderful universe?"

"Sanatan, you are right. You will find good and bad natured people everywhere, whether we are in America or in India".

Four evenings later everybody sat in Ivan's car. Ivan was taking them on a trip to see all the wonderful sights of the area. The car drove off.

After passing Michigan Lake the car turned. They passed Sheriden Road, and a little further away they found a magnificent building, Bahai Mandir, very near to Linden Avenue. The car stopped. For many centuries human beings have been constructing temples, mosques and churches to show their faith and devotion to God. The Bahai Mandir is an extraordinarily beautiful temple of the Bahai Community. Some of the temple is made up entirely of glass. On the summit there is a big dome, and there is a delightful garden nearby. It took about 40 years to construct these nine gates in Mandir. The religious-minded people are attracted by seeing Baha-Ul-Allah slogans on the walls and doors.

Everybody descended the staircase with Ivan. Pointing his finger at the mini theatre, Ivan said,

"Come on, in this theatre the wonderful past of the Bahai community can be seen on the screen."

After seeing the film on the Bahai community, everybody emerged from the theatre.

Ivan said, "In the Bahai Religion, more attention is given to the 'family unit'. Give justice and love to all human beings. It is clearly said in the religion that if you are committing sins, then you have no right tarnish the image of others who have also committed sins. In this religion there is a lot of importance placed on maintaining good relations with the people of other different religions."

"Don't you feel that the majority of human beings are becoming more conscious about religion?" Sanatan commented on seeing more and more people enter the Bahai Mandir.

"It is difficult to say. But I must say that many people are attracted to religion, and more and more religious buildings have been constructed!"

After pausing for a while Ivan continued.

"Sanatan, you know very well that religion and science are very closely related. In my opinion science is not right without religion and religion is not perfect without science."

They all went into the garden and spoke about various issues.

All of a sudden a snowfall started.

Trembling with cold all hurried out of the garden and sat in the car. The car drove away.

The car stopped after crossing Jackson Street and then stopped again at the corner of Franklin Street. When they got out of the car, the snow had stopped.

In the opposite direction, there was a wonderful Ambassador hotel. They all went there to have their dinner.

After finishing their meals, they reached home. It was about 11 p.m.

On the following day both friends went to college together. They spent a few hours in the library and then went to the cafeteria when they talked about their studies. Sanatan asked his friend,

"Do you know Ivan, that from 1939 to 1945 research and development work in the field of atomic energy was carried out in Britain?"

"What areas did those studies cover?"

"Well, according to the reports available, they fell into two distinct categories. The Cavendish Laboratory in Cambridge, the Birmingham University and the National Physical Laboratory were engaged in that Research and Development work. This covered nuclear physical studies, the development of analytical methods and investigations of the chemical and physical properties of uranium and its compounds."

"And what was the second feature of the research work in England?"

"The second aspect of the research work was related to development work undertaken in industry aimed at the achievement of an industrial process for the production of high purity uranium metal. Presently, extensive work is also being carried out in the development of methods for separation of uranium isotopes. Besides, developmental work is in progress on the manufacture and properties of uranium hexafluoride and electrolytic cells for the production of fluorine."

"But will such developmental work lead to the ultimate production of the atomic weapon system?"

"Why not, but only if wisdom prevails over the minds of the political leaders."

Days passed by. One morning, Sanatan and Ivan were sitting on the sofa in the drawing room, reading newspapers. All of a sudden Ivan saw news about atomic research inventions. He asked Sanatan,

Have you looked at this report?"

"No, my friend, please read it."

"Six international committees were established to assess the Biological Effects of Atomic Radiation, which is also called by its acronym—BEAR. The committee was to provide a thorough review on the effects of atomic radiation on living organisms. The Committees on BEAR was put together in 1955." Ivan paused for a breath and then added, "Under the provisions, six committees were formed to investigate various problems arising from the release or presence of radiation in the environment. Each of these committees are studying the following—the Pathologic Effects of Atomic Radiation; Meteorological Aspects of the Effects of Atomic Radiation; Effects of Atomic Radiation on Agriculture and Food Supplies; Disposal and Dispersal of Radioactive Wastes; and Oceanography and Fisheries. The findings of all these committees are expected to provide valuable insight into various kinds of adverse effects of atomic radiation on human lives. These committees are expected to submit their preliminary reports finally within the next three years. Besides, the studies conducted by the Committees on BEAR do not overlap with the studies conducted by the Atomic Bomb Casualty Commission."

Ivan looked quizzically at Sanatan. Then he asked, "What do you make of it?"

"It is clear that two distinct thought processes are simultaneously developing in the world today, especially after the nuclear attacks by America on Japan. The first line of thought is that the economically developed nations of the world have come to realize that nuclear supremacy is essential for maintaining their supremacy in the world and for keeping the underdeveloped countries under their thumb."

"And what is the second line of thought?" Ivan asked anxiously.

"Well, you just read the second report. The sane people of the world have come to grips with the devastating effect nuclear energy could have on mankind at large, if used indiscriminately."

"But then, should we do away with the research and development of nuclear capabilities?" Ivan was perturbed.

"No, I'm not in favour of giving up the development of nuclear capabilities. However, a lot of effort and research is needed to fully develop the potential of nuclear energy. The last decade of physics has been very exciting. Undoubtedly the future will come with many more surprises. The best we can do now is to get ready for the challenges ahead."

After giving his views, Sanatan fell silent.

Everybody then sat on the dining chairs to enjoy some tea and breakfast.

At night, Sanatan and Ivan came back from the college. In the drawing room Radha, Tapan and Kanaiyalal sat talking and enjoying the music coming from the record player.

Later, they ate dinner and then everybody stood up.

Suddenly the ring of the telephone disturbed the calm of the drawing room. The Valet appeared and picked up the phone. He listened to the voice on the other end of the line, and then turned to Radha, "It's for you, Ma'am, from India."

She picked up the shining brass receiver.

"Hello, it's Radha," she said hesitantly.

"Hello Radha, it's Shalin here. How are you, Radha?"

"I'm fine, Shalinbhai. I have just been thinking of you all. How is everything there?"

"Is Sanatan there?"

"Oh yes, he is right here." Sanatan was standing near Radha. She placed the receiver in his hands. Sanatan placed the receiver to his ear and said, 'Hello, this is Sanatan . . . ."

"Listen Sanatan, I have sad news for Radha and you. My mother died yesterday afternoon after a brief illness."

"Oh my God, how did that happen?" Sanatan uttered these words painfully. Shalin told of the incident in detail.

"Oh, I'm very sorry to hear it." He turned to Radha and said, "Speak with Shalin. But have courage. Your mother is with us no more."

Radha found it difficult to suppress her sobs as she began speaking to Shalin, "Hello Bhaiyya, how did all this happen." With that, she began to cry aloud.

Chapter 17

Sanatan turned his attention to Radha who was crying inconsolably, sitting on a sofa nearby. As gently as possible, he tried to tell her what Shalin told him and the futility of travelling to India. He explained that Shalin had called up after the funeral was over.

After some time when she became quiet, Kanaiyalal came forward and placed his shaking hand on her head and said, "I can understand how you feel, when your dear one departs. Please have peace. Pray that the God gives your mother a place in heaven. She was an angel."

Radha let out a small sob and wiped tears from her eyes. Little Tapan was perturbed as to what was happening to his mother as he observed that she was crying so much. Seeing his mother so upset, he also cried. Suddenly gloom spread over the house. Ivan offered his consolation and asked her if he should organise for her to travel to India, which she quietly declined.

After some time, Sanatan along with Radha and Tapan went to his bedroom.

That night, Radha found it hard to sleep. But little Tapan, who realised that something unpleasant had happened, had fallen asleep. Sanatan sat in the bed holding Radha in his arms who wept intermittently as she found it difficult to endure the pain of separation from her mother, which could never be bridged during this lifetime.

She said, "Before we left Bombay, I went to meet my mother. She was not well, despite that, she enthusiastically asked Madhavi Bhabhi to prepare excellent food for her. Although the doctor had advised her not to eat sweets, she asked me to place a small piece of Barfi in her mouth. She then told me, 'I don't know if I'll ever see you again. Let me have my favourite sweet at your hands.' She knew, Sanatan, that sweets were not recommended for her health."

Sanatan stroked her arm to console her and said, "Look Radha, I understand how you feel. But crying any longer won't get your mother back. Moreover you have read the Geeta. It is said that the bodies of the embodied-self can neither be slained nor can it be the slayer. The embodied-self casts off its worn out bodies and enters others which are new. Weapons kill the body, not the soul.

The soul is eternal, all-pervading, stable, immovable and ancient. We are all mortal beings. Whoever is born has to die one day. In fact, there is no wisdom in crying over a loved one's death, but it is better to cherish one's good ideals and adopt virtues from life."

Radha unsuccessfully tried to stifle her sobs and said slowly,

"I am aware of the truth in your words. Despite that the thought of her not existing within this world is unbearable." Sanatan pulled her close to him and said soothingly, "Radha, my dear, when you understand so much, why do you cry so much? Yes, the thought of not being able to see her alive anymore is certainly painful. But Radha, are you not the same brave person who had given me moral strength and courage to complete my M.Sc. and reach these heights of my career?"

Radha looked up at Sanatan and smiled wanly, "It was because, I was aware of your inherent strength. My role was merely supplementing your conviction within you."

"Should you want to go to Bombay, I'll make the necessary arrangements for you and Tapan." Sanatan said soothingly.

"No, not now. Shalinbhai said that there is no need to rush back to India. The only thing is, my father is probably deeply upset. But, my going there could not help him emotionally at this time. You realise, Sanatan, that ours is a very closely-knit family. Even if I'm not there in person, my family members still know that I am with them emotionally in these moments of anguish."

Sanatan did not say anything but simply nodded his head. He was staring ahead at the wall at the far end of the room. Radha was also silently looking at a point on the ceiling. After some time Sanatan lifted her hands and held his face in her two palms. Sanatan looked down at her and lowered his head to kiss her on her forehead. Radha pulled and pressed his head to her chest for a very long time. Sanatan felt the tension of her body relaxing somewhat as she loosened her grip on his head. Sanatan lifted his face and looked at Radha. He tenderly moved his forefinger on her eyebrows one after the other. She closed her eyes and pulled him down on her. He extended his left arm to switch off the table lamp. Darkness descended in the room. The silky blue light of a night lamp soothingly illuminated the darkness of the bedroom. Sanatan enveloped his arms around the slim body of Radha as she snuggled to close to him.

She tenderly uttered, "My dear Sanatan, make love to me tonight; I want you to relieve me of all the tension that mounted up in me since the evening." Sanatan kissed her tenderly as she responded warmly with her quivering lips. Radha was bitterly tense and she wanted anything that could relieve her of her anxiety and uneasiness. The news of her mother's death had cast a deep blow to her psyche. The pain resulting from the thought of not being ever able to meet or see her dear mother alive ever again was unbearable. She felt as if her mind had been thoroughly paralysed. She felt that the numbness of her mind would immobilise her physically. She wanted to be relieved of the deep ache thrusting up her entire body. She urged Sanatan to relieve her of the growing tension within her.

Sanatan understood how she felt. He understood the complex desire of his dearest wife. With great tenderness he kissed her again on her lips. Radha closed her eyes and a teardrop escaped from the corner of her eyes. Her lips parted a little to reveal her even white teeth. Both bodies were indulged in one other for a long time.

Sanatan went to the bathroom after some time. When he returned to the bed he found her sitting in the bed covered up in the quilt he had wrapped her in.

Radha told him hesitantly, "Sanatan, I feel guilty."

"For what?"

"After hearing the news of my mother's death, I couldn't control myself from having sex."

"Why should you feel guilty? What we did was purely an act of releasing mounted tension within us—you and me. You needn't punish yourself by feeling guilty."

"But . . . Sanatan . . ."

"No buts and ifs . . . ; what we have done is natural. And remember the dictum—'Sex relieves tension.' You were very tense when the news of your mother's death was given to you. Perhaps, the sex helped you to relieve your tense nerves." Sanatan said soothingly.

"I guess you are right. I was very tense."

Sanatan stroked her back consoling her. She got up and went to the bathroom. After about five minutes when she emerged, she found Sanatan already asleep.

The next morning, at the breakfast table Ivan asked Sanatan, "How is Bhabhi?"

"She is asleep presently. She was unable to sleep until late last night."

"I was extremely sorry to hear of her mother's demise. I know how lonely she must be feeling at such a time."

"Yes, she has found it hard to deal with the shock. But, I think she will recover from it."

"Will you come to the college today? I think, you better keep her company for a day or so. When she regains her composure, you can resume attending your classes."

"That's what I have been thinking." Sanatan replied.

After about an hour Larsen brought a tray of breakfast for Radha.

He said, "Ma'am, please accept our heartfelt condolences on the demise of your mother. We're all upset at your grief."

Radha said, "Thank you, Larsen. Thanks for your condolences. But, please take this breakfast away. I don't feel like having anything to eat now."

"Oh ma'am! It happens." Then, placing the plate in front of her, he said, "I know how you'd be feeling. Look, I've prepared a very simple breakfast for you today. Do you know that a good breakfast is necessary to sustain yourself? Moreover, even if you give up eating, it would not get your mother back."

Radha looked up at Larsen and smiled, "You're not only a good cook; you are an excellent philosopher." She picked up a slice of bread from the plate.

Larsen didn't say anything but bowed to her respectfully and left.

Ivan returned late in the evening from college. Upon his arrival he found Sanatan and Kanaiyalal talking in the drawing room. Not seeing Radha he asked Ivan,

"How is bhabhiji?"

"She is well, Ivan. She is writing letters to her father and two brothers in her bedroom." At that moment Larsen entered to announce that the dinner was ready. Ivan asked him to lay the table. A couple of minutes later both friends went to Radha's room.

"Come on Radha, dinner is ready." Sanatan said.

"You may proceed. I don't feel like eating today."

Ivan looked at Radha and insisted. "Please take some food."

"I have no desire to eat, Ivan. My mind is somewhat unhappy today." Radha said.

After some coaxing, Radha finally joined everybody for dinner.

"We fully appreciate your mental state. But, despite that, I won't allow you to kill yourself of starvation." Than adding in jest Ivan said, "Do you know what the people would say? They would say a woman guest died of starvation in my penthouse. How do you think any girl would consider marrying me after hearing of that?"

Everyone around the table laughed. Radha too gave up her grim composure and smiled. Sanatan applauded, "There you are, smiling like a bright star." He lifted a glass of red wine before him and said, "Radha, I see the sun in your smile and light in your eyes!" He emptied the glass in one gulp.

Everyone laughed happily including Kanaiyalal and Radha. Ivan lifted his glass up high, bellowed "Cheers!" and gulped down his wine. The tension in the atmosphere that had loomed large over everybody quickly dispersed as Ivan laughed aloud.

After partaking of dinner everybody departed. Sanatan told Ivan, "Today I telephoned Ronaldo and I must meet him tomorrow at 10 a.m. in his office."

"OK." said Ivan and he went into his room.

Next morning Sanatan arrived at the University and punctually entered Professor Ronaldo's cabin. Professor Ronaldo extended his hand and welcomed Sanatan.

"How are your studies progressing, Sanatan?"

"Very well, sir. This nuclear subject is so wide and so complicated that even if I spend my whole life on researching it, there would not be enough time for me to digest it fully."

"You are right. Tell me now what you wanted to say."

"When the atom and nuclear properties are separated from heavy water then how is the transformation of nuclear energy from the Atom created? When I was making notes of my observations in the laboratory, I realised that the creator of this universe is fantastic! Moreover the work done by the great scientists of America and other countries are praiseworthy and I salute them."

"Sanatan, you know that the roots of the suspense of science have come from the ancient saints of India who created Vedas. Because your country was under slavery all your inventions were taken out of your country and studied in detail by the German, Russian and American scientists."

"In your opinion, who created this universe?" Sanatan asked this question of Ronaldo with anxiety.

"It is said that 12 billion years ago the universe was formed. The scientist Stephen Hawking believes that the planet earth was originally a small piece which was hanging in space. Once upon a time it was blasted and then eventually it spread all over. Because of the high temperature, stars, planets, galaxy and clouds were formed. Hawking believes that because planet earth is developing faster and faster, there will be no end to this universe. He believes that planet earth was formed and that someone must have created it. The famous scientist Francis Mason says that the universe was formed by God. One powerful creator works in the universe, who we know as a spirit. The achievement of Him creating the formation of the planets is an example of his greatness. All are a small sign of His power. The scientists from all over the world are working very hard to find the secrets of the universe."

Proessor Ronaldo talked in detail about planet earth and the creator.

Sanatan was so fascinated with what Professor Ronaldo was saying that he asked many questions which were cropping up in his mind.

"Sir, if we think about speed, surface geography and our relations with one other, and if we study this minutely, only then can we understand individual uniqueness and we can observe it. What do you think?"

"You know that the sun is just like a round ball. The external temperature of the sun is 1000oC and the internal temperature is about 15 crores degree centigrade. The sun is thirteen lacs and ninety thousand kilometres away from the planet earth and the diameter of the sun is 8 lacs and eighty thousand miles. The heat of the sun is distributed very widely. The earth gets only one 220th crores of the temperature of the sun. It barely takes eight minutes for the heat of the sun to reach the earth. Because of this, human beings, vegetables, animals, birds and all creatures thrive. You know this universe has a good environment, is stable, in an orderly fashion and well controlled. We can see this universe because of the invisible Almighty. I remember the physicist Francis Thomas who has written many verdicts about the universe. Everything in our society is joined together, whether it is big or small. Their relation with each other is strong and positive. Because of the Almighty, all these things are happening in a systematic way". Professor Ronaldo spoke for a long time and then waited.

"Basically Sir, as you are aware, I'm extremely interested in and am pursuing my research on 'Harnessing power from solar energy', although, my main interest area remains Nuclear Physics. Today, I propose to discuss with you research in the fields of low temperature atomic physics and solid state physics."

"As a nuclear physicist your interest in Solar Power and even Solar Rays is but natural. However, let me tell you that the research in the properties of solar power and solar rays is very much in the nascent stage. Oh! But before we touch upon that, you need to understand about the magnetic properties of the fields of the Earth and the Sun. Basically, the Sun's magnetic field plays the most significant role in all of these."

"Sir, I've heard that the Earth's magnetism does not remain constant; and its polarity is to undergo some changes. What are the reasons for these changes?"

"Your information is correct. In fact, as long ago as 1838, the German mathematician Carl Friedrich Gauss was the first person to devise a method of analysing the Earth's field mathematically and estimating its strength. After that, in more recent times, in 1952, Jan Hospers, studying basalts in Iceland, came up with convincing proof that there existed long periods in the past, when the north-south magnetic polarity of the Earth was reversed."

"It's very surprising!" Sanatan could not suppress his wonderment. Professor Ronaldo continued speaking.

"Comparing Carl's observations with recent ones shows that the north-south field of the Earth is weakening by about 5% per century; maybe even a bit faster. No one of course guarantees the trend will continue for another 2000 years, until the poles are reversed."

"But how does the magnetic field of the Earth change; I still cannot understand that." Sanatan interjected.

"What it all suggests is that, flows of liquid iron inside the core of the Earth, create the currents responsible for the magnetism of the Earth. Now, these flow patterns can be quite complicated. This is because there may be several independent currents or eddies as we call them, out of which some are stronger, and others are weaker, which changes the pattern. I hope you understand."

"Yes sir; it's clear. Fantastic!" Sanatan exclaimed.

"Sanatan are you aware of how you can create electric currents?" Then replying to his own question, Professor Ronaldo said, "One way is by using a battery, which creates an electric current through chemical processes. The other method is known as 'dynamo.' All dynamos are based on principles found by Michael Faraday that, an electric current is created in a wire or electric conductor that moves through the region of magnetic forces or magnetic field. In 1832 Faraday himself tried to measure electric currents created this way, by the flow of London's river Thames across the magnetic field of the earth. The circuit was completed by a copper wire, strung across Waterloo Bridge in London with its ends dipping into the water. The current was too weak to be measured, but the principle was correct. All dynamos work on this principle."

"But how would you explain the change in the Sun's magnetism?"

"I'm coming to that. You are aware of how the uneven rotation of the hot gases on the Sun—the fastest near the equator, as the motion of sunspots show— helps create electric currents in this manner."

"But all the details of the electricity on the Sun are not available to the scientific faculty."

"That's true. Not all details of the process are understood, because we can only guess what goes on in the regions we cannot see, under the surface of the Sun."

Professor Ronaldo looked at Sanatan.

He continued, "Sanatan, Mathematics was one of your favourite subjects, besides Physics. Here, you can use your mathematical skills intricately to learn how the current is produced within the Earth and the Sun. For your mathematical calculations you need a magnetic field, as well as the flow of liquid iron under the surface. This magnetic field is none other than the one created by the currents themselves!"

"Sir, your explanation really makes sense. I have found my direction for my research. But, I wonder, if the magnetic fields of the Earth and the Sun could not be used as carrier waves as a mode of communication?"

"I am not aware of any research being made in that direction. But in case you propose to undertake research in that field, I would like to draw your attention to the study on Alfven waves. Recent observations of oscillations in magnetic loops of the Sun's coronal atmosphere have established the basis of coronal seismology."

"The study of the Sun seems very intricate." Sanatan observed.

"The Sun does not like to share its mysteries." Professor Ronaldo chuckled heartily. Then he added, "Haven't you read what the famous solar physicist, E.N. Parker once said—'The Sun has proved to be a skilful and tricky customer.' Our current knowledge needs to be continuously developed and frequently revised. This is especially true for the corona." Professor Ronaldo concluded in a tone of finality. "The tremendous energy being released by the corona could become a source of energy in the future."

"It's very similar to nuclear fission. I think that I've found my way. Many thanks, Sir." Sanatan said.

"I have great hopes in you, Sanatan. Feel free to approach me should you need me at any time." Professor Ronaldo said looking at his watch.

Sanatan thanked Professor Ronaldo again before his departure and he went into the college library. After borrowing a few books Sanatan came out of the college campus. When he reached home it was around seven in the evening.

On seeing Sanatan, Radha smiled at Sanatan and asked, "How was your day, Sanatan?"

"It went very well!" Sanatan paused and added, "You know Radha, today during my discussion with Professor Ronaldo, I found a new clue for my research. If Dr. Bhabha learns of this, he would be very pleased."

"Really; what is it?" Radha asked curiously.

"As you are aware, I have been thinking of undertaking research on using the omni-present magnetic properties of the Sun."

"Yes, you did mention that during a speech in an International Seminar held at Bombay about three years ago."

"That's right. At that time, it was merely a passing thought. But today, after my discussions with Professor Ronaldo, my conviction has been strengthened."

Two days passed. On Sunday morning there was a chilled cold. Because the heater was working, sound sleep was obtainable in this cosy atmosphere. However, as per his daily practice Sanatan woke early. He came into the drawing room and picked up the newspaper. On the first page one news item caught his attention. The headline shouted,

"John Gacy, accused of 27 murders, caught."

Chapter 18

Sanatan sat up and read, 'Police have found the remains of twenty-seven young men in the basement of a building owned by John Gacy, a building contractor. In the last six years Gacy had allured young men to come to his house on some pretext. After that he would force them to commit unnatural sexual acts with them and then kill them. Since he possessed a large house, no outsider ever realised his heinous acts. In society, he was considered a highly respectable and prestigious wealthy person.

One day, a fifteen-year youth, Robert Piast went to Gacy's house. Before he left his house, Robert told his mother about the whereabouts of Gacy's house and said that he had was offered a job by Gacy. That day happened to be the birthday of Robert's mother. He assured her that, he would return on time for the celebration. When Robert didn't return home, his parents were worried. Robert was working in a medical store as an assistant. They made enquiries at the medical store initially. They learnt that Gacy had visited the shop in the early evening and asked Robert to accompany him. Robert's parents lodged a complaint with the police.

When the police made enquiries and investigations at Gacy's house, they found a receipt from a photographic laboratory, where Robert had left in a camera film to be developed. The police conducted extensive investigations in and around the house. They detected a basement, where they found the skeletons and remains of twenty-seven young men. The police arrested the serial killer John Gacy on the charge of murdering of those ill-fated men.'

Sanatan murmured, "Oh God!"

Ivan who had just emerged from his room asked, "What happened, Sanatan?"

Sanatan handed the newspaper to Ivan. He read the news item and his eyebrows shot up in surprise. He blurted out, "Oh my God! How could he do that!"

"Do you know him?"

"Oh yes, I know him quite well. We already met once."

Sanatan looked at Ivan, dumbfounded.

"Oh, but how do you know him?" Sanatan was visibly shocked.

"Don't get worked up, Sanatan. I am no friend of his. He happened to know my father. We had a few business meetings with one another."

"Oh, I see!" Sanatan exhaled his breath slowly.

"However, what shocks me is that he was a perfect gentleman during our meetings. He seemed absolutely suave. I am really stunned to learn that he was actually Saitan in the disguise of a gentleman."

"What will happen to him now?"

"Well, it appears from the news article that an electric chair is awaiting him round the corner. The police seem to have a foolproof case against him. Nevertheless, Gacy can appeal against his sentence for around fifteen times under various pretexts and in this way can extend his life for another eight to ten years."

"If such a thing happens, don't you think it would make a mockery of the law?"

"Yes; it certainly would! You may be surprised to learn that, out of the fifty states of America, only thirty-eight have the provision for the death sentence. Suppose that having committed a murder in Illinois a person escapes and gets caught in the neighbouring state of; say, Wisconsin; he won't be sentenced to death, but instead would be sentenced to life imprisonment."

"It is quite a weird law," Sanatan said. "Such a dangerous criminal must not be spared and should be sentenced to death!" he declared with a hint of suppressed anger.

"Calm down, Sanatan; you are far too emotional." Ivan laughed lightly.

"I can't bear injustice and inhumane acts, whether they are committed by people or by states."

"Are you a reformist or a scientist?"

"Well, isn't a scientist a reformist in a way?"

While they were talking, Radha and Larsen arrived with breakfast and tea. While eating '*upma*', they talked among themselves.

After some time Radha said,

"Tapan and Daddy are ready now. Be ready, both of you, so that we can go to the airport to catch an aeroplane to New York."

At 8 a.m. everybody was ready. When they landed in New York they were delighted to see the magnificent skyscraper buildings. They entered 5th Avenue and as the car passed 42nd Street, Ivan said,

"In the opposite direction you see a most beautiful building carved from Marble. That is the biggest New York Public Library, which was built in 1911. It is said that more than 4 crores of books are stored in this library."

The car stopped when they reached 34th Street. Ivan asked everybody to get out of the car. All alighted from the car and went on the opposite direction towards a very tall building. Ivan said,

"In 1930, this 102 storey building "The Empire State Building" was constructed in just 14 months. At a height of 1472 feet, it is one of the world's tallest and most splendid buildings."

Everyone followed Ivan and they all entered the building. Suddenly there was a strong gust of wind. Radha caught Tapan's hand. There was an observatory on the 102nd floor. Everybody got into the lift. About 40 people can fit into the lift. Looking at such a huge lift, everybody was amazed. Ivan said,

"In these buildings there are a large number of offices. This plaza's construction is eye-catching and magnificent. From this building business worth billions of dollars is carried out. In this building there are 73 lifts altogether, some big and others small."

On reaching the observatory, everybody enjoyed themselves. Using transparent glasses Manhattan could be seen to the North, Brooklyn to the East, New Jersey to the West and New York and the Atlantic Sea to the south. Everybody was delighted to see eye-catching sights in all directions. After seeing many beautiful skyscraper buildings nearby, Sanatan asked Ivan a question,

"At the time of constructing such fantastic tall buildings, architects have to prove their ability. Isn't that right?"

"Of course. In Park Avenue and Medicine Avenue there are many buildings that are taller. We cannot forget that. Just see that building. It is Manhattan's main office of the UNO, which is 39 storeys tall. It can be seen clearly from here."

Kanaiyalal was amazed to see all these sights. He thought that if he had not come, he would have missed so much. He would have missed how the Americans lived their lives in the midst of wealth. Moving around Ivan pointed his finger at Hudson River, which was a long distance away.

Ivan said, "See in the distance. In the Atlantic sea on Liberty Island you will see the Statue of Liberty. This is the symbol of the freedom of the country. The height of 'The torch' is 93 metres from top to bottom. In 1886, France gave this monument to America."

"Shall we go down," Sanatan said as he looked at his wristwatch. "Radha has to go to meet her friend Jyoti in Queen's. After taking our meals we have to catch a plane to Chicago from Lagudia Airport."

"Yes. I am ready." Ivan said.

All descended to the bottom floor. They left the building and got into the car. The car started moving, and Radha said.

"Ivanbhai, the feelings of love and generosity you have shown us are wonderful. I have no words to thank you. I feel that in this foreign country you are really an angel in the form of a man".

"Bhabhi, you all came to my home and stayed with me. I feel as if you are my real family. I have done my duty as a friend. You are under no obligations to me." Looking towards Radha he said,

"I am interested to see India. When I come there I will surely be your guest."

While talking they reached to Jyoti's apartment in the Queen's area. All got out of the car. As they were going towards the bungalow, another car arrived and stopped at the same time. For a moment, everybody was looking at the car. Nilay came out of the car and went to Radha and asked,

"If I am not mistaking, are you Radhaben?"

"Yes."

"Come on! Welcome. Jyoti is waiting for you all."

After saying this Nilay switched on the remote control. The door opened automatically. Radha and Kanaiyalal saw this with astonishment.

While talking, they all reached the big drawing room. Everybody took their seats on the sofas.

Nilay said, "Please sit down comfortably. I will be back in a moment. Jyoti is busy in the kitchen. I will send her into you."

As Nilay went away, Kanaiyalal asked Sanatan,

"I saw for the first time that the main door can be opened and closed by remote control. How does that happen?"

"Daddy, this is a new invention. As currents develop in the air, it makes it possible. Through currents and waves the rays of light was converted into energy and sound waves spread in the air. This process is used in telecommunication systems. When I studied this, I was very excited. The inventions of television and radio are possible because of currents and waves. This is a new invention." Sanatan gave details of recent technical developments in the world.

Both of them were talking when Jyoti and Nilay came over to them. Radha introduced everybody. Before Radha could introduce Ivan, Nilay introduced Ivan to Jyoti.

"Jyoti, this is Ivan. He is Sanatan's friend, and so he is ours too. He is our first ever Malaysian guest."

"Welcome Mr. Ivan! I'm glad Radha brought you along. In fact, I am very pleased."

"It's my privilege." Ivan smiled, bowing slightly to Jyoti.

"Jyoti, despite living in America you haven't changed a bit," Radha hugged her old friend.

"And Radha, you too are the same. We could not forget our culture and upbringing so easily!"

"I strongly believe that if we reside in any place in the world we should never forget our culture."

When the guests were comfortably seated, Nilay asked Tapan, "Young boy, I am sure that you would like to watch some cartoon films, wouldn't you? Follow me; I'll switch on the TV for you in my study."

Tapan was pleased. He followed Nilay to the study room. After a while Nilay returned to the spacious drawing room. Everybody was talking happily. Jyoti and Radha went into the kitchen.

Nilay joined everybody in the conversation. Their talks ranged from Nilay's business to Sanatan's research, life in America, the policies of the Indian government headed by Pandit Jawaharlal Nehru, his stand on the tenets of Panch Sheel and efforts at improving relations with China.

All this time, Ivan remained a silent listener. But at the mention of China he broke his silence, "Gentlemen, I think your prime minister, Nehru, has committed a political blunder on the Eastern border connected with China. The Indian political design does not suit them and one day or the other China will act against Indian interests."

"Well, I don't think that's possible. Chou En-lai arrived in Delhi just last week on 19th April. From the tone of the Chinese premier it is evident that he needed peace with India. He has reportedly stated in Delhi that he finds no reason why any conflict between the two nations cannot be settled reasonably through friendly consultations in accordance with those principles of Panch Sheel." Sanatan remarked.

"Perhaps, you are influenced by what you read in the newspapers. The reality is just the reverse. You need to read between the lines. Did you not note the statement made by Nehru when he said, 'unfortunately other events have taken place since then which have put a great strain on the bond of friendship and given a great shock to all our people.' In fact, the Indian refusal of the summit meeting of both nations brought the diplomatic game to stalemate. Meanwhile China continued to treat the McMahon Line as the de facto boundary in the eastern sector and the western sector unchallenged by anyone. I want you all to understand that inwardly China has not taken kindly to India accusing it of 'aggression' for the Chinese presence in Indian claimed territory."

Ivan gave his version of the political understanding.

"But what is wrong with India's position as far as its stand on the border issue is known?" Kanaiyalal asked.

"That is the crux of the problem, Uncle," Ivan said vociferously, "the Indian Government is adamant that there could be no general boundary negotiations. The boundaries had already been delimited and China must withdraw before any discussions can take place."

Sanatan remarked, "But why doesn't China accept the McMahon line?"

"China would accept the McMahon alignment in the western sector, but India should drop the claim to Aksai Chin. Chou En—Lai has maintained the position that he has taken ever since his first meeting with Nehru, that although the Chinese did not accept the McMahon Line as fair, the Chinese Government would accept it because of its friendly relations with Burma and India." Ivan, who was taking a keen interest in world politics, expressed his views.

There was silence for some time. Ivan vociferously agreed with the three Indians and cautioned seriously,

"The Chinese will surely take military action against India."

When Jyoti and Radha returned to the living room Ivan was saying,

"In politics the friends of today could become the foes of tomorrow."

Jyoti called out,

"Alright, it is time for a ceasefire! Please come into the dining room. Your meals are ready". Everybody laughed at her remarks.

Radha called Tapan from the study room. All occupied the chairs around the table. Everybody enjoyed the food, hot 'puranpoli' and 'surati undhiya', which is a dish prepared by baking various vegetables, beans, roots and other such ingredients. Everybody was hungry.

Following the sumptuous dinner the evening was over. Everybody thanked Nilay and Jyoti. Then they arrived at the LaGuardia Airport. Ivan sent back his friend's car, which he had used for the whole of that day.

When they arrived at Chicago airport, Ivan's driver was present with the car. Everybody reached Ivan's home safely.

The next morning, while going to the University, Ivan turned the car away from the usual road. Sanatan was perplexed, but didn't say anything. After a short drive Ivan stopped the car opposite a white palatial house.

Sanatan asked, "Whose house is that?"

"It's the same house which you read about in the newspaper yesterday."

"Oh! It's Satan's house! Let's go. I'm disgusted."

They drove towards the university.

After parking the car both students went to the college. Sanatan asked,

"Well, I was thinking that I have been living at your parents' house for almost four months now. It will take at least two to three more months for me to get my Doctorate degree."

"So, are you thinking of paying off the rent now?" Ivan asked mockingly.

"No, I was saying that I don't know when and how I will be ever able to repay my debt to you?"

"Good thinking!" Ivan chuckled. "There is one way you can repay your debt, if you consider it a debt."

Sanatan looked sharply at Ivan, "What do you expect of me? How do you want me to pay you?"

"You must dedicate your research to the good of the community of the world. That's, in fact, what my father and I have been dreaming about. You can help us fulfil our dream."

Sanatan was not sure what Ivan wanted of him. As a scientist from the Atomic Energy Establishment, he was committed to put his research to the good of India. He found it hard to understand what Ivan wished him to do.

He cautiously replied, "Sure, Ivan. I share your ideals. We'll certainly explore how we can work together in future."

Ivan extended his right hand and said, "Many thanks, Sanatan!"

The next three months were extremely crucial for those two research students as they were entering the final phase of their research studies. In fact, Sanatan was a little ahead of Ivan. He had prepared the first draft of his thesis. Sanatan and Ivan spent most of their days in the library and laboratories of the university. Although, the subjects of their research were different, Sanatan and Ivan would spend many hours together in the physics laboratory.

In the fortnight that followed, Professor Ronaldo suggested some changes in Sanatan's thesis. For the next seven days Sanatan industriously and neatly retyped the entire thesis. It was late in the evening. Far below, the streets of the city were glittering in the streetlights which were already ablaze. He extracted the last page from the Remington typewriter, read it carefully and placed it with a pile of other typewritten papers. He stretched his tired limbs. Putting his arms up above his head he yawned. He felt a tender touch on his shoulders. He turned around and saw Radha smiling at him.

"Are you tired?"

"Yes, a bit. But, I have completed my work. I've finished writing the thesis", said Sanatan and yawned again.

"When do you propose to submit it?"

"Maybe tomorrow. Now, I'll have to call up Professor Ronaldo and find out if he is available. After he signs this thesis, it can be submitted."

"Would you like some tea; it could recharge you?"

"Sure; I would love it, Radha."

Radha went to the kitchen to get some tea for him and returned quickly. Meanwhile, Sanatan stacked the papers together and neatly piled them in a file. Radha placed the tray of tea and cookies before him. She said,

"I don't have the slightest doubt about you earning the Doctorate."

"I don't know if I will succeed in my efforts or not, but I have researched certain theories, which could change the future course of the way the world looks at India. I have gone beyond Atomic fusion and nuclear fission and have explored ways using the solar waves for energy development."

Next day Sanatan talked on the telephone to Professor Ronaldo.

"Sir, I've completed my thesis. It's ready for submission. I have carried out all the changes that you suggested."

"That's wonderful! When do you propose to submit it?"

"Sir, I thought of handing over the file for your review today, if you are not too busy."

"Not at all, Sanatan; I am not too busy for you. Can you make it at three in the afternoon today?"

"Oh yes, Sir, I will be with you punctually at three in the afternoon. Thank you, Sir." He replaced the receiver.

Sanatan entered Professor Ronaldo's office at the appointed time. Professor Ronaldo enquired about his research and his family and then opened the voluminous thesis file placed before him. Gradually turning the pages the professor scrutinised the work of his pupil and when he closed the file with a deep sigh after a full twenty-five minutes, a smile lit up his studious face.

Professor Ronaldo had turned fifty-eight a week previously. Before starting his teaching career, he had worked in the American Defence Research Laboratories at the Pentagon. Removing his glasses he looked up at Sanatan.

"Excellent, my boy, excellent! It's revolutionary."

"Thank you Sir, But I owe this credit to your able guidance."

After three months Sanatan was conferred with a Doctorate by the Chicago University. That evening at a small party organized by Ivan, Sanatan announced his decision to return to India. The following week was spent in booking tickets, shopping and farewell parties.

After a fortnight, Sanatan and his family boarded the flight for Bombay. Before getting on the plane, Sanatan affectionately hugged Ivan. Tears welled up in everybody's eyes. The public address system gave a final call for the passengers heading to India to board the plane. Ivan warmly shook hands with everybody one by one. The flight took off within thirty minutes of Sanatan and his family boarding it.

Chapter 19

On the following day, Sanatan went to meet Dr. Swaminathan. Seeing Sanatan arriving in his office, he got up from his chair, came forward, hugged him and said.

"I was waiting for you".

Sanatan sat in the chair opposite to him, and Dr. Swaminthan said with a smile.

"Well done Sanatan. Welcome to India on earning your Doctorate degree. I am really proud of you. Bravo for you!"

"Many thanks, Dr. Swaminathan. So, what's the latest news of the AEC?"

"Well, to begin with; last year we commissioned Cirus, a 40 MW natural uranium fuelled reactor and ten months later, we commissioned Zerlina, a zero energy experimental reactor. Also, the Construction of the Plutonium Plant at Trombay has begun. I am happy to inform you that our nuclear research programmes are progressing in the right direction."

"By the way, read this." Dr. Swaminathan handed a paper to

Sanatan. It was a copy of a secret report datelined 2nd July 1961. It read, 'The US State Department has instructed its members in Europe, Karachi, Colombo, New Delhi and Bombay to report any information of India's nuclear programme, its capability and probable intentions.'

Looking up, Sanatan exclaimed, "So the Americans are already sniffing around our installations!"

"Our present worry is the chance of a Chinese nuclear attack. There are possibilities that at any time a battle may take place with China. President Eisenhower has assured Prime Minister Nehru of America's support against any possible Chinese nuclear aggression when he visited New Delhi in 1959."

"Oh! Things are gradually heating up!" Sanatan observed.

"Oh! And by the way here is an order pending for you." Looking at Sanatan, Dr. Swaminathan continued talking. "I have been assigned a new task of project coordination. A core team has been commissioned by the Chairman, Dr. Bhabha to spearhead the nuclear capacity of our country. The team comprises of Dr. Vikram Sarabhai, Dr. Sethna, Dr. Khan and other prominent scientists including you."

"Oh really! I'm very pleased!"

Afterwards enjoyed tea together and then departed.

That evening, as they had decided, everybody went to Chowpatty to meet Vasudevbhai. When they entered the home this time, Laxmiben was not there to welcome them with a smile anymore. Madhavi welcomed everybody. After a long time, Vasudevbhai arrived and was happy to see everyone. He hugged Kanaiyalal. Sanatan came forward and bowed his head down to the toes of his father—in—law. Within a short time Shalin and Pulin also came from the office. Everybody sat together and ate dinner. Time passed quickly. Late that night Radha, Sanatan and Kanaiyalal took their leave and went home.

Next day the Chief of Atomic Research Centre, also known as the ARC, Dr.Homi Bhabha called Sanatan into his office. Sanatan talked about his experiences during his stay in America. He appreciated his best friend Ivan very much as well as his guide, Dr. Ronaldo for the successful completion of his thesis. After a while Dr. Bhabha congratulated him on achieving his Doctorate degree and said,

"Sanatan, I have taken many responsibilities upon my head and so I am always very busy nowadays. I wish you will handle the research laboratory I have established from now on."

"But sir . . . ." Sanatan began.

Dr.Bhabha intervened and continued further,

"At present ten scientists are working in the Atomic Research Laboratory. From now on the scientists who are conducting research on nuclear energy will work under you."

"Sir, I will do my level best to fulfill whatever trust you put in me."

"Pay more attention to other subjects" Dr. Bhabha told him, "Nuclear reactors are working day and night to obtain Uranium and Plutonium. I am confident that because of our newly established reactors, 'Cirus,' then 'Dhruv', and now 'Apsara', we are now capable of starting a new atomic era. I am fully confident that you will succeed in all of your responsibilities."

"Sir, I know that my responsibilities are increasing more and more. But I promise you that I will accomplish all these tasks to the best of my ability, and I will sacrifice my own body and soul to do so."

"Very good. Now, listen. Nuclear energy can be used constructively for medical, agriculture and industry. In future, there will be a shortage of nuclear energy in India and so we have to develop many nuclear reactors at various places in the country. For this project many thoughts are cropping up in my mind."

"Sir, through nuclear energy you have a dream to bring about a green revolution in India. I assure you that I will not disappoint you in achieving your goal."

"I am very proud of you, Sanatan."

It was evening time when Sanatan left the office of Dr.Bhabha.

Time passed.

All of a sudden war was declared with China.

On October 21, the Chinese attacked the two-infantry battalions and some Assam Rifles, and were beaten off with heavy losses on both sides. The festivities of Diwali were marred by the news of the deaths of several Indian soldiers on the NEFA border.

Late that night Nehru made an urgent and open appeal for the intervention of the United States to take action against the Chinese with bombers, and fighter squadrons. Nehru requested fifteen squadrons and appealed for American aircrafts to undertake strikes against Chinese troops on Indian Territory and to provide cover for Indian cities. In response, an American aircraft carrier was dispatched from the Pacific towards Indian waters, but the crisis passed twenty-four hours after Nehru made this appeal, and the aircraft carrier turned back. The world learned on November 21, 1962 that the border war was to be ended by China's unilateral ceasefire and withdrawal.

Much later, the Defence Ministry released the figures of the losses of the Indian soldiers: 1,383 killed, 1,696 missing, and 3,968 captured.

The Indian government had doubled the budget allocation for strengthening the defence forces. Because of their defeat in war, Nehru was very nervous. The Prime Minister had personally convened the meeting of the top echelons of the Atomic Energy Commission, the DRDO and the senior officers of the three wings of the military. He emphasized the lesson to be learnt from the 1962 debacle. He instructed the top scientists of AEC and DRDO to work in tandem for the development of the nuclear armament capability in the shortest possible time. At this juncture Dr.Bhabha agreed and said, "If you give us permission, we will make an atom bomb in a short period of time."

Before the atom bomb could be created, Pandit Jawaharlal Nehru suddenly died on 27th March 1964 of a cerebral hemorrhage followed immediately by a heart attack. The children of India lost their 'Chacha', meaning uncle. The whole nation was griefstricken. On the back of the river *Yamuna* in Delhi, the cremation ceremony was held of the adored leader Nehru.

Following the death of Nehru the political situation of India was worsened. The politicians of different parties tried to capture leadership. The ruling elite became more corrupt and India was less governable. Under such turmoil, Lal Bahadur Shastri became the Prime Minister. He was very polite and a nation lover. Because of this people liked him. At that time Pakistan was thinking about launching an attack on Kashmir.

Sanatan was feeling more and more dejected and sad reading in the newspapers that anti-Hindu demonstrations had erupted in Madras. Opposition to the Congress Party grew tremendously and the state of Punjab was partitioned into the Hindi-speaking Haryana and the Punjabi-speaking Punjab.

There was no safety on the borders so India thought that Pakistan could attack at any time. In few days this news spread to other countries through India. America had to sell weapons, fighters, and war submarines so that if there happened to be a big war between India and Pakistan, America would gain a big advantage financially.

In the past Pakistan captured lot of land from India of which 5180 square kilometers of land was given to China as a gift. So China supported Pakistan. As China was supporting Pakistan, it was arranged that they would fight with India.

The Prime Minister, Lal Bahadur Shastri, talked to Dr.Bhabha and asked him to go ahead and make an atom bomb. Scientists worked day and night for this mission. In 1965 India was thinking of examining the ruinous strength of the atom bomb, at the same time as Pakistan attacked the border.

Taking advantage of the traumatic political state of India, Pakistan initiated skirmishes in April 1965 in the Rann of Kutch, a sparsely inhabited region along the West Pakistan-Indian border. In August fighting spread to Kashmir and to the Punjab.

When Sanatan left home one morning at that time he realized that Pakistan would something unusual. Almost all the headlines that were published in the newspapers read:

'Pakistan will attack India at any moment!'

'Critical conditions on borders'

'Pakistan is fully prepared to take Kashmir'

For the past week, the Government gave suggestions to the Indian public on how to protect themselves when the siren voice is heard, and how to go about their business with the help of candles, chimneys and lanterns, how to blacken out their houses, and not to listen to rumors. All these suggestions were often given in either newspapers or on the radio.

Military sources were sent to India on the borders of Kutch, Punjab and Rajasthan to protect the water reservoirs, the full blossom atomic research centers at various places, army quarters and the electricity supply stations. Sanatan's laboratory and other research centers incurred problems because of these conditions.

When Sanatan arrived home in the evening, Radha and Kanaiyalal asked him many questions about the situation.

Replying to Radha, Sanatan said, "There is danger present because of war. You go to our house in Chowpatty along with Tapan and my father. I may be engaged in the office and that is why I may come home late at night. Alternatively they may call me on duty at any time. Because of that, if you all are at Chowpatty, it will be easier to hear from one another."

"Alright," Radha replied.

It was arranged that everybody would go.

Radha said, "Please telephone me regularly. We will be worried about you"

The following day everybody went to Chowpatty to stay there.

In September 1965 the Pakistani and Indian troops crossed the partition line between the two countries and launched air assaults on each other's cities.

Pakistan bombed the Jamnagar Airport. The Indian army troops compelled the Pakistani soldiers retreat through fighters. Thousands of soldiers were ready to fight strongly for the sake of their country.

After three days Pakistan attacked Dwarka once again.

Their intention was to demolish the Vikrant Submarine. The Indian soldiers strongly attacked with their aircrafts and the Pakistani soldiers were forced back.

After a week, there was another attack on Jamnagar.

Using a helicopter, an explosive device was dropped, and as it slowly spread over the land after hitting the ground, the light that came from it made it look as it was the day time.

Pakistan saber jet fighters once again bombed the Army Airport. This time the Indian air force and Army were ready for the attack. The brave soldiers of the Navy defending the Vikrant submarine crushed a Pakistan airplane. Pakistan desired to destroy the airport. In retaliation, the brave Indian soldiers destroyed the important airport, Sargodha, in Pakistan. The brave aircraft soldiers showed their brilliance through the use of anti—aircraft guns and the Pakistanis were disappointed.

Many days passed in this way, and both countries continued to attack one another's cities. After threats of intervention by China, the United States and Britain, Pakistan and India agreed to an UN-Sponsored ceasefire and withdrew to the pre-August lines.

Within a short while the war had ended but the noise of war echoed in Sanatan's ears for many days. That day Dr. Swaminathan called Mr. Sanatan into his cabin and said,

"Sanatan, the Government has asked us to invent new weapons. We rapidly have to make new nuclear weapons. If Pakistan attacks us suddenly and if at that time we show carelessness or if we have not enough weapons, how can we fight them?"

"Sir, as far I know we are ready enough to fight. Our army and navy can fight at any moment. We can give a strong response if we are attacked. Our soldiers are ready for this. Now think about nuclear weapons. Sir, you know we can develop these nuclear weapons in a very large way. Our defence department is working hard to accomplish this. Our scientists are striving to the utmost to develop chemical weapons and biological weapons and to produce them in a bigger quantity."

"Speaking truthfully, it is not necessary to produce atomic weapons but as many countries in the world are developing nuclear weapons in a big way, a large country like India cannot rest." Dr. Swaminathan replied.

"I fear sir, that when the time of war comes in the future, that with these new modern nuclear weapons planet earth will be destroyed. Because of this, new inventions in nuclear weapons will be a problem for human beings." Sanatan described in a soft manner what could happen in the future.

"Sanatan, I understand your feelings of pain. The government says that if you are not ready for the aggressive fight with modern nuclear weapons, then other neighboring countries will challenge our country. We do not use these weapons for killing, but it is essential to show our readiness. Only these purposes is the Government spending billions of rupees for the development of such nuclear weapons." Dr. Swaminathan gave an accurate picture of the government.

After leaving Dr. Swaminathan's cabin, Sanatan went towards his own office. He was very sad at that time.

Prime Minister Shri Lal Bahadur Shastri of India and President Ayub Khan of Pakistan met in Tashkent, USSR, in January 1966. Both leaders pledged continued negotiations and respect for the ceasefire conditions, and signed an agreement on 10th January 1966. But unluckily for India, the night after the agreement was signed, Shastriji died in Tashkent.

The news of Lal Bahadur Shastri's death struck India like a bolt from the blue. The entire nation was plunged into grief. Some people suspected foul play behind his death. Gone was the war hero and the messenger of peace, and gone was the great statesman who restored to India her honor and self—respect in the assembly of nations.

One Saturday morning Sanatan was summoned by Dr. Bhabha to his residence. Dr. Bhabha liked to meet his fellow scientists rather informally. Sanatan reached the bungalow of Dr.Bhabha at eight on a wintry January morning. The maidservant asked Sanatan to wait in the terrace garden. Sanatan was enchanted to see the lush green hills of Trombay in the far distance. Beyond the hills he could see the sun steadily rising in the east and its reflection on the creek just beyond the hills. Sanatan found the cool breeze quite invigorating.

Suddenly he heard a voice from behind, "Don't you think the scenery is enchanting?"

Sanatan turned on his heels and found himself face to face with his boss, Dr. Homi Bhabha. Bhabha was wearing white flannel trousers and a red striped shirt and a maroon jacket. He looked handsome in his sports outfit. Sanatan moved forward and shook hands with him.

"Good morning, Sir!" Sanatan said.

"Good morning, my friend! Come, let's take a stroll in the garden. I have something important to discuss with you."

Dr. Bhabha and Sanatan descended from the terrace directly into the garden using a winding metal staircase.

"Look Sanatan, it's like this. Pakistan has not taken their recent defeat lightly. Moreover, it is wary of our growing nuclear capabilities. And since China has begun to lend technological and scientific support to them, the situation for our nation has assumed tremendously alarming proportions. You are next in seniority to me in the AEC. Last week, during my meeting with the prime minister designate Indira Gandhi, I suggested your name as the vice-chairman of the AEC."

Sanatan was about to say something. Stopping him with a gesture of his hand Dr. Bhabha continued, "No need to thank me. In fact the nation deserves a person like you. A meeting of the governing council of the UN's International Atomic Commission is being convened at Geneva next week. I thought of sending you to represent India. I have lots of other engagements in India in the next few weeks. But, Mrs. Gandhi is of the opinion that as a chairman of AEC, I must represent a case of the progress that has been achieved by India in Atomic Energy and make an effective representation of Indian interests."

"I think that she is absolutely right. When will she be sworn in as the Prime Minister?"

"I believe she will be sworn in on 24th January, before the Republic day. Another thing, I was planning to leave India by night flight, but since I have certain important tasks to complete, I've delayed my departure by twenty-four hours. I propose to leave tomorrow."

"When do you propose to return, Sir?"

"The meet at Geneva will last for a week. After that, I propose to visit the Alps on my return journey. I have been looking forward to capture the scenic beauty of the Alps on canvas and on my camera."

"That's a very nice idea, Sir. I am aware of your passion for nature and painting."

"Yes Sanatan! As man is achieving progress in science and amassing things of material needs, he is fast losing contact with Mother Nature. If only we learn to love nature with the advancements that have been made in science, life would become all the more beautiful and worthy of living."

"Sir, but the blatant materialism and greed to conquer nature and the resultant erosion of forests is posing a grim future for mankind." Sanatan commented.

"It would be better if mankind understood this fact. Otherwise, it will be too late and planet earth will be turned into a barren planet like Mars."

"I believe that we scientists need to really do something in this direction and strive to preserve the ecological balance of the earth." Sanatan echoed the thoughts of his superior.

"Sanatan, I want you to convene a meeting of all our senior officials and during the meeting we'll plan the strategy of the development of nuclear armament. I've promised Mrs. Gandhi to present the first nuclear device for weaponry system to the nation by the end of next year."

"Sure, Sir. In fact, nothing should deter us from developing such technology within six months. After that we shall have to carry out the mandatory tests before we finally test-explode the nuclear bomb."

"Well then, let's return. You will have a lot to do before we meet once again."

Sanatan returned to his office at nine and immediately he passed the order for an emergency meeting of the top echelon of the AEC. The staff members of the AEC offered their homage to the departed Prime Minister of India, Shastriji.

On the night of 24th January 1966, Dr. Swaminathan, Dr. Sanatan and other dignitaries were at the airport to wish Dr. Homi Bhabha Bon Voyage.

Then the call came for him to board the Air India Boeing 707 plane. He shook hands with everybody and walked briskly towards the aircraft.

The flight took off on time and headed westbound. The whole night passed peacefully. Only a journey of a few more hours was left to reach Geneva. Outside the plane, clouds obscured the view of the peaks of the Alps. All of a sudden there was a fireball. The Boeing 707 with 116 people onboard passing Mount Blanc crashed into a peak of the Alps. All 116 persons onboard the ill-fated aircraft perished. The enchanting heights of the Alps had been turned into a bloody graveyard.

The demise of Dr. Homi Bhabha, who had shown the way of the peaceful use of atomic energy to the world, was a huge shock for the people of India were jolted with shock on hearing the news of the death of Dr. Bhabha.

Addressing the gathering Sanatan appealed to his fellow scientists and technocrats at the Tata Institute of Fundamental Research and AEC, to work even harder and strengthen the nuclear capability of India as was envisioned by their departed chairman. The entire staff at both establishments worked all day to pay homage to Dr. Bhabha in the most befitting manner.

On the fourth day, Sanatan was summoned to Delhi by the Prime Minister's office.

Chapter 20

When Dr. Swaminathan and Dr. Sanatan arrived at Delhi, cold winds blowing from the North welcomed them. They found that, despite their warm clothing, they felt their limbs were being numbed with cold.

The First Secretary, Rajiv Sharma from the ministry of Defence, awaited their arrival. When both came out from the airport he guided them to a black Ambassador car waiting for them. Carrying the three passengers the car drove sedately towards Akbar Road.

Reaching the south Block, Sanatan and Swaminathan were ushered into a moderately large conference hall of the Defence Ministry.

When they entered the conference hall Sanatan noted that the nine officers were already seated around the large oval table. The First Secretary, Rajiv Sharma, introduced the duo from the AEC to the others. Sanatan and Swaminathan took their seats. For the next two hours Dr. Sanatan and Dr. Swaminathan listened to the secretaries' briefing with rapt attention. At times, they interrupted the speakers to elicit more information or to clarify a point or two, which they jotted down on the writing pads before them.

At around 11.30 am the meeting was concluded. For the next half hour they were engaged in informal talks. Sanatan and the others had a generous share of refreshments with more tea. At noon, Mr. Sharma asked the duo from the AEC to accompany him to the Defence Minister's offices on the first floor of the building.

The Defence Minister, Mr. Yashwantrao Chauhan, was seated behind a large oak table. After shaking hands with both the officials of the AEC, he guided them to the rather informal seating arrangement of sofa and chairs in the corner of the spacious room.

For a while the minister enquired about the activities at the Atomic Energy Commission, short for the AEC. Then he gazed at both scientists and said, "The nation is passing through a troubled phase. The war with Pakistan is over. The Pakistani forces were taken aback at the way our defence forces dealt with them, especially after the setback we had endured during the Chinese aggression in 1962. The defence preparedness and strength that our military forces have mustered during these three years speak volumes about the great chivalrous valour of our soldiers. We are all aware that Pakistan's pride has been badly wounded and the present political leadership of that nation will not remain idle for long. A gambler, who has lost the first round of their game, then plays for double with the hope of recouping his loss. Our intelligence reports indicate that Pakistan could wage another decisive war with us. Because of this, we cannot afford to slacken our defence preparedness."

The minister paused for a while to take a deep breath and then continued, "I am deeply upset today in remembering Dr. Bhabha, who died so suddenly only a few days ago. As he has made a magnificent contribution to the development of atomic energy, the Prime Minister, Indira Gandhi, has decided to change the name 'Atomic Research Centre' to 'Bhabha Atomic Research Centre', which will also be known as BARC. The Prime Minister is keen that work in the sphere of development of nuclear technology will not slacken. She will see both of you today in about half an hour."

"Sir, I would like to assure you that as a pioneer in the field of atomic energy, Dr.Bhabha had certain dreams, and my colleagues, Dr. Bhatnagar, Dr. Shethna, Dr. Ramanna and the other scientists of the AEC as well as myself will not leave any stone unturned to accomplish and fulfill his dreams. We will not hesitate to sacrifice ourselves for the sake of our country".

"Thanks, Dr. Sanatan, we expected such assurance from you. I have been briefed on your research in the US and also on your exemplary contribution in the devclopment of nuclear technology."

"Sir, I have not done anything extraordinary. It is my wish to see that our nation once again becomes a wealthy, strong and powerful one."

"Our prime goal is that we have to establish more and more research as well as the development centers of nuclear weapons. As we obtain more Uranium and Plutonium, we have to expand our working nuclear reactors. Under your leadership establish more and more atomic research centers of nuclear energy at various places in the country. Scientists have a wealth of intelligence, so find more clever and brilliant scientists and employ them. In the future, Pakistan, China and America may harass us with the Kashmir issue. We have to be ready for the possibility of war in the future. If we have not sufficient arms, how can we fight with them? For this reason it is essential for you to create nuclear weapons on a large scale."

Both scientists were listening to the Defence Minister, Mr. Chauhan, in silence. A few moments passed quietly and then Sanatan said,

"Sir, I fully agree with your suggestions. For your information I can inform you that all three nuclear reactors are working at full strength. I assure you that there will be a gradual and positive growth in the production of nuclear weapons. Our beloved and intelligent Prime Minister is a very inquisitive woman with a sharp mind and can grasp the most difficult subjects like your nuclear technology. I will see to it that she is assured of what you have been telling me. Indeed, she is very aware of the projects being executed at the AEC. In fact, I once had an occasion to meet her when she was heading the Science and Technology Ministry and also the I &B Ministry in Shastriji's cabinet."

"Let us go to the Prime Minister's residence where she must be waiting to talk with you." The Minister said as he stood up from his chair and checked his wrist watch.

The Defence Minister's motorcade sped towards Janpath, the official residence of the Indian Prime Minister, with Sanatan and Dr. Swaminathan on board.

At 10 Janpath, security was very tight indeed. But the motorcade of the Defence Minister was allowed past the gates without any checks. The Defence Minister and Dr. Sanatan walked together, with Dr. Swaminathan closely matching their sedate steps. They were ushered into the inner rooms of the sprawling residence where the Prime Minister met her very important visitors.

The personal assistant of the Prime Minister, George Abraham appeared and bowed down slightly to the Defence Minister. He said, "Sir, Madam will be with you in a few minutes. She is presently with the Nigerian President."

"We will wait here, George," the minister said.

"Shall I send you something to drink? It's bitterly cold today."

"Sure George, please send us some tea."

"Certainly, Sir." He looked at the other two.

"They are Dr. Sanatan and Dr. Swaminathan from the AEC."

George shook hands with them, one by one and left them alone in silence. Soon, a uniformed bearer carrying a tray with tea and biscuits appeared. He handed the cups to the visitors and, with a bow to the minister, left the room.

As Sanatan was taking his last sip of tea, Mrs. Indira Gandhi entered the room with her usual briskness and soon reached the far end of the room.

All of the dignitaries got up from the sofa. The Defence Minister introduced both the scientists to Mrs. Gandhi. After some time Mrs. Indira Gandhi sat in the revolving chair near the window.

"Welcome, Dr. Sanatan, the nation is proud to have great scientists like you."

"It is my privilege and honour to be in your presence, Madam Prime Minister." Sanatan said, "It is great of you, Madam, to appreciate what we do at the AEC. Madam, I present Dr. Swaminathan, an accomplished nuclear physicist and the Chief of Co-ordination at the AEC."

"Chavanji must have told you how anxious I am about our nuclear programme."

"Madam, we are all aware of the nuclear policy of the developed countries of the West. There is one, and only one option, before us and that is to achieve absolute self-reliance in producing enriched Uranium. Our first task is to take effective steps to procure as much Uranium as possible, because that will ensure the growth of our nuclear capabilities."

"I'm glad to hear that." Mrs. Gandhi said. "I was told that you had been assigned something different by Dr. Bhabha."

"Oh yes, Madam," Sanatan said, "I am working on harnessing Solar Waves for the generation of electricity as well as using them in telecommunication."

Mrs. Gandhi's eyes sparkled, "Very interesting! So, is Dr. Swaminathan also with you on this?"

"Yes, Madam," Sanatan said cautiously, "Our research is still in its nascent stage. We cannot say with absolute certainty today if we shall achieve success."

Mrs. Gandhi interjected, "Why not? Where there is a will, there is a way; I'm sure you know that. I have read the report on your research and that is why I had requested for you to meet me."

"Madam, the matter is absolutely Top Secret. Nevertheless, we will brief you broadly on what it entails." Dr. Swaminathan interjected.

"Go ahead."

"Well, Madam, as you are aware, the Sun radiates solar waves. But, there are so many different kinds of 'solar waves'. So one needs to be specific about the sort of solar waves one requires. But I will try to give you the general idea of my hypothesis on using the solar waves for the generation of power and then using them as a medium of telecommunication." Dr. Swaminathan spoke as if he was conducting a class on physics.

"But don't we use the air as a medium for transmission purposes? Is it possible to use the solar waves in a similar fashion?"

"I told you, Madam, that's our hypothesis on which we are currently working," Dr. Swaminathan replied, waving his hand at Dr. Sanatan. "Why don't you tell Madam how we were prompted to undertake this research, Dr. Sanatan?"

"Sure, Dr. Swaminathan," Dr. Sanatan turned to Mrs. Gandhi, "Madam, I will tell you how the science of oscillation, or the vibrations in the Sun, has prompted us to undertake a deep study of Helioseismology. This is a science of oscillations and those oscillations are caused by waves in the Sun, known as solar waves."

As Dr. Sanatan slowly explained the project they were handling, the thoughtful Mrs. Indira Gandhi looked at him intently listening with rapt attention, as if she was reading the entire script written in his mind.

Sanatan said, "The Sun's acoustic waves, though, are at frequencies too low for humans to hear. So we have to 'speed up the waves' in order for us to hear these solar waves. There are also deep Sun-penetrating gravity waves with gravity as the restoring mechanism that generates the oscillation standing patterns called 'g-modes' that have not been accurately detected yet. They are hypothetical at this point, but we are looking for them diligently."

All this time, Mrs. Gandhi had fallen silent and she looked out of the windows thoughtfully. Sanatan waited for the effects of what he had said so far to be absorbed by her sharp mind.

Slowly Mrs. Gandhi said, "Dr. Sanatan and Dr. Swaminathan, after having listened to both of you, I am sure that your research will change the course of power generation in the future. Dr. Sethna was not going overboard in his praise of you. He has recommended you, Dr. Sanatan, for the post of the Secretary at the Department of Atomic Energy in the Indian government."

"Thank you, Madam," Sanatan replied, "I will strive with all my ability to justify the trust you have placed in me."

"Dr. Sanatan, I am delighted that Madam has chosen you for this position of great responsibility." Yashwantrao Chauhan, the Defence Minister, said.

After taking leave of Mrs. Gandhi and the Defence Minister, the two scientists arrived at Ashoka Hotel.

By six that evening they were aboard the Bombay-bound Indian Airlines flight.

Swaminathan observed his silent colleague for a while and then asked, "What are you thinking about?"

Indicating towards the sky through the porthole, Sanatan said, "This vast expanse of the sky is filled with innumerable stars, planets and the sun. At times I wonder why Mother Nature created all these and when? How many secrets are stored in the depths of that empty looking sky? So many questions are still unanswered today and nobody can say for certain if answers to all these questions will ever be obtained at any time in the future" he added wryly.

"Russell once said that God can act without violating the laws of physics." Swaminathan quipped. "Science does not provide validation of the existence of God, but those who believe in his existence or in the divine essence, certainly provide logical justification. In other words, such logic cannot provide definite justification about the existence of God or the Supreme Divinity, but it certainly indicates that there is a divine presence and that there is a way in which one can search for the divine existence." Dr. Swaminathan continued.

Both of them fell silent and slipped deep into thought. Sanatan was awoken from his reverie when Dr. Swaminathan remarked,

"Religion says that there is enough strength in the universe and you will always find this strength in every human being. We know that there is big powerful force in the universe. The power of energy remains silent in a person's mind. Perhaps you may know that the scientists who are studying in depth the electric power in the human body are of the opinion that our physical frame works with just one lakh volt of electric power. The science of physics shows that there is enough strength in the center of an atom. There is even heavy energy in every cell of our bodies. As it is on the inside, we do not experience it but sometimes nature breaks this law and at times we hear about incidents where some coverings of body cells either becomes loose or detached, for reasons that are unknown. When this happens, terrific electricity emerges from the body cells and burns the body of the human being to ashes."

Dr. Sanatan was listening to what Dr. Swaminathan said carefully. Both fell silent for some time. Then, looking at Sanatan, Dr. Swaminathan continued,

"Recently I read a bizarre news item in a magazine. In 1966, Dr. John Irving Bentley who was 93 years old and a past medical practitioner was living alone in Crowder Sport at Pennsylvania. In his house such an incident happened to him. On receiving news that something was wrong at Dr. Bentley's house, police and a group of emergency personnel soon arrived. They checked the house minutely and they soon discovered ashes in an area on the ground. Then they saw that half of a right foot with a boot still attached was the only part of the person that had remained unburned. Afterwards they found that this person was Dr. Bentley and the unburned half of a right foot with the boot was that of the same person. This fire had been so acute that all the bones of his body had turned into ashes."

Dr. Sanatan was listening attentively and he looked at Dr. Swaminathan.

Dr. Swaminathan asked a passing air-hostess to bring them two cups of coffee. They started drinking coffee after she gave it to them. Finally after finishing his last sip of coffee, Dr. Swaminathan looked at Sanatan and continued talking,

"Our human body is a kind of a moveable electric house. If we are able to utilize this electricity in other areas, it would be capable of doing the same things that a powerful powerhouse could do. I shall tell you about another incident, if you are not tired of hearing about the subject."

"Not at all. I am intrigued in hearing about it. Please relate this incident to me."

"Listen. On the night of 1st July 1951 the same type of incident happened at Saint Pittsburg in Pennsylvania. Mary Reaser, who was a 67-year-old widow, sat on a spring chair. All of a sudden her body burst into flames. Within minutes Mary's 80 kilogram body had been converted to merely 4 kilograms of ashes. The fire only spread a meter in diameter. The investigation was handed over to the Forensic Scientist Dr. Wilton Cragman. Mary's skull had contracted and had been reduced to an orange shell. The ordinary law of science dictates that it should have either been swollen or turned into pieces. Usually at the temperature of 3000oF the bones of the body are not converted into ashes for 12 hours, but here, Mary's bones were lying in ashes. When we read about these types of incidents or hear or experiences, then we have to believe that like God, there is a powerful spirit who also runs the outcome of the universe." After telling such a long story, Dr. Swaminathan looked at the sky from the porthole.

"From this it is clear that it is not possible to understand the mystery of the universe." Dr. Sanatan gave his opinion.

Dr. Swaminathan continued his talk of such mysterious occurrences, and said,

"Sometimes surprisingly unforgettable incidents have happened. If you touch somebody's body you will get a severe electric current. A lady named Janney Morgan got this power when she was 13 years old. Just by touching it with one hand, she was able to light a 100-volts electric bulb. To examine Janney's energy, one scientist took her hand in his and he got such a sudden shock of electric current that he became unconscious for a few hours. Scientists in the world do not understand how these types of incidents occur."

After talking for so long, Dr. Swaminathan kept quiet.

Sanatan was also in deep thought. Many thoughts were cropping up in his mind. The Prime Minister appointed him to the seat of Dr.Bhabha and thereby gave him a great responsibility. Lots of thoughts were whirling in his mind of how to meet this responsibility.

For the last two years India progressed so much in atomic areas that many scientists were coming to India to study modern technology. In the beginning, a power reactor was established in Rajasthan. The design for this reactor came from Canada and the Indian scientists worked hard and succeeded in the atomic area. The scientists of India started a nuclear physics training programme.

In 1964, in order to receive the collection of data of neutron beams from the nuclear reactor, the Philippines and other neighbouring countries ordered a spectrometer through the International Atomic Energy Agency and they supplied it. When the Rutherford Application Laboratory of London needed the same type of spectrometer, Indian scientists made the spectrometer with their own design and skill and supplied it. India supplied atom technology with conditions to Thailand, Indonesia and Egypt.

"Sanatan, you are thinking a lot. What do you propose to do now?"

"About what?"

"About your new responsibility!"

"You know, Madam Prime Minister wants us to develop our nuclear armament capabilities. I have been thinking about it."

Swaminathan said, "Sanatan, I am more concerned about power generation using nuclear technology. The development of arsenal is a destructive activity, whereas, the development of power should be considered as a first step in terms of the economic growth of the country."

"I am reminded of the words uttered by Dr. Bhabha. He once said, 'we may have to repent if we fail to produce nuclear energy in our country. When every country is striving to achieve selfreliance we cannot afford to do nothing.'"

"You are right, Sanatan. Dr.Bhabha started the process, which was extraordinary. I salute him with love. Now, I will reply to the questions you asked earlier. In 1945, the Tata Trust invested money and started the Tata Institute of Fundamental Research Centre. Then in 1948, the Atomic Energy Commission was established. Scientists doing research work in nuclear physics joined the Atomic Energy Research Centre. The 'Atomic Energy Establishments' is progressing steadily. We need to review the working of the nuclear centers of Indore, Kalpakkam, Calcutta and Hyderabad. Financial help is given from the department of Atomic Energy, to the Institute of Physics, Bhuvaneshwar, the Mehta Institute of Mathematics, Allahabad, the Shah Institute of Nuclear Physics, Calcutta, the Tata Memorial Centre, Bombay and other institutes. The nuclear reactor, Dhruv, was imported. As nuclear reactors 'Cyrus' and 'Apsara' are being made ready in a modern way."

Sanatan was listening to Dr. Swaminathan's lecture with anxiety, and then said,

"Next week, please call a meeting of the Chief Officers and scientists. I request you to prepare an agenda for the meeting. After our discussion, we can finalise our plans."

"O.K." Dr. Swaminathan said. All of a sudden Dr. Sanatan said,

"Recently Pakistan became a headache for all of us."

"There is a reason for that. When Hindustan was divided in 1947, they did not get Kashmir at that time."

"I feel that our politicians are guilty. As Pakistan became independent, it attacked Kashmir. On account of the army expenses, Pakistan's bank balance was almost nil. India gave Pakistan a sum of twenty crores of rupees in advance. The remaining 55 crores of rupees were to be given with some conditions. Mohammed Ali Jennha realised that Pakistan needed those 55 crores of rupees very badly. Sardar Patel opposed this, so Gandhiji went on a fast. When Gandhiji was asked to retire from the fast he did so, on seven conditions. The Indian Government did what Gandhiji had asked and thus Gandhiji saved Pakistan from bankruptcy. From this money arms were purchased from foreign countries and India was targeted. Because of this, up untill now Pakistan has remained our enemy." Sanatan spoke in a sad tone.

"You are telling the truth, Sanatan. Because of Gandhiji's ideology, Nathuram Godse and Narayan Apte were disappointed and excited. In fact, Godse was Gandhiji's pupil, and he also went to Jail for the freedom of his country. He was Hindu and unless he was not allowed to read one lesson of the Geeta or Rugved, he would not eat anything. He could not tolerate Gandhiji's ideals in favour of Pakistan and he aimed his pistol at Gandhiji and shot him. After a while Dr. Swaminathan looked at Sanatan and continued to speak,

"Now the ruler of Pakistan understands well that if they want to rule the country of Pakistan, the burning issue of Kashmir must be at the forefront of their agenda."

After listening to Swaminathan, Sanatan expressed his views.

"India is a secular country. Here the Muslim gets equal rights just like the Hindu; but sometimes he gets even more special rights, fame and goodwill. In India, a Muslim can become President, Vice President, and he can obtain other such important titles. In Pakistan the conditions of the Hindu is not good. They cannot achieve fame or any special rights in Pakistan."

"Perhaps, the disposition of the rulers of Pakistan has become less favourable and they are more wickedly inclined. Moreover, China and America, who both gave support to Pakistan, accelerated the hostility against India. In fact, both countries needed the support of Pakistan. This time, in the war with Pakistan in 1965, if the army of India wanted to take back our own Kashmir, which they occupied before, they could do so. But because of our good nature and generosity we signed the Tashkent agreement and we have forgiven them." Dr. Swaminathan said.

"Perhaps they will perceive our peacefulness as our weakness." Sanatan continued.

"Our country is peace-loving. We believe in co-existence, so we will never start a war. Still we have to produce atomic arms. The advanced countries who produce these atomic arms know that if the atomic war takes place, the whole earth will be destroyed. Everybody knows that the fight with atomic weapons will turn the earth to ashes. Still America, Russia, France, Britain and China, because they are large advanced countries, wish to be superior to other countries in the production of nuclear weapons and would like to keep them under their thumb. If all countries, keeping humanity in mind, utilize atomic energy in favour of the good of human beings then war will never take place and world peace will be maintained forever. People can live in happiness and prosperity."

Swaminathan said, looking at Sanatan's face with love and then he said, "This is only a dream, but I have got full faith that one day my dream will come true".

Sanatan said, "I now recollect my childhood which was spent with my friend Iqbal. Last month when I went to my native place Umreth, I found out through my friends that he had also become a very famous scientist. In 1947, when Hindustan was partitioned because of communal rights, he went to Lahore." After saying this, he told of how he had studied with Iqbal, and how his Abbajan had sacrificed his life for him. He spoke with a heavy heart as he reminisced.

The cabin lights were dimmed off. Soon the aircraft swung to the right in a slow descent. In no time, the aircraft landed. When both scientists came out of the airport, darkness had fallen.

Chapter 21

Radha was worried as Tapan, who had gone to school, had not returned yet late in the evening. She was not able to concentrate on her cooking. Time and time again she would return to the drawing room from the kitchen with worry written large on her face. Sanatan had gone to Calcutta on official purposes. He was to return on the following day. Kanaiyalal was reading a newspaper seated on a swing on the balcony. Radha could not hide her anguish and discomfiture from him. She went up to him and said,

"Bapuji, Tapan hasn't returned from school yet. I'm deeply worried about him."

"You needn't worry, Radha. He might have been engaged with his friends or teachers. You know that he is always punctual and values discipline." Checking his wrist watch he added, "It's already seven. Let's wait for half an hour more . . ."

"You know well that he is back at home by five everyday."

"Let's wait for a while more. If he does not return by then, we will search for him."

Kanaiyalal's words failed to provide any comfort to the worried Radha. After another fifteen minutes she rushed to the drawing room as she could not control herself. She telephoned Tapan's close friends—Jatin and D'Souza. She learnt that both of them had returned on time to their homes. However, on listening to what D'Souza said at the end of their conversation, Radha's worries eased to some extent.

"Tapan might have gone to a cinema to catch the latest English film." Before leaving school he had asked D'Souza to join him, but he declined, telling him that the family of his uncle had come from Allahabad to stay with them for four days.

Listening to D'Souza, Radha was somewhat relieved. Generally, whenever he would be delayed, Tapan would send a message or inform somebody of his plans by telephone. Replacing the receiver on the cradle she returned once again to the door of the balcony.

Radha turned to Kanaiyalal to say, "Tapan's friend, D'Souza believes that he has gone to watch a movie with his friends."

"He should have called up to inform us. Well, now your worries are over, right?"

"That is the trouble with the present generation. Generally he calls up whenever he is delayed in coming home. But he didn't call, and I was deeply worried."

"Well, he is, after all, an immature child. Sometimes, children act in such a way. You should tell him not to do so in future." Kanaiyalal advised Radha.

Since, they were discussing Tapan, Radha expressed her opinion,

"I feel, Bapuji, that Tapan is much cleverer than his father at his studies. If we examine all his school results to date, we can see that he has constantly maintained first or second place."

"Yes, he is very diligent. After returning from school, he will not sit idle until he has finished his homework."

"It is true," Radha said, "He remains engrossed in reading after he finishes his homework and doesn't while away his time in roaming around the area with his friends."

"Radha," Kanaiyalal said, expressing his opinion, "Tapan has inherited his love for education from Sanatan—that is what I feel. In two months' time his H.S.C. examination is scheduled. I am sure his name will feature in the merit list."

"I hope what you say will happen, Bapuji. Although the days of his exams are nearing, he was on a couple of picnics with his friends. Once he was to the Elephanta Caves with them and then later he joined them on a three-day outing at Matheran."

"So what?" Kanaiyalal interjected. "One must go out and about every now and then. What is the problem if he goes to see a movie with his friends? We are very much aware that he is not careless in his studies. Besides, he is no longer a child. We should give him some liberty."

"I agree with what you say. But he is at a certain age, and at times I am worried that he will get into the company of undesirable friends."

"You needn't worry on that count. Tapan is a clever boy and has an excellent knowledge of the difference between right and wrong."

"His father, too, desires that he studies well and becomes a great scientist like him, and that he attains a place of honour in society."

"Just you wait and see, that will happen," Kanaiyalal assured her with confidence.

"His father was telling me that he has already decided on a college at which he will seek admission for Tapan."

"That's wonderful," Kanaiyalal smiled.

After some time Radha was in the kitchen and when the dinner was ready she called out,

"You better have your dinner. You can't say when Tapan will arrive."

Kanaiyalal accepted what Radha said and sat down to partake of the meal. Generally, every night they used to have dinner together. But Sanatan had gone to Calcutta and Tapan had not yet arrived home.

While eating his meal Kanaiyalal was lost in thoughts of Tapan. If he gets entangled in bad company being of an immature age, his whole future would be ruined. As soon as a child attains an age of understanding things, the virtues of good behavior and ideal character must be instilled in him. The good qualities imbibed during his childhood enables a child to scale greater heights of success in life.

Proper care was taken in Sanatan's upbringing. While studying by the light of earthen lamp and hurricane lamp, Sanatan had achieved a higher degree of knowledge. As a result, he received an opportunity to study in America, and today he had obtained a higher position in the country. He had been the darling of many people and qualities that were worshipped by millions of people were evident in him. While partaking of his meals, Kanaiyalal was thinking that achieving a great place in society or country depends upon the willpower of an individual. This becomes possible only through great efforts, dedication and integrity.

They were all acting carefully in the matter of Tapan's upbringing. Tapan too, was a boy of understanding and he was clever. Therefore, whenever Radha expressed her feelings of doubt about Tapan, Kanaiyalal felt that it was unnecessary.

Finishing his meal, Kanaiyalal got up. He came to the drawing room to switch on a radio. Enchanting old film songs were being broadcast on the radio—Binaka Geetmala. He settled down on a sofa to enjoy the music.

At around nine-thirty Tapan arrived home. Before Radha could say anything, he said, "Sorry Mummy; I am late because I went to watch a movie with friends."

"You should have telephoned at least! You could have sent a message through somebody. I was deeply anguished worrying about you."

"We suddenly made a decision to watch the movie. Having reached the theatre, I tried to telephone you from the Irani Hotel, but could not get the call through. As the movie had started, I didn't try again."

"Now wash your hands. I'll lay the plate for you."

"Did grandpa have his meal?"

"He was waiting for you to have our meals, but when he learnt that you possibly went to the movie, he finished his meal. Now, I'll sit with you for the meal", Radha replied.

The mother and the son settled down to have their meals.

Radha could not control herself and said,

"As you hadn't returned by seven in the evening, I was deeply worried. Having spoken with your friend, D'Souza, my worries were eased. Should you make such arrangements in future, you must immediately telephone to inform me."

"Sorry, mummy; but that movie revealing the secrets of science was highly recommended to us. My friends and I suddenly decided to watch it. But in future you won't have to worry about me as I will always contact you to let you know if I am delayed."

After having his meal Tapan got up to wash his hands. As he was moving towards the washbasin, the telephone rang. Kanaiyalal picked up the receiver.

"Tapan, it's for you."

Tapan spoke on the phone for a while and then replaced the receiver on the cradle. Suddenly Radha asked, "Who was that, Tapan?"

"Mummy, it was my friend, Swati, who is studying with me. Tomorrow, I will give her my chemistry notes. She called me up to remind me of that."

"Look, Tapan, your exams are nearing. Instead of remaining involved with your friends you had better concentrate on your studies. Avoid going to the cinema or the theatre until your exams are over."

"Mummy, don't you trust me? I will certainly pass with the highest possible marks."

"Tapan, I trust you without a doubt. I just hope that you too will become a great scientist like your father."

"Mummy, I'll never disappoint you on this. I'll strive to the best of my ability to do so. I believe in doing my work and one always enjoys the fruits of one's labour."

The following day, Sanatan arrived from Calcutta. He had been planning to evolve strategies to develop nuclear armament on a large scale. He initiated action to open Research and Development centers on nuclear weapons and nuclear energy at various places in India. Due to his exemplary work he was honoured with many higher awards. In order to increase the production of nuclear energy, Sanatan had to undertake tours of many important cities of India. The government was desirous to ensure that the shortcomings of 1965 following war with Pakistan did not remain unresolved and the country should become stronger. It was necessary for the country to develop enough strength to buttress the attacks by neighbouring countries as and when they ventured to do so.

Time flew by. Tapan took his HSC examinations. He had done well in them. Everybody in the family was happy. Soon the results were announced. Tapan missed first place on the merit list by just four marks. A wave of happiness spread over the family. Friends, relatives and all dear ones came to congratulate him on his wonderful success. Many of them conveyed their congratulations through telephone calls. On the third day after Tapan passed his exams, on a Sunday, Sanatan organised a party at his home.

Tapan was somewhat sad as he had failed to attain the first position.

On the day of the party Sanatan observed that Tapan was lost in thought.

Sanatan asked him, "What are you thinking about, son? Shake off your sadness and anguish."

"Daddy, I've been thinking, why didn't I get the first position on the merit list despite all my efforts and work? If my dream would have come true, how happy I would have been!"

"You are right. I understand your anguish. But being placed at second position on the merit list is no mean achievement, and is a source of happiness. You still have to acquire higher education in the college. Your studies, from now on, are of more importance. You have my blessings for your glorious success in the days to come. If a man works harder and with diligence, no work is difficult for him."

It was time for the party. Slowly, the invited guests began to arrive. The entire family of Vasudev had come from Chowpatty to celebrate the joy of Tapan's great success. The bosom friends of Tapan—Jatin, D'Souza, Swati, and Mohini were present. The principal of the school arrived and congratulated Tapan on his grand success. Many of Sanatan's friends from the scientific field attended the party and congratulated Tapan. In this way, the party to mark Tapan's grand success was organized with great enthusiasm and splendour. On this occasion dinner was arranged. The guests enjoyed the party with joy and gaiety until late that night.

In the month of June the colleges re-opened. Tapan was admitted to the science faculty and he began to attend the college regularly.

One night Sanatan and Radha met in the bedroom. Radha seemed to be very happy. She rushed to embrace Sanatan with a wave of emotion. Taking her in his strong arms Sanatan asked,

"What's the matter? Why is my queen is so happy today?"

"Tapan resembles your personality and is like you when he speaks. But today . . . ."

"Hmmmmmmmm . . . . Why did you stop?"

Radha's countenance showed great happiness. She said, "No . . . no . . . I . . . . I was telling you, just something else." Radha stopped.

"Why did you stop? Tell me what you wanted to say," Sanatan laughed.

Radha blushed and then said, "I wanted to share good news with you."

"Why don't you tell me? What do you wish to say?"

Lowering her eyelids Radha replied, "I am going to be a mother."

Upon hearing her, Sanatan immediately took her face in his hands and kissed her several times.

"Why did you wait so long to tell me?"

"I suspected and that is why this evening I was examined by the lady doctor, Dr. Bhanuben Kapadia and my doubt became reality."

"I'm thankful to God for listening to our prayers. I pray God that your desire to be the mother of a daughter will at last be fulfilled."

"You know, Sanatan, that for many years I have been longing to be a mother of a daughter."

"Have faith in God. You'll have a daughter."

Everybody was happy with this news. Although Sanatan remained very busy in his work, at times he would take time off to come home for lunch in the afternoon. Also, he tried to arrive home early at night.

Sometimes Radha would comment, "I am aware of your responsibilities. Do your work first. You needn't worry about me. I don't like that you come home early because you are worrying about me."

"But what if I like to?" Sanatan smiled and said as he looked at her. "I come home for lunch, since we live in the campus of Anushakti Nagar."

Radha couldn't suppress a giggle.

"I can always phone you if ever I should need you."

"But I come home early because I like your company."

"Let it be. Nobody can win against you in arguments."

One day Radha said,

"So many years have elapsed. I had almost given up the hope of becoming a mother again. After so many years God has heard our prayers. Now, I only wish that God blesses me with a daughter."

"Radha, it is not in our hands whether you give birth to a son or a daughter. Everything depends upon the mercy of God. Still we can nurture hope for the birth of a daughter."

The days passed happily. Radha used to consult the doctor as and when she felt any discomfort and be examined.

One day, due to severe labour pains, Radha was admitted to the maternity hospital of Dr. Bhanuben. News of Radha's condition was conveyed to the house of Chowpatty. Madhavi rushed to the hospital. She uttered a few soothing words, which comforted Radha a great deal.

When Radha experienced waves of labour pain twice, she was taken to the labour room. Tormented by severe pain, Radha would cry out aloud.

It was twelve midnight. Radha had been suffering labour pains for the past six hours. The doctor made every effort for the normal delivery of the child. At last, the circumstances were such that the original plan had to be changed. Hence, the doctor summoned Madhavi to her consulting room.

The doctor told Madhavi, "There is no alternative but to perform a Caesarian operation." She stopped for a moment and asked, "Where is Dr. Sanatan? He is not here!"

"He has gone to collect the medicines prescribed by you. He should be here at any moment."

At that precise moment, Sanatan entered the room.

Dr. Bhanuben explained to him the seriousness of Radha's health. She informed him that there was no recourse except a Caesarian operation.

Listening to the doctor, Sanatan became sad. He asked worriedly, "Doctor, surely nothing will happen to Radha?"

"Look, Radha's condition is serious at this very moment. The child is in an oblique position within the womb. Just pray God that everything will be alright."

Sanatan signed the form supplied by the doctor. After a while an Anesthetist arrived. When Radha was wheeled into the operation theatre she was blabbering with pain. The doors of the operation theatre were shut. The eyes of Sanatan and Madhavi were fixed on the red lamp glowing above the doorpost of the operation theatre.

When the operation was over, Dr. Bhanuben emerged from the operation theatre. Sanatan and Madhavi who were seated on a bench got up with a start. Looking at the serious countenance of the doctor their hearts sank.

The doctor came over to them and said, "I'm sorry, Dr. Sanatan. I had to sacrifice the female child in order to save Radha's life. Out of the two, only one could survive and so I chose to save the life of Radha."

Hearing the doctor, Sanatan became speechless. Tears welled up in his eyes. He thought of how Radha had longed to be a mother of a daughter and what her reaction would be when she would learn this.

While Sanatan was thinking this, Dr. Bhanuben said, "I must tell you another thing, Radha will never be able to have another child."

Sanatan was stunned. Madhavi placed her hand on his shoulder in a gesture to console him.

Disappointed, Radha returned home. Gradually, she was relieved of the anguish. Two years elapsed since then.

"You were supposed to go to a conference at Geneva. What happened to that?"

All of a sudden Sanatan remembered Dr. Homi Bhabha. While talking to each other in praise of Dr.Bhabha, Dr. Swaminathan said to Sanatan, "In 1955 when the UNO arranged an international Conference on the 'Peaceful Use of The Atom' at that time the leading worldwide atomic scientists were present. Dr. Homi Bhabha, being the president, gave such a marvelous and fantastic lecture that appealed to all the representatives present there." Sanatan's face was sad because he recollected his memories of Dr.Bhabha. Instead of Dr. Bhabha, he had to go and attend the International Conference at Geneva. After some time he said to Radha,

"Perhaps, I shall have to go in November."

Time elapsed. Tapan had passed the intermediate exam with very high marks. On that night, Sanatan asked Tapan in Radha's presence,.

"Look Tapan, this is the most important turning point of your career. You need to take a decision as to which faculty you will choose. As you have opted for the 'B' group, you can easily gain admission to the medical faculty."

"Daddy, you know very well that I have been thinking of becoming a scientist like you and serving the nation as you do. I don't have the slightest desire to become a doctor."

"You are the master of your wish. Your decision will be accepted by us all."

One night, Sanatan arrived home and suddenly declared,

"On 26th November an international conference on Nuclear Arms and Disarmament will be held at Geneva. Next Monday, I shall fly to Geneva to participate in this conference."

Chapter 22

When Sanatan arrived in Geneva, the city located amid the enchanting natural scenic beauty of Switzerland, it was seven in the morning. For a long time Sanatan continued to watch the beautiful houses located on the banks of the lake. Mother Nature had showered all her splendorous beauty on the lake and the hills surrounding it with lush green forests. Foggy clouds could be seen on the peaks of the distant mountains. Sanatan had learnt that Switzerland was located on the mountain tops. Today, he was watching it in person. Naturally, he was reminded of Shrinagar and Kashmir. During college time he had visited Kashmir, accompanied by some of his friends. Tall pine, oak and fir trees on either side of the wide roads, beautiful green grassy patches amid snow—covered mountain peaks and natural beauty spread all over made him experience the heavenly joy during his visit to Kashmir. Today, when he saw the natural and beautiful wealth of nature, his heart danced with happiness at the handiwork of the supreme creator.

Accommodation was provided to the representatives of many countries in that grand hotel. In every room, a folder containing detailed information and instructions was placed on a table. Sanatan carefully read it. After a while he entered the bathroom. The warm water bath spruced him up. As he was tying a knot of his tie before the mirror, the phone rang. One of his two assistants, Mr. Deshpande, was on the line.

"Sir, Dr. Gangadharan and I are awaiting you in the visitors' lounge."

"Alright, I'll be with you in five minutes."

Sanatan put on his coat. He looked out of another window. He could see a beautifully laid-out garden. Some visitors were wandering here and there. Suddenly, his glance rested on a person and a wave of joy went through him. Quickly he reached an elevator and went down to the ground level. As soon as he emerged from the elevator he almost ran towards the garden. He looked carefully at a person standing against a pillar.

The man was wearing a brown suit and had a fawn colored toupee on his head. His eyes rested on the distant mountain peaks. Very cautiously Sanatan walked up to him and when he realized who he was, he thumped his palm on his right shoulder. The other person seemed irritated by such rowdy behaviour. For a moment red hot anger flashed in his eyes, but the moment he saw Sanatan before him his eyes twinkled with delight.

"Oh, Sanatan! You are in Geneva too?"

"And how about you, Iqbal?"

Their eyes were filled with tears of joy. The two friends were meeting after many years. They embraced each other for a long time. They missed each other for so long that when they finally met again their joy knew no bounds.

"Dear friend, Iqbal, you left Umreth for Pakistan but I found out this news too late. Whenever, I happened to go to Umreth I always asked our friends about your whereabouts, but nobody knew. Moreover, you did not give your address in Pakistan to any of our friends" Sanatan complained.

"That is true, dear Sanatan, there is a reason, it took a long time for us to settle in Lahore. Moreover a ban was imposed by both countries on the exchange of letters and afterwards when the ban was lifted, even then there was censorship. Months passed by and then I thought that having completed your study in Bombay you might have left Umreth permanently and settled in Bombay with your family. In addition, I did not know your address or your whereabouts. So where could I write a letter to you? Because of such reasons we were unable to contact each other" Iqbal replied in detail.

"Anyhow, how is your mother, Sairabanu? How are Uncle Rahim and Zubeida?"

"I am sorry to inform you that Uncle Rahim is no longer in this world but the rest of the family members are well". Iqbal replied hurriedly.

"Oh!" Sanatan said, looking at his wristwatch. "I will be late for the meeting. So please meet me in my room later on. I will be waiting for you."

After leaving Iqbal, Sanatan went into the visitors' lounge. He asked Deshpande and Dr. Gangadharan to accompany him. It was about nine o'clock by the time they had finished their breakfast. Leaving the restaurant, they walked towards the United Nations building, where the first round of the conference was to begin. All the representatives of the nations were asked to reach the conference hall by nine-thirty. It was the first time that scientists from all over the world were gathering in such a large number.

The President of the United States, Mr. Samuel, delivered his welcome address. He explained the purpose of the conference and welcomed the scientists to express their views. Many countries expressed concern that the process of producing weapons would pose a threat to humanity. This was a burning question at the conference. The chemical weapons can destroy mankind living on this planet. Within a fraction of a second, the chemical weapons could cause mass annihilation of millions of people or subject them to die a painful slow death. Talking about the need of world peace the United States advised other nations not to produce atomic bombs as well as other atomic weapons. On one hand the US advised other nations to refrain from producing nuclear weapons whereas on the other side they developed newer weapons almost regularly and tried to exercise control over other countries by selling them those weapons. Why does the United States advise other nations not to buy weapons from other nations or hoard them? Such issues were discussed at the conference.

Participating in the discussion Sanatan observed that man on Earth today is constantly living a terrified life.

"If the super-powers like America, Russia, France, Britain and China do not stop developing and manufacturing nuclear weapons and atom bombs, the peril of mass annihilation hanging over the mankind is never going to subside. If progress is to be made in the direction of disarmament and establish world peace the citizens of all the countries will have to live with a sense of non-confrontation and peace. The mass production of weapons of mass destruction being carried out all over the world will have to be suspended forthwith. We all have to apply our minds to this issue and question ourselves, what we are doing is right or wrong. Nothing would ever be achieved by discussions or passing resolutions at such conferences. We shall have to use our strength to stop the eruptions of battles and wars in the world. The production and development of newer weapons must be immediately suspended. The purpose of this conference is to ensure nuclear disarmament and that would only be achieved when we discuss measures and modalities to ensure an atmosphere in which the entire humanity could live in peace," Sanatan said.

Listening to Sanatan's explicit thoughts, the eyebrows of the representatives of many nations were raised. Sanatan's purpose behind criticizing countries like America was aimed at showing how material prosperity increases through the production of nuclear weapons. Nations like America were becoming financially prosperous by earning billions out of the production of weapons. Not only that, but the sale of weapons is the main source of income for America and out of such earnings it has established an armament industry which has resulted in the establishment of other industries related to aviation, shipping, automobile and ancillary industries to produce other ingredients of weapon systems. America began to provide these weapons to the other nations supporting her. As a result America earned immense wealth. Following the World War II the American presidents took leadership of the world politics. They hoped that the world politics would come into prominence as a collectivist policy of America during the period from 1950-60. Until 1954, America claimed to have stabilized political powers in 64 nations.

To date how many countries did the US enter into armed conflicts with? America intended to establish a status of sovereignty of the world by imposing itself on others.

America had attacked many countries to date with her combatant soldiers, military aircrafts and ships. She engaged in war in 1945 with China, in 1948 with the Philippines, in 1950 with Korea, in 1963 with Vietnam, in 1964 with Congo and Laos and lastly, at the time of war between India and Pakistan and India and China, she supported Pakistan and China against India, and thus had interfered.

To date, Sanatan had studied about America in great detail. Moreover, when he had stayed in America, he had minutely studied the diplomacy of America and her desire to gain control over the entire world. And that is why in his lecture, Sanatan described America as an arrogant, selfish, self-centered and crafty country as well as a nation that was detrimental to world peace. In his lecture Sanatan severely criticized other super powers as well. Lastly, he concluded his lecture with a question.

"Can we all take positive steps in the direction of world peace by putting a stop to the production of nuclear weapons and burying our mutual quarrels as well as our differences?"

After Sanatan's lecture, the proceedings of the Conference came to an end for the day.

When Iqbal came to Sanatan's room as planned, he was writing his memories of the day in his diary.

Placing his diary and pen to one side, Sanatan welcomed Iqbal.

"Welcome Iqbal . . . . you are most welcome! We have met at leisure after so many years. We have suddenly obtained an opportunity to talk peacefully."

"You are right, my friend. Seeing you I am reminded of our schooldays, our worthy teacher Vidyacharan Sharma, Bhatt Saheb and all our friends—Bansi, Bipin, Fakruddin, Dhimant, and Rehman."

"Wonderful! I'm glad that after so many years, you can remember everything."

"Who can ever forget the days of one's childhood? We can never forget those fine memorable days of our childhood, even if we grow up to be great men and achieve greater heights. That Bhadrakali Vav step-well of Umreth, those mango trees with lots of mangoes, the lake and especially our Jubilee school come alive before my eyes even today. Tell me Sanatan, how are your parents?"

Listening to Iqbal, Sanatan was lost for words. He didn't even know where to begin. After remaining silent for a while he said,

"My father lives with me in Bombay. But my mother passed away many years ago. After you left, I was married to Radha. My son, Tapan, is studying in a college. He is as clever as we were. He has all the characteristics of becoming a scientist."

Sanatan paused, looking at Iqbal. Then he asked,

"How's aunty Saira? I believe that you too must be married like me. How's Zubeida?"

"Thank God we met here by chance today. Many times Ammijan remembers you. For the last two years she has not keeping well. She has succumbed to an attack of paralysis. She is tired of life. Zubeida is married now and is living with her inlaws. In 1952, I was married to Mumtaz. These days, my son Karim and daughter Zohra are studying in a college."

"Alright, Iqbal, tell me truthfully, how was my lecture today?"

"Wonderful!"

"In my lecture this morning, I intentionally lashed out at America's policy of double standards. How can it be tolerated that America makes other nations dance to her tune? How can we tolerate the double standards of America when she at one time supports your nation and at other times thrashes you with a cane?"

"In this matter, not only America is to be blamed, my friend," Iqbal opined, "In fact, our own politicians are largely blameworthy."

"You are right. Even in India, the politicians are engaged in shameful acts like corruption, scandals and other such treacherous activities. Such destructive activities are going on in most of the countries. If they are not stopped, the devastation of entire humanity is a matter of absolute certainty."

"What can we do?" Iqbal asked seriously.

"A lot! We had decided to live life within the basic ideals of world peace. Do you remember that?" Sanatan reminded him of the past talks of their mission.

"I not only remember, but every word of our mission is engraved on my heart. Today after meeting you my happiness has doubled."

"Since we have met today suddenly, we should part after making plans for the future, so that we can proceed in the direction of our mission." Sanatan expressed his viewpoint.

"We both are individually connected with the politicians and that is why we are very well aware of their good and bad sides. If we cannot foil their destructive policies devastation would spread over the earth." Iqbal expressed his opinion.

"For this purpose we will have to engage in a candid discussion. Go to the depths of the problems and explore their reasons and only then will we be able to move in the direction of the perfect solution." Sanatan said.

"You are telling the truth. With the partition of India we all have become very unhappy. How happily the Hindu and Muslim communities once lived together with a sense of co-operation, peace and understanding! But look at us today! The minds of the Pakistanis have been slowly poisoned in such a manner that they look at India with disgust and hatred and consider them as born enemies."

"I feel, Iqbal, that the basic reason for this is the Kashmir issue. Both the houses of parliament have accepted through an unanimously passed resolution, two decades ago, that Kashmir is an inseparable part of India. India's stand on the issue of Kashmir is very clear today. India does not want any sort of mediation from anybody, whether it is China, America or the United Nations. India has the right to protect her sovereignty and that is why the Indian rulers repeatedly demand the return of the part of Kashmir occupied by Pakistan." Sanatan presented the true picture of Kashmir.

"You are aware that the military rulers mostly run the political administration of Pakistan. If they continue to keep the Kashmir issue alive and continually spew venom at India, the people of Pakistan will allow them to rule, and such circumstances have been created," Iqbal said.

"In India, the politicians pamper the people of minorities and selected castes to ensure the growth of their vote-bank. Their act is like feeding milk to snakes. In 1947, when India was partitioned, the British kept the issue of princely states fomenting. Due to the iron-like policy of Sardar Patel the questions of the princely states were resolved. The Prime Minister, Jawaharlal Nehru, lodged a complaint with the United Nations when a problem was created in the Kashmir issue. This way, despite the fact that Kashmir was united with India, an uncertainty was created about it. During these days, the final shape was being given to the Indian constitution. In order to ensure that the confidence of the people of Kashmir was not shaken, it was accorded a special status through an inclusion of section 306 in the constitution. This section later came to be known as a section 370. This section provides the Indian constitution, or none of the laws of the Indian parliament would become applicable to Kashmir. In this way, Pakistan fought the war in 1965 on this question of Kashmir." Sanatan expressed his frustration about the politicians.

"In such a situation, the helpless people of Kashmir have to suffer. The Muslims of Kashmir have been settled there for many years. They were living in brotherly love with the Hindu Pandits for many years! Now only time will tell if such brotherly feelings, such accord and such peace will ever exist." Iqbal presented a pathetic picture of the people of Kashmir.

"Whatever will be, but the problem of Kashmir is getting more and more complicated with each passing day. America plays an important role in this. The American President, John F. Kennedy once told the

Ambassador of Pakistan, stationed in Washington that, "America is not interested in Kashmir but is interested in the problem of Kashmir. The American policy is aimed at making India and Pakistan fight with each other. On one hand, the ever growing grip of Russia on Kashmir is reduced and on the other hand, Pakistan buys weapons from America and other countries." Sanatan exposed the American policy.

"Nowadays, many times war has erupted between groups of Shia and Sunni sects in Pakistan. The Pakistani rulers try to cause mischief for Afghanistan. This way, instead of resolving the domestic issues, our political leaders act as pawns in the hands of the super powers and make wrong decisions, left and right." Iqbal criticized the rulers of Pakistan.

"I believe that the Muslims living in India enjoy many more privileges than those in Pakistan." Sanatan said.

"Your observation is correct." Iqbal said.

"A Muslim living in India with the proper qualifications can reach the highest and best position in the nation, whereas, despite all the talk of a highest position for a Hindu in Pakistan, they have to live a miserable life."

"Very true! When Khuda created this universe, he has created the bad mind of the man in such a manner that he is not able to come out of the web of his selfish, crafty and deceitful attitudes." Iqbal put forward his philosophy.

Concluding their discussion Sanatan asked,

"Now, tell me Iqbal, what should we do to achieve our mission that we have been cherishing since our childhood days? If you have ever thought about it, please tell me."

"I get many thoughts, but have not been able to arrive at any decision." Iqbal said.

Looking at Iqbal, Santan said,

"Iqbal, we have four days on our hands. How can we suspend the devastation of mankind through contemplation, deep thinking and the exchange of views? How can we avert the nuclear warfare forever? How can we avoid annihilation of humanity which could be engineered through nuclear weapons? How can we make the entire humanity fear free through peace and harmony? How can such circumstances be restrained through the scientific intentions? Several such questions are cropping in my mind. Let us pray God so that we can get proper answers for such questions."

They were tired by the activities of that day. They wished one another 'Good night!' and parted.

Chapter 23

The international conference on atomic weapons and disarmament that had been going on for the last three days was progressing in an interesting and thrilling manner. Most of the nations were in favour of finding a way to eradicate the fear of devastation created by nuclear weapons. But certain other nations, who were aiming at overflowing their offers with plentiful earnings through the sale of nuclear weapons, missiles, warships and atom bombs, opposed them, so that the production of nuclear weapons and atom bombs would remain within their control and thus were trying to tilt the balance in their favour.

Putting forward arguments on behalf of India, Sanatan pointed out several times that if humanity was to live in peace, the research and production of nuclear weapons must be suspended forthwith. If all the nations of the world created a multitude of bombs and missiles as a measure of self-defence in order to save itself from a nuclear attack, the day would come when the World War III would be fought solely with nuclear weapons. Then, the existence of entire humanity could possibly become endangered and massive devastation could ruin the earth. The scientific inventions must always be used for the benefit of man and if the need arose, nuclear weapons for protection.

Supporting the arguments of the American representative Dr. Asif on behalf of Pakistan said, "The greatest fear that any country could have, would be from their neighbouring countries. If a neighbouring country wages war, one needs to be fully prepared for that. This way, every country will have to have stock weapons and arms. We buy weapons from America and other nations for self-protection and not to attack others with them."

This way, each one presented one's views in the conference. A lot of discussion took place in favour, as well as against, the nuclear weapons but no proper decision was in sight. The following day was the concluding day of the conference. That night when Iqbal went to Sanatan's room, he was jotting down notes of the day's events in his diary.

"Welcome Iqbal, come in! Now, in two days we shall have to part."

"Yes."

"I could not digest what your boss, Dr.Asif said. He talked of having your cake and eating it too."

"You are well aware of the attitude of our rulers! If Dr.Asif did not talk in such a manner the people of Pakistan would never pardon him and he would become a subject of grave humiliation."

"True, now, you tell me, how would you proceed in the direction of world peace living amid such political rulers of your country?" Sanatan asked the question that was disturbing him.

"Yaar, you are lucky that millions of people are present in your country to support your viewpoints, but in my country it is so different! In spite of that, I remember our mission and some way will have to be found." Iqbal paused and then continued, "After tasting defeat in the war of 1965, the Pakistani rulers have poisoned the minds of the people to such an extent that they look at the Indians with absolute contempt and hatred. Even through the text books taught in the schools are totally incorrect, a sense of enmity and repulsion have been invoked among the students against India. Besides, the politics of Pakistan is responsible for the feuds between the Shia and Sunni sects. Since the Sunni population is larger in Pakistan, every now and then tyrannical incidents take place in the Shia mosques and public places. Smaller castes like Ahmedia have been totally wiped out."

"I've heard that Mohammed Ali Jinnah basically belonged to the Shia sect. But, his two sisters were converted to the Sunni sect following their marriages; is that true?"

"Yes, in 1948, when Jinnah left for the heavenly abode, a feud ensued on the issue of his will. His close relatives wanted to execute his will in accordance with the regulations of the Shia sect. Recently, an individual called Husain Ali Amanji Valji has protested against that and has contested the court order. Manji Valji said that Mohammed Ali Jinnah and his sister Fatima were converted from the Shia to the Sunni sect of Muslims. Hence his entire properties will be disposed of in accordance with the Sunni regulations."

"Then what happened?" Sanatan was interested in what Iqbal was saying.

"The case continued, but the people of Pakistan were dissatisfied. In fact, Mohammed Ali Jinnah was the resident of the Paneli village near Porbander City, in the Gujarat state of India. Originally he belonged to the Vaishnavaite sect, and Lohana community of Hinduism. Later, he was converted to Islam and became a Khoja Muslim. He followed the Shia sect of Islam. The present-day Pakistan wants to eradicate his identity as a Shia Muslim."

"I heard that the Mujahids living in East Pakistan and Afghanistan also nurture severe opposition and anger towards the Pakistani rulers." Sanatan said.

"Its basic reason lies in the divisive attitude of the Muslims and internal politics of Pakistan. The students of Pakistan are being taught that not only the Hindus but every other person is engaged in perpetrating a conspiracy against the Muslims or Pakistan. When I hear or see such things my heart suffers deep anguish at how mankind resorts to so many false beliefs!"

"Iqbal, since you are talking to me candidly and frankly, I can tell you that our politicians, too, are not wedded to the truth. Many politicians are seen to adopt corrupt and unpatriotic activities by snuffing out the voice of their inherent spirit to occupy and sustain the position of power. How proud we felt for our motherland when we were studying in school! Today, the politicians are engaged in activities which are considered shameful not only for individuals but for the entire nation."

"What is your opinion on the question of Kashmir?" Iqbal asked.

"The politicians are responsible to a larger extent in resolving this issue at an early opportunity. Having the issue of the Kashmir problem alive and burning, not only India but Pakistan also will have to expend billions. I feel, due to these politicians the Kashmir issue will develop into a grave crisis in a few days. As I believe, the Inter Services Intelligence (ISI) of Pakistan has given orders to provide teachings against India in the Madressa and foment a holy war 'Jehad.'."

"I am of the belief that America has played a decisive role in fomenting bitterness against India." Iqbal commented as he looked at Sanatan.

"Dear brother, America has been taking care solely to enhance her financial prosperity and economic prowess. She earns trillions through the sale of armaments. The US ensures that both our nations have to spend a large chunk of the budget on defence by instilling a fear of war in both countries and in this way ensure that we never become economically prosperous."

"Sanatan, I have noticed that Pakistan has been spewing a language of revenge considering India as her arch rival. None of the leaders of Pakistan have condemned this, but instead abuse India in one way or another. Even after snatching away half of Kashmir they don't seem to be satisfied. They are plotting to devastate India." Iqbal expressed his anguish.

"I have heard that according to the new game-plan of the ISI, in order to economically devastate India, a plan to circulate fake currency in India has been perpetrated. Planning is being thought out to establish Madressa in Pakistan, Jammu, Kashmir and in Kerala to misinform and incite poor, illiterate Muslim youths to undertake subversive and terrorist activities in India. The ISI is scheming to divide the masses, ignite communal violence, spread fear phobia through bomb blasts and encourage the smuggling of drugs and arms. This way, ISI aims at spreading deep roots of devastation in India by encouraging terrorism." In a very serious tone Sanatan was squarely accusing Pakistan. For a while Iqbal kept quiet and then looking at Sanatan's face, recalling the past he said,

"Sanatan, we had envisioned the dream of world peace since our childhood. The time has arrived to proceed in the direction of the mission that we have thought about. The work henceforth is of great difficulties. It may take many years to accomplish that. Now, we must move ahead after taking a firm decision."

"You are absolutely right." Sanatan said in a tone of agreement. "Now, we shall not have to wait for many years. When I was studying in America, I met Ivan. His father, Mr. William is the owner of an island called Sohali, close to Malaysia. I have his invitation to visit that island, which has a population of one million people. They both, like us, are lovers of world peace. I have exchanged views with them about world peace. They have promised to spend billions of dollars on our mission. Not only that, they will provide complete co-operation with us in our mission. At an opportune time we will go to the Sohali Island."

Listening to Sanatan, Iqbal heaved a sigh of relief. He suddenly said, "Presently, I live in Islamabad, but my conscience pricks me. Hearing the meaningless orders of the politicians, my conscience is anguished. Whenever they express hatred, enmity and wicked thoughts about my motherland, India, at times, I feel as if each and every cell of my body is on fire."

For a while Sanatan gazed at Iqbal's face and then he said,

"Iqbal, I am very sure that we won't have to wait for long to initiate the activities of our mission. We met here and exchanged thoughts; I consider all that as a Divine beckoning. You can write down the details of the Sohali Island, name, address, and code number— everything in your diary."

Listening to Sanatan, Iqbal noted the details of Sohali Island in his diary.

"Sanatan, is it not possible for both of us to create a unique universe through our work in which mankind can live in peace and with harmony?"

"Dear friend, it is an uphill task to create such a universe. If I put forward the concept of such a universe in my country the people would whole-heartedly welcome the idea, but you can never think of spreading such concepts in Pakistan. You know very well that the Pakistan government provides full support to the ISI in its meanest, dangerous and terrifying activities."

"Then what should we do?"

Sanatan was lost in thought for some times. Then he said, "You are aware that the Muslims are temperamentally fierce."

"Yes."

"During the days of Ramzan large sized drums were played throughout the night. Do you remember when Tajiya was brought out in procession in Umreth, how the Hindus used to hide themselves in their homes out of fear? Our Muslim brethren would inflict various forms of tortures in the memory of Mohammed, the holy prophet, and endure physical pain. I watched the fierce Muslims from the terrace of my house and experienced great fear."

"The Pakistan rulers understand very well such fierce temperament and that is why they continue to rule over Pakistan by pouring poison in their ears."

"Dear friend, as a matter of our friendship I would like to tell you that in the coming few years India will attain the highest place in the field of nuclear energy, and I don't have the slightest doubt about that. But your country, Pakistan will have to either beg or steal the necessary uranium or plutonium and plans of nuclear reactors from the countries for the development of nuclear weapons."

"Sanatan, what you say is, true. I am required to frequently visit Iran, Holland or China as per the instructions of my boss."

"As far as I know, you don't posses supplementary information of the nuclear reactor to produce nuclear energy."

"How did you learn of that?" Looking at Sanatan, Iqbal asked.

"The way your country handles espionage work, my country too has an espionage network, which provides us with all the supplementary information. In our hearts there is no other thought except the exploration of world peace. My heart is anxious to see the day when divine rays of the serenity of humanity spread all around from the evolvement of a new universe." Sanatan replied.

"Sanatan, I am sure that Allah would help us to attain our aim as has been greatly desired by you."

Keeping his mission in sight, and taking a step in that direction Sanatan said,

"Look Iqbal, listen to me carefully. This discussion will remain our closely guarded secret. This is necessary for the success of our mission. You are living in Pakistan and are placed at a premium position as a scientist. You will continue to receive all the information as to how and what steps Pakistan is taking to develop and produce arms for self-protection. The first step of our mission would be to concentrate on the minutest details of the goings—on in Pakistan. We shall continue to maintain our contact and make plans for the future."

"The concept of world peace is foremost in our hearts. Let's strive together to create a world where peace, prosperity and humanity prevail that for a long time now, I anxiously await to see. I am ready to sacrifice anything for the accomplishment of our dreams." Iqbal said, overcome with emotion.

It was almost midnight as they continued to talk. Both friends came out to the balcony. The cold wind sent a chilled shiver up their spines. Immediately, they closed the doors of the balcony and went back into the room. Their eyes rested on the full moon visible through the window. All around the moonlight was spread like a bright white sheet stretched over the tall trees in the garden. Uttering 'Good night!' Iqbal left for his room. The entire city was fast asleep. Everywhere total silence prevailed. Walking around the room, Sanatan bolted the door, switched off the lights and stretched out on the bed and instantly fell asleep.

Next morning, the conference entered its final day. Discussions ensued throughout the day. Certain resolutions were passed. Some of the resolutions were passed without much discussion, whereas a few others were resolved after more discussion.

Sanatan addressed the gathering expressed his views explicitly, clarifying various issues about India.

"None of the powerful and big nations have any right to attack smaller or weaker nations. When will mankind ever prosper? It will be when we all strive together to establish a peaceful new world. We should bury the mutual hatchet and enmity, forget our bitterness and make efforts to instill the virtuous qualities of ideal attitude, behavior and character, so that all the people of the world can exist with mutual trust, peace and fearlessness. This will only become possible when all of us permanently stop the research and production of nuclear weapons. India has never believed in violence. She has never attacked other countries. India is the birth-place of Buddha and Mahavir and a land of non-violence of the father of the nation, Mahatma Gandhi. We have to produce arms and even hoard them, but that is only for self-protection. If all the nations of the world stop producing weapons and understand the significance of world peace, India would not be required to do all that. Besides, I would like to make it explicitly clear that although we believe in non-violence, if any country attacks India without any reason, instead of remaining quiet, we would retaliate and provide a befitting answer. Nevertheless, I would like to reiterate that establishing supremacy over other nations by annihilating innocent masses and conquering them is not a characteristic of a wise man."

When they sat down for lunch Sanatan said, "Iqbal, tonight I shall leave for India and you will return to Holland. Convey my best wishes to all. I wish to meet aunty Saira, but you are aware that we have become pawns in the hands of the politicians. Give my regards to Mumtaz, Karim and Zohra."

"Sanatan, having met you after so many years the burden in my heart has been eased. Whenever, you call me, I will come up. Convey my affectionate 'salam' to Radha, uncle Kanu and Tapan."

"Many times I think that if India and Pakistan bury their hatchet and enmity the people of both nations can become happy and live in peace. The prosperity and happiness of the people of the world cannot be achieved unless casteism and communalism are given up. When Hitler perpetrated his satanic plans and organized mass killing of the Jews how painful the cries of severe anguish from their hearts were! Don't you think that the creator of this universe has evolved a great wonder by creating the mischievous mind? What a mass-massacre was perpetrated by America when they bombed Nagasaki and Hiroshima in 1945?"

They continued to talk until they had finished lunch.

At night, when Sanatan sat in a car to leave for the airport, tears welled up in Iqbal's eyes. His throat was choked with a surge of emotion. As a reflex action he lifted his right hand to bid farewell. Tears rolled down from his eyes. He turned his face sideways. The car carrying Sanatan sped away.

After returning to India, Sanatan became extremely busy with his work. He went to Delhi accompanied by Deshpande and Dr.Gangadharan, to meet the Defence Minister. He conveyed his report on the nuclear weapons and disarmament conference to the Defence Minister, orally as well as in writing. His father, Radha and Tapan were quite well.

The days flew by. Once, Radha complained that during Sanatan's absence, Tapan used to roam frequently with his friends until late at night. Once, he had been on a three-day picnic to Matheran accompanied by his friends. At times, Tapan did not pay any attention to what Radha said, and did whatever took his fancy. Listening to Radha's complaints, Sanatan was deeply perturbed.

Chapter 24

One evening as Tapan was going out, Sanatan stopped him and requested,

"Tapan, come here and tell me where you are going now?"

"Daddy, I'm going to meet Ramamurti at Matunga."

"Ramamurti? Do you mean the man who heads the Microfilm Department in the Bhabha Atomic Research Center?"

"Yes."

"What do you have in your hand?"

"Two physics notebooks."

"Why are you taking them with you? Are you going to give them to somebody?"

"Yes . . . no . . . no . . ." Tapan stammered.

Sanatan emphatically asked,

"You are going to meet Ramamurti's daughter, Rita, aren't you? Tell me truthfully."

Listening to Sanatan, he nodded his head with an expression of fear on his face.

"Look, Tapan, these are your student days. For a long time I have been observing that as well as studying, you have been spending time wandering about with others. If you wish to become a great scientist like me, you ought to concentrate your mind on your studies now. Does Rita study with you?"

"Yes Daddy, she needs my notebooks. I was going to give them to her."

"Alright, you may go. But remember, you shall achieve success in life only if you have good studious friends at college, and only then will you be able to achieve your aims in your studies."

Radha emerged from the kitchen as the father and the son were talking. She suddenly asked,

"Tapan, tell me, who are Rita and Mohini, who repeatedly call you on the phone?"

"Both of them study with me."

"I've heard that you have been going around more and more with Rita these days. Is this true?" Radha asked.

"Mummy, as we study together at college, we often meet each other. Sometimes we share snacks in the canteen, and at other times we read together in the library. As a matter of fact, Rita is also as clever and as bright a student as I am."

"Look son, you are at such an age that if you become distracted from your studies, we will be very upset," Sanatan said.

"But daddy, don't you trust me?" Tapan asked somewhat testily. For a while he fell silent. Then he added, "I don't deny that I meet and spend a lot of time with Rita. But my aim is to pass my exams with the highest marks possible. Since, my B.Sc. exams are nearing; Rita and I read in the library of Ruia College until late at night."

"Don't misunderstand us. We are telling you all of this for your benefit."

"I can assure you that, Jatin, D'Souza, Rita, Mohini and I are currently extremely busy in reading and preparing for our examinations. We don't have any time to catch movies or enjoy picnics anymore. We don't while away our time on futile talks."

"That's wonderful. Yesterday when I called Ramamurti into my office cabin about some work, I learnt about Rita and your other friends while talking to him. Without elaborating, I would like to advise you to concentrate on your studies." Saying so much, Sanatan fell silent for a while. Then he said softly,

"You can go now, but don't be late."

Tapan kept quiet. He slipped on his chappal and went out.

"The food is ready. Shall I lay the plates?" Radha asked.

"No, not now." Sanatan paused for a while before blurting out, "These young ones of the present-day generation don't seem to understand anything and enter into useless arguments."

"These days are not like ours. Even the values of education have not remained what they were in our time. How reverently we worshipped our parents, elders and our teachers!" Radha remarked supporting Sanatan's viewpoint. She added, "I would like to say that the modern values have not affected Tapan to that extent. He is very much a person of great understanding. Also, he is very wise, clever and very good at his studies. To date he has never disobeyed us, but sometimes . . . ."

"Parents can never think of anything else except the happiness of their children. Besides I hope that Tapan will strive to fulfill my dreams, my wishes and aspirations in ensuring peaceful lives for mankind for which I am working very hard. I believe that God's grace always helps us in such noble deeds."

"Sanatan, you are right. These days we often hear cases of wayward and rogue children; and that is why it is natural that we get worried about our son. I firmly believe that Tapan would never act in a manner which would tarnish our reputation."

After a while both sat down to have their supper. Suddenly the doorbell rang. Tapan had returned within an hour. All the three of them settled down to have supper. They talked while eating their meal. At that time the telephone rang. Sanatan placed the receiver to his ear and listened. Kanaiyalal, who had gone to meet Vasudev at Chowpatty, was to stay there for the night.

The next day Tapan and his friends were seated under a tree in the compound of Ruia College. D'Souza blurted out,

"Why is nobody talking today? Why are you all silent?"

"It's Jatin . . ."

"What's happened to Jatin? Why has he not attended college for a week? Is he not keeping well?" D'Souza fired his questions.

"Jatin was admitted to the Sion Hospital a week ago. All of his pathological reports have been received, and he was diagnosed as suffering from blood-cancer." Mohini, who was Jatin's neighbour, informed them

All the friends became serious listening to what Mohini said. The date of the exam was nearing. While every one of them were engrossed in their studies, such serious news saddened them.

"Rita and I were at to the hospital this morning to meet Jatin. His case is worsening day by day. The doctors have given up hope. Blood transfusions are being carried out. The doctor says that as the disease has reached the final stage, there is hardly any chance of his survival." Mohini said.

Tapan suddenly said,

"Then why don't they move him to the cancer ward in the Tata Hospital?"

"They have been thinking of that. Initially they couldn't detect the disease. When the reports were received just two days ago, the doctor pronounced the case as a serious one."

"What should we do now?" asked D'Souza.

"Blood transfusions will have to be carried out on a daily basis; that's what I understand. Let us get our blood groups checked, so that we all can donate our blood."

That evening all the friends went to the hospital, where they learnt that as Jatin's condition had worsened, he had been transferred to the Tata Hospital.

They all reached the Tata Hospital soon.

Jatin's parents and sister, Sweety, were crying bitterly. When the friends reached the hospital Jatin was in a coma and fighting for his life. All the friends were engulfed by sadness at the plight of their friend.

For the last three years, all five friends were going about and studying together and shared in each other's moments of happiness and sadness. Although Jatin was not as clever as the others, they were sure that by remaining with them he would be able to improve his learning as they would help him. Tapan and Rita were the most studious of the group. They would earnestly discuss study matters with Jatin whenever he needed it. In this way Jatin was progressing well in his learning, but suddenly he was taken ill.

When it became very late that night, Jatin's parents requested his friends to return to their homes. All of them, except Mohini, left for their homes. Mohini stayed behind to provide consolation and warmth to Sweety who had been crying incessantly.

Very early the following morning, the phone rang in Sanatan's house. Tapan got up quickly and placed the receiver to his ear. It was Mohini, who informed him in a serious tone,

"Jatin's condition is critical. Come soon!"

Tapan woke up his mother softly. He told her about Jatin's condition and that he was going to visit him at the hospital.

When Tapan reached the hospital, Jatin had already left for the heavenly abode. Tapan fell silent. His throat was choked with emotion and he sat down on a bench. D'Souza placed his hand on Tapan's shoulder saying,

"Have courage, friend, our beloved friend has left us to depart for the divine world."

The bitter crying of Jatin's parents filled the hospital. Mohini was trying to pacify the inconsolable Sweety, by holding her arms.

At twelve that afternoon, Jatin's dead body was taken to the crematorium. For Tapan, this was his first experience of visiting a crematorium. Jatin's dead body was placed on the pyre. Logs of wood were placed around the dead body. After a while it was set alight. Watching the flames of fire leaping to envelope Jatin's body, Tapan was thinking,

"One day, ultimately, a man has to succumb to death. Why can't the scientists who do so much research, try to find a medicine that can cure a person of cancer?"

By evening when a crestfallen Tapan reached his home, his heart was very heavy. He only had some milk and went to bed to sleep.

Somehow, a week passed melancholically. Slowly Tapan emerged from the influence of grief. Once again he became busy with his studies.

The exams of the B.Sc. were over. Tapan had done well in the examinations. On the last day of the examinations, he was to see a movie at the afternoon showing with D'Souza and Rita at 3.00p.m. Due to unforeseen circumstances, D'Souza could not attend the movie. Therefore, only Rita went to the movie. After the movie was over, they went to the King's Circle garden and sat on a bench.

"How have you done in your exams, Tapan?"

"Excellent! How about you?"

"I found the Physics test a bit tough. But I did well in the chemistry test." Rita replied.

"Now, what are your plans for your further studies?"

"I am going to wait for the results to be announced first. I'll think about my future plans after that. Hmmmm . . . what are your plans?"

"You are aware that I propose to become a scientist like my father. That's why instead of seeking admission to the medical faculty I chose to do my B.Sc."

"I feel that you will achieve first or second place on the merit list, won't you?"

"How can I say that for certain? Nevertheless, I can say with confidence that my name will appear in the top five."

"Tapan, I would like to congratulate you in advance. I pray God to help you in fulfilling all your wishes."

"Will God listen to your fervently made prayers?" Tapan jokingly asked, looking at Rita's face. This made Rita blush. But she commented,

"You just crack jokes at any time that suits you."

"That is not so, Rita."

For a while both fell silent. Then Sanatan asked,

"Shall we get up now?"

"Oh, no."

"Hey, it's getting darker already. Our folks at home will be worried about us."

"You've told me that you have already phoned your home, didn't you?"

"That's true, but it's better if we arrive home early at night."

"Why don't you like my company?"

"Rita, you know that we've been together since noon. If I didn't like your company, why would I agree to go for a movie with you?"

Listening to Tapan, Rita heaved a sigh of relief. She giggled and Tapan lovingly watched the dimples on her cheeks as she did so.

Once again they fell silent.

Rita was reminded of the discussion she had with her father.

"Rita, what do you think of Tapan, who studies with you?" Her father, Ramamurti, had asked.

"He is nice."

"You must be aware that his daddy is the most honoured person, I feel that instead of studying further you should find a life partner for yourself."

"Papa, I think that I'm too young to get married."

"My dear daughter, that's what you think. Do you know, if you get married, how many of our worries would be eased?"

"So, you think that I'm a burden to you?"

"No, you misunderstand me. That's not what I meant to say.

If we get you married, we will be relieved from our responsibilities."

"But, tell me clearly, what do you wish?"

"I shouldn't say, but since you are asking, I would like to say that one cannot find a good boy like Tapan easily. I would say to that extent that if you like Tapan you shouldn't delay. Instead of thinking of studying further, get married to him."

"Shall we get up now?" Rita was woken up with a start from her revelry by Tapan's words. Getting up she asked,

"Can I ask you something?"

"What is it . . . ?"

Slowly they came out of the gate of the garden.

The road was lit by the streetlights. Tapan sat into a taxi to meet a friend. Suddenly, Tapan asked,

"What was it you wanted to ask?"

"Oh nothing . . . . nothing . . . . not now . . . . Some other time." Rita blurted out, waving joyfully and then fell silent as the taxi drove away.

The days passed.

One day the results of the B.Sc. examination were announced. Tapan stood at second place in the Bombay University. Everybody was overjoyed in the house. Everybody congratulated him. Granting her blessings by placing her hand on Tapan's head Radha said,

"Son, may you live long and glorify your father's name! Besides, may you have great inspiration to serve society at large and our nation. May you become an accomplished scientist like your father and produce great inventions. These are the words of my blessings."

"Mummy, my Daddy is a unique person. He has devoted his entire life in search of world peace. The modern techniques that he has evolved to develop nuclear weapons by transforming the atomic energy into power are quite unique and unparalleled. To tell you the truth, I am not qualified enough to fit into my father's shoes."

"Don't think in that way, Tapan. Should you have devotion and dedication, you will do even better than your daddy."

"As a matter of fact, through experimentation, I would certainly like to explore the secrets of atomic energy. And to that end, my daddy will always remain my ideal."

"Tapan, may I ask you a question?"

"Ask it."

"Will I get a reply?"

"That depends on what sort of question you are asking."

"I've heard that Rita is a clever student and she stood at eighth place on the merit list."

"Yes, that's true."

"I've learnt that you like her. Is that true?"

"Oh mummy! Why do you ask me such a question?"

"I'm just asking if you like Rita or not?"

"There is no question of liking or disliking. I want to study further. I shall have to concentrate more on my studies. Presently, I have no time to think of such frivolous things."

"You may not know, but Rita's father, Ramamurti, spoke with your daddy about your marriage to Rita."

"And then?" Now it was Tapan's turn to be surprised.

"Your dad had replied that you should wait until the results of your exams were announced, and if you both agreed, they would think about it."

"This means that so much discussion took place without my knowledge?"

"Oh, your grandpa is pestering me every day on this issue. He wants you to get married before he leaves for the heavenly abode. He wants to see you married and your wife in this house, which will make him very happy."

"See mom, I have an ardent desire to study further. Until such time as my studies are complete, I don't want to think about it."

Two to three weeks passed.

One day, when Tapan arrived home he received news that his grandfather Kanaiyalal was admitted to the Sion Hospital. He complained of chest congestion and loss of breath, so he was admitted to the ICU. After two days, his health had recovered and he returned home. The grandpa had an honest talk with Tapan,

"Son, won't you fulfill the wish of this old man? Why are you avoiding getting married?"

"I'm not refusing. I'm only requesting to extend the time. Let me pass my M.Sc. examination first. Only then will I think about it."

"No, Tapan, no. I cannot trust my health any more. I cannot predict when I will be swallowed by the jaws of death . . ."

The words of his grandfather compelled Tapan to think.

Views and thoughts were exchanged in the house and at last, a unanimous decision was taken with regards to the marriage of Tapan and Rita.

Within a week, the betrothal took place and a month later the marriage was celebrated.

The marriage function was a grand event and everybody within the family was very happy. On the following day Tapan and Rita were to go to Nainital together for their honeymoon. Everybody was tired after the day's marriage ceremony. Sanatan had gone to bed early as he was very tired.

It was almost past midnight when the telephone rang. Radha lifted the receiver. Quickly she passed it to Sanatan and said,

"It's a call for you, from New Delhi."

It was an urgent message from the Defence Ministry. "According to the information we have received, Pakistan will declare war on India, at any moment. The Defence Minister, Mr.Bajaj wants you to fly out to Delhi, accompanied by Dr. Swaminathan, on the first available flight."

Chapter 25

Early the next morning, Dr. Sanatan and Dr. Swaminathan occupied their seats in the Boeing plane. After some time when the aircraft leveled out at 32000 feet altitude Sanatan unfastened his seat belt.

"I cannot understand why Pakistan causes such mischief so often. In 1965 it lost the battle, yet again, why do they want to take such a foolish step as to wage a war with us?"

"Sanatan, you know and understand the rulers of Pakistan. Ever since the day Bhutto was placed at the helm of affairs as the President of Pakistan, they have been thinking day and night of snatching Kashmir away completely. Moreover, the Pakistan Army Chief, General Yahyakhan is publically making announcements and misguiding the masses that they will not rest until they can retain control over Kashmir".

"That will remain their dream. It's never going to happen. Do they think that we will quietly watch them when they attack to gain control over Kashmir? We 'll make them pay heavily for such a mistake".

"The Pakistani rulers have created these circumstances themselves. In order to rule and keep their people in good humour, they would be dethroned in no time if they don't flex their muscles at India. This fear causes great discomfiture to the Pakistani rulers". Swaminathan observed, looking at Sanatan.

"Pakistan's economy is in a shambles", Sanatan replied "Six years ago Pakistan suffered a great defeat in an attempt to snatch away Pakistan. Hundreds of soldiers and innocent citizens were massacred. They have no shame in falling to their knees before America and to beg for armaments help and monetary loans. Isn't that a surprise?"

"Where is their true democracy? For most of the time, Pakistan has been ruled by military dictators. They are only hungry for power and rule with absolute disregard for the good of their people. Their political state is akin to the Moghul rule, where their reign was inspired through ghastly acts of conspiratorial murders".

Expressing his grief Sanatan observed, "Would they not be thinking as to how their people can live in happiness and peace and their nation can progress? Can they not see the painful days that will be endured following the days of war?"

"Sanatan, are you not aware of the cruel temperament of these Muslims? Despite having tasted defeat several times they continue to chant 'Kashmir . . . . Kashmir!' incessantly for many years. They have already snatched away a part of Kashmir. Now, if they gain control over the rest of Kashmir their long cherished dream would be crystallized".

"What's the use in having such childish dreams? What can we gain by locking horns with the mighty and powerful India? As a matter of fact, it is Pakistan who will sustain greater damage in the war. Why can't they understand such a simple matter as this? The neighbouring China and America often instigate the Pakistani orders to declare war against India. Other Islamic nations also lend their support to Pakistan. Due to these reasons Pakistan declares war". Sanatan said looking at Swaminathan.

"If Pakistan declares war this time, either the whole of Pakistan would be broken into pieces, or will give up battles for good. You know how well our military has progressed!" Swaminathan said.

"I am aware of that. As many submarines have been inducted into the Indian Navy, the soldiers are willing to put their lives at stake in the war. If Pakistan commits a mistake by engaging India in war, it will sustain terrible devastation. As the Pakistani rulers have failed to resolve their domestic issues, they create such plans of war to divert the attention of their people from their problems", Sanatan said.

"Incidents of communal violence between the Shias and the Sunnis in Karachi, Mujahirs fighting against the policies of Pakistan in Afghanistan, the people of East Pakistan raising their heads against their oppression and seeking liberation, the opposition parties throwing spanners in the works of the government, and such tormenting problems cannot be resolved by the Pakistani rulers. They even fail to realize that India has superior military and better armaments. Why do they invite trouble and devastation in this way? I just fail to understand this!" Swaminathan turned his eyes from the port window and looked at Sanatan. He paused for a while and then continued,

"You know well that if war breaks out, our government is totally prepared to put up a good fight! Last month, when I accompanied the Defence Minister to the advanced borders, our military commanders were telling us that if Pakistan committed the error of waging war against our nation, they would erase its existence from the world-map".

"The Indian rulers are far better in that they are not planning to attack other nations. Moreover, our administrative system shows to the world that even a Muslim or a Christian or any non Hindu can occupy any high position of power, without any discrimination of caste, community or religion. This shows our religious tolerance towards all communities irrespective of them being Hindus, Muslims, Christians, Sikh or Parsi". Sanatan said.

"Who will explain all of this to the Pakistani rulers? For how long will the ruling Janta in Pakistan continue to satiate its thirst for human blood through its oppressive murderous rule? In 1965 Pakistan sustained grim defeat and the Tashkent Treaty was signed, but they still don't want to forget the Kashmir issue." Swaminathan said.

"Hindustan was partitioned and Pakistan was carved out. Kashmir was merged with India because of King Hari Singh. This fact pierces the hearts of the Pakistani rulers. No country wants to make them understand and accept this matter and soothe their feelings. On the contrary, they instigate Pakistan against India.

This is our misfortune", Sanatan pointed out emphatically.

"We've studied Indian history in our schools. The Moghul emperors used to fight battles to exercise control over the whole of India. Those Moghul emperors used to bribe many of the commanders of the Hindu Kings and win them over to their side. Many times among the Muslims, the killings and murders of brothers, fathers or sons would often take place due to a lust for power. All of these human weaknesses are

explicitly seen on the negative side of human nature".
Swaminathan expressed his viewpoint.

"I would like to go a step further and add that the
British have gifted a bloody and tarnished independence
to us. The result of such liberation is still being endured
by us today!"

"Is there no way to save ourselves from all this or to
save mankind from this?" Swaminathan seriously looked
at Sanatan's face.

For a while Sanatan was lost in thought. He bit
his lower lip in concentration and then resolutely said,
"How can that be predicted? Man always strove to
find solutions to whatever problems were created with
the evolvement of this universe. The objective of my
life is to somehow stop the warfare that could cause
the devastation of mankind. How can mankind ever
experience the joy of world-peace?" Having talked at
length Sanatan stared at the horizon in the distance
through the window. The plane had almost reached
Delhi.

A short time later, as the plane landed at the airport
in Delhi the land, buildings and the runway glowed in
the bright sunrays of the rising sun. A car drove them to
the office building of the Defence Minister, Mr. Bajaj.
When they reached the Defence Minister's office, Mr.
Bajaj welcomed them warmly.

"Dr. Sanatan, I am proud of you that you have
attained greater heights of acclaim through your
experimentation in the field of nuclear technology. I
have learnt from our undercover agents that Pakistan is
likely to attack India with double the force they did in
the 1965 war".

"Sir, I can foresee that if Pakistan casts her evil glance at Mother India, her devastation will be a certainty".

"Look, I have completed all my discussions with the chiefs of the three wings of the military on the impending war scenario. All three chiefs say that our soldiers are ready to even sacrifice their lives in order to protect the honour of our country. They are eagerly awaiting orders from their superiors". Then the Defence

Minister continued, "The reason behind my summoning you both here urgently was that you will have to stay in Delhi until the war is concluded, so that in the case of an emergency, your help could be of use to us".

"May I suggest something, Sir?" Sanatan asked.

"Yes, what is it?"

"Let no mistakes that were committed during the 1948 war be repeated. Pakistan had taken a large part of Kashmir under its control, which came to be known as Independent Kashmir. Ensure that such an incident is not repeated. With such incidents, the morale of our soldiers and commanders will be shaken".

"I would like to opine to that extent, that this time we must recover the area taken over by Pakistan and in addition snatch away some of the area under their rule. When such a thing happens, the morale of our defence forces will be enhanced". Dr. Swaminathan commented in support of Dr. Sanatan.

The Defence Minister continued, "This time the Muktivahini Forces of East Pakistan has requested our help. That is why counter-attacking Pakistan would be an easier course of action. In return, the Muktivahini

Forces have great expectations of us. Most of those people are from Bengal. It is our duty to help them".

"The administration of East Pakistan is just as bad as that of West Pakistan. The people of East Pakistan have so many problems that the government does not pay any attention to them. Now, East Pakistan is seeking liberation. One of the popular leaders of East Pakistan, Janab Mujib-Ur-Rehman has been seeking justice from the ruling party on behalf of the people of East Pakistan. If Pakistan starts a war it will be broken into two separate nations". Sanatan expressed his viewpoint.

"When India was partitioned lakhs of Muslims had migrated from the Bengal region to take refuge in East Pakistan. Many times those Mujahirs requested the ruling party to let them live a life of happiness and peace, but their pleas fell on the deaf ears of the politicians of the ruling party. This way, the Muktivahini Forces, also known as the Liberation Force, was established. They are willing to fight for their rights until the last drop of their blood is shed". Dr. Swaminathan presented a pathetic picture of the Bengali refugees.

"Taking advantage of this we earned the confidence of the Liberation Force. The strategy of the war has been planned out following discussion and the exchange of viewpoints with the three chiefs of the Army, Air Force and Navy. While the Pakistan army fights in Kashmir, our brave soldiers will cross over the Bay of Bengal and fight deeper into Pakistan. The ruling party will not have the slightest knowledge of this. Moreover, when our Indian Army attacks with great force using modern weapons, the people of Pakistan will be struck with a terrible sense of fear. Our defence forces are fully equipped to devastate their forces in Kashmir", The Defence Minister, Mr.Bajaj, provided a glimpse into his formidable strategy.

Suddenly the telephone rang. There was news from the frontier. Having completed his telephone conversation, the Defence Minister said.

"Today, it is 3rd December, 1971. The defence forces of Pakistan have gradually gathered closer to the border. There is news that they may attack either Bhuj or Jamnagar at any time tonight".

"Sir, when our preparations are absolutely complete, why should we be afraid? For many years now we have known that our chivalrous soldiers have always been standing alert in Kashmir braving severe cold in the region where snow does not melt for six months of the year. They are protecting our borders at the cost of their lives." Dr. Swaminathan said as he looked at the face of the Defence Minister.

"This time a good strategy for war has been prepared. Not only will Pakistan face a very tough time, but will never think of engaging India in war ever again. After this war their aggressiveness will subside like a wet cat", the Defence Minister said, rising from his chair.

Sanatan and Swaminathan also got up from their seats and said, "Best of luck!" The Defence Minister went into the adjacent large room where the three chiefs of the Military were waiting for him. A discussion ensued. Having listened to them peacefully, the Defence Minister smiled serenely. He experienced great solace within on hearing what they had to say. This time the Pakistani soldiers would be facing the hardest fight of their lives.

That night, Pakistan attacked the Kutch-Saurashtra region. The Indian Army was well prepared for such an eventuality. The brave Indian soldiers pushed back Pakistan's large-scale attack.

The instructions given by Lieutenant General Jagjit Singh Arora to the Indian soldiers were duly followed. The Pakistan Army quickly lost all of their enthusiasm. The Indian defence forces gave them a befitting response. Their attacks were thwarted by counter-attacks.

On the other hand, having made an agreement with the Muktivahini Forces, the Indian Army began its forward march to take control of the Pakistan territory. This was an event which caused grave concern for the Pakistani rulers. No advance preparations had been made by them to thwart the armies advancing towards East Pakistan. The valiant Indian soldiers were advancing forward in Azad Kashmir and other parts of Pakistan to exercise control over those regions. Under the guidance of the commander-in-chief of the Eastern Command, Jagjit Singh Arora, the brave Indian soldiers were moving ahead fearlessly.

The war continued for fourteen days. Pakistan realized that they had lost the war. The realisation dawned on them that thousands of soldiers would be killed mercilessly and that the Indian Army would take control of Lahore in Pakistan if the war continued any longer. Because of this, Leiutenant General Pheroz Khan, heading the command of the military forces in Pakistan, accepted his defeat.

Instead of surrendering to an enemy, Pheroz Khan wanted to die, but in the time of war, mental stability needs to be maintained. The deaths of thousands of other soldiers would be a certainty if he proceeded with the war. That is why, swallowing his bitterness, he chose to surrender to the Indian General.

Every cell of Pheroz Khan's body was on fire when Pakistan extended their hand for the truce, and General Arora agreed to concede.

Talks were held at Simla between the two nations. President Bhutto and his daughter, Benazir Bhutto, were present accompanied by other diplomats on behalf of Pakistan. At last, the Simla Agreement was given a final shape. According to the agreement that was reached between them, it was decided that the Indian soldiers would return all conquered territories to Pakistan. The issue of Kashmir would be resolved, according to the provisions of this agreement. Also, it was decided that East Pakistan would be rechristened as Bangladesh and Mujib-Ur-Rehman would be made the head of the newly formed sovereign country.

This way the people of East Pakistan were delighted with the creation of Bangladesh. Large processions were brought out onto the roads and streets and shouts of 'Long live Mujib-Ur-Rehman!' filled the air. The creation of Bangladesh was like pouring boiling oil on the hearts of the Pakistani rulers. But they were all helpless to change what was occurring. For no reason they had cast an evil look at Mother India and initiated the first attack. In return they had earned severe disrepute. Such an insult was intolerable but they had no other choice but to accept it.

A bloated back mark of shame had stuck to their head with this defeat. One more incident had taken place in the life of Pheroz Khan that forced him to swallow his bitterness.

That day Dr. Sanatan and Dr. Swaminathan arrived to meet the Defence Minister Mr. Bajaj. He was in a very happy mood.

"Sir, we did not know that Pakistan would surrender so soon", Sanatan said.

"There was no other way for them. If they had continued their mischief Pakistan could have suffered grave damage. We had reached the outskirts of Lahore, and Lahore airport was under our control. The devastation of the Pakistani army would have surely happened, and our defence forces could have taken control of the Pakistani territories.

Looking at the Defence Minister's face, Dr. Swaminathan observed, "Since Pakistan has suffered such a severe defeat, it would certainly try to take its revenge".

"That's all in God's hands. As a neighbouring country we can only pray that the Almighty give wisdom to them. If both nations—India and Pakistan—remain peaceful and exist with co-operation billions of rupees being spent on defence could be saved. Instead this money could be used for the development of happiness and wealth of the countries. Every now and then the Pakistanis' intellect becomes deranged. That is why we are required to spend billions of rupees on defence forces and on the purchase of nuclear weapons". Expounding on the Indian economy, the Defence Minister expressed his viewpoint.

Dr. Sanatan and Dr. Swaminathan returned to Bombay on the evening flight. When Sanatan reached his home after having been away for so many days his family were very happy. Rita had mixed very well with the family by now. At times when Rita uttered something out of feminine weakness, Radha would bear goodnaturedly with her. Radha was very much aware that such silly issues didn't become mountainous problems.

In spite of such understanding, one day a small quarrel erupted between the daughter-in-law and the mother-in-law.

That night Tapan told Sanatan and Radha,

"Tomorrow we will leave this house to live in a new house".

This was shocking news for Sanatan and Radha.

———◈———

Chapter 26

Rita refreshed herself by taking a shower in the early morning. Having offered her prayers and worship, she entered the bedroom and saw that Tapan was still fast asleep. It was Sunday, and so there was no hurry for him to wake up and leave for work. The previous day they were at a party hosted by Ramamurti for his birthday and because of that they had stayed back until late that night at Matunga. Whenever Tapan visited his father-in-law, he always received a warm welcome from him, and his mother-inlaw, Sulabha, took elaborate pains to give many varieties of food to Tapan. Ramamurti would talk with Tapan about varied subjects ranging from nuclear weapons to political events taking place in India and all over the world. However, Ramamurti always ensured to support whatever viewpoint Tapan expressed to him and never contradicted him.

"Hey, don't you want to wake up today?" Rita cooed in Tapan's ears tickling him on the ribs.

"Oh, let me sleep more, Rita. It's Sunday, today." Tapan turned on his side.

"But why don't you just look out . . . . It's already nine," Rita said, drawing the curtains. Suddenly the room was filled with a dazzling bright light. Tapan sat up in the bed.

He got out of bed and prepared for the new day ahead.

He brushed his teeth and settled down to read his newspaper with a cup of tea on the side table. Yesterday at the party he had a couple of pegs of whisky when his father-in-law insisted. At that time he was reminded of his parents. He had left his parents because of Rita, but it was against his wish. Only for the sake of Rita's happiness had he agreed to live in a new house with her.

"Rita, it's almost eight months since we came to live in this house. I don't know why, but somehow, today my heart has become heavy with the memory of my parents."

"Look Tapan, I haven't come here at my free will. In fact, we both had decided to leave your parents and live in this house. It was only then that we left your home."

"My poor mom! How she always cared for my progress! In the morning, as soon as I would brush my teeth and get freshened up, she would always be ready with tea and breakfast."

"Am I not providing you with tea and breakfast?" Rita was annoyed.

"I don't know why; but I no longer feel the happiness and serenity that I experienced in my home."

"That is your psychological blockage, Tapan. Nevertheless, after coming here I have always maintained relations with your parents. Whenever you have asked me, I've always invited them to our place and I've never refused to visit them."

"Rita, I understand all that, but I don't know why my disturbed mind . . . ."

"By thinking in such a manner you are tormenting yourself. You know very well before we left that house how far I had tried to compromise with your mom. She was always prepared to interfere in my work on a flimsy pretext. At last, when I could not tolerate any more, I convinced you to reside in this house with me."

"That event still pierces my heart today. Many times I felt that you were trying to make a mountain out of a molehill, but mom, the poor soul; was always worried about how she could make everyone within the family live a comfortable and happy life."

"This means, you wish to say that I am to blame that we've come to live in this house! You feel that only I am blameworthy?" Rita said heavily with unhappiness. Abruptly she got up. Tapan too followed her. Placing a hand on her shoulder he tried to console her, "Rita, I don't like you crying over such insignificant issues."

"Then why are you going back on our agreement concerning that house and upsetting me? In order to make you happy in every way, I am making all the efforts; whereas you . . ." Rita began to cry.

"Last week I went to meet mom. You know that Daddy wasn't at home. She was feeling lonely and was very dejected due to her feelings of loneliness. I even told her to come to our house as often as she liked."

"Then?"

"Quickly she told me that Dad hasn't approved of us leaving that house. He was prepared to cut off his relationship with us."

"Tapan, why has our decision to leave your parents caused such trouble to your father? Besides, do we not visit them now and then? Moreover, point out to me one family where the sons are not leaving their parents. Why don't you reply?"

"You might be right in what you say, Rita, but parents always think of the happiness that they can obtain from their children."

"I don't understand why you become sad by remembering the past? Besides, I might be blamed if

I didn't take care of your needs, or if I didn't cook or love you. Then you would have a reason to remain unhappy."

"Whatever you may say, Rita, but one thing I wish to explicitly bring to your notice is that during the last eight months of our stay in this house there hasn't been a single day when I didn't remember my parents."

"Alright, now tell me, what do you propose to do? Would you like to return to your parents' home?"

"If I reply to your question in the affirmative you won't like it, and if I answer in the negative I won't be happy either."

"What has made you think of such things since this morning?"

"It's because daddy has gone to Delhi for two days and mom would be alone at home and unhappy thinking about us. I became emotional thinking of her sadness."

"But, why didn't you tell me two days ago? Had you shown your desire we could have spent Sunday with her."

"I asked mummy, but she didn't approve of my plan. Hiding her anguish she merely told me with a heavy heart that she hopes we live happily in our house. There was no need for us to go there."

"That means that mummy does not approve of us going to their house."

"It is up to you what you think. But, it is certain that if we go there in the absence of daddy, mummy wouldn't be happy, since daddy doesn't approve."

Listening to Tapan, Rita became very unhappy. Leaving Tapan alone in the hall she went into the bedroom. Putting the newspaper aside Tapan was lost in thought. Every now and then he was reminded of his mother and his heart cried out. His mother had showered all her love and affection on him and made him study well. She always smilingly ensured that her son never had an occasion to be unhappy because of her actions. As Tapan grew older he came to realize that due to his difficult temperament there was a little bit of friction between his parents. Due to his whimsical nature his daddy would work until late in the office. As his mummy had said, his daddy would remain in a library studying as part of his higher education. That is why his benevolent mummy was worthy of all the credit for whatever success and achievements that his daddy had achieved. Tapan, too, intended following in the footsteps of his daddy, but, now he felt that Rita's temperament was an obstacle to his path of progress. He felt severe pang of unhappiness. He began to feel that he had hastened unduly in choosing Rita as his wife and agreeing to get married so soon. At times he would compare Rita's temperament with that of his mother and realized that nobody could equal the affection of his mummy.

He got up from the sofa and went to the balcony. He looked up at the sky and fixed his gaze on the row of tall trees. Watching the greenery of the trees amid the concrete buildings his anguish was eased, and he forgot his unhappiness. He began to understand the all pervading divinity of the Almighty. Having remembered the creation of the supreme divine, he silently offered his prayers.

Having acquired his graduation in the science faculty he secured employment with the B.A.R.C. He still continued to pursue his studies for his Master's degree. In his studies he had been following in the footsteps of his father. Akin to his father he too was a brilliant student. His daddy had always been a studious pupil. His father had to stay away from home and at such times his mummy would prove a great help to him. His mother had never compromised in bringing him up. His grandfather had told him about the days of troubles that his mummy had endured while Sanatan was in America twice, and that made him worship her.

Whenever he returned from school, his mom used to keep snacks and a glass of milk ready for him. Leaving his school-bag at home, he used to run out of the house to play with his friends. His mom had always helped him to finish his homework assigned by his school-teacher. When he began attending college, he was instilled with such virtuous qualities that he considered a matter of great honour to pass with the highest possible marks. His mummy had never taunted him for not studying properly. At times, his mom would compare the style of studying of the bygone days with the present system of studying and thus cited examples so that, without deviating from his pursuit, he could study well.

Tapan was reminded of an event of his schooldays. On that particular day, his schoolteacher had taken his students on a picnic to the Madh Islands. His grandfather had gone to Umreth on some work. For about three to four days previously his mummy had fallen sick as she complained of a fever, cough and cold.

"I won't go on the picnic. Since you are not well, I will cancel my plans to go to the picnic," Tapan had said.

"No son, for the last fifteen days you have been anxiously waiting to go on this picnic. Usually you are never otherwise free from your studies or reading books. Since this is a picnic with your class-mates, it would be better for you to leave aside the books and enjoy the picnic."

"But mom, you aren't well in any way. So, I won't go on the picnic. Mummy, I am not going, so don't insist that I do." Saying this he placed his palm on her forehead. She had fever and he noted her temperature using a thermometer. It was 100oF.

"You don't have to worry as I am taking medicines prescribed by Dr. Sharma. If I need anything I'll call up my papa and get the things I need from there."

Due to her insistence Tapan decided to join the picnic. He could hardly realize how quickly the day passed playing with his friends in the lap of the beautiful natural surroundings. He had thoroughly enjoyed the picnic with his friends. At last, when they were preparing to leave the picnic spot, someone brought terrible news,

"Sir, Ramesh and Vinod, who had entered the sea to swim, have drowned."

Sudden gloom enveloped all the students. All of them were shocked and they rushed towards the sea-shore. People had gathered around the two dead bodies of their friends. The teacher asked Natu who was already there,

"How did this happen?"

"Sir, the five of us friends came wandering down here. Since I couldn't swim, they all entered the sea. Vinod and Ramesh swam out deep into the sea. Many of us warned them not to go any further. But they were in no mood to listen to us. Suddenly a big wave swept them away. Two fishermen standing on the beach saw that they were drowning. They jumped into the sea to save them. They eventually brought them to the shore. They laid Ramesh and Vinod down on their bellies and managed to push out some water, but despite that their lives were not saved." Natu described the incident in detail.

The teacher let out a sigh. He knew that such incidents had taken place there in the past. That is the reason why he asked all the students to avoid swimming in the sea. But those five students, disregarding his instructions, had headed off towards the sea. The teacher sternly scolded Natu and his two other friends. Whatever was destined to happen had happened. There was no point in lamenting any more.

Tapan and his fellow students became very unhappy. Since morning they had gathered and had been enjoying the picnic with all sorts of fun and frolicking. Thinking that a pall of gloom would envelope the households of Ramesh and Vinod, every student felt a deep sense of dejection. At that, Tapan was reminded of his mummy. For the last hour or so, he had been thinking of returning home and then such a ghastly incident had taken place. The police arrived. The relatives of Ramesh and Vinod had also arrived and everyone else waited with them. The panchnama of the dead bodies of the boys was carried out. The dead bodies of the boys were received later that night only after the post-mortems were performed.

When Tapan arrived home it was twelve mid-night and Radha lay in bed writhing painfully. Radha's brother and his wife were standing close to the bed.

Moving her hand soothingly on Radha's head, Madhavi was trying to console her. The moment Tapan entered the house, Radha smiled brightly looking at him.

"Why have you been delayed?" Radha's father, Vasudev, asked.

Tapan narrated the incident at the picnic in detail. When Tapan finished, Madhavi asked,

"Tapan, why did you go to the picnic when your mummy wasn't well? Do you know that after you left, your mother's fever increased and she continued to endure it until the evening? Thank god, your neighbour, Kalyani learnt of her condition and telephoned us to arrive here quickly. That is why we all rushed here. Meanwhile, somebody brought news that a couple of students, who had gone for a picnic at the Madh Islands had drowned. Hearing the news, Radha fell unconscious. Immediately we summoned Dr. Sharma. He administered an injection to her and gave her some medicine. She was asleep for the last two hours. She has just opened her eyes. Now, finding you beside her, her health will improve swiftly . . . ."

Madhavi described the condition of Radha at length. Tapan was sad to hear that because he was delayed, he had failed to telephone his house and repented his folly.

The next day morning Radha woke up refreshed. She had been given sedatives the previous night and because of this she had a sound sleep. Before going to his clinic, Dr. Sharma arrived to check on Radha's heatlh. After conducting his checks he said,

"Radha's fever is rising and falling intermittently. We had better get her blood checked." That evening her blood report was received. Radha was diagnosed to be suffering from Malaria.

Madhavi told Radha, "Radha, it is better that you come with us to our house in this condition. If you stay here, who will look after you?"

"Madhavi, Tapan's exams are nearing. It will be very difficult for him to travel down from Chowpatty to Chembur everyday to attend his school."

At last, it was decided that Madhavi would stay with them until Radha regained enough strength to walk about.

Getting news of her indisposition, Kanaiyalal rushed back from Umreth. Sanatan had also arrived from Delhi.

Within a week Radha regained her good health.

Tapan became sentimental thinking of his mother who was a living image of pure maternal love and affection. There were many such incidents when Radha had striven hard for Tapan's higher studies and his progress, and she ensured he became an idealistic and patriotic person.

He had always carried the guilt and pain of leaving his mother.

A lot of time elapsed. One day, when Tapan returned to the BARC after having met a colleague, he was shocked and pained to hear jolting news.

Important microfilms had been stolen from the Microfilm Department and the police had arrested Ramamurti on suspicion of his collusion in the theft.

Chapter 27

That night Sanatan summoned Tapan to his house. Tapan had also been allotted a house within the BARC Complex at a distance of a five to seven minute walk. Sanatan's name was a force to be reckoned with among the great scientists of the world. Sanatan was appointed to the post of Scientific Advisor to the Defence Research and Development Organisation, also known as the DRDO. The Government held such a dynamic position in high esteem and honour. Due to this, as soon as Tapan joined the BARC, within a short time he was given living quarters.

"Tapan, I have heard that your father-in-law, Ramamurti, has been arrested. Is this true?"

For a moment Tapan looked at Sanatan and nodded his head in affirmation, lowering his eyes.

"As a matter of fact, such an act can only be considered as treachery. How could such a traitor enjoy better treatment than most?

"Daddy, I told Rita about it. She could not believe that this news was true. She could not imagine that her father would stoop so low."

"Somehow I refuse to agree with what you say. When Rita decided to leave this house for petty reasons all of a sudden, I smelled a rat."

"Believe me, Daddy; I can vouch for Rita's integrity in this matter. Yes, I have not forgotten the way in which we left this house. Such a hasty step is unforgivable. One who cannot live with their goddess-like mummy should only be considered an idiot and a grossly ignorant person."

"Then why, for the last ten months, couldn't you convince your loving wife that the steps she had taken were unjustifiable, and you should both have returned to the house?"

"To be honest, many times we've had heated discussions between us on this issue. This has at many times caused a rift in our marital life. For many days at times we do not talk to one another. I am in a great dilemma; I cannot leave her, nor can I forget you both." Tapan paused and then looking around he asked,

"Daddy, where's mom and grandpa?"

"They have gone to meet Vasudev. They should arrive at any moment now. I have been to Thana in the suburbs of Bombay and as soon as I came home, I called for you to come and see me."

"Daddy, what will happen to Mr. Ramamurti now?"

"The law will run its course in this case. I have been fighting all my life against treacherous activities. Such traitors are only worthy of disregard and hatred. I hate such people."

"But, what if he is proved innocent? Rita believes that her father cannot be guilty of such a crime."

"I hope that Mr. Ramamurti is innocent, but the police are not so foolish that they would arrest someone without any evidence. Moreover, people worship money in this world. Many aspire to become millionaires overnight without sweating and that is why such incidents take place. It is possible that Mr. Ramamurti thought in this way."

"What should I do now?"

"Just wait and see. The matter will go to the court of law and the police will keep him on remand until the outcome is decided."

"Oh! I have heard that police sometimes use the third degree to extract information from suspects."

"You are right. In order to extract the truth from suspects, police resort to harsh measures and make use of thrashing. But without that, the criminals would never confess to having committed the crime they have been accused of."

"Let's assume that a criminal admits to the crime he was under suspicion of having committed, what would his punishment be?"

"Only the judge can determine the punishment depending upon the crime committed."

"I cannot believe that Mr. Ramamurti would have committed such a crime."

"Tapan, let me tell you that understanding the mind of the man is as difficult as penetrating a thick steel wall. There are many incidents told on the pages of history about people who had always lived a life of integrity and dedication but due to their mischievous minds, were incited to undertake deplorable acts when their circumstances changed. In this way, the man's mind is responsible for instigating him to commit wicked deeds."

"Will you come to the police station to meet Mr. Ramamurti tomorrow?"

"You know well, Tapan, that ever since the day you left this household with Rita I am filled with disgust and anger for you both. Due to social customs I have always maintained cordial relations with Mr. Ramamurti's family. Mr. Ramamurti used to often come to this household. I always welcomed him happily. But, today having heard of this news my heart is filled with absolute disgust and hatred for him." Sanatan expressed his explicit viewpoint.

"Daddy, because of Rita's insistence I left this house, which was a grave mistake. I realise that now. But if you don't stand-by my mother-in-law, Mrs. Sulabha, and my brother-in-law, Vinaykant, they will be devastated."

"But what can I do about it? Are you asking me to compromise my principles?"

"Daddy, my request is not so difficult. I am just asking you to try your best to help Mr.Ramamurti be freed."

"I cannot make any decision at this stage. I will act in accordance with my conscience. Hmm . . . . Where is Rita?"

"When you telephoned, she was getting ready to visit her mother's house. She expressed her desire to accompany me to see you, but I asked her not to come with me."

"You did well."

Suddenly the door-bell rang. The servant, Govind, opened the main door. Kanaiyalal and Radha entered the house. On seeing her son, Radha's eyes danced with joy.

"Tapan, son, when did you arrive?"

"About an hour ago."

"Hasn't Rita come? How is she?"

"She is alright. She has gone to meet her mom and I have come to meet you."

"How have you been?"

"Good, Mom. But for the last two days I have been suffering from a cough and cold."

"Have you taken your medicines?"

"Yes."

"Have supper before you go. I have prepared your favourite item—Patra."

"No . . . no . . . mummy. I have to go home now." Tapan said.

"But why are you in such a hurry? Rita isn't home yet."

Tapan remained silent. He was helpless before his mother's affection. Sanatan went into his room and picked up a foreign magazine to read. Radha went into the kitchen. Tapan and Kanaiyalal were left alone together.

"So, how are you, Tapan?"

"Everything is fine, thank you, grandpa."

"Have you settled in your office?"

"Yes grandpa, I must regularly go to Bombay city to attend classes for obtaining my M.Sc."

"Where do you attend these classes?"

"I go to the Indian Institute of Science at Kala Ghoda, near the Regal Cinema."

"How are your studies progressing?"

"Excellent. Sometimes I also go to the American Library to read. How have you been keeping, grandpa?"

"Not so good, Tapan. I am prepared to go whenever the Almighty sends his call. I am just thankful to him for letting me live for so long. In addition, my whole life was spent happily and contentedly. That is something I have great happiness about."

"Grandpa, when I was very young you loved me a lot, didn't you?"

"Son, if you were Radha's son, you were also a part of my heart. Your father was always busy with his work and that is why you were like a distraction for both of us."

Listening to what his grandpa was saying, Tapan laughed aloud.

"Are you making fun of me, grandpa?" he said.

"No, I am not making a joke out of you."

Before Kanaiyalal could say any more Radha appeared at the door. She said,

"Tapan, your grandpa and you can finish the supper. After that you both can continue talking."

"Why won't daddy join us to eat with us?"

"He is busy reading, so he won't eat right now."

Tapan got up for his supper. After supper, he once again returned to his grandfather's room. Kanaiyalal, who had been lying on the bed, sat up. Talking to his grandson again, Kanaiyalal asked,

"Tapan, may I ask you something?"

"Ask it."

"Do Rita and you get on well with one another?"

"Yes, why do you have to ask?"

"It's because you have come alone today. How's Rita?" Kanaiyalal asked Tapan as he looked at him.

"She's fine!"

Meanwhile, Radha came from the kitchen and also sat down.

"As Rita has gone to her parents' home, I've come here now." Tapan replied to the other part of his grandfather's question.

"Is everyone well at your in-laws' home?" Kanaiyalal asked.

The innocent question asked by his grandfather caused great anguish to Tapan. For a moment he felt silent. Then he said seriously.

"Mom, grandpa, I cannot hide anything from you both."

"What's happened?" Radha asked worriedly.

"It's about my father-in-law, Mr.Ramamurti . . . ."

"What has happened to Mr. Ramamurti?" Radha asked quickly.

"This evening, the police arrested him at the BARC office at Chembur."

For a moment both were speechless on hearing what Tapan said.

"Why did they arrest him?" Radha asked.

"He is accused of having stolen microfilms," Tapan replied. "That is terrible! It must be as if the heavens have fallen on Sulabha and Rita. Vinaykant must have been shocked. Does your dad know about it?" Radha asked in a voice mixed with fear and anguish.

"When he learnt about it, he telephoned me and called me here."

"And then?"

"We discussed the matter at length. Mom, you know well that daddy has lived a good principled life. He never compromised his principles for any selfish motives. I requested him to help free Mr. Ramamurti from the police station, but he is not ready to take any decision at this stage."

"But, our relations with your in-laws is considered even thicker than blood relations. It is our duty to stand by them at such difficult times."

"Mom, you understand, but dad does not think in that way. What should we do?"

"Alright, I will talk to your daddy, and ask him to make enquiries about this case and free Mr. Ramamurti from police custody if he is innocent."

"Yes mom . . . . please try your best to convince daddy of this tonight."

"Leave it to me and don't worry, son. If we cannot help you at this critical period, when can we?"

"Well, I will leave now, mom."

"Sure. Don't worry and keep your cool. Tell Rita that we are thinking of her and her family at such a trying time." Seeking the blessings of his father, Tapan headed towards Sanatan's room accompanied by Radha.

"Sanatan, Tapan is leaving." Radha said.

"He may go." Leaving the magazine on the table, Sanatan emerged from his room.

After Tapan left Radha asked,

"Shall I lay a plate for you, Sanatan?"

"Yes." Saying this, Sanatan took his seat at the dining table. Radha disappeared into the kitchen. After having his meal, Sanatan returned to his bedroom.

After finishing her work, she became tired and entered the bedroom where she found Sanatan reading a magazine.

"Tapan told me everything. Now, what shall happen to Mr. Ramamurti?" Radha asked her husband.

"Whatever happens shall be in accordance with the law."

"But due to our relations with the family, is it not our duty to support them in their time of need?"

"At times, we have to endure hardships by associating with unsuitable people. Whoever has done wrong will have to bear the punishment for their crime."

"Look, if anybody indulged in criminal activities, such a person should be punished by all means and I believe that firmly. But, as Mr. Ramamurti is related to us, I am worried about the criticisms of us by people in society."

"You must understand one thing very clearly, Radha. If Mr. Ramamurti is guilty of this crime I will stand aside. Nobody can ever save him." Sanatan angrily ground his teeth.

"You are very obstinate. Why don't you understand what am I saying?"

"Well, tell me what you want me to do."

"I want you to go to the police station. Go and meet Mr. Ramamurti and try to understand what he has to say for himself. After that you can decide what you wish to do."

"Since you are insisting so much, I will go and see him, but it still would be against my principles."

"Mr. Ramamurti and you have been working in the BARC for so many years now. Have you heard if he has ever engaged in such activities?"

"I have not heard so. But at times I would hear something about him every now and then, which tarnished his image. However I never gave credence to such baseless talks and I did not take them seriously."

"It is for that reason that I am asking you to go to the police station to meet him. After talking to him, if you feel that he is innocent, try to have him set free. Millions are aware of your name and reputation, so they will listen to you." Radha slowly tried to convince him.

Inhaling a deep breath, Sanatan turned and tried to sleep, but he spent the whole night in mental agony. He deeply hated anyone who acted against the nation's interests. Despite that, honouring his promise to Radha, he went to the police station next morning. The police officer, Sadashiv Kulkarni, knew him well. Immediately he made arrangements for him to meet Ramamurti.

On seeing Sanatan arrive to meet him, Ramamurti lowered his eyes in shame and guilt. As he had been unable to sleep well the previous night, Ramamurti looked haggard and his eyes and face showed no feeling.

"Mr.Ramamurti, being the father of your son-in-law and your well-wisher, I want to know the truth in the allegations leveled against you. I have absolute regard and love for you. Because of this, I ask of you that you tell me everything, without hiding anything; so that I can help you."

Listening to Sanatan, Ramamurti was flustered. He struggled within his mind to answer Sanatan's question. At last, he said in a pathetic manner,

"Important documents pertaining to the military bases and defence airfields were handed to my department for microfilming. My associate Mukherjee and I worked together in preparing the microfilms. Before I could return the microfilms and the documents they were stolen."

"How did that happen?"

"Mukherjee vanished from the scene in the same way as the pictures and films did. I heard that he flew to Dubai the day before my arrest."

"This means that Mukherjee is guilty and since the person responsible was not found, the charges have been brought against you and you are being framed."

"Your assumption is absolutely correct. I am totally innocent in this matter. Please help me, Mr.Sanatan."

"Look, Mr. Ramamurti, if you are guiltless, no harm will come to you."

The case was brought before the court of law and Ramamurti was set free in the absence of evidence. More time elapsed. One day, Sanatan received concrete information that Mukherjee and Ramamurti both were working as ISI agents. Having learnt of this information, Sanatan was shocked.

———◆◇◆———

Chapter 28

"Tapan, I thank your daddy sincerely. I believe that my papa was released because of your daddy's efforts."

"Look Rita, it is the judge in court that declares a person as innocent. In spite of that, my daddy certainly helped the release of your papa by going to the police station and speaking on his behalf."

"Maybe, but if your father didn't intervene the case would not have been disposed of so quickly."

"I spared no effort in convincing my dad, but his principles were creating obstacles for him. At last, I had to pass the work of convincing him to my mom."

"Then?"

"It's a big thing for me that mom could convince my highly principled daddy." Tapan paused and said, "Rita, by now you must realize what a good-natured person my mother is. You might say that she does not have a good relationship with you, but didn't she rush to help your family folk in the time of their anguish and trouble?"

"When I heard that, I was pleasantly surprised. Truly, your mummy is certainly benevolent. As soon as she heard of my papa's arrest she came to our house and consoled my mother and brother. I now realize she is certainly a benevolent, helpful and great person."

"In that case, avoid entering into conflict with her. If you wish, we can return to our old home." Pausing for a while Tapan continued, "It's your choice now. It is you who had chosen for us to move to the new house. Now, it's only you who will have to make the decision to return."

"I'll meet mummy during the week. At noon today, I am going to meet my papa. If I get delayed, heat the food I've kept for you; and eat it." Rita told Tapan who was tying the knot of his tie and preparing to go to the office.

"Alright." Tapan replied.

Soon Rita reached her parent's home. Since Ramamurti was sleeping in the other room she talked to her mother.

"If he was not innocent the court would not have set him free," Sulabha said.

"Amma, you are an absolutely innocent and gullible person. What I've heard about papa makes me hang my head in shame," Rita said.

"What have you heard about him?"

"I have heard that papa is not innocent."

"Surely Mr. Sanatan has not turned you against your papa?"

"Oh hell! It's due to him my papa was released."

"But uptill now, you were talking against Sanatan."

"He might be a principled and obstinate person but he nurtures great love for his family ties. If that was not so, he would not have gone to the police station to have papa released."

"This means that due to Sanatan's efforts, your papa was released?"

"I firmly believe so. Up until now I found him to be a stern person, but, today I realize that I had erred in understanding him."

"Why have you suddenly begun to speak in favour of Santan?"

"Amma, my in-laws are certainly worthy of reverence. Tapan, too, played a significant role in convincing his daddy and mummy. It's only because of him and his mother that Mr. Sanatan went to meet papa in the police station the next day."

"Hello Rita, when did you come?" Ramamurti emerged from the inside room, where he had been sleeping.

"I arrived just a short while ago. You were asleep, so I was talking to Amma. How's your health?"

"It's better now.

Why are you not going to the office today?"

"I am not in the right frame of mind yet. I propose to rest for a week and only then attend the office."

"If you remain at home you will be engulfed by all sorts of negative thoughts. Don't you think it would be better if you go to the office and devote yourself to work?"

"Even if what you say is correct, my heart pains me thinking about the way I was arrested and how my reputation was tarnished."

"But why should you worry about social criticism, when you have been released by the court due to the lack of evidence against you?"

"I am presently mustering my confidence. I will attend the office at the right time."

"You may both continue talking. I'll go and get some coffee . . ." Sulabha said and walked to the kitchen.

The moment Rita was alone with her papa, she asked him,

"Papa, tell me truthfully, whether you are innocent or guilty of the crime?"

Listening to Rita's question, Ramamurti was flustered. He began stammering,

"Why . . . why . . . . don't you trust your papa? I was pronounce innocent by the court. Surely, you are aware of this. Then why do you ask me such a question?"

"You have been released in the absence of evidence against you. My faith in you has been shaken and that is why I feel like repeating my question; Papa are you absolutely innocent?"

For a long moment Ramamurti stared at his daughter. On seeing that, Rita continued, "I have already seen the look of a criminal in your face. How long will you go on hiding the truth about yourself from Amma, my brother and me?"

"It seems that you are a victim of some sort of misunderstanding."

"In that case, resolve my misunderstanding."

"Rita, dear daughter, don't cause me pain by accusing me in such a manner."

"Papa, a man becomes happy or unhappy only through one's *karma*. A man becomes great through his good deeds, whereas through wicked acts a person becomes shallow, poor and becomes castigated by society. I am very sorry to tell you that Tapan and Mr.Sanatan have become aware of your misdeeds."

"Oh, my child!" Ramamurti's eyes filled with tears.

"Papa, as I am your daughter please bear with me if I point out your faults. But, I call upon you to put a stop to the treacherous activities that you have initiated against the nation. Apply your mind to where the good of your family lies."

"Is it really a fact that Tapan and Mr.Sanatan are aware of my activities?"

"If that was not so, why would I have explicitly asked you today? Why don't you realize that a daughter would never wish anything so undesirable for her papa?"

"No . . . no . . . . my child! It is I who is the sinner and a crook. How shall I ever be able to show my face round your house ever again?"

"Papa, have faith in the Almighty. If your conscience is clear, God will show you the way. Now it is you who will have to decide if you want to become a traitor or a patriot."

"Perhaps you don't know that the people in whose hands I have become an instrument, will never ever forgive me. They will never allow me to be a patriot. I have become a victim of circumstance. I would like to assure you that I will certainly strive to extricate myself from the clutches of these dangerous and crafty criminals."

"Bravo, Papa, bravo! Now, I am with you. Does Amma know of this?"

"Yes, Rita. Your mom knows this. But she is confident that I will come out of this mess soon." While they were talking Sulabha entered the hall with a tray carrying mugs of coffee. Sipping coffee, Sulabha said, "Rita, now that you have come, do not go until you join us for dinner."

"That's what I had intended."

When all of them finished their coffee, Sulabha picked up the empty coffee mugs and the tray. Holding the tray in her hand she said,

"Rita, would you like to come out with me?"

"Where, mom?"

"I am going to meet my friend, Dipti. Her son has been blessed with a baby boy. I thought I would go and see the child and play with him . . ."

"No, mom, I won't come."

"Alright, in that case stay and talk to your papa. I will return in less than an hour." After Sulabha left, the father and daughter were alone again.

"Papa, how did you get yourself entangled with those dangerous hoodlums?"

"You must be aware that last year I visited Delhi, accompanied by Mukherjee."

"Oh yes, and after being to Delhi, you went to Jammu via Katara on the pilgrimage of the goddess Vaishnodevi. I am aware of that."

"Mukherjee and I were anxious to reach our hotel at Jammu via Katara, because, Mukherjee was expecting his friend to meet him there. Because of this, Mukherjee was in a hurry to reach the hotel on time."

"What happened then?"

"We reached the hotel. Afterwards the doorbell rang. Mukherjee himself opened the door. A tall and well-built man about six feet tall was standing in the doorway. Shrikant Mukherjee introduced him to me and said that his friend, Ramesh\ Shetty was living in the Lalbaug area of Bombay. I told Shrikant that I had never seen his friend in Bombay, nor did he ever refer to him in my presence. Replying to me, Mukherjee had said that he had also gone there on pilgrimage and was to leave for Bombay on that night. I shook hands with Shetty. For a while we talked about insignificant things. After a while, Mukherjee got up and told me that he was going to the market to buy toothpaste and shaving cream, and quickly left us alone, closing the door behind him." Saying so much, Ramamurti picked up a glass of water and drank it with a quick gulp.

"You must have been perturbed then?"

"Of course, I was surprised that after introducing me to a total stranger, Mukherjee had left us alone and suddenly went out of the hotel room. For a while I stared at his face. Instead of looking soft his face seemed crude. His eyes seemed to show cruelty behind his face. He began to talk to me as soon as Mukherjee left us alone." Saying so, Ramamurti was lost in thought.

Shetty had asked, "Mr. Ramamurti, surely you haven't had any trouble to have to go to darshan at Vaishnodevi? I hope it wasn't because you had any problems?"

"No . . . no . . . we could offer our prayers to the Goddess Vaishnodevi with absolute devotion. In fact, I'm thankful to Mukherjee that he planned this trip to Vaishnodevi. Whenever he had to visit, he made it a point to visit Vaishnodevi, without fail."

"Do you know how much Mukherjee earned last year?"

"Well, I don't know that, but last month when I attended his son's birthday party at his home, I felt, he was living a luxurious life."

"Did it not occur to you how that was possible?"

"It did cross my mind that how could my subordinate officer organize such a lavish bash?"

"Didn't you ever ask him?"

"Why should I poke my nose into anybody else's private business?"

"Don't you feel like making more money?"

"I don't follow. What are you hinting at?"

"I am being very clear in what I am saying. If Mukherjee is rolling in so much wealth, it is because of our grace. Now, if you just follow Mukherjee's example, you too will be able to earn so much wealth."

"Mr. Shetty, I have always lived a happy and contented life. I don't have the slightest desire to earn money through unfair means."

"I have come to know that you head the department of microfilm processing. You can have whatever you wish for."

"I do not follow. What do you want to say?"

"Mukherjee has brought you here by our request. Whatever he does, he gets paid for doing it."

"Tell me clearly, what do I have to do?"

"You must have heard about the Inter Service Intelligence, didn't you?"

Hearing that Ramamurti began to perspire and shake badly. He found it difficult to say anything. Somehow, mustering courage he had said,

"I am aware of the activities of the ISI. I read about them through newspapers, that the terrorists have attacked at Punjab at some times, whereas, at other times they have attacked Kashmir."

"Perhaps you may be aware, Mr. Ramamurti, that the ISI has spread a wide network throughout India and can get anything done."

"What does that mean?"

"We pay heavily in return of the work we get done, but if it is not done the payment is death!" Shetty threatened.

"What do you expect me to do? Tell me in detail so that I might think about it and let you know."

"There is no question of thinking about anything. Mukherjee has been doing all sorts of tasks, and we have been paying him well. Recently, we have heard that photographs of military bases and airfields will come in your hands very shortly for microfilming. We need those microfilms at any cost."

"You should have assigned that task to Mukherjee. Why am I needed?"

"Mukherjee had said that if we don't take you into our confidence, such a task was impossible." Saying this Shetty opened his briefcase.

"I am giving you an advance of one lakh today. The balance payment of four lakhs will be paid in Bombay when the job is accomplished."

Listening to Shetty, Ramamurti turned white with sheer fear. He had always lived with integrity and truthfulness all his life. Now, what should he do?

"And what if I refuse to do as you say?"

"Mr.Ramamurti, there is no question of you refusing to agree with what we are asking you to do. Besides, you are well aware of the consequences of refusing our 'requests'. It is better you accept our proposal with no opposition."

"Mr.Shetty, I have no cravings for money. I have no desire to become a millionaire overnight. Let me live my life as I want."

"Mr. Ramamurti, you don't have to do anything. You will have to simply turn a blind eye to what Mukherjee will do."

When they were talking about this, Mukherjee returned.

Shetty told him, "I have briefed your friend about everything. My job is to get you people organized at a suitable time." On saying this he left the room.

Listening to her father's story Rita was badly shocked. She could not believe that her father would ever undertake an activity that was against the nation's interest.

"Papa, this time you have been released and declared innocent, but at any time an avalanche of trouble could be heaped on you."

"I am fearful for that reason exactly. Sometimes I think about committing suicide so that my family will not be dragged into this situation."

"Don't you ever think in that way, Papa. You must learn to face the difficulties cropping-up in your life. Sanatan thought that I was associated with your undercover activities. But somehow, I took an oath of truthfulness and convinced him of my innocence".

"How I will show my face to Tapan and your father in law now? I will resign from my job tomorrow."

"If you do that, the matter will be out of your hands, and the authorities will think that you are guilty. Until such time as Mukherjee is traced in Dubai you do not have to worry. But I am afraid that after taking away all the documents from Mukherjee, they might kill him."

"Alright, since you advised me, I will return to the office from tomorrow onwards."

Meanwhile Sulabha returned. That night all of them had dinner together. After the dinner was over, Vinaykant escorted Rita to her home.

The next day, Sanatan summoned Ramamurti to his office and said,

"Mukherjee is guilty and you are innocent."

Listening to Sanatan, tears welled up in Ramamurti's eyes.

Chapter 29

The nooks and corners, as well as the streets of Karachi, which were usually alive with the jostling and bustling of people, were once again embroiled in bloody communal violence between the Shia and Sunni communities. Once again the police were compelled to use force to quell the violent mobs. As the news of the violence spread like wildfire, the shopkeepers pulled the shutters one after the other. As the hoodlums joined the communal rifts, the violence that followed turned too murky for the common man. The police commissioner began to issue orders one after another in rapid succession to ensure that the violence did not spread into other areas of the city.

A little distance away from the villa of General Pheroz Khan, one could see the dancing waves of the Arabian Sea. Aziz Maqbool went up to the window. The sun was setting on the horizon and the atmosphere, coloured in the vivid hues of the setting sun, looked enchanting. For a few minutes Aziz stood looking out of the window watching the splendourous beauty of nature. When the sun had vanished on the horizon, he turned and went to a room, where his father Pheroz Khan lay on his sick bed, worshipping Allah. He had been confined to bed for the last twenty days. Once a physically strong and well-built man, Pheroz Khan had joined the army as a private and gradually rose to become a General. In 1971, despite the fact that Pakistan had been defeated, he used to twirl his moustache proudly and say,

"Since our own brethren of East Pakistan turned traitors and joined the Indian Army, we had to taste shameful defeat. But now, if war breaks out once again, I will devastate India . . . ." Pheroz Khan indulged in such day-dreaming.

One day he suddenly fell sick due to Typhoid. The unrelenting fever weakened him. Gradually his booming voice was reduced to the meek voice of an old man. He lost his love for food and even his appetite. Also, he had no desire to speak to anybody with affection.

Aziz Maqbool's mother Nafisa somehow controlled her emotions and advised her husband, "You have spent your entire life fighting with India. Now, when you are helpless owing to your ill-health it is better to concentrate your mind on the worship of Allah and seek His refuge."

"I know, Nafisa, that whoever is born ultimately goes to the realm of Allah. I have no qualms about it. I shiver at remembering the scenes of war of 1965 and 1971 that I fought with India. In the war of 1971, I had to endure the insult of surrendering myself to India. That scene of surrendering to India always torments me."

"But, please do not trouble yourself by thinking so much about past events."

"Nafisa, you do not understand how those flames of insult have been burning me from within. The thoughts of my insult don't allow me peace. I just hate my hapless condition."

"I just know this much; that my enmity can never be obliterated by more enmity. Therefore, we must thank the

Almighty for whatever life remains and also express our gratitude that he has given us birth as human beings."

"You do not understand me, Nafisa."

Then addressing his son, Aziz, he said, "Aziz, my son, I have great respect for you and I love you from the bottom of my heart."

"Abbajan, the doctor has advised you not to talk much. Anyway, you are physically very weak."

"Just do one thing, call Mastan, the first ISI officer to come and meet me."

"Abbajan, it would be better for if you take a rest."

"I will have eternal rest when I go to the realm of the Almighty after my death. The thoughts buzzing in my mind today will not allow me to lie here in peace. My heart will not be at rest unless I speak and reduce its burden."

Aziz dialled Mastan's number and spoke to him.

After some time Mastan arrived. Aziz got up to leave the room. Pheroz Khan addressed him, "Aziz, you too are to sit here and listen to what I have to say."

Aziz once again sat down on the sofa. Turning his eyes to Mastan, Pheroz Khan said, "I feel that I'm not going to live for long. You are my close friend and that's why I've asked for you, so that I can unburden my heart."

"As soon as I learnt of your health, I rushed here. I'm sorry to notice your fragile health. What did the doctor opine, friend?"

"The doctor has assured me that I will once again recover from my illness, but I have no hopes of my survival."

"Don't say that, friend. We both have vowed not to rest until we have the whole of Kashmir under our control. A great number of plans have been prepared to liberate Kashmir and when we are in need of brave soldiers like you, you are stricken with such an illness! I pray Khuda for your quick recovery."

"You don't have to worry, Mastan. Our intentions are noble and clear. Kashmir has always been ours since 1948 and will always remain so. Kashmir could be considered ours, ever since the day Jawaharlal Nehru referred its question to the United Nations."

Listening to Pheroz Khan's views, Mastan expressed his views on the Kashmir issue. "Every son of each Pakistani soldier is willing to sacrifice his life, even today, for Kashmir. Red hot blood flows within their chests to become martyrs, and that is why I can tell you with certainty that one day either Kashmir will emerge as an independent nation or the whole of Kashmir will be annexed to Pakistan."

"Mastan, what you are saying is true", Pheroz Khan said. He added after a pause, "It is a daunting task to extricate Kashmir from India. India is a very powerful and a large nation. Despite its smaller size Pakistan must maintain a large military and buy modern weapons and armaments in large numbers. In this way because of India, our country can neither be developed nor achieve progress."

"After fighting two wars with India in 1965 and 1971, we all have to think of new strategies against India. Just four days ago many important decisions were taken in a meeting of the top officers of the ISI."

"Mastan, tell me quickly, what decisions have been made?"

"It is our experience that by entering into battle with a largesized nation like India, a smaller country like ours always sustains great loss and damage. Fighting with India openly is like pushing daggers into the chests of our millions of soldiers. That is why we all have decided to wage indirect war with India and cause as much damage to them as possible and weaken them."

"How would you accomplish that? Have you thought of some scheme?" Pheroz Khan asked, looking at Mastan. "Organise infiltrations in Kashmir in the name of Jihad, the holy war. We will provide training on terrorism by Madresas at various places. Hire the services of Afghani, Irani and Sudanese mercenaries and train them to spread terrorism in Kashmir. In the initial stages, Madresas will be established in the major cities of Pakistan. Then this will be followed up by the establishment of Madresas in the occupied Kashmir. Teachings against India will be provided in these Madresas, and military training will also be imparted. mGradually such activities will be expanded and then trained terrorists will be infiltrated in large numbers in Jammu and Kashmir as well as the other cities of India."

Excited by what Mastan had said, looking at him, Pheroz Khan said, "I feel that the Inter Services Intelligence is far better than I had imagined."

"You know well, friend, that Pakistan was established in the name of Islam. We all, the followers of Islam, have become ardent enemies of the Hindus and Hinduism. When Pakistan was carved out of India, the issue of Kashmir was not a hindrance. But these days, the Hindus and the Congress are obstacles in our way and will remain so. That is why if we continue to shout day and night about Islam, the people of Pakistan will understand the significance of the military."

"I feel that what you say will play a significant role in getting Kashmir liberated."

"Pheroz Khan, following the partition of India, general elections were not held in Pakistan for many years, nor was the constitution of Pakistan created. In 1958, when the first constitution was placed before the nation, leaving aside the convening general elections, President Iskandar Mirza established military rule in Pakistan. Sending him to London, General Ayyub Khan later promulgated Marshall Law. We are well aware that the people of Pakistan believe that the military is supreme and all-powerful and that is why they are attracted towards military rule."

"I am of the opinion that the first thing we should do is to turn the world-opinion in our favour. The other nations of the world should make India understand that it is a prerogative of the Kashmiri's, in whose favour they should vote and that is an internal matter as well as their natural right. In this way we should create a suitable atmosphere for election. If India does not bring about a solution to this issue directly, we shall recruit terrorists within our military forces. Then these terrorists will be infiltrated in Kashmir initially, followed by other cities of India to undertake subversive activities on a large scale."

When Mastan felt that Pheroz Khan was experiencing some trouble after taking a long time to reply, he said,

"Dear friend, you had better take some rest. Recuperate your physical and mental health." "Don't worry about me. Listening to you every cell of my body is filled with happiness. Besides, if your plans come to fruition, I think that Kashmir will come under our control. The first thing that we must do is win over the hearts of the Kashmiris and invoke faith in their hearts for us. Moreover, if the need arises, we can prepare at least one young person per family to sacrifice themselves according to our plan of terrorism, and we can by all means emerge victorious." Pheroz Khan spoke up with emotive enthusiasm.

For a while silence descended in the room. Suddenly, looking at his son Aziz, he said, "Aziz, you must bear in mind that the dream of snatching away Kashmir from those old men is in the hands of young men like you. Each one of you should be ready to sacrifice your life to the end."

"Abbajan, you are well aware that your ideals and mine are exactly the same."

"Friend, you must be aware that we have the full support of America. On many occasions, America has criticized India and favoured us. Why should we be afraid of any country or any economic problems when a great super-power like America is supporting us? You said that our military has all sorts of modern weapons. Moreover, in order to enable us to compete with India in matters of armaments and missiles we have star scientists. Besides, most of the Islamic nations are with us, so why should we be afraid of India?" Mastan elaborated as to how the country can remain safe.

The telephone rang. Aziz picked up the receiver. Continuing his talk, he turned to his father and said, "Iqbal and his companion Ahmed intended meeting you."

"Let him come." Pheroz Khan said.

"Oh, no! We have been talking for so long. You must rest now. Call them tomorrow." Mastan intervened.

Pheroz Khan was lost in thoughts for a while. Then he said," Ask them to come at ten tonight. I will sleep for an hour."

Aziz conveyed the necessary instruction and replaced the receiver.

"Iqbal will come at ten tonight to meet you."

"Shall I leave now?" Mastan asked slowly.

"Yes."

"Friend, you had better take some rest."

"To tell you the truth, I got bored of resting so much. You have almost spent an hour talking to me, but I was not bored even for a minute."

"It is because, we are committed to snatching away Kashmir and these words are engraved on your heart."

Saying this, Mastan rose and taking his leave of the other family members he bade them "Khuda Hafiz" and went out.

His car sped past a few military vehicles on the roads of Karachi. The roads and streets of Karachi were full of Military Personnel and vehicles. The communal violence between the Shias and Sunnies was at its height. Curfew was imposed in many parts of the city.

At ten that night, Iqbal and his scientist friend Ahmed arrived at Pheroz Khan's house. At that time, Pheroz Khan lay awake.

"How are you feeling now?" Iqbal asked.

"Not so well; but tell me, when did you come back from Holland?"

"Just yesterday. I learnt you weren't feeling well."

"Tell me if you experienced any hindrance in developing your nuclear weapons?"

"Absolutely not. We received excellent guidance and encouragement from China and Holland. Even the President accorded us proper honour."

"Iqbal, the military is very happy with you since you have become a Joint-Chairman of the Pakistan

Power Commission. When billions are being spent and invaluable human brainpower is being put to use for scientific experiments in the world, it would not be proper for our nation if we retreat in acquiring that information."

I am aware of that, sir. I am indebted to the government for appointing me as a head of this department of modern nuclear weapons and also for evaluating my capabilities and qualifications. I am well aware that our government has decided to acquire modern armaments for our military forces otherwise we shall never be able to counteract any attack by other countries. This way, I will strive to work in the direction of strengthening Pakistan with modern weapons and armaments.

"Excellent! To that end it is immaterial if we have to extend our hand like a beggar to other nations to obtain Uranium and Plutonium. Until we become self-reliant, everything is of no use to us."

"You will be pleased to know that my latest visit to Holland was quite successful. I was able to take into our confidence certain officials working on nuclear technology."

Listening to Iqbal, Pheroz Khan smiled.

"But Sir, I cannot understand one thing; why does one nation collide with other nations with a sense of enmity? Why are no efforts being made to spread world-peace?" said Iqbal.

"Just take the example of our neighbouring country, India. When that country is sparing no effort to develop most modern weapon and armament systems and nuclear capabilities, how can we afford to remain a peaceful spectator? Shouldn't we be prepared to meet the challenge of a sudden attack by our neighbouring country? Iqbal, you may be the top scientist of our nation, but let me say that you are not aware of the political lessons."

"I am merely interested in my work. I might deeply involve myself in the development of nuclear weapons technology, but I will always cherish a dream of propagating world peace."

"You had better give up such madness. There is hardly a country in the world, where great efforts have not been made in the direction of developments of newer horizons of scientific progress. Those countries which do not possess such capabilities run their administration on the support of other capable nations."

Iqbal remained silent. Such talks of politicians and the superior officers of the military never appealed to him. He had always been wondering why no efforts had been made by the nations by which entire humanity could live and prosper in peace. But Iqbal knew that the Almighty had played the biggest trick by creating the human mind.

As Pheroz Khan was tired after talking for so long, he said, "I feel so tired. I need to rest now."

Immediately Iqbal rose to his feet. He took leave of Aziz Maqbool and Nafisa and left the house.

At around midnight, Pheroz Khan who was already in pain, opened his eyes. His movements caused Aziz and Nafisa to wake up. Pheroz Khan's fever had increased. At the same time he complained of severe chest pains. Immediately a phone call was made to the doctor. He called Aziz and Nafisa to come closer to him. Pheroz Khan began to stammer with a heavy tongue.

"Aziz, I will not survive now. The veins of my temple are on the verge of splitting apart."

"Don't talk like that, Abbajan. You will surely be cured. The doctor should be here any moment now."

"I am in severe physical discomfort and my mind is not at peace. After my demise . . . ."

"Tell me, Abbajan . . . !"

"Aziz, you are the Air Marshall today. I wish to give you a responsibility."

"What is it, tell me."

"Aziz, promise me that you will not rest until you avenge the insult meted out by India to me."

"Abbajan . . . . !"

"Yes, Aziz! You will never turn away from any difficulties which you may encounter, even at the cost of your life, and fulfill your promise to me."

Aziz stared at Pheroz Khan's face which had become contorted with extreme pain. He was also a brave soldier. Looking at the condition of his father, he was filled with sorrow. The moment of ultimate separation had arrived. In a split second he took a decision and spoke in a voice trembling with emotion,

"Abbajan, I promise you that I will avenge your insult that you had to endure when you were shamefully defeated in the war with India in 1971 at the cost of my life. Now, my only aim will be how I can inflict a mortal blow to India."

"Listening to Aziz's words, Pheroz Khan breathed his last. The faint smile on the face of the now dead Pheroz Khan was reflecting his conquest.

Chapter 30

The news of the explosion of the first ever atom bomb by India on May 18, 1974 at Pokharan spread all over the world like wildfire. All the nations looked at this achievement of India with a sense of awe. The credit for such noteworthy success in the field of nuclear technology went to the Bhabha Atomic Research Centre. Following America's example where a large number of nuclear scientists were working, over six thousand scientists and technocrats were working at BARC. The Uranium used for making atom bombs was produced at this center. This nuclear center bothered Pakistan like a piece of dust in an eye. India had advanced very much ahead of other nations in the field of nuclear physics. When the people of Pakistan learnt of India's magnificent feat, they were overcome with sheer jealousy. The Pakistani scientists knew well that they were miles behind the Indian scientists in the matter of the development of atom bombs and nuclear armament technology. For many years they had been striving hard to achieve self-reliance in the field of nuclear energy. In order to make the nuclear centre at Kahuta work efficiently, the Pakistani scientists travelled about the world to many countries in Europe to gather spares and technology to make an atom bomb. On the other hand some scientists were striving hard to win sympathetic support from Holland and China.

Immediately after receiving the news of the atomic blast at Pokharan, the Chairman of the Pakistan Power Commission, Dr. Asif, summoned an emergency meeting of scientists. Many issues were discussed at that meeting. At last, summarising all the points discussed in the meeting, Dr. Asif said.

"Friends, henceforth the work of the Kahuta Power Commission will have to be enhanced. A new nuclear centre at Golra will be activated. I am pleased to say that after spending some time in nuclear research activities at Elmilo in Holland Dr. Iqbal has returned. He has developed amicable relations with the scientists in Holland and in that way has been successful in obtaining secret information on nuclear technology. I am confident now the creation of the Islamic atom bomb will be possible. When China sends certain vital technical information to us, our dream of making an atom bomb will be ultimately realized.

From the scientific viewpoint India is superior to us, but the patriotism of the subjects of Pakistan is still with us and that is the reason we shall achieve success in defeating a large-sized nation like India. You must be well aware of how a tiny mouse can fell a large-sized elephant.

Now we have received a challenge from India, and we all have to collectively face that with due courage. We will have to work day and night to produce atom bombs, even if we have to depend on other nations for that purpose.

India always brags as if it is a superior nation to us and makes efforts to emerge as a super-power in the world. When India is busy blowing its trumpet and beating the drums of its great achievement by conducting the nuclear test at Pokharan, we cannot afford to remain mute spectators. We need to keep our armaments in absolute readiness. It is my appeal to all the scientists present here, at this meeting, to work hard for the creation of Islamic bombs, so that no country can dare to look at us.

Since, Air Chief Marshal Aziz Maqbool is away from Pakistan he has not been able to attend this meeting. Nevertheless, his best wishes are always with us."

After presenting his views in detail Dr.Asif fell silent.

After that a few questions were asked and satisfactory replies were provided to them. In this way the meeting came to an end.

On the following day Dr. Asif summoned Dr. Iqbal to his cabin. He said,

"Iqbal, the Islamic atom bomb must be developed at the earliest possible time. If it is not done soon, the people of Pakistan will never forgive us."

"Talks with China are continuing. After we receive certain technical information, it will become easier to develop the bomb."

"If it is necessary, it would be better for you to go to China and gather all the things necessary to develop the bomb."

"All the necessary drawings will be made available during this week. If that does not happen I will go to China."

"All right!" Once again remembering Aziz, Dr.Asif said, "It would have been better if Aziz could have attended the meeting yesterday. You are well aware that Aziz Maqbool has gradually earned the trust of the Prime Minister. Since his father, Pheroz Khan died, he seems to be walking around like a zombie."

"He was very dear to his father. Following the death of his father the Prime Minister has promoted him to the Chief of Air Force." Iqbal said.

"He has been repeatedly talking of destroying the military powers of India. He has been planning to infiltrate the trained terrorists in Jammu-Kashmir and then spread a terrorist network in all the major cities of India.

"It is easier said than done."

"Aziz Maqbool believes that if one is mentally resolute nothing is difficult. Until such time as terrorism is not spread in the most important cities of India like Delhi or Bombay, we shall not have Kashmir under our control. When the masses of India cry out in protest and anguish against the terrorist activities and then force the government of India to forsake the Kashmir issue, only then will our task become easy." Dr. Asif unveiled the picture of terrorism.

Iqbal didn't like to hear about such things nor did he approve of putting that plan into action. All of these things were in the hands of the politicians. He had to merely dance to their tune. He was against the creation of the Islamic bomb. Rather he was more anxious to see unity between the Hindus and Muslims. He was aware that he was placed at a very high position in the nuclear research field and only for that reason he ensured to hide his viewpoints and thoughts from certain Pakistani officials.

Many times he would engage in discussions with politicians. He would carefully present his views on forging an atmosphere between the two communities, but nobody paid any heed to his views.

There was another problem. The mentality of the people of Pakistan was moulded against India. Absolutely distorted and false lessons were taught to the students while teaching them the subjects of geography and history. Instead of imparting truthful facts, false information was being fed to the students with the intent of spreading lies. Different types of pictures were drawn up so that hatred for India would be invoked among the Pakistani youth. Derogatory terms were often used in speeches and lectures and in that way venomous feelings against India were exhibited. In this way, the Prime Minister and the military rulers had been accomplishing the task of keeping the Pakistani subjects under their thumb.

Looking at Iqbal, Dr.Asif remarked, "I can see that you are lost in thought."

"Yes".

"What are you thinking about?"

"Sir, you know well how deeply I am interested in establishing world peace. The entire world is engaged in the arms race. Can we not create a universe where world peace and universal brotherhood prevail, where no feelings of enmity, hatred or bloodshed exist?"

"That will never be possible. Iqbal, mankind will always remain power-hungry and greedy for wealth. If you refer to the Moghul history, you will find instances where a son has usurped the political powers and reign of the Kingdom by imprisoning or killing one's own father. Who can ever change such ancient history?" Dr. Asif expressed his thoughts.

"Many times, I am reminded of my past. When I remember the days before the partition, my heart cries out in pain. Under the British rule, everybody was so happy and prosperous. The Hindus and Muslims shared in one another's pains and happiness. How gladly they mutually participated in religious festivities! But today? Both communities have become arch enemies."

"Iqbal, don't ever express such views before the Pakistani politicians! Since you are my good friend, I am merely advising you." On saying this Dr. Asif fell silent and looked at Iqbal.

He continued, "I may agree with what you are saying. But why don't the Indian rulers come to a compromise on the Kashmir problem? They continue spending billions of rupees in order to increase their military power. If such an amount of money could instead be spent on the public welfare, how happily people could live! We should let the people of Kashmir take a decision of whether they wish to merge with Pakistan or live with India. The Indian rulers have proved themselves to be very obstinate and egoists by giving so much credence to such an insignificant issue as Kashmir."

Iqbal was prompted to reply, but he remained silent.

After that, many years passed. The policies of the democratically elected prime minister were proved wrong. Corruption spread wide in all walks of life. Inflation grew unchecked. The people were severely tired of such democracy. At an opportune moment General Karim Abdullah showed his true colours. He revolted against the Prime Minister. The Chiefs of the army, navy and air force, had all colluded with General Karim Abdullah. The Prime Minister was placed under house arrest. In this way, the end of democracy was brought about in Pakistan and the era of military rule dawned. Suddenly the political picture of Pakistan underwent a great change. As soon as the reins of the nation fell into the hands of the military, anti-Indian propaganda adopted an aggressive outlook. In order to distract the attention of the people of Pakistan, the Kashmir issue was brought to the fore of the propaganda. Terrorists were infiltrated in India in a large number. Massacres occurred in Jammu and Kashmir on a daily basis. The banks were plundered. Great turmoil broke out in Kashmir. The issue of Kashmir was discussed heatedly in the Indian Parliament. It was not possible to solve the Kashmir problem.

The military ruler, General Karim Abdullah, took harsh administrative steps, which agitated the people of Pakistan. He ordered the scientists to produce an atom bomb in a certain timefame.

A few days later, General Karim Abdullah summoned Dr. Asif and Dr. Iqbal to his cabin.

"Following the Pokharan Test, the confidence of our people has been badly shaken. Because of this, I want you to produce an atom bomb quickly," General Karim Abdullah said.

"My associates and I are working day and night to achieve that. Dr. Iqbal is conducting different kinds of experiments in order to convert the nuclear energy into power. I am confident that in a short while we shall acquire capabilities to become a member of the world's atom club," Dr. Asif replied.

"We will think of becoming a member of the Atomic Club later. But considering our domestic problems we must immediately explode an atomic device like the Indians did. If this is not done, the people of Pakistan will be angry with the Pakistani rulers."

"I do understand, sir, but such work takes a lot of time." Dr. Asif said.

"No, Asif. I have given all sorts of liberties to you and your associates. Go abroad, beg, borrow or even steal if you have to, and win over the officers of the other countries by providing them with any inducements. I am interested in the production of the bomb at the earliest possible opportunity." General Karim Abdullah declared emphatically.

"I realise what you say, Sir. Tomorrow we will discuss among ourselves, prepare a new plan and implement it."

"I may have to go to America next month. You can consult Aziz Maqbool in my absence. Alright, now get busy with your production of an atom bomb." Having said this, General Karim Abdullah left to attend another meeting.

Dr. Asif took the chief scientist, Dr. Iqbal, to his office. Dr. Iqbal began talking.

"Sir, General Karim thinks that an atom bomb can be produced in a jiffy. Is there no other way to satiate this thirst of severe hatred against India?"

"Iqbal, since when have you begun to argue in such a foolish manner? You know well that the people of Pakistan do not want anything less than Kashmir. The Indians too do not want to accept the idea of Pakistan slipping through their fingers. It's only because of this that enmity has grown between the two countries since the attainment of Independence."

"But our rulers have played a significant role in fomenting such hatred."

"Why do you say that, Iqbal?"

"Sir, the rulers of the nation should have devoted their attention to developing agriculture, industry and society, so that the people could live happily and prosperously. Instead they waste billions of rupees on the procurement of armaments. Our soldiers are guarding our frontiers round the clock. Now, the minds of our people are polluted to such an extent that the youth is openly instigated in the Madresas to start the insurgency of arms against India. Terrorists are being created in large numbers. I feel that due to such painful oppressive attitudes, the people of Pakistan will never be able to heave a sigh of relief again" Dr. Iqbal presented the picture of prevailing circumstances.

Dr. Asif was not only his boss, but also a good friend, philosopher and guide. They were very close as they had worked together for a very long time.

"Iqbal, as your friend, I must advise you to have a valorous attitude to involving yourself in combat, otherwise, what you are saying could be construed as a treacherous act against the people of Pakistan."

"Let me speak today and unburden myself. You know very well that the public opinion of the people of Pakistan is never a mature one. Besides, the religious fanatics and fundamentalists are abounding here in large numbers. The people of Pakistan are less worried about their hunger than war and they seem to love bullets more than bread. They seem to be more worried about revenge than their own miseries. It is not proper in any way!] Pakistan fought three wars with the Indians, but what has ultimately been achieved by us? Nothing, except shameful defeat and absolute disappointment!"

"In battles, only one of the two nations emerges victorious. Why do you forget that?"

"What I want to point out is that it is we who have to suffer damage by fighting with a large country like India. You are well aware, sir, that we are already engulfed by problems such as largescale poverty. Afghan, Taleban, the Shias and the Sunnis, need to resolve their war problems. India is a non-secular nation. Two billion Muslims live in that country. If we drop a missile or an atom bomb on any of the Indian cities, several Muslims could die, and thousands of Mosques, a large number of copies of the holy Koran and a great many educational institutions will be destroyed. Is this not an act against the holy tenets of Islam?" Iqbal expressed his suppressed anger. He paused for a moment and continued, "Whenever I am alone, I think of the well-being of the people of Pakistan. But when thinking of the devastation perpetrated by the armed conflicts and war, I become badly shaken. I wonder why the politicians don't implement the wisdom they learn from the religious treatises. Take for instance the holy Koran, the Geeta and the Bible; which religious treatise advocates humanity to perpetrate wars?"

"Iqbal, listening to you, I feel that you are under the deep influence of the Gandhian thoughts on non-violence."

"Don't you think, sir, that we need to adopt such policies by which the people of both nations can live in peace? What has our religion, Islam, taught us? Gandhiji had not only read all the religious books, but had imbibed within him the wisdom derived out of them. And that is why he could inspire a non-violent revolution. It is only for this reason that he has been recognised as Mahatma—meaning the greatest spiritual soul—by the world at large. While he was alive, he never once showed an interest in bloody revolution. When India was partitioned, and Pakistan came into existence, the massacre of the people on both sides and communal violence caused him severe anguish and mental torture."

"Truthfully speaking, Iqbal, your thoughts are absolutely Gandhian. Our rulers would never be able to tolerate such thoughts. Not only that, but if they even happen to learn of your viewpoints or ideas, they would withdraw you from the field of nuclear technology."

"I am very much aware of that. I might have attained great achievements as a nuclear physicist, but if I cannot do anything for the benevolence of humanity during my lifetime, the Khuda will never pardon me." Saying this, Iqbal's eyes filled with tears.

Many times, whenever such discussions took place with Dr. Asif, Iqbal's heart would become anguished with such thoughts.

More time elapsed. The military ruler, General Karim Abdullah, took steps to bring about an improvement in the worsening economic conditions. In order to develop friendly relations with other countries he undertook several frequent foreign tours. The Air Chief Marashal Aziz Maqbool dreamt of crushing India under the soles of his boots. He continually propagated against India and thus, poisoned the minds of the Pakistanis. While worshipping Khuda, he would pray, "Oh Khuda, please grant me strength, so that I can fulfil the promise I made to my Abbajan."

One day, when Aziz Maqbool was exchanging his views and thoughts with Dr. Asif in his cabin; he received shocking news.

His mother, Nafisa, had been admitted to the Saifuddin Hospital as she had suffered a massive heart attack.

Chapter 31

Following the Pokharan test, a disenchanted Sanatan would return home from the office and sit quietly in his room for a long time. The other members of the family, including Radha and Kanaiyalal understood his sadness. They tried to help him out of his melancholic state, but soon he would be caught in the floodgates of mental anguish and sadness again. Whenever he sat down for his meals, he could not eat as he did before. His anguish was tormenting him from within.

Once, when Radha went to her bedroom to sleep, Sanatan was reading the book 'War and Peace' by the great laureate Leo Tolstoy. It felt as if the great devastation taking place in the book was actually being experienced directly by Sanatan as he read. Reading about the terrible destructions in war, his heart was filled with deep anguish. He closed the book and was lost in thought. Why are human beings so cruel? Why do the super powers perpetrate mass annihilation of the innocent masses just to acquire a piece of land or to satiate their hunger of supremacy over other countries by turning the small nations into their scapegoats? Since the time of Mahabharat several wars have been fought in the world, but what has humanity at large achieved?

Germany was devastated due to the war. Over a million innocent women, men and children were annihilated by the airborne attacks of Britain, France and America. On the other hand four million German soldiers were deprived of their life on the battle-fields.

The German autocrat Hitler massacred legions of Jews in the gas chambers. The devastation, perpetrated on Hiroshima and Nagasaki by the atom bombs dropped there, is still not forgotten by the world. Several wars and battles ranging like the Iran-Iraq war, the Vietnam-America War, the Arab-Israel war and the India-Pakistan war have been fought and humans have been mercilessly killed. If we bring such cruel, murderous, painful scenes before our eyes, we would realise that the enemies of humanity is humanity itself, which is filled with a sense of power-hunger, religious fanaticism and severe hatred towards other human beings.

When Sanatan was exhausted thinking about this for so long, he switched off the table-lamp. Darkness descended on the room. The dim light of the night-lamp spread all over the room. He rose to his feet from the chair and went to bed. He lay beside the already sleeping Radha. Still he was lost in thought. He stared at the ceiling. Suddenly, Radha opened her eyes. She saw that Sanatan was wide awake. Patting him on the shoulder she softly asked,

"Why are you still awake?"

Turning on his side facing Radha, Sanatan said, "I am not able to sleep despite my best efforts."

"I can see that, for the last few days, ever since the Pokharan test, you seem to be moving about in a daydream. Although you attend your office regularly, when you return home, the bright pleasure and joy that was evident on your face in the past, is absent these days."

"How can you perceive happiness on my face? Disappointment and unknown fear has engulfed my heart and my mind is in turmoil because I remained engaged in finding out the secrets of atomic and nuclear science as a nuclear physicist without any consideration for day or night. With the help of my other associates we developed capabilities in nuclear power, nuclear weapons and achieved success in developing the atom bomb.

I have been thinking that by unveiling the secrets of the atomic system we shall be able to convert nuclear energy into power, which could be put to use for the benefit of mankind. Despite this, it is also very true that in order to protect our nation from other countries, we have to either manufacture or purchase modern nuclear weapons, fighter aircraft or guns for our military. If we don't do that other countries could attack us and conquer us; and once again we will be subjected to slavery. I have only one worry and that is about my dream of world peace."

"You will have to prepare yourself that it will only remain a dream. I believe that none of the nations will agree with your thoughts of world-peace."

"What you say is right, Radha. When I went to discuss it with the higher officials, defence minister and the Prime Minister, nobody paid any heed to what I had to say. They were not interested in listening to my views."

"Oh but, just remember what you observed during your two periods in America? Why does America spend billons of dollars on scientific research? Why do several factories manufacture modern armaments and have the Pentagon working day and night? Large nations like America wants to make the other countries of the world dance to her tune. That country is an expert at forcing two other countries engage in battle. This way, America is playing strategic games to make other countries continually fight with one another. If that doesn't happen who would buy the armament developed by them? How would they prosper financially?"

"Radha, these worries are preventing me from enjoying tranquillity. I want to complete research that would ensure happiness and peace for entire humanity. I feel gagged and suffocated amid the crowds of politicians. I feel, as if my view points of achieving world peace are falling on deaf ears. Having performed the nuclear explosion at Pokharan, we have tested our capability of making the atom bomb. Now atom bombs will be produced in large numbers. After that, won't the ordinary people have to live under the shadow of fear with the creation of atom bombs?"

"But, who understands all this?"

"I believe that atom bombs will be manufactured everywhere in the world in this manner and when atomic warfare takes place the entire world will be devastated. Entire humanity, animals, birds and vegetation will be obliterated from the face of planet Earth. This thought frightens me."

"Sanatan, I will only say that you will have to find your own way to live differently. God always helps us in our noble tasks. Hence, without losing heart, move ahead with courage and confidence and achieve what you aim for."

"How wonderful, Radha! Although, I might have achieved so much in the atomic field, when I listen to your thoughts, I realise that you have perfectly imbibed within you the ideals of life. You have passed your graduation exam in economics, but you seem to be an expert at psychology."

"Well . . . . Well . . . . , it is already midnight. Let's sleep now."

"The reverberations of what you say pierce my chest and strike my heart. I am sure that my cherished dream will gradually be crystallized before me."

Saying this, Sanatan chuckled and took Radha in his arms.

Both were lost in romantic bliss.

The next day, as Sanatan sat having tea, the colours of the rainbow were reflected on his face, one after the other. His countenance did not show the sadness that was visible in the last few days. He was talking to Kanaiyalal with his normal enthusiasm and a smiling face. Suddenly, Kanaiyalal had an asthma attack. Sanatan was baffled. He stood beside Kanaiyalal and moved his hand softly on his back. He said, "I'll call the doctor."

"No . . . . no . . . ." Kanaiyalal said, "There is no need to call the doctor. It's because of my age that such bouts of asthma bother me. I'll take my inhaler and soon I'll recover. I get such breathing problems because it is the winter season."

"Nevertheless, do take care of your health. If you feel like describing your symptoms to the doctor tell Radha or me without any delay."

"Sure."

As he said this, Kanaiyalal picked up a newspaper, went to the drawing room and sat on a sofa.

At around four in the evening when Radha went to Kanaiyalal's room with a cup of tea, she was shocked when she looked inside the room. Tears were rolling down the cheeks of Kanaiyalal. Radha turned pale with fear. Placing her hand on his shoulder, she asked,

"Why are there tears in your eyes? What happened?"

"I was reminded of my past. Today is your mother-in-law's anniversary. Because of that, her memories made me emotional."

"Oh sorry, Papa. Every year I used to remember the anniversary of her death, but today it just slipped my mind." Radha's voice became husky saying this.

Today your mother-in-law is not in this world anymore and I am reminded of the happier days I spent with her. Besides, I am reminded of a childhood friend, Arvind, and his wife, Madhu. Now, what is left for me at the end of my life, other than fond memories of the past?"

"Papa, at the end of life, the happy memories of the past become our treasured possessions that please our hearts and soul."

When they were talking, the doorbell suddenly rang. Quickly, Radha went to open the door. To her pleasant surprise, she found uncle Arvind standing before her.

"How wonderful, uncle! Welcome! Just a moment ago papa was talking about you."

"Oh, really! For a week, I had been remembering Kanu. All of a sudden I was reminded of Kusum's anniversary and so I thought of coming to meet him." Radha led him to Kanaiyalal's room. She said,

"I will get something for you to eat. Meanwhile talk to your friend."

"No Radha, I ate on my way. I am not hungry. Better serve some tea." Arvind said.

"Arvind, you won't believe how much I have been thinking of you since this morning" Kanaiyalal said.

"Call it Telepathy and that's why I am here."

"We both are unlucky. Many years ago I lost Kusum and some time ago your wife, Madhu, died."

"Friend, who is immortal in this world? We all have to leave this world for the heavenly abode. In fact, for many days now, I have been thinking of you and Kusum. I thought of meeting you on her anniversary and that is why I have come here."

"That is very nice of you. What else do we have except remembering and thinking of our past?"

Meanwhile, Radha appeared with two cups of tea and some refreshments.

"Papa was deeply anguished remembering my mother-in-law. Thank God you have arrived."

Radha left them alone and they began talking.

After staying with them for four days, Arvind talked of leaving for Umreth. Kanaiyalal and Radha insisted he stay for a few more days but Arvind decided to return to Umreth. The sweet smell of the earth of his birthplace was beckoning him. Kanaiyalal, too, thought of visiting Umreth, but it was not possible for him to do so due to his ill-health. Moreover, Sanatan was spending his days in a disturbed state of mind.

One day Sanatan summoned Ramamurti to his cabin. When Ramamurti came in his face showed sadness.

"Hmmmm . . . , how is everything? Is everyone at home well?" Sanatan asked.

"Yes." Ramamurti gave a short reply.

"Look, I heard that you are not able to pay attention to your work as before. I can see that your face is drained of colour. Can you tell me what are you worried about now?"

"It is nothing like that. I do my work in the department with all my heart and soul. The problem is that the stain of past events has been etched on my heart for life."

"Don't have such thoughts in your mind. Your case is over now. So, it is better for you to concentrate on your work with happiness."

"Sanatan, I shall remain indebted to you for life for the help and support you have given in my case."

"You must thank God that the original convict, Mukherjee, was arrested when he came to India and the charges against you were withdrawn." Sanatan paused for a moment and then asked,

"How are Sulabha and Vinaykant?"

Both are well. If you visit us one of these days accompanied by your wife, Radha, we shall be very happy."

"Certainly, we will come." Sanatan replied.

"May I leave now?" Ramamurti asked.

"Just sit here for a while. Listen attentively to what I have to say."

Placing the empty teacup on the table Ramamurti looked at Sanatan.

"It has been five months since the Pokharan Test was carried out. My mind is not at peace. I am planning of going abroad for a few months."

"That's a good idea. Will you go abroad with Radha?"

"Oh, no. It is because of my father's old age. Somebody, namely Radha, is needed to look after him."

"When do you propose to leave?"

"It's not yet decided. But I plan to go in a month or so. I haven't spoken to Tapan and Radha about it yet. But I'll tell them soon. Now, please concentrate on what I am going to tell you now."

"Yes, what is it?"

"I've heard that the Inter Services Intelligence agents always adopt various techniques. If you are, once more, entangled with them, it will be very difficult to extricate yourself from their clutches. Therefore, do your work diligently. I hope that you will consider this advice and I ask you not to ignore what I say."

"Why, Sanatan! I will always remember your advice. How can I ignore the advice that you are giving for my benefit? You shouldn't worry. I'll follow every word of what you say."

Then he continued,

"What do you think of the political scenario in Pakistan? The people there seem very happy with the imposition of military rule."

"You know that by keeping the Kashmir issue alive Pakistan continues to foment hatred against India. Just look at their cunning tricks. Every now and then they try to bring up the Kashmir issue for discussion in the International forum. To hell with them; it is their old habit. But tell me, following the Pokharan test, what counter steps can they take? Do you have any idea?" said Sanatan.

"I have heard that they are seething with anger at our progress in nuclear technology. They are filled with jealousy at our progress. It is unpredictable when their anger will become ugly."

"I have heard that they have engaged all of their scientists to make atom bombs. This is their old habit.

If we buy aircraft or armaments, they will strive to buy armament and aircraft of a superior quality. As we have made an atom bomb, it will now be their aim to make an atom bomb also. It is immaterial if they have the required technology or not, they would organise it somehow by procuring spare parts, machinery and technical knowledge either by stealing, cheating or by smuggling from other countries."

"What you say is true, Sanatan. They are not going to remain quiet after our Pokharan test."

After some time Ramamurti left. Sanatan was reading an important file. That very night Sanatan had a telephone conversation with Iqbal, who was living in Karachi. Then he arrived home.

While dining Radha asked,

"What are you thinking of?"

"I am really tired of work. I feel like visiting Malaysia to have some peace of mind."

"That's a good idea. You should certainly go."

"One of my friends is in Malaysia. We have kept in touch for years."

"When do you propose to go?"

"We propose to go in a month's time. I have to finish some of the pending work before I can leave."

After a few days, Sanatan's air tickets were received.

The day of departure arrived a month later. While driving the car on the way to the airport, he advised Tapan, "You must work carefully and diligently. You must remember that the number of friends is much smaller than that of the enemies. Because of this, be very careful."

He told Kanaiyalal to take care of his health.

He also asked Rita to live in peace and understanding with Radha. Before entering the customs hall, his and Radha's eyes met. A tinge of sadness made their hearts heavy. He told her, "Be brave, Radha. It is not befitting for you to shed tears like this."

But when Sanatan disappeared from view in the customs hall, tears rolled down Radha's cheeks and then she found it difficult to stop weeping.

When Sanatan reached Malaysia, Iqbal was waiting for him as they had planned in advance. From there, they left for Sohali.

When the two friends landed at Sohali Island, Ivan was waiting to welcome them, with a broad smile on his face.

———◈———

Chapter 32

"It is a unique experience to look at such lush greenery and trees growing around this Island," Sanatan observed, peering at the forest vegetation on two sides of the road, through the car window.

"This whole Island is full of such abounding greenery. After driving for about four kilometers we can see such a dense forest on the left, which presents us with spellbinding scenery." Ivan laughed.

"Wonderful . . . . ! Absolutely exciting . . . . !" Iqbal exclaimed.

"It is only for this reason that my daddy wanted you to visit us and have a peaceful vacation."

Soon they reached William's fortress-like sprawling residence. Instructing the driver Ivan said,

"The guests are to be conveyed to the guest house. So, just wait out here."

Sanatan was surprised to enter the palatial villa.

"The house seems very large and magnificent and it seems to have many rooms. It is as if we have entered a building like red fort at Delhi or a palace of a Moghul Sultan." He said.

"Sanatan, we heard our teacher talking of the grand palaces and the splendorous regal lives. I feel as if we have come to a dream world." Iqbal supported Sanatan's observation.

In a moment, they were ushered into a spacious hall. William rose from a sofa and welcomed them affectionately.

"Welcome to Sohali. I hope that you had no trouble on your way."

"Absolutely not. Ivan came with us from the airport. Before we arrived here, we thoroughly enjoyed the scenic beauty of your island. As a matter of fact, this has been the most enchanting experience of our life." Sanatan paused for a moment and then looking at Iqbal, he added,

"My childhood friend, Iqbal, an eminent scientist of Pakistan and I are deeply pleased and awed at watching the splendorous scenic beauty of Sohali Island."

"You will find serenity on this island that is unavailable anywhere else in the world. You may be tired after your journey. Have a rest, and then we'll meet."

Ivan led the two guests out of the house and took them to the guest house located some distance away. Instructing Rodricks at the door he said,

"Take proper care of the guests. See that they have no trouble."

Passing through a large hall, when Sanatan and Iqbal arrived in their allotted suites, they were awed by the great splendour of comfort, which had the facilities of a five-star hotel. A colourful, costly Iranian carpet was laid on the floor. The ceiling had intricate designs that compelled the eyes to continue looking at them. The massive ostentatious chandelier hanging from the ceiling added more beauty to the majestic room. A switchboard was timed to automatically open windows and doors. Placing the luggage in the grand suite-room, Rodricks said,

"Sirs, do call me, should you need anything. Four of us are at your disposal round the clock."

After Rodricks left, Sanatan had a bath. He took a hot water shower for a long time. Fitted with several electronic gadgets, the bathroom looked glamorously beautiful. Looking up at the ceiling Sanatan was shocked. The blue sky with clouds outside was reflected on the ceiling. He felt as if he was bathing under the sky. Having his lazy bath Sanatan thought,

In the last decade or so, science has been greatly advanced. Man seems to be competing with nature to achieve greater success in science.

He was pleased to note that today's scientists had developed certain gadgets harnessing the light and sound waves.

The next morning when Sanatan woke up from his sleep, his heart was filled with vibrant happiness hearing the sweet sounds of birds.

Mother Nature had scattered all her bountiful gifts around this place, which was located far away from humanity. He was pleased to see the lush green trees and greenery through the window. There is a great joy in living in seclusion. The atmosphere around abounded with natural beauty.

William came to see them in the morning. He asked Sanatan and Iqbal to accompany him for a morning walk. Looking at Sanatan he asked,

"Can you sleep well at night?"

"Yes."

"When we take a little walk our bodies and minds will be filled with freshness and vigor."

"In fact, only the lucky ones could find such a place to live in. Iqbal and I never imagined such a place on the earth which could have so much beauty around and so much comfort. We are enjoying the heavenly pleasures of this paradise."

"This afternoon, I wish to show you a library situated about half a furlong away. Almost all the books published in the world could be found there."

"How wonderful!" Iqbal stared at William's face.

"It must have taken many years for you to develop this Island!"

"No. When control of this island fell into my hands its modernization had already taken place. All the newest inventions taking place in the world are quickly introduced here. The establishment of regality had taken place several centuries ago."

"The serenity on this island is quite unique whereas, the Sohali Township is enchanting owing to the modern electronic gadgetry. On one hand, the luxuriant growth of vegetation is pleasant on the eyes while on the other hand the flora and fauna adds to the grandeur of this island. I feel strongly that, after coming here one's mind begins to dwell in the higher realm", Sanatan expressed his joy.

When they visited the library, Sanatan's joy knew no bounds. Most of the valuable books which had been published all over the world were to be found there. Sanatan was extremely pleased to find the rare books, which were in the science section of the library. Expressing his appreciation to William, he said,

"Sir, you have certainly done great work. I have never seen such a large collection of books to date."

"I have been thinking that the desired things should be made available to anybody who visits this island. And that is why I have been asking you to come and stay here."

"Now, I firmly believe that we shall be able to achieve our aim of world peace in the atmosphere of this place."

Sanatan and Iqbal spent some of their days going around the Sohali town, meeting people, observing ultra-modern electronic equipment, studying books in the library and trekking through the tracts of the dense forests.

One evening, after returning from the library, Sanatan sat on a bench underneath a large tree.

"Iqbal, we have been here for almost twenty days now. The atmosphere is such that it attracts us like a massive magnet. What do you say?"

"Should I talk of the heavenly beauty of this island or the hospitality accorded by William and his son, Ivan? I am at a loss of words in appreciation of either."

"What do you think of our dream of 'the search for World Peace' that we have cherished since our childhood?"

"Sanatan, I firmly believe to that end we can never find such a nice atmosphere or people of such a sweet nature anywhere on the face of the earth."

"Ivan was just asking me yesterday when we are going to crystallize our dream of establishing world peace."

"What was your reply?"

"I told him that I'll think about it and then let him know."

"Have you thought of anything?"

"Yes, do you remember the large open ground amid the dense forest that we had seen? We should build a most modern underground laboratory below that open ground. We should get a few scientists who can understand our feelings of world peace and our aims. What are your views on this? What do you feel?"

"It's an excellent idea. If we are true to our resolve we shall certainly be able to achieve our aim. We will not leave any stone unturned in saving humanity by propagating the message of peace in the world. If our aim, resolve and integrity will be true and pious, Allah will lead and direct us on the right path. I firmly believe this", Iqbal expressed his views positively.

"Are you thinking of returning to Pakistan?"

"No, friend. You know well that when we left our motherlands we resolved that we will not leave this land until our aim is achieved."

"Are you missing your wife Mumtaz, Zora and Karim?"

"What can be done if I am? Tell me; don't you also miss your wife, Radha? In fact, Zora and Karim are dearer to me than my life. But our mission is more important than our memories." Iqbal said.

"What you say is right. I am also reminded of Tapan, Radha, Rita and my father. But let it be, let's talk about our work."

"How long will it take to create certain kinds of virus by conducting research of harnessing the sound and light waves and their frequencies?" Iqbal asked.

"It will take at least five to seven years and I believe that if we are lucky, we can achieve success much earlier."

"This means that we will have to stay here somehow until we achieve our aim."

"Of course, but it is very necessary to figure out how shall we live here, hidden from the world, for all these years." Sanatan looked at Iqbal's face.

"Let us go now. After a couple of days' of hard thinking, we will find a suitable solution."

Both of them stood up from the bench and strolled towards the guest house.

One evening, William called Sanatan and Iqbal for a meeting. Ivan, too, was present.

All four had gathered to exchange serious viewpoints and thoughts.

"Sanatan, you can initiate the discussion. Let us unanimously arrive at a decision" William smiled, looking at Sanatan.

For a while, Sanatan was lost in thought but he spoke out,

"You all are well aware that the world today is becoming selfish and craves the domination of other countries. The scientists of all the nations have become pawns in the hands of the politicians. Everybody knows that grave devastation and destruction would be the result of wars, and especially nuclear warfare. Innocent humanity would be annihilated and the earth would turn barren. Many would be deprived of their dwellings and would become homeless. They would be affected by such grievous diseases that they may be forced to live the remainder of their life in severe pain and sufferings as diseased persons. Iqbal and I are of the opinion that the only way to come out unscathed from all these troubles is the search for world peace. Iqbal, too, says that, the rulers of Pakistan are fundamentalists and religious fanatics. As such, they are determined to unfurl the flag of Islam religion throughout the world. In order to spread their reign over the world, they have initially steadied their sights on Kashmir. Misguiding the masses, confusion has been established and misleading teaching is being provided in educational institutes in order to snatch away Kashmir from the fingers of India. They aim at spreading an atmosphere of violence in all the larger cities of India in the future, especially by sending terrorists to Bombay, Delhi, and Jammu-Kashmir. The rulers of Pakistan will produce nuclear atomic weapons in large numbers and if they cannot do so they will procure them either through smuggling or by importing. This way, it will establish its strong image as a terrorist state in the world". Having expressed his wide-ranging thoughts, Sanatan paused for a moment. He sipped water from a glass and then looking at Iqbal, he asked,

"Iqbal, have I understood your viewpoint correctly or not?"

"What you have said is absolutely perfect."

"Now, let me talk about certain weak points of my country. The rulers of my country are in no way less mean and cunning. The legal system is so loose that a great many offenders manage to escape unscathed. In order to strengthen their vote bank those who are in positions of power get suitable resolutions approved of with a majority in the upper and lower houses of parliament. Not only that, a scenario is actually enacted as if the political rulers are plundering the national coffers. It will cause no surprise if, in the future, corruption and nepotism grow enormously due to the moral turpitude of such rulers and a great number of politicians emerge in the country who would eat away the national wealth as a termite would bore through a piece of wood. As soon as the position of power is achieved, many of them will begin to think of how to amass wealth that actually belongs to the poor masses of the nation, and spend lavishly on luxuries, partying and lavish lifestyles. Such unscrupulous politicians would only think of stashing away their ill-gotten gains in Swiss banks and they would have no qualms, whatsoever, even if the country becomes heavily burdened by financial debt or falls back on the path of progress. The national rulers would ensure that they have a constitution that enables them to achieve quick satisfaction for their selfish motives. In this way, considering the current situation, I feel that Indian politics will be severely degraded. Moreover, in the absence of proper education the people will turn out to be powerless and cowardly. Thus, if there is any recourse that is left to save oneself from such evil elements and protect the other nations from them, it is the message of the world-peace." Without hesitation, Sanatan presented a clear picture of a future India.

"Sanatan, having understood so many details, we should come to a conclusion that in order to achieve our aim, we must initiate construction of the laboratory."

"Very true! As well as that, we will have to fabricate a story and spread news that Iqbal and I do not exist in the world anymore." Sanatan replied.

"What is the reason for that?" Ivan asked anxiously.

"That is to prevent the top political leaders or the members of our family from calling us as and when needed. Due to this, I propose that we continue to remain underground on Sohali Island until our aim is achieved. What do you say, Iqbal?"

"I fully agree with you." Iqbal said.

"There is another issue of getting the scientists to this place. We must recruit the best scientists from all over the world. We need to make arrangements to allow them to stay on Sohali Island until our research is concluded and they should be compelled to take an oath of secrecy."

"I would like to say that I would not mind paying those scientists a little more", William chuckled.

"Now, I have to declare the third and most important point of our discussion. After Iqbal and I disappear from the public eye we will have to assume new names and we will have to change our appearances with plastic surgery."

"Why are all these things necessary?" Ivan asked.

"It is necessary. When our existence is obliterated, why shouldn't our names be too? For this purpose, new names will be necessary." Sanatan replied. Then looking around, he gradually explained the whole plan to everyone. Each of them agreed with Sanatan's views.

Within a week construction of the underground air conditioned laboratory had begun at full swing, as per the plan.

One morning, news spread through newspapers, radio and television, which shook millions of people in the world.

"A helicopter burst into a fireball following a fall into deep ravines of a mountain after crashing into high peaks on Sohali Island."

The news in detail was as follows;

"The Chief Controller of the Indian Defence Research & Development Organisation, known as DRDO, and the Principal Scientific Advisor to the Government of India holding the Cabinet rank, the famous nuclear scientist Dr. Sanatan, who was the key—figure of the Pokharan nuclear test and Dr.

Iqbal, the Joint-Chairman of the Pakistan Atomic Commission, who enabled Pakistan to achieve prominence in the field of nuclear technology, were one-time childhood friends. They were on a visit to the Sohali Islands on holiday. The helicopter flying them crashed into a mountain peak. Both scientists were burnt to death in the fire that enveloped the helicopter."

Chapter 33

Having returned from the hospital the mother and daughter entered the house. Rita went straight to the bedroom to change her clothes. Sulabha sat in a chair placed near Ramamurti. Ramamurti asked,

"How is Rita? What did the lady doctor have to say?"

There's good news. Soon you are going to become a grandpa."

"Wonderful! You certainly gave me very pleasant news. I hope everything is normal with her!"

"Oh yes! I have registered Rita's name in the Vibha Maternity Nursing Home."

"That's good. When will she have to go for a check-up again?"

"Once every month. However, one can visit any time if necessary."

"Is her mother-in-law aware of the news?"

"Yes, she is aware that Rita is three-months pregnant. Before getting Rita's name registered, I informed Radha of the news."

After a while Sulabha rose to her feet and walked to the phone. She picked up the receiver, and dialled a number. When she heard Radha's voice on the other hand, she said,

"Radha, we've arrived home. Dr. Vibha has told us that there is nothing to worry about. Rita's health is perfectly normal. Please, come and see us as often as possible."

"Certainly, I will come," After saying this Radha replaced the receiver on the cradle.

The next day, when Ramamurti returned from the office, he seemed very tired. Sulabha prepared tea for him. The telephone rang before he could place the empty cup on the table. Ramamurti picked up the receiver and said,

"Hello . . . ."

"It is Ramesh Shetty here. Have you done my work or not?"

"No", Ramamurti replied in a trembling voice.

"When will it be done?"

"I am doing my best."

"Two months have elapsed in mere talking. I am giving you two final months. If I do not get the maps of the spots of the nuclear reactors and the formula for producing nuclear weapons and if I don't get the microfilms on these two items by that time, be ready to face the consequences."

"Shetty Saheb, try to understand what I am saying."

Ramamurti spoke fearfully in a trembling voice. "The work that you have asked me to do is so difficult that . . . ."

"Look, I am not interested in hearing you cribbing. It is your problem as to how well you accomplish that task. Shrikant Mukherjee was far more courageous than you. If he was not behind bars, this work would have been accomplished a long time ago. Now, you only have to finish the work. It is up to you to meet Sanatan or use Tapan to do the assigned work. What I have told you to do must be done instantly."

"My life will turn into a living hell once again."

"Aren't you getting money in return? Didn't you receive Rupees five lakhs last time?"

"I don't want any money. My conscience will not allow me to do such work."

"Ramamurti, just bear one thing in mind, we won't listen to such talk. Just take your money and enjoy it."

"I am deeply afraid."

"Whether you are afraid or not is not our concern. Just do what I have asked you to. Do you care for the well-being of your family or not?"

"Brother, please don't be so cruel. My reputation has already been tarnished earlier. If I act on your orders, I don't know what will become of me!"

"Ramamurti, just remember; if you don't decide to act as we say, you may have to forfeit your life."

"No . . . . no . . . . Shetty . . . ."

"Then, get on with the assigned task immediately."

Before Ramamurti could think of any reply the telephone line went dead. Shetty had terminated the connection.

It was fortunate that while the telephone conversation has been taking place, Sulabha was busy cooking in the kitchen.

Ramamurti was lost in deep thought. At the time of the theft of the microfilms, the chief culprit was Shrikant Mukherjee. Ramamurti was forced to indirectly help him. He had thought that by helping him once in such a shameful deed, he would steer clear of such people in future. If necessary, he would resign from his job. But before he could act as he had thought, Shetty cornered him.

Sanatan had gone abroad, so it was not possible to seek his guidance and advice. He was left with only Rita and Tapan. He knew that Tapan was an ardent idealist and a patriotic person. If he confided his secrets to him, the whole thing would fall flat on its face. Besides, Tapan had such patriotic fervour and an idealistic temperament that he would sacrifice his life to stop any act that was against the national interest or security.

For a long time Ramamurti pondered over his problem but when he couldn't think of any solution, he asked Rita to come over on the next day. That day Sulabha had gone to the market. Ramamurti wept bitterly before his daughter. Rita was a strongwilled person and was shocked to see him crying. She fetched a glass of water from the kitchen. Ramamurti took two sips.

"Daddy, why are you weeping? What's happened? I'm frightened. Tell me, why have you called me? Where's Mummy?" Rita asked many questions rapidly.

"My dear child, I'm in a deep quagmire of trouble." Ramamurti replied "Look; please tell me calmly everything that has happened. Then, we both will think of how to tackle the problem."

"I just can't think of any solution. At times, I think of committing suicide."

"What is bothering you that you are talking of committing suicide? Tell me quickly, what has happened? What is making you so unhappy?"

Without hiding anything, Ramamurti revealed all of his secrets to his daughter. Having heard him unburden his soul, Rita said,

"I warned you earlier and advised you to resign your job. But you didn't pay any heed to my advice."

"If I had resigned then it would have been very good; but since I was released as a guiltless person, I thought that I wouldn't have any such trouble in the future, and that I wouldn't have to do such work ever again."

"If you just had followed my advice, the turmoil that has engulfed your life could have been avoided."

"Dear daughter, I feel ashamed and hate myself for performing such treacherous and unbecoming acts. It's better if the Almighty calls me to the heavenly abode."

"There wouldn't be anyone living unhappily, if one could die by asking or praying God for it. As a matter of fact, it was your grave mistake to accept rupees five lacs last time. Anyway, now without cribbing about what has happened, let us think of a solution to extricate you from this situation."

"You are right. Many times I had thought of avoiding doing such work, but I couldn't restrain myself and now I am in a terrible situation."

For a long time Rita pondered over the problem and then she asked,

"How about seeking the advice of Tapan?"

"I am totally lost and perturbed. I am willing to do anything you say. I am so afraid of ruining your peaceful life just because of my stupid act. I don't mind if I have to die."

"There is no use in repenting for your misdeeds, Daddy. Now, you must take your next steps with the utmost calmness and understanding."

"Does Tapan know that I had taken the bribe of rupees five lacs?"

"No, we never discussed it following your release by the court of law as innocent of the crime."

"I simply feel deep shame at such things."

"But now, what's the way out? Now, you will have to tell the absolute truth to Tapan."

"Do I have to tell him about taking rupees five lacs? Nobody, except you, is aware of it."

"I think you may avoid mentioning about rupees five lacs, but you will have to reveal the rest of the matter. In the future, at an opportune time, you may inform him of this issue of rupees five lacs."

"Whatever you advise me I'll do, my child. But now my mind is severely agitated and disturbed. I wish for this problem to be resolved soon."

Tapan had to leave town on an official visit, so he couldn't be reached. Rita went to stay with her parents for four days. Rita and Ramamurti would have secret discussions while Sulabha was oblivious of what was going on. With each passing day Ramamurti felt as if his weight was dropping. He didn't feel like venturing out or talking with others. He felt drudgery in attending the office. He was really tired of life.

When Tapan returned, Rita left for her home. One day, when Tapan returned from the office, he found Ramamurti seated on a sofa. He paid his respects and asked him about well being of the others. After they partook of tea and snacks, Rita emerged from the kitchen and sat on the sofa. She said,

"Daddy is very nervous. He has come to seek your advice."

"My advice? How can I advise my elder?"

"For the last week or so daddy has been severely confusion. In fact, he has become a victim of time and circumstance."

"That seems so; I can see that he has become pale. What's happened so suddenly?"

"To be frank, I will have to tell you everything because he feels quite uncomfortable as to how to relate it to you."

"All right, tell me" Tapan looked at Rita's face.

"You are well aware that he was arrested for the theft of the microfilms but later, for want of incriminating evidence he was set free by the court of law."

"Oh yes, I am aware of it."

"But there is something you aren't aware of. The ISI agent Ramesh Shetty is after daddy now."

"ISI agent!" Tapan exclaimed. "Why is daddy in contact with such characters? Tell me clearly so that I can understand the whole thing properly."

At length Rita narrated the matter to him and then she asked him,

"What should be done to extricate daddy from this situation?"

"I don't know where my papa is. Listening to all of this I am also deeply confused. I don't know in which country my papa is; otherwise we could have contacted him for his advice. Could we not wait for a while?"

"No, Tapan, no! That is not possible. That hoodlum is making repeated telephone calls to threaten him. He has given him until the first of next month. If daddy doesn't accomplish the work as he has instructed him, Shetty might kill daddy and also create immense problems for us."

"I don't know what to say, Rita. I am really confused. It is very difficult to take such threats lightly."

"Tapan, hasn't your papa given his telephone number where he can be contacted?"

"Oh, no! When he was leaving I asked for his whereabouts and phone numbers, but he had replied that he would call back as and when necessary."

"That means, even your Mummy is unaware of it."

"Yes, that's true. Even mom doesn't know." Tapan lowered his head with sadness. His tone was serious.

For some time nobody spoke. Each one was in turmoil and thinking. Some time later as if finding a clue Tapan said,

"How about seeking the advice of the RAW, the Research and Analysis Wing,—the Indian Secret Service? Just a couple of months ago I happened to meet an officer of RAW, Mr.Subodh Banerjee, in papa's office."

"Supposing that after we talk to him, they arrest daddy on some pretext?"

"That may be possible. However, taking into consideration his friendship with my papa, perhaps he might prove to be a true help for us. Besides, instead of succumbing to the threat of that hoodlum it is better to seek the refuge of the RAW." Tapan expressed his view.

"My mind cannot think properly since I heard of this. Now, only the Almighty can save us from all of this" an ashen faced Rita piped up. She turned to Ramamurti who was silent all this time, and asked,

"What's your opinion, daddy?"

Suddenly silence descended in the room. The ring of the telephone startled them. Tapan jumped to his feet and rushed to the other room to attend the phone. Rita meanwhile thought of something and turned to her father.

"Daddy, I feel that you must tell Tapan about that rupees five lacs now and even reveal it to Subodh Banerjee, if necessary" Rita said.

"Do what you feel is right. I have left the decision to you."

When Tapan returned to the room, Rita told of the incident of Jammu in greater detail, and spoke of how Ramesh Shetty had cornered her daddy and how he was forced to accept the bribe money of rupees five lacs.

For a moment Tapan was tense. His face clearly showed his feelings of disgust and anger at his father-in-law for engaging in such traitorous activities. Every small line on his face showed his suppressed anguish.

"Daddy, I am younger than you, so bear with me if I have to advise you. But please remember that if you try to hide any fact from an officer of RAW, it is you who will have to repent for such an act. It is needless to say that if you reveal everything to Subodh Banerjee truthfully, you might get proper guidance in the matter. On the other hand, after listening to us, instead of taking pity on you, he might arrest you. Hence, we had better think of all the possible consequences." Tapan said excitedly looking at Ramamurti.

Hearing Tapan, Ramamurti could not help crying out aloud. He spoke with a choked throat,

"I have already said that I have made a grave mistake and I am willing to accept any punishment meted out to me."

They then discussed various other matters and resolved to fix a meeting with Subodh Banerjee at the earliest opportunity.

Usually Banerjee preferred to spend Sunday with his family, but when Tapan insisted on a meeting, he couldn't refuse.

On the appointed Sunday, accompanied by Rita and Ramamurti, Tapan reached Banerjee's office. Welcoming them, he said,

"I am pleased to receive you all. Where is Sanatan these days? I've heard that he is abroad!"

"Yes Mr. Banerjee; he is abroad. But none of us in the family are aware of his whereabouts."

"It is of the utmost necessity to maintain secrecy about certain national issues. Perhaps you may be aware of that. Sanatan too is possibly abroad on such an issue. Even my wife and my sons don't know that I've come to the office for this meeting."

"Mr. Banerjee, let me introduce my wife, Rita, and my father-in-law, Mr. Ramamurti."

"If my memory doesn't fail me, I think he is the head of the department of the Microfilm section of BARC. Besides, you are the same Ramamurti who was found not guilty of the theft of the microfilms, by the court of law. Right?"

"Yes, I am that unfortunate Ramamurti."

"Sanatan had taken my guidance in your case as he is a friend of yours, Mr. Ramamurti. Anyway, what brings you to me, Tapan?"

Tapan narrated every detail of Ramamurti's problem. Banerjee was stunned by what he heard. He received more evidence of how ISI was spreading its tentacles all over the nation. Banerjee thought seriously and then said,

"Look Tapan, my friendship with Sanatan is obstructing my duty. In fact, I should put hand-cuffs on Mr. Ramamurti's hands and put him behind bars. But, I won't do that. There is no doubt about Mr. Ramamurti's guilt. However, in order to save him and apprehend the culprits, I will have to formulate a plan."

"What plan?"

"You see, Mr. Ramamurti is acting in collusion with the ISI agents and he is engaged in activities against the national security. In fact, the officers of RAW aren't aware of this matter. Hence, Mr. Ramamurti will have to maintain his friendly contact with the ISI agent. This way he will have to make a show of friendship with them and keep them in oblivion."

"But if he does so, don't you think, Mr. Banerjee, that Mr. Ramamurti would be in grave danger?"

"That is very possible. However, I will have a candid discussion with my associates. I'll let you know of the decision tomorrow."

When they took leave of Mr. Banerjee, all three of them were filled with anxiety. Ramamurti was deeply fear-stricken. He couldn't believe that he would have to nurture a friendship with such a cruel ISI agent.

On the following day, Tapan went to see Mr. Banerjee. He explained to Tapan to instruct Ramamurti as to how he should act further. That night, Tapan met Ramamurti and explained to him what Mr. Banerjee had instructed in detail.

A few evenings later, Ramesh Shetty called up Ramamurti on the phone. He asked Ramamurti to meet him the following night. Listening to Ramesh Shetty, Ramamurti began to sweat profusely.

Chapter 34

One day, when the news of the deaths of Dr. Sanatan and Dr. Iqbal—the greatest contributors to the area of atomic weapons was announced, the whole world was stunned. The morning newspapers vividly described the friendship between Sanatan and Iqbal and a detailed account of their childhood spent in Umreth village was described. Many journalists, while expounding the significance of unity between the Hindus and Muslims, had recounted the incident of bloody, macabre and murderous communal violence during the partition of India when Iqbal's father, Yakub, had saved young Sanatan's life by shielding him from the dagger thrown at Sanatan, sacrificing his own life. In this way they had acclaimed the Hindu-Muslim unity.

Certain hypercritical newspapers had published editorials describing the achievements of both the scientists, but severely criticized the atrocity of such scientific advancements.

Many others newspapers publishing more details about the two scientists had written that, despite being very close their families had been separated for over thirty years. In spite of that, why and how those two scientists had decided to meet at Sohali Island was a source of mystery for everybody.

One newspaper had written that following the death of Dr. Homi Bhabha, Dr. Sanatan had been appointed in his place. Dr. Sanatan had made great progress advancing Dr. Bhabha's unfinished tasks in the field of nuclear technology. In Pakistan,

Iqbal also had made tremendous efforts to make an atom bomb and he was expected to achieve success within a few days' time. Both nations had suffered irreparable loss due to the deaths of those two scientists and the vacuum which had been created in the field of nuclear technology would be extremely hard to fill. A pall of gloom enveloped both nations on receiving the sad news of those two scientists.

Although the Pakistanis had been defeated in three wars against India, they did not give up in voicing their support and chanting for seeking rule over Kashmir out of sheer jealousy and hatred towards India. Several times whenever democracy had emerged, in the Pakistani political life, the general public would enjoy peace and tranquility. But then the bigwigs of the military would itch to usurp the political powers and that would ensure the demise of such democracy. Because of this, the people of Pakistan had to endure military rule for many years and less of the civilian governments' rule. On the other hand, India always had witnessed a healthy democratic system since gaining their Independence.

Nevertheless, the rich became richer and the poor became poorer under this democratic system. A large number of corrupt and scam merchants were in control. The political system of India was gradually degraded. There always were ugly goings-on to attempt to usurp the seat of power by fair or foul means. Instead of healthy competition, the erosion of character was the order of the day. Besides the public appearance of the politicians full of shameless, unbecoming and reproachable behavior tormented the people at large. The government officials plundered the government exchequer as if it was their own property. The people of India were silently enduring the anguish when they realized the wicked, shameful and truthful picture of India that was being perceived by the world. But a volcano of dissatisfaction was simmering within their hearts. Nobody knew when the layers of lava building up within their hearts would erupt in the form of a volcano. When the sorry state of India and Pakistan was exposed in the newspapers, the people of both nations suffered agony.

Having received the news of Sanatan's death, poor Radha had almost become insane with grief. She cried so loudly that the walls seemed to shake and at times she banged her head on the walls in the depth of her sorrow. Her feelings were lost in a vacuum of senselessness. Tapan and Rita maintained their calm and tried to console her, but Radha felt as if her entire world had fallen apart. It was as if the sun that had illuminated their marital life from the mid-heavens had suddenly set. Sudden darkness descended in her life. Crying bitterly, she clung to Tapan.

She wailed, "Son, I've lost everything. I don't know what sins I must have committed that the almighty is punishing me!"

"Mom, happiness or sadness, are subject to our past Karma of previous birth. What can we do if we were destined to enjoy lesser happiness? Therefore, have patience and try to accept the unhappiness that has been heaped upon you."

"But how can I live my life all alone?"

"Why do you think you are alone? Aren't Rita and I here with you? Even grandpa is with us! Look Mom, we both are going to live here with you now. So don't you worry!"

For a long time calm prevailed. Suddenly the telephone rang. Tapan picked up the receiver. It was Ivan calling from Sohali Island.

Handing over the receiver to Radha, Tapan said, "It's Ivan."

"Hello . . . ." Radha's crying voice trailed.

"Bhabhiji, I know how you must feel. It must seem as if the heavens have fallen on you. But we are helpless before the wish of God. Keep up your courage."

"Where can I muster courage from? My whole world has collapsed. He left us a few weeks ago saying that he was going to Malaysia. How and when did he come to you?"

"He came to us two days ago. Iqbal was with him. Both of them left to view the scenic natural beauty of the island. Suddenly their helicopter collided with a high hill. We made extensive efforts to retrieve the dead bodies from the deep ravines, but with no success."

"Ivan, how is your daddy?"

"He is deeply shocked by this incident. I pray to the almighty to give you strength to bear with these painful moments."

After that Ivan spoke to Tapan, and then he hung up.

Later, Ivan phoned Dr. Iqbal's family to console his wife.

Kanaiyalal found it hard to endure the loss of his only son, Sanatan. He thought that it was he who should have died at that age. But all of a sudden such an incident occurred. He strived to control his grief. At night, when he retired to his room to sleep, his eyes would fill with tears. It looked as if God had spoiled his old age. He also realized how grieved Radha was. They both tried at times to ease their sorrow by reading the holy Geeta. He used to fall sick quite frequently in those days. Due to his old age his immunity system too, had gradually weakened. Whenever, he saw Radha clad in a white sari, making her looking like a hermit, her bare forehead and bangle-less hands, his heart bitterly wept within. Gradually, one after the other the days passed. Somehow, they endured the shock of Sanatan's death.

After about three months or so, suddenly one night, Kanaiyalal complained of severe chest pains on his left side. He was sleeping alone in the room. It was almost midnight. Within minutes he was sweating profusely. Somehow, he pressed the bedside switch. The room was illuminated quickly as the fluorescent tube lit-up. He frantically tried to locate a Sorbitrate tablet to place under his tongue, but failed. His hand swept away a jug of water placed on the side-table and it fell on the floor with a loud clatter.

Hearing the sound of the water jug falling, Radha rushed into the room. Pressing his hand on his chest, Kanaiyalal lay in the bed. She called out loud to Tapan and Rita, who appeared within minutes. Rita mopped the water from the floor. Tapan telephoned the doctor and requested him to come immediately.

Kanaiyalal lay on the bed in a state of semi-consciousness. His eyes were roving here and there. Although he tried to speak, he couldn't utter a word. Inaudible words emerged from his quivering lips. Radha located the Sorbitrate tablets and placed one in Tapan's palm saying.

"Quick! Place this tablet under his tongue."

Tapan did as instructed. Meanwhile, the doctor rushed into the room. He held Kanaiyalal's hand to feel his pulse and checked his blood pressure using the stethoscope.

"It's a massive heart-attack." With these words, he began massaging Kanaiyalal's chest. Eventually, the heavily breathing and anguished body of Kanaiyalal turned calm and lay flat, before the doctor could administer any further treatment. The doctor declared Kanaiyalal dead. Radha and Rita cried inconsolably.

It was hard to believe the sudden death of Kanaiyalal just four months after the demise of Sanatan, but everybody felt helpless before destiny. Soon, Radha controlled herself and consoled Tapan and Rita.

A few days later, they had almost overcome their grief.

One day, when Tapan returned from the office he didn't find Rita at home. He asked Radha, "Mummy, where has Rita gone?"

"She had to consult the lady-doctor. That is why she has gone to her mother's home."

After a while Tapan said, "Mummy, I feel that we have become hapless following the death of papa. After the demise of grandpa, the house seems empty, doesn't it?"

"You've done well that you have decided to come and live here with Rita following the death of your papa. At this moment, I'm thinking, without you two, what would I have done?"

"Look Mom, you have taught me that the cycle of happiness and sorrow always revolve during our lifetime. You have taught me not to let happiness go to my head and not to lose heart in time of despair. We come into this world with our share of happiness and unhappiness."

"What you say is correct, but son, when we lose our loved ones, all these words of wisdom suddenly become meaningless and the mind becomes imbalanced. Anyway, now Rita's delivery date for her child is fast approaching. It is better if she lives with her mother."

"She refuses to leave you on your own."

"But you know well that my health is good. Besides, our houses are not very far away. If necessary, either we can call her or I can go there. Let her stay with her mother. I have no problem. Here, because of the deaths of your papa and grandpa the atmosphere is already heavy with sadness. Let her be away from it. It is imperative for her to change the place and to be away from such a gloomy environment. Explain that to her."

"Yes Mom, I'll explain that to her when she returns home."

At night, Rita returned home very happily. Radha advised her about the care she needed to take during her pregnancy. Rita used to get overwhelmed by her love for Radha. Her feelings and attitude towards Radha had totally changed. Radha had considered Rita even more precious to her than a daughter.

That night, Tapan conveyed his mother's thoughts to Rita.

Rita replied, "All right, Tapan. I will do as you and your mummy say, but listen to me now."

"What is it?"

"Ramesh Shetty is pressurizing my daddy and now he is unable to bear it."

"A week ago when your daddy met me in the office he had told me about his meeting with the RAW officers."

"When I went to our home, he opened his heart to me. He cannot talk to Amma about all these things. Tapan, hearing my daddy I am also afraid of the situation. In fact, he met the RAW Official, Subodh Banerjee, and acted as he had advised."

"What did he say?"

"He advises to stretch out the time as much as possible and then attack at the opportune time."

"What does that mean?"

"Daddy told me that if we don't decide on anything in this matter, we might lose the gamble."

"You are right, Rita. Those ISI agents are so ruthless and cruel that if things don't happen according to their wish, they will not hesitate to use guns. They move about without a care for their own lives."

"Do you think Pakistan will succeed in snatching away Kashmir from India?"

"Only the future has the answer to that. But doesn't Pakistan control over half of Kashmir presently? The rulers of Pakistan have been taking undue advantage of the goodwill of India. It's a pity that the central government cannot lift the section 370 for Jammu and Kashmir that was imposed five decades ago. Even these days billions of rupees are spent to conduct the administration of Jammu and Kashmir every year."

"Where is the peace in the lives of Indians, and especially in the lives of the Kashmiri people despite such massive expenditure?"

They continued talking past midnight.

The next evening, when Tapan went to leave Rita at Ramamurti's house, they found Ramamurti seated lost in deep thought. Greeting them he said, "Welcome, Tapan and Rita."

They went to the inside room.

Ramamurti said, "Thank God you have come. I have been thinking of telephoning you today."

"Why, what has happened?" asked Tapan.

"Today, I was at the RAW office. They have drawn up a plan."

"I see!"

"Yes. Now, when Ramesh Shetty calls. I will have to obtain information about the meeting time and the venue. I will have to proceed carrying the original microfilms. The RAW officers would be lurking around in plain clothes. They will move in at an opportune time. Just thinking of it, I shiver with fear."

"Daddy, if you stay courageous, we shall be able to conquer them."

For a long time, Ramamurti and Tapan discussed the situation. Four days later, Ramamurti called up Tapan. He informed him of his scheduled meeting with Shetty in the dilapidated temple on the back of Surajkund Lake in Thane.

Tapan reached his home early in the evening. Radha was surprised to find him at home early.

She anxiously asked, "Are you all right, son?"

"Oh yes, Mom!"

"Why are you home early today?"

"I have got to meet someone now. That is the reason why I am early."

"Would you like to have tea?"

"Sure."

Sipping tea, Tapan was lost in thought.

Suddenly he asked his mother, "Mom, one thing which pains me is, why do some of our Indians turn traitors?"

"Maybe they were nurtured on evil ideals."

"But shouldn't man nurture ideal thinking to make one's life progressive?"

"All that depends upon the individual. Although your papa has passed away, his good deeds are still remembered with reverence in this country. No Indian would be unaware of your papa's work. Dr. Bhabha, who acted as an inspirer and a dreamer of atomic age strived hard to usher in the green revolution in India. This way, your papa too, worked day and night to crystallize the unfulfilled dreams of Dr. Bhabha. I suffer from only one thing and that is the fact he could not realise his dream of evolving world peace during his lifetime. Although, he achieved glorious success in the field of nuclear technology, remaining dedicated to the nation but he couldn't unite all the nations of the world."

"Mom, I promise you that I will spare no effort to crystallize papa's dreams. The ideals cherished by papa are inspiring me within every moment."

At five in the evening he left his home. Tapan had resolved that at night he would follow Ramamurti, without telling anyone, in order to protect him.

Ramamurti had told Subodh Banerjee that Ramesh Shetty would arrive at nine o'clock that night. Subodh Banerjee had made complete arrangements to nab the ISI agent. He took four policemen along with him in his jeep. He instructed two senior police officers to arrive there on motorcycles. By eight o'clock inbthe evening, all of them reached the forest and hid behind the bushes.

Take up your positions! Subodh Banerjee gave the order. At forty-five minutes past eight promptly,

Ramamurti reached the dilapidated temple. He gazed around with a sense of fright. His heart was pounding violently from within. He was experiencing discomfort in such an eerie place.

Meanwhile, Ramamurti heard somebody's footsteps. He was alerted. Banerjee too was ready. A man with a masked face moved forward. It was difficult to recognize his face. He came closer to Ramamurti and asked hoarsely.

"Ramamurti, have you brought the original microfilms?"

Ramamurti recognised the cruel voice of Ramesh Shetty.

Ramamurti replied, "Yes, I've brought it."

"Excellent! Hand over the cover to me. We'll check the microfilm. If it is found to be original, money will be sent to your home. If you try to play any tricks, you'll pay for your act."

Ramamurti moved forward holding the cover in his hand. He was trembling with fear. Before he placed the cover in the outstretched hand of Ramesh Shetty, a bullet whizzed past the ear of the stout man in the darkness.

"Hands up and surrender at once. You are surrounded from all directions!" a loud powerful voice said.

"That won't happen!" Angrily Altaf, the terrorist, who had accompanied Shetty in case Ramamurti would double-cross them, opened fire indiscriminately and shot in the direction of the sound. Two accomplices had also joined Altaf and Shetty, and were hiding in the bushes to protect them.

For a moment everything was quiet. The sudden change in circumstances prompted Ramamurti to escape with the cover of microfilm in the opposite direction. Altaf fired at the escaping Ramamurti. He fell to the ground. Seeing this, Subodh became alert.

Two motorcycles sped ahead. The policemen from the jeep also began to fire.

"If you want to live drop your guns and raise your hands!" one of them said.

For some time silence descended. Slowly four men emerged from the bushes with their hands raised. The policemen moved ahead to arrest them but, suddenly, the stout man called Altaf emerged from behind the bushes holding Tapan by the neck. He moved ahead closer to the four men.

One man placed the revolver on Tapan's temple and shouted, "If you fire at us, this man will die."

Subodh Banerjee was shocked. How did Tapan fall into their clutches? His imagination ran wild, but there was no time to think.

One of the four men kept the barrel of the revolver to Tapan's head. They laughed cunningly. Once again the revolvers shone in their hands.

"Mr. Banerjee, we thought, what if Ramamurti was deceiving us? Thinking thus, we abducted this man and kept him with us as a hostage. If you venture to shoot us he won't remain alive." They said of Tapan.

"Uncle Subodh, don't worry about me. I am willing to accept martyrdom for the nation, but either capture these terrorists or kill them."

After everyone heard what Tapan said, the atmosphere became still.

For a moment Tapan thought and then he tried to snatch away a revolver from the grip of a terrorist standing close to him. Altaf was very alert. He pointed his gun at Tapan's temple and fired three bullets in rapid succession. Blood spurted out.

Immediately Subodh Banerjee moved forward quickly with the policemen. Headlights were switched on. Surrounding the terrorists from all sides they began firing. All five terrorists were killed, and, three policemen lost their lives.

Late that night when Radha was informed of Tapan's death, she felt as if her world had truly ended. The cruelest blow of destiny shattered Radha's heart.

⊰❈⊱

Chapter 35

Hearing the news of Tapan's death Louis alias Sanatan experienced grave shock. He was thoroughly shattered. The brave hearted Sanatan couldn't control his tears. Patrick alias Iqbal, Ivan and William expressed their condolences.

"Mr. William, I fail to understand for what sins God is punishing me. I wanted to accomplish a unique and auspicious task for entire humanity. Why does the almighty place obstacles in my way?"

"Louis, don't you forget that God always tests only good men."

"Just four days ago, after the inauguration of the laboratory, having begun the work for world-peace, I was happy thinking that a great task for the benefit of humanity at large was being accomplished by me, at the cost of my kith and kin. But today, having learnt the news of the death of my dear son, Tapan, I am shattered."

"It doesn't befit a person like you who is an accomplished scientist, and has great understanding and wisdom. Wipe your tears and compose yourself."

William wiped the tears rolling down the cheeks of Louis.

"I am thinking that at this time I should be beside Radha, but I cannot do so."

"Oh yes! It is necessary. But a few months ago, in order to initiate a mission for the sake of humanity at large, you and Iqbal declared yourselves dead and assumed the new names of Louis and Patrick. Since that day Sanatan and Iqbal have been dead from the world. Hence, how could Louis be with Radha at such a time? You will have to remain engrossed in your work, in order to forget your anguish." William said gravely, patting Louis on the back.

"Mr. William, I had with great difficulty swallowed the bitterly painful decision to declare Radha a widow in the public eye. That was followed by the news of the deaths of my father and then Tapan. Now, Radha has turned helpless. How will she be able to live?"

"Louis, tell me something; do you have faith in God or not?"

"I do, I absolutely have faith in the almighty."

"Now, my second question is; do you want to crystallize your dream of ushering in world-peace or not?"

"I have relinquished my household and came here only for that purpose."

"Lastly, my third question; won't you consider yourself lucky for the life that you have lived when you will ultimately achieve success due to your expansive invention made through your efforts put in over the years?"

"Mr. William, you are absolutely right; but at times it becomes difficult to restrain the mind. Not only patriotism, but also the mantra of world-peace is engraved on my heart."

"In that case forget everything, and get on with your work."

"I don't know why the thought of meeting Radha came into my mind?"

"After all we are ordinary mortal beings. Besides, you needn't be worried. Ivan and I often make phone calls to India and will continue to do so." William said, placing his hand on Sanatan's shoulder.

"If you will allow me, I'll go to India and meet Radha," Ivan said.

"That's a good idea, Ivan. Certainly, you should visit India accompanied by Mr. William. You both will be able to greatly contribute to easing Radha's pain." Louis said, his face brightening.

As they were talking, the telephone rang. William picked up the receiver, and said "Hello!"

The telephone operator of the laboratory asked from the other end, "Sir, is Mr. Louis or Mr. Patrick there?"

"Yes, they are both here!"

"Would you kindly send them to the lab, please?"

"Sure!" William replaced the receiver and said, "We will talk later. You both are required in the lab."

Sanatan alias Louis and Iqbal alias Patrick headed towards the underground laboratory.

The work in the laboratory was going ahead slowly but very well. A team of select scientists from all over the world were working there. Everyone was busy with their work. Louis and Patrick ensured that no obstacle stood in the way of the laboratory. Whenever anything was needed those instruments or implements were quickly brought to the laboratory.

While interviewing all the scientists who were working in the laboratory, Louis had told them, "I want all of you to bear in mind that the work being carried out here is solely meant for world-peace and is very secret. Do the work allotted to you with the utmost diligence and integrity. I am hopeful of your wholehearted co-operation."

All the scientists were diligently working on their tasks. All their needs were regularly provided. They had chosen to come and stay here, leaving their homes and families for the realization of the great mission of world peace. They all knew that only in the case of an emergency could they leave the island, but only on condition of maintaining absolute secrecy about their stay there.

In this way, all the scientists were living there together under an oath of secrecy.

All the scientists were dedicated to their work. Arrangements were made for their entertainment at various places and no time restraint was placed on them, but even so, most of the scientists remained engrossed in their work without consideration for day and night. They were striving to complete their allotted tasks as soon as possible.

Louis and Patrick received daily reports about their families from Ivan and William and felt happy. They were sure that they would be able to achieve their aim in no time if the scientists continued to strive in that manner.

Louis and Patrick regularly received news of what was going on in the world, but nobody on the outside had any idea of the activities going on at the laboratory on Sohali Island.

One evening William and Ivan talked to Louis.

"Louis, we will depart for India tomorrow. We will return in about four days. Do you want me to say anything in particular to your family?"

For a while Louis thought deeply with his head lowered.

Then he said, seriously, "Radha took pride in her son, and often said that if my mission of world peace remained unfulfilled, Tapan would accomplish it. But destiny had a different plan. While conveying your words of condolences, tell her explicitly that the dream of world peace will be surely fulfilled."

"Louis, leave it all to me. We will definitely succeed in healing the wounds that have been inflicted on Radha's heart."

"Mr. William, you are like my father. Since you cherish the feelings of world peace in your heart, you have dedicated all your wealth to such a noble and benevolent task."

"The sacrifice you and Patrick have made is much greater than my sacrifice. I understand your anguish." William said. "The ardent desire to do something spectacular for the nation and leaving your loved ones and cutting off all contact with your family for the new dawn of entire humanity will never be forgotten by the coming generations."

"I am merely striving to my best abilities for world-peace. I don't know how far I will succeed in my mission. I just need blessings of the elders like you. May I say something to you, Mr. William?"

"Yes, you may say it."

"There is hardly anyone, among the wealthiest and richest in the world, who would ever think of using wealth for the benevolence of others. When I think of your noble contribution, I feel that I shall always be inferior to you. You shall always remain great, in my eyes."

"Louis, you might consider me to be a great man but the feeling of love for the world community is greater than the love for one's family. The former is in abundance in your heart. The challenge that you and Patrick have accepted to make a place for yourselves in the hearts of the lovers of World Peace, and your dream of world-peace that will crystallize, will never be forgotten by the people of the coming centuries."

"Mr. William, I believe that the reason for being born as a human is to be benevolent to everybody in the world."

"Well . . . . well, we have talked enough. You and Patrick must have your dinner with us tonight." After a while William added,

"I hope that you didn't have any difficulty in procuring things for the laboratory?"

"No."

"Just ensure that the work does not become stagnated at any time. If you face any difficulties, let me know in person."

"Mr. William, you provide everything for me before I need it, so what need do I have to complain?"

As they were talking, Patrick came to them, almost running.

He said, "Louis, a large fire broke out when Joseph and Roberto were carrying out some experiments in Lab 3. Thankfully, the fire was extinguished before it spread. Otherwise, it would have affected other laboratories and would have become very dangerous. Joseph and Roberto have been admitted to hospital with severe burn injuries."

"Patrick, let's go to the hospital." Then looking at William, he added,

"Mr. William, see you at the dinner."

Both of them reached the hospital. The doctor said,

"As timely treatment was received Joseph and Roberto have been saved. Both are out of danger."

After returning from the hospital accompanied by Patrick, Louis reached the damaged laboratory.

The next day, William and Ivan left for India from Sohali Island. During the flight both had extensive discussion as to what and how much to tell Radha.

Placing his luggage in the suite of Hotel Oberoi Towers, Ivan dialed a number. Hearing a familiar voice, he said,

"Bhabhiji, it's Ivan. I have just arrived in Bombay."

"How nice! Welcome! How is Mr. William?"

"He is fine. He is here with me."

"How lovely!"

"We're here on a business trip. We're planning to be here for at least four to five days."

"In that case, why don't you come directly to our home?" Although these words slipped readily from Radha's lips, she immediately turned sombre remembering Sanatan. Then she quietly asked,

"When are you coming over here?"

"At four o'clock this evening."

Before she could replace the receiver, she couldn't suppress a sob. Her throat was choked with grief.

Ivan called out from the other end, "Are you crying, Radha?"

"What else can I do? God's games are strange. If he bestows happiness on us, he drenches us in oceans of joy and when he chooses to heap sorrows on us, there is no limit to it. I have lost Sanatan, his father and by the time I overcame the sorrow of losing them both, my son also left for the heavenly abode leaving his wife, Rita and me, hapless. To whom can I tell my tales of woes?"

"Look Radha, have courage. If you break down in this manner, what will happen to Rita?"

"I just cannot understand what sins `God is punishing us for." Radha couldn't suppress her sobbing.

"Radha, have patience. Daddy and I will come to you at four in the evening at your house."

Quietly Radha replaced the receiver. Rita was seated beside her. Both were weeping. Who can console whom?"

At four in the evening accompanied by William, Ivan reached Radha's house. Seeing them her eyes welled up with tears.

Ivan said, "Whatever was destined to happen has happened. We are all just helpless."

"Ivan, you know how contentedly I was living. After Sanatan left, I told myself to spend my life with Tapan's support. But that dream, too, is shattered."

"My dear daughter," William said looking at Radha's haggard grief-stricken face. "We are all helpless before God's wish. Sanatan had ignited the torch of world-peace. I'll continue to strive to keep that torch burning. Have faith in me."

"Bhabhiji, shake off your sadness. Have faith in God. He will have mercy upon us all." Ivan tried to console Radha.

As they were talking, Rita entered the drawing room carrying a tray with tea and snacks. She smiled respectfully and gracefully at the guests. Looking at beautiful Rita, William said, "Dear child, you also need to have courage. Don't forget that you must take care of your health, too."

"Mr. William, we somehow manage to gain strength to live through each other's warmth and affection.

Although, the doctor said that Rita is due to give birth in four days, she has decided to live with me, instead of living at her mother's home." Radha said.

Having enjoyed tea and snacks, William said, "The door of my home is always open to you. With just one call from you, your brother Ivan will come rushing to you to help you. The chain of love and affection that unites our two families will never be broken."

"It is certainly my great luck that I have received the warmth and affection of an elderly person like you who is so religious, benevolent and affectionate. Many times Sanatan was most appreciative of you. I hadn't met you then. But having met you now, I realize how correct Sanatan was! Mr. William, you certainly are divine . . . . an angel!"

"I fully intend to crystallize Sanatan's dream one day. Dear Radha, I can only assure you that I will certainly ensure the realisation of the dream of world-peace cherished by Sanatan." William pronounced firmly.

Listening to William's words, Radha's face glowed with happiness. As Ivan and William rose to their feet to leave, Rita said,

"We won't ever forget that you have come to our home all the way from Sohali to console us. We've received additional strength to live our lives by your coming."

"Now that we have strengthened our business relations with India, we'll have to come here often." Ivan said.

Before the guests left, Radha and Rita insisted that they would come for dinner on the following day, to which they agreed. They didn't wish to hurt the feelings of Radha and Rita by refusing the dinner.

On the following day, Ivan and William arrived for dinner at Radha's house. She introduced Shalin and his wife Madhavi, who had come to help Radha with the household work.

As Rita did not appear for dinner, William asked, "Where has Rita gone?"

"She has been admitted to the maternity home, just this afternoon."

After the dinner the guests left in the happy atmosphere.

The next day, Ivan and William were due to depart for Sohali Island. On that day, Radha telephoned them and gave them the good news.

Rita had given birth to Tapan. Jr. and both the mother and the newborn son were hail and hearty.

———◆———

Chapter 36

When Aziz Maqbool reached the Saifuddin hospital the sun had already set. When he entered the special room he found his mother, Nafisa, whose eyes were fixed on the white walls of the room. On seeing Aziz Maqbool, her eyes twinkled for a moment with unsuppressed pleasure. With a wan smile she welcomed him.

Brushing his hand on her head Aziz said, "Don't you worry at all. You will get well soon. I pray to the Almighty Allah to enable you to move around healthily."

Nafisa, who was experiencing difficulty in breathing, lay quietly. Suddenly, the doctor entered the room.

Aziz asked him, "How is she now?"

"It was a serious asthma attack. For a while it was necessary to place her on oxygen. Let's wait for the night to pass. Tomorrow we will see what should be done."

"Even at home she often experiences breathing problems. But after using the pump, she feels better."

"Some blood tests were required to be performed for a proper diagnosis. We will receive all the reports by tomorrow."

When the doctor left, Aziz also came out of the room. A nurse was looking after Nafisa.

After some time the chairman of the Pakistan Atomic Commission, Dr. Asif reached the hospital. Aziz affectionately received him. Having looked at Nafisa briefly, they came out of the room and sat on a sofa in the waiting area.

Aziz began talking against India.

"Would you believe that for me every moment is highly precious? The inferno of the feeling of revenge has been burning incessantly within me round the clock since the day I made my promise to my father on his deathbed. Until I have my revenge on India, I won't be able to have mental peace. Everyday I make plans and disregard them at night. Yesterday I met uncle Mastan. By the time I had conjured up a new plan and put that into action, I received the news of the serious illness of my mother and that made me rush here."

"What do you have to do now?"

"As soon as my mother returns from the hospital my plan will be ready. I just hate India. I won't be able to rest in peace until I destroy that blasted country."

After a couple of days a meeting was fixed in Dr. Asif's cabin. The moment Aziz entered, Dr. Asif asked how Nafisa was. While they were talking, the Air Marshal Salim arrived with a scientist friend, Ahmed.

"Ahmed, I've heard that your trip to Holland was successful and I believe that you propose to visit China. Is that true?"

"Earlier, I thought of going to China; but I will not be going now. I am continually talking to the Chinese officials, who are India's greatest enemy. China provides us with excellent cooperation and support.

"Isn't it true that the last time when you accompanied Iqbal to China, you obtained a satisfactory amount of technological information on nuclear technology?" Dr. Asif asked as he looked at Ahmed.

"Yes, Iqbal and I had developed a much closer friendship with the Chinese officials. But now I can decisively say that we may have to exercise greater patience as Iqbal has died. But I can assure you that in a short while, we shall be able to manufacture the atom bomb indigenously."

"Ahmed, an atom bomb must be made as soon as possible." Aziz piped up.

"We already have procured enriched Uranium to make atom bombs. The reactor at Kahuta is working at full production. The scientists are working with all their hearts and soul. Soon we shall be able to produce atom bombs."

Listening to Ahmed, Aziz was filled with a feeling of happiness.

A couple of months later, General Karim Abdullah summoned Aziz to his office.

"Sir, you still remember me after such a long time has passed." Aziz said.

"Aziz, since we met last, what progress have you made?"

"Sir, I make plans almost every day and disregard them. But truly speaking, my soul is restless. Until such time as I bring India to its knees, I won't have peace."

"Why don't you meet Dr. Asif for this purpose?"

"We had at least three meetings. Nevertheless, even after thinking a lot, I have not been able to evolve a plan that would be firmly set in my mind. But I am certain that I shall be able to think of a viable plan. You may not realise, but I am just worried I might die . . . ."

"Oh hell, Aziz, such thinking doesn't befit you. Don't you ever think in such a way. Aziz, you are aware that next month I will be proceeding on a tour of

America as well as other Islamic nations. In my absence you will have to protect our nation. The ISI officer Mastan was telling me that hundreds of terrorists have been infiltrated into Kashmir to perpetrate heinous and bloody skirmishes in the valley." General Karim Abdullah presented his plan for the future.

"Sir, kindly do not worry at all. I am in touch regularly with the Chiefs of the Army and Navy. At the right opportunity, I will strike India. Not only that, but after striking it, I will devastate it and thus avenge the insult of my father."

"I know, Aziz; the blood of Islam flows very quickly through your veins. I am also aware that you will even put your life in danger to accomplish your oath."

"One thing I can definitely say that I no longer care for my life, but if I cannot devastate India, it would be the greatest setback of my life."

"I am sure that the Allah will guide you perfectly towards your aim."

"At times, I wonder if we could somehow have a technique by which we could jam the radars of the enemy and bombard their strategic targets and installations. I am filled with such intense desire to accomplish my task."

"Whatever you propose to do should be done only after considerable thinking. Besides if necessary you should seek the advice of Dr. Ahmed, Dr. Asif and Mastan. But do remember, if we drop a bomb in the Indian territories, their military is not going to remain silent. They might strike back vehemently and we may have to lose Pakistan."

"Due to such fears, I encounter difficulties in putting my plan into action."

"In the last war that we battled with them, we sustained greater damage than any expected benefits. Thousands of our soldiers had to surrender to India, and were imprisoned. Our general soldiers lost their lives. Pakistan's economy also suffered quite a devastating blow. Our nation has come to be recognized as a terrorist state. Henceforth, the action plan should be such that our nation has to bear a lesser brunt." Karim Abdullah grimly painted the realistic picture before everybody.

"Sir, is it not possible to engage India in battle with the support of other nations?" Aziz asked as he looked at the General's face.

"The purpose of the forthcoming trip is aimed precisely at mustering the support of other nations in our crusade."

"America supports us in all sorts of ways. If our defense forces are fully prepared and remain alert round-the-clock, it will be due to the American support." Aziz said.

"But, Aziz, why do you forget that America virtually cuts off our hands. In order to keep close tabs on the movements of the defense forces of India the American military officers and most of the secret service agents strive to spread their roots very deeply. We have to pay a heavy price to procure the latest weapons."

"Anyhow, we cannot do without the American support presently. In order to enhance our economic prosperity we will always get support from the Islamic nations, so we shall soon be able to recuperate our economic strength." Aziz corroborated the viewpoint of the General.

"In fact, we have extended our hand of friendship towards the Gulf countries a number of times and many of the nations have provided us with a large amount of support." After a short pause Karim Abdullah added,

"Most of the nations cannot help themselves from indulging in the large-scale annihilation of mankind. Just remember your own past. This has been going for over thousands of years. Everybody wants to spread their own kingdom. In order to develop one's empire, the roots of the religion should spread deep and wide."

"Sir, can't we aspire to unfurl the Islamic flag all over the world?" Aziz asked.

"Every religious leader deeply aspires for such a thing. But when different sects of religion violently quarrel among themselves, how can such days ever emerge? You are well aware that, just recently, violent skirmishes occurred between the Shias and the Sunnis in this very city of Karachi. Many lost their lives. Curfew had to be imposed in different parts of Karachi. Now, if the religious leaders continue to fight among themselves how can the Islamic flag flutter all over the world?" Looking at his wristwatch General Karim Abdullah suddenly said,

"Aziz, no matter how long we keep talking, we will not have enough time to discuss this. Before I leave for America, it would be better if you show your plan to me. If that is not possible you may proceed ahead with the assistance of Dr. Asif or Mastan, during my absence. Well, I wish you the best of luck for the success of your plan."

Aziz rose to his feet with a smiling face. After shaking hands with the General, when Aziz left the office the darkness of night had already enveloped the earth. When he went and sat in the car he experienced tremendous pressure from within, until he reached home. He kept his eyes tightly closed; lost deep in thought.

Time elapsed. Gradually and slowly Aziz's willpower began to falter. Many times he would stumble into his house in a mentally deranged state. Despite conducting meetings with Dr. Asif and Mastan, the ISI officer, he couldn't arrive at any conclusion. Aziz desired to apprise General Karim Abdullah of his action-plan before he left for America. But somehow his mind remained in turmoil. With the onset of night he would lose control over his composure and he would drown himself in bouts of drinking.

One day, as he was talking to his mother, he suddenly experienced a severe chest-pain. He pressed his left chest with the palm of his right hand. He was sweating profusely. Nafisa was bewildered. She made him lie down on a bed and summoned the doctor on the phone. The cardiologist took his cardiogram. He was given medicines and an injection. The doctor gave certain instructions to him in a sombre tone. He asked for Angiographies to be performed as he suspected blocked arteries. The decision of performing by-pass surgery was to be taken only after the results of the Angiographies were received. The doctor forbade Aziz from straining himself and ordered him to avoid drinking liquor.

Aziz heard the doctor's instructions but didn't pay any heed to them. Disregarding the advice of his mother, he began to go around after just three days of rest. At times he suffered from bouts of severe migraine and he used to clasp his head with two hands.

Razia was a secretary of the President. Sitting before a computer she used to handle all the tasks assigned by the President. Since the President, Farokh Azam was on a tour of the Gulf countries, she was relatively relaxed.

Razia had a love affair with Aziz. Taking advantage of that, one night Aziz called her to a room in a hotel. After they enjoyed their time with one another, he asked,

"Razia, would you do me a favor?"

"Tell me."

"Promise me; after I complete what I have to say, that you won't turn your back on me."

"What's so important?"

You must promise me first. Only then can I tell you my plan." Saying this Aziz placed a bag full of wads of currency notes in front of her. Seeing so much money, Razia was taken aback. After a while she said,

"All right, I promise, but tell me what I have to do?"

"You will have to send a coded message from your computer to my office."

"I do not follow."

"Send me a coded message—"The sky is red," which will be received by me at the nuclear center. Immediately I will go into the private office of the President and type the message, as given by you, into the computer there."

"Then?"

"Instantly a message box will appear on the computer screen that a jet fighter plane is ready to take-off. Immediately, I will press the red button and fly the jet fighter plane loaded with atom bombs hidden in the hills of Baluchistan, and attack Ahmedabad."

"So, you are planning to go to war with India."

"Yes Razia, I don't know how long I have to live. I have already had a heart attack. On my father's deathbed I promised him to avenge his insult that he had to bear during the last war of 1971. Now, the time has come to fulfill that promise."

"But, the President, Farokh Azam and General Karim Abdullah are both out of the country. Would you dare undertake such a tremendous risk at this time?"

"I have already had discussions with Dr. Asif and the General. Today, I have this golden opportunity. I will fly the aircraft and if necessary, accept martyrdom."

"No, Aziz no! Before undertaking such a dangerous mission why don't you seek some proper advice?"

"The plan I have decided on is absolutely perfect. I just need your co-operation. I have brought all the money I could find in my house, in this bag, for you."

"I am deeply frightened."

"Razia, you don't have to worry. Tomorrow you will get your passport and air-tickets for London."

Late that night, when Razia left Aziz she was lost in deep thought.

Two days later, Aziz Maqbool was ready to undertake a very dangerous and drastic deed, after he received a coded message from the President's office.

Carrying a megaton bomb, Aziz Maqbool flew the jet fighter high into the skies. He muttered under his breath praying to Allah,

"Oh Khuda, please have mercy on me. Please grant me enough strength to fulfill my promise made to my father."

Traversing through the skies of Jodhpur the jet fighter cruised towards Ahmedabad. The radar of Jodhpur had hit a technical snag that night. Suddenly, the brave Indian soldiers saw an unidentified aircraft flying overhead. Having confirmed the availability of a service revolver, headgear, a radio, and telephonic equipments, as soon as Brigadier Jimmy received a scramble signal, he ran towards the jet fighter. Immediately he flew his plane in the sky. Jimmy began firing with an automatic gun. Fighting ensued in the sky.

When Jimmy did not receive any response from the Chief Air Marshal seated in the jet fighter, he began firing from the 30mm gun. Suddenly, the sounds of a siren echoed throughout the city. Before anyone could understand, Aziz Maqbool dropped a bomb on the lands of Ahmedabad from an altitude of twenty thousand feet from a burning bomber aircraft.

❖

Chapter 37

Terrible dreadful night!

Painful cries of deep anguish!

On that fateful night when the atom bomb fell on Ahmedabad City in the famous Manek Chowk, millions of men and women and children were fast asleep. All of them perhaps, had been dreaming of the wonderful morning when they would awake, but contrary to that, those sleeping and dreaming people of Ahmedabad would never wake up again.

It was as if a massive wall of heavy atmospheric pressure had suddenly been built. It moved forcefully ahead for two and half miles within ten seconds. All the buildings and structures that came in its way were flattened to the ground, like a house of cards. People living in those buildings met their end without any inclination of their fates. Many were buried alive under the debris of the crumbled buildings.

The spot where the atom bomb had struck generated heat measuring 5000 degrees Celsius. Fire spread all around due to a sudden windblast, which spread devastation for miles.

The explosion of the atom bomb created radioactive waves, which shattered the physical constitution of the human beings. Besides, the radioactive waves adversely affected the landmass and water bodies. Suddenly, the water was sucked away. From nowhere black tar rains lashed the grounds. The long-term effect was to be felt by the people of a future generation in the form of serious ailments like cancer.

Massive buildings crumbled as if they had been shaken by tremors of a ruinous earthquake. In the spot where the bomb had struck, a thousand square feet ditch two hundred feet in depth was created.

So many buildings, such as a mosque located near Dhalnipol and Astodia Chakla were turned into ruins. All the way from the Railway Station, ST Stand, Law Garden, Vadaj to the Dariyapur gate, all the buildings standing tall came crashing down. While thousands of people were fast asleep, enormously heavy and gigantic debris crushed them alive. Initially, some noises were heard from all around, but soon they were followed by a few cries of the trapped victims. And then very soon absolute silence descended akin to the eerie silence of crematoriums. All around spine-chilling stillness prevailed.

Intermittent painful cries and terrified shrieks added ghostliness to the stillness of the night and the entire atmosphere seemed frozen up throughout the city. Soon the appalling cries of pain ended with the ultimate arrival of death. The devastating power of this fusion bomb was far greater than the bombs dropped on Hiroshima and Nagasaki in 1945. Nobody in the world, except the Japanese, had ever seen such a brutal and crass dance of the God of Death. Over three million people died from their injuries, within just minutes. The thermo-nuclear heat of the bomb and the shockwaves began to create a mushroom of dark cloud high above the sky of Manek Chowk.

Gradually, the devastating effect of the atom bomb began to spread. In all the areas within three kilometers radius from Manek Chowk as the center point, comprising of Mani Nagar, Juhapura, Ghatlodia,

Nehru Nagar Char Rasta, Naranpura, Sabarmati, Bapunagar, Saraspur, all the large buildings and towers standing tall didn't collapse, but not a single creature or a human being living within them survived due to the tremendous amount of heat generated by the nuclear explosion. In a few seconds millions were swallowed up in the jaws of death. In the first three seconds, due to the tremendous pressure of twelve pounds per square inch exerted by the tornado of heat wave created by the bomb explosion, the walls of the buildings within a region of three kilometers were blown up. Vadilal Hospital was razed to the ground whereas several floors of the civil hospital crumbled up as if a giant hand had swept them away. The powerhouse was reduced to rubble. Electrical and water supplies were irreparably damaged. Those who were saved from being buried under the debris of the buildings caving in were burnt alive by 5000 degree Celsius of heat generated by the explosion. Such a horrible and dreadful dance of death had never been seen before.

When daybreak came, the entire Ahmedabad city was enveloped by darkness and for many weeks to come the city was not to see the light of the sun. All the water bodies like the rivers, wells and lakes for miles on end were polluted by radioactive dust released by the explosion of the nuclear bomb. It was to be the beginning of a months-long severely cold nuclear winter. The atmospheric temperature was to plunge below—300 and the city was to witness a tremendous amount of snowfall. A heavy dark cloud of smoke of over a thousand tons was suspended in the sky, which was to block the sunrays passing through the ozone layer. As the ozone layer over the city was torn apart by the nuclear explosion, the ultra-violet rays of the sunlight were to bring with them certain dangerous ailments, such as cataracts, cancer, and other serious diseases for mankind. After many months, when the clouds suspended in the sky descended, serious epidemics were to spread in the villages, towns and cities in the vicinity, which caused cases of dysentery, diarrhea, hemorrhage, hair loss and even blood cancer.

Though, Aziz Maqbool dropped an atom bomb in a fit of madness, the Indian soldiers did not falter. The President and the Prime Minister of India made a joint decision and within minutes, an atom bomb was thrown using an intercontinental ballistic missile fired on Karachi. Several areas of Karachi such as Bunder Road, Soldier Bazar and the Military Cantonment were enveloped in blazing fire erupting from the burning buildings and armament depots. Millions lost their lives and thousands of buildings crashed down.

Suddenly gusts of wind began to blow at a speed of 500 miles. The chilling cold winds virtually froze the people to their bones. Fiery fires were burning in and around Karachi city and in the adjoining towns. Thousands were running away from the devastation wherever it was possible.

Within hours, the entire world was discussing the war which broke out between India and Pakistan. Most of the nations thought that Pakistan was merely threatening India with a nuclear attack, but when Pakistan dropped an atom bomb on the Indian soil, all the people of the world sat up in shock and disbelief. A mentally deranged, psychotic and unbalanced Air Chief Marshal Aziz Maqbool of Pakistan had shocked the world by his suicide bombing. He fulfilled the promise he made to his father at the cost of his life, but in doing so he had pushed millions of innocent lives into the crushing jaws of death.

Beholding such a terrible facade of death and devastation, entire humanity trembled with fear for days to come. Thousands and thousands of people left their villages, towns and cities fearing that devastation was following them. The grief-stricken people left their native places and without caring to look back for their kith and kin, just plunged ahead to save themselves with whatever little they could carry with them. Their hearts were pounding with fear. The roads and streets were filled with the corpses strewn about. Within seconds, thousands stopped breathing and dropped like flies owing to the grave misuse of the scientific invention. Hundreds and thousands of fear-struck men, women and children were running away as fast as their wounded limbs could permit. Everyone was aiming for the zone of safety far away from the devastation behind. It seemed that their fearful cries were frozen on their lips. Their bewildered eyes were wide with terror as if they had sensed death jeering them and running alongside them at a rapid pace.

Professor Bansi Patel, with the group of running people, too, was trying to muster as much strength as possible to increase his pace. He was bewildered to see a sea of corpses of human beings and carcasses of animals strewn about on the road. What was ironic was that even the birds of prey like vultures, kites and crows were also roasted to death, swept away by the heat waves!

Stumbling and falling in the darkness, Professor Bansi Patel was craving water and suddenly he felt dizzy. He seemed to lose his balance, and fell to the ground. Leaving behind the limping Professor Patel who had become weakened by hunger and thirst, all his companions ran ahead.

Who could ever stop human beings from perpetrating such horrible acts? Perhaps, we cannot change the history but can wenot make efforts to build a better future? Luckily, an ambulance drew up on the road and the driver saw Professor Patel stumbling and falling on the road. He stopped the vehicle to pick up the limp body of Professor Patel.

When Professor Bansi Patel was admitted to the hospital of Dr. Sukumar Trivedi in Bharuch, located in a safety zone and far away from devastation, he was unconscious. Dr. Trivedi immediately administered emergency treatment to him. The whole hospital was filled with injured and sick people. The atmosphere of the hospital seemed terribly grim with the cries of pain and the suffering of the sick and injured. Dr. Trivedi, his associate doctors and nurses, devoted themselves to the services of the grief-stricken teeming crowds of patients with dedication.

The next day, Professor Patel slowly opened his eyes. Dr. Trivedi rushed to check on his condition. He checked his pulse and heartbeat. Then he asked, "What's your name, Sir?"

"B . . . . a . . . . n . . . . si . . . . Pa . . . . te . . . . l!" he stammered. A moment later he asked, "Where . . . . Am . . . . I?"

"You are in the hospital. You will be better soon," Dr. Trivedi said, and gave some instructions to the attending nurse and sped off to attend to other patients.

Suddenly at midnight, Professor Bansi Patel awakened from his sleep. The dreadful scenes he had witnessed a few hours previously flashed before his eyes, and terrible memories saddened him. He had been appointed a lecturer at Petlad College. He would commute daily from his residence at Vallabh Vidyanagar to Petlad.

He stayed back at Petlad the previous night at his colleague, Professor Rajni Shah's house after the conclusion of the cultural program in the college. In the morning, after his bath he had dressed and was thinking of leaving for Vallabh Vidyanagar, when he saw groups of terrified people running for safety. Talking to a neighbour, Bansi Patel realised the seriousness of the situation and ran for safety. Today, he had been saved. He stared at the ceiling for some time.

Suddenly, hundreds of thoughts swarmed around in his mind. The memories of the atom bombs dropped by America on Hiroshima and Nagasaki in 1945 came back into his mind. One and a half lacs people out of the three and half lacs population of Hiroshima and three quarter lacs people out of two lacs of Nagasaki were killed. Following that, three million more Japanese citizens met a tragic death by succumbing to the thermo-nuclear effects of the bomb. Having visions of such terrible scenes often shook his whole being.

He was vividly reminded of a news story he had read of a nine-year old girl, Kim Hook, who had fallen victim to a Napalm Bomb dropped by Captain John Plamer. Kim was surrounded by gasoline smoke and fluids. As she was running away to safety, her clothes were set alight. When the entire garment covering the little girl got burnt her skin began to melt away also. The pressreporter, Paula Siemens, who was covering the war, was also running away to safety and when she turned around, she saw the naked Kim running desperately and as fast as she could, crying in terrible pain. Paula immediately pointed her camera at her, and froze that fateful picture of the burned and naked Kim Hook running to save herself from death. As if driven by some supernatural power, Kim Hook managed to escape from the destructive reach of the bomb and then collapsed out of severe exhaustion. The unconscious Kim had been transferred to a hospital, where her life was saved.

This report that he had read in a newspaper came alive vividly before his eyes. Like Kim Hook, he also fell unconscious after reaching the safety zone and luckily his life had been saved. Silently he prayed and thanked God.

For a while he lay in silence. The cries of pain from a woman in the nearby bed shook him. Bansi was filled with deep sorrow hearing about her pathetic condition from her relative. The woman was Nikita, who had sustained several burn injuries. Her wounds were bleeding profusely. Dr. Sukumar quickly appeared. He administered an injection to her to prevent infection. When silence prevailed, Bansi tried to sleep, but failed miserably. Vivid visions of the terrible scenes he had witnessed flashed through his mind like a horror film. Suddenly he let out a suppressed sob and silently prayed God.

"Oh, God! If so much devastation can be caused by an atom bomb of such small power, entire humanity as well as the birds, animals, insects, and vegetation would be completely destroyed if all the atom bombs made by man are released. Why can't the scientists think of creating an invention which can cause the death of the person who plans and engineers such ghastly and demonic weapons and resultant mass destruction?"

Shortly he was reminded of his childhood friend, Sanatan, who was living in Bombay. He had gone to express his condolences to Radha upon receiving the news of Sanatan's tragic and accidental death. Radha had been living with great expectations of her son, Tapan. People generally reflect that angelic human beings are needed more in the heavens and so God calls back such people from the world. If Sanatan had been alive today, wouldn't he have striven to alleviate the suffering masses of the world?

Thinking about this, he stared at the hospital walls.

A nurse approached his bed. Moving a hand lovingly on his head she said, "We have informed your wife at Vallabh Vidyanagar. She should arrive at any moment now."

"Thank you, sister!"

"For a long time I have been observing you. You seem to be lost in thought. Are you not able to sleep?"

"No sister, so many thoughts have engulfed my mind, and because of that it is impossible for me to get any sleep."

The terrible memories and your perception of what you have just been through are still fresh in your mind. I will administer an injection to you that will help you sleep well."

The injection had its desired effect. Bansi Patel slid into a deep sleep. Early the next morning, when he opened his eyes, he saw that his wife, Usha, and son, Vishal, were standing before him. Seeing them, tears welled up in his eyes.

He spent a fortnight at the hospital. At last, Dr. Sukumar Trivedi allowed Bansi Patel to go home.

Exactly two months later, he visited Radha at Bombay. He was shaken by what he had heard from her. Her youthful son, Tapan, was also dead. It was as if Radha's world had fallen apart.

"Radhabhabhi, I have personally experienced the devastation that can be caused by the terrible powers of war. What a great misfortune occurs when a man becomes an enemy of another man! Sanatan had been asking me to come to Bombay to listen to him talk about world peace, but I couldn't make it. And when I have finally come here, neither Sanatan nor Tapan is alive. How sad!"

Saying this Professor Bansi Patel began to weep aloud. After a while, he described the situation of Ahmedabad and the devastation caused to the city.

Listening to him, tears trickled down Radha's cheeks. When he saw Radha in tears, Professor Bansi Patel said, "Radhabhabhi, whatever was destined to happen has happened. Wipe away your tears."

"Bansibhai, while you were talking I remembered Sanatan. He couldn't fulfill his dream of World Peace that he had cherished since his childhood. Our aspiration that his son, Tapan would fulfill his dream has also been shattered. His life has been taken by God's wish. Now, I don't know if Tapan's son will be able to realize his grandpa's cherished dream," Radha said and began to weep aloud.

"Radha, control your emotions. God shall give you justice even if he is late in doing so. Besides, a cycle of happiness and sadness alternates in the life of a man. If your life is tragic today; it will become happier tomorrow. Perhaps, the sunrise of tomorrow could bring some joy for you. God always tests his people at every moment."

"Bansibhai, I am aware of what you are saying. I wasn't pained so much by the death of Sanatan as I was pained by Tapan's demise. He also had dreamt of spreading world peace; but now will such a dream ever be realized?"

"I am sure that his dream will be realised some day. I am sure that God will listen to our prayers. The seed of world peace had been sown in Sanatan's mind ever since his childhood days. Somewhere in the world its echo will be heard." Bansi said.

"It will be sufficient if man is humane enough. Our popular poet has expressed the true religion of humanity, but right from day one Pakistan has been acting against the religion."

"You know very well that ever since the day the Kashmir issue was referred to in the UNO, Pakistan has considered India its arch enemy, and has been abusing India. No noble task is being undertaken by Pakistan, but they just abuse India. Despite usurping control over a part of Kashmir they still are not satisfied."

"How long will this continue? The people of both nations have to live with intolerable pain due to such enmity. Why can't they understand such simple logic?" Radha asked as she looked at the Professor's face.

"All of these Pakistani leaders have such logic, but they selfishly crave controlling other political powers. The Indians and the Pakistanis have both been born from the same soil, so why do they fight as enemies?"

"The basic reason for the enmity is the different religions of both communities. We are Hindus and they are Muslims. We worship cows, whereas, they eat the flesh of cows."

"I know, Radhabhabhi. Iqbal and Sanatan were not only great friends, but they were as close as real brothers. If this wasn't so, Iqbal's father, Yakub would not have shielded Sanatan from an assassin's dagger during the communal violence that broke out following the partition of India and Pakistan in 1947. In fact, many Muslims today are very anxious to see the flag of friendship unfurling with their Hindu friends. But, as the scheming of the Pakistani rulers is failing in Kashmir, their intelligence agency, the ISI, has been perpetrating secret insurgency operations for a long time now. The ISI agents are trying hard to spread their network from Kashmir to Kozekode and Mehsana to Meghalay. Their sole aim is to eat up India from within, like a termite."

"That may be so, but what I cannot understand is why the Muslims of Pakistan dropped an atom bomb on India and caused the heinous annihilation of the peacefully living Muslim subjects of India? Around twelve crores Muslims are living in Pakistan, but in India, around sixteen crores Muslims are living in peace and prosperity. In the large cities and towns of India and especially in Ahmedabad, we can see mosques in almost every street. We also see so many temples alongside them." Radha said.

"I feel that the Pakistani leaders are fooling their subjects. The majority of the Pakistani population believes that such an attitude of hatred and enmity with the neighbouring nation is in no way desirable. I believe that the mass devastation caused by the atomic bomb dropped in Karachi will cause an eruption of dissatisfaction among the people of Pakistan. I wouldn't be surprised at all if the ordinary masses of Pakistan declare Jihad against their corrupt political leaders." Professor Bansi Patel expressed his opinion with a belief that the picture of Pakistan would undergo a drastic change.

After a while, he asked Radha, "Have you heard any news about Iqbal's family?"

"No, I have received no news." Radha said.

The next day, Uncle Poonamchand telephoned Radha and gave her sad news.

"Ashwin and his wife Prachi are no longer in this world."

On hearing the news, Radha was shocked.

———◈———

Chapter 38

"Iqbal, ultimately Aziz Maqbool dropped the atom bomb on Ahmedabad city. Lacs of innocent people died and millions were rendered homeless. For several years millions of people will continue to suffer from incurable diseases. It was almost as if the people were living a bad dream." Sanatan said with a gloomy heart.

"It was not a bad dream, it was reality. You are aware that the rulers of Pakistan teach young children to wage Jihad against India. The former Prime Minister of Pakistan, Zulfikar Ali Bhutto, had publicly announced during his reign that if necessary the people of Pakistan will eat grass for one thousand years but will not rest until they gain Kashmir. In Aziz's case, the most important aspect was the revenge of his father's insult." Iqbal gave his opinion on Aziz.

"Was it not because of this madness that India dropped a bomb on Karachi? My heart trembles while thinking about the destruction caused on both sides."

"Look here, Sanatan, what has happened has happened. Now we will have to concentrate more on our aim of world peace."

"Were Mumtazbhabhi, Zora and Karim in Karachi?"

"I discovered that when the Karachi port was destroyed, all three of them were in Lahore. I pray God that they are safe and happy wherever they are."

William and Ivan came in while this conversation was going on.

"I have tried to impress on Iqbal that before the conditions in the entire world deteriorate further, we must try to save mankind through new discoveries and concrete steps," Sanatan said.

"Look here Louis; to begin with, avoid addressing each other as Iqbal and Sanatan. Everyone here knows you as Louis and Patrick. It is better for everyone that way. Now let's talk about research. We gather from your conversation that all the scientists are devoutly and continuously doing the tasks assigned to them," William said with a smile.

"Dad, if we are to gain control over sunrays then the maximum credit goes to Louis. Even Patrick studies all the scientific books throughout the day and presents his summaries to Louis," said Ivan.

"I am sure Ivan, that one day we will succeed in our task," William spoke with resolute confidence.

Looking at Patrick, Louis replied, "All nations armed with nuclear weapons were in high spirits until now. But now they are panicked while thinking about the destructive power of even an ordinary bomb. Patrick and I are thinking about only one thing and that is how to destroy all the world's nuclear bombs, nuclear weapons and missiles. When we are able to destroy all nuclear weapons the nations spending billions on nuclear weapons, will start spending the same money on social welfare and public benefit instead."

"Louis, your ideas are fantastic and superior. God be supportive in turning your ideas into reality," William said, looking at Louis.

"My heart misses many a beat when I think about the catastrophe that has fallen on millions of people because of nuclear bombs. What I think is this. Many died within a second. It was a quick death for them. They did not suffer neither did they see any suffering. But now, how do we save millions of people from lifethreatening illnesses and diseases arising out of nuclear radiation. That is the biggest challenge." Louis spoke with genuine worry.

"America, Russia, Britain, France and China are afraid that if chemical weapons are not banned, then they will loose their supremacy. 140 nations have signed the Geneva Treaty, yet many of these nations are making chemical and biological weapons considered as the ultimate threat to mankind," Patrick expressed his concern over these dangerous weapons.

"Chemical and biological weapons can wipe out mankind from the face of this planet within a moment. A single chemical weapon can evaporate millions of human beings from this earth. America acts like the Godfather to the world but it has different teeth to show and different ones to chew. America preaches peace and wages a tirade against the production and sale of weapons. On the other hand America has established a military industry. They supplied such weapons to nations who support them. This made them financially very rich." Louis spoke angrily about America's policies.

"America talks about peace and understanding between India and Pakistan after selling weapons millions of dollars worth to Pakistan. How do they have the nerve to do this? India should not make a nuclear bomb and she should not buy these weapons from other nations. American administration keeps talking about such things. In reality America does not like the fact that India buys weapons from France, Britain and Russia. America has sinister plans for India and Pakistan. America hopes that India and Pakistan will continue to fight over the issue of Kashmir; and that these two keep buying weapons from America and therefore will be continuously ruined. America has ulterior motives. I personally believe that America is responsible for Pakistan's bomb on Ahmedabad city," William said while talking about India-Pakistan relations with America.

"I strongly believe that America is helping China and Pakistan to stop India from becoming a self-reliant and powerful nation. India is constantly being made to worry about protecting its borders. America wishes to see India and Russia divided into several parts. America hopes that smaller states like Sikkim, Nagaland, Tripura, Mizoram and Manipur break away from India and become independent nations. But mark my words . . . America's desire to break India will never succeed," Louis said passionately.

"Louis, it is now in our hands to spread peace in the world. If nuclear wars continue like this, the earth will be destroyed. Scientific discoveries which can give peace and happiness to human beings must be made very quickly," said William, regarding world peace.

"Have you noticed one thing . . . that America has not allowed any war on its own land for almost a century? In 1939 when the Second World War began, America was the world's most important country economically. America was saved from the two World Wars. During these two Wars all the big cities of Germany were destroyed by heavy bombarding. Innocent German men, women and children died in air attacks. Every home in Europe had someone fearful of dying in the war. Japan was ruined in the World

War. If we are not able to contain America's blatant arrogance then we will not be able to save the world from destruction." Ivan criticized America's policies and remained quiet for a while.

Then he added, "The entire world knows that war only brings devastation. Even then mankind cannot refrain from war. How many wars have been fought in this world? How many millions have been killed? Yet it seems that mankind is never going to change."

"At this moment I am reminded of a great novel about the World War I "All Quiet On The Western Front"; written in 1928. I will never forget a war scene depicted in that novel," said Louis.

"What was so special about that scene?" asked Ivan.

"German soldiers are advancing to attack their enemy. One of the German soldiers is wounded. While running away, he saw something which made him forget his pain. One lance corporal was running alongside him. His entire head was blown away by a bomb shell. There was nothing like a face on his shoulder. Even then his body kept running and blood was gushing out from his mouth."

Everyone was shocked to hear this. There was silence for few moments, and then Louis continued.

"When I read that I could not sleep for an entire night. That lump of flesh, the blown out eyeball, the arm, those limbs . . . they just kept coming before my eyes. How could a headless body run with such speed? It was very painful to imagine all this. I was determined at that very moment that people must be taught about the fierceness of war and that I must even put my own life at risk to avoid all types of war. I believe that God always helps in such good causes. I am sure that we all will be able to play a role in keeping peace in the world." Louis looked at everyone with some hope.

"Even today the effects of that novel have not diminished from my mind," he added.

"My heart is disturbed whenever I remember the images of war ravaged Europe. The most beautiful and magnificent cities of Russia and Germany were severely damaged during the two World Wars. The ancient city of Warsaw in Poland was destroyed by heavy bombarding. The famous cathedral of Monte Carlo, which was like home to the people of Europe was destroyed. We shall never see anything as beautiful as that Monte Carlo cathedral ever again. Famous architectural monuments of Italy, France, Germany and other European cities were ruined in the war. Several art treasures were robbed. Many works of art were burnt in the bombardments. The entire Berlin Museum was burned to ashes. On 6 May 1945 bombs were dropped over the famous Berlin Museum. 434 precious paintings were turned into ashes. Classic paintings by famous French and Italian painters like Bottichelli, Caravazio, Titian, and Veroniz as well as German masters like Kanach and Menzel were lost during the war. The war turned art into ashes," said William talking about war and art in Europe.

Everyone was listening intently to William.

"Mahatma Gandhi waged a non-violent war against the British to free India from their slavery. However, the debate on who would become India's first Prime Minister became very critical. Gandhi advised Nehru to let Mohammad Ali Jinnah become the first Prime Minister of India. But Nehru was determined on becoming Prime Minister. Gandhi warned that this may result in civil war but Nehru remained adamant. Nehru became the first Prime Minister but Hindustan was divided into two parts; India and Pakistan. Today, the same Pakistan has waged a nuclear attack on India and the results of that act are before our eyes. Elimination of nuclear weapons is the most important aspect of world peace," said Louis.

"The United Nations was formed after the World War II. The idea of complete disarmament was mooted. But we all know how sincerely this idea was implemented! Several nations went to war and the United Nations was a complete failure in avoiding these wars," said Patrick about the UN.

"As you all know, the six permanent members of the Security Council make 80 per cent of the weapons manufactured in the world and they even export arms. Except for Japan, all major powers possess nuclear weapons. That the policies of the UN have been nothing more than phony can very well be understood from this," said Louis.

"There are no limits to this hypocrisy! From 1965 to 1967 America relentlessly bombed North Vietnam. But the Vietnamese were indirectly supported by the Chinese. So the major arms to Vietnam were provided by China. On several such occasions the Chinese openly challenged the Americans. Even then America could not do anything to China. How can we enforce world peace without mutual respect, trust and faith?" Patrick said.

"America is the biggest arms dealer in the world. It is playing a dangerous game of buying and corrupting the political leaders of the world and inciting them against each other. If the other nations are not careful about this, America will continue to become rich and other nations will become poor. There is a definite possibility that the world's arms dealers may have bought out the leaders of India and Pakistan. The wealth of Europe and America is derived from their arms exports. The weapons industry determines the politics and the economy of Europe and America in such a manner that the African and Asian nations will continue to fight with each other for years to come. If you pay careful attention to what I am saying, the reason why world peace is not becoming a possibility or why the poverty of nations is not reduced will become clear to you," Louis said.

"I believe to that extent that if India and Pakistan decide to live peacefully with each other and reduce their expenditure on arms significantly for five years, the populations of both nations will be able to live happily and peacefully. But if this happens, how can the wealth of America be sustained? America clearly understands that world peace and economic inequality affect the entire world. And that is the reason why America ensures that it influences the entire planet through its coercive powers," said Patrick.

"I understand that the Pakistani secret service, the ISI, have gathered the terrorist army comprising of Sudanese, Afghani, Lebanese, Egyptian and Bahraini professionals near Jammu and Kashmir. Whenever they get an opportunity to dodge the Indian armed forces, they sneak into the territory and kill innocent Kashmiri Pandits."

"Pakistan has a clear cut policy on this issue. They want to keep the issue of Kashmir burning at all costs. They want to gain publicity in the international forums and force India to accept the mediation of the United

Nations or even America and China," said Ivan. He paused for a while and said, "India has announced on several occasions that there can only be bilateral talks on the issue of Kashmir. India will never accept the mediation of any third party or other nation," he said.

"Pakistan wants to take advantage of India's stated policy. Pakistan hired terrorists to kill Hindu Pandits in Jammu and Kashmir one by one. They want to spread terror so that the remaining Hindus also leave the valley. And if under any external pressure a plebiscite is taken in future then only the Muslim population will remain present to cast their vote so that Pakistan can push forward the Islamic Nation theory to strengthen its claim that the local population want to merge with them," Louis explained Pakistan's policy.

"So it is important that we now concentrate our efforts to bring lasting world peace," William said as if summing up the entire argument.

"Louis, I am not able to understand why God is testing us so severely! After Tapan's death I went to India with my father. There I met Radha and Rita. As long as I was staying in India, I could never imagine that Pakistan would ever do something as drastic as dropping a nuclear bomb on Ahmedabad," said Ivan looking at Louis.

"I knew Aziz Maqbool for many years. Therefore I can definitely predict that his father's ghost weighed so heavily on his mind that he could have gone crazy any day," Patrick said candidly.

"Louis, you go ahead in your work. And if you face any difficulties, let me know," said William.

Ivan and William rose to leave.

As they were about to go out the door, the telephone rang. Ivan picked up the receiver. He heard the familiar voice of Radha talking at the other end. Ivan's heart shuddered, listening to the stories of the tragic atomic war waged by Pakistan.

Chapter 39

On hearing the news of the sad and sudden demise of Ashwin and Prachi in the bomb blast, Radha went to pay her condolences at Uncle Poonamchand's Andheri residence. She was visibly disturbed by what Uncle Poonamchand had to say. Even Vinod came home from America to console his father.

Although two months had passed, Poonamchand and Vishakha were still unable to overcome the grief of the sudden loss of their children, Ashwin and Prachi. Vishakha would often miss them dearly and would burst into tears. Poonamchand would console her by telling her, "It was predestined. Why are you still brooding? We were living such a good life. Nature got jealous of us and took our children away."

Vishakha cried in response.

"We have to assume that they were destined to have a very short life span." Poonamchand said.

"You try to understand that we have lived our life to the fullest. But they were so young. It was our time to go, not theirs. They were still like a bud, waiting to blossom into flowers and yet were nipped in the bud." wailed a dazed Vishakha.

"I understand your sorrow, but we are slaves of destiny," said Poonamchand.

"Pakistan will be destroyed because of the way they killed lacs of innocent people. On the spur of the moment I agreed to send them for the pious darshan of Shrinathji and their fates were sealed at that moment" There was regret in Vishakha's voice.

"Time and tide wait for no-one. They were destined to leave us. They would have died in a crowded street in Bombay. Circumstances are just excuses and we are mere puppets in the hands of the Creator. After darshan the bus reached Ahmedabad. The bomb blast occurred and killed them mercilessly", said Poonamchand resignedly.

"They were coming from the divine land when the blast occurred and their last vision was of the beautiful Lord", said Poonamchand.

"Before they understood what life was, their lives were extinguished by being burnt and charred to death. Oh! What a gruesome sight it must have been!"

"It is no use to continue crying. Let us thank God, that the heir of our dynasty, our other son, Vinod, is still alive. Lacs of people have died without heirs to carry on their legacy. This war has left many homes orphaned," said Poonamchand.

"It is difficult to accept the truth. The Indian army took revenge by bombarding Karachi, so that they also understand how painful it is", sobbed Vishakha.

Rasikbhai also faced a similar tragedy when his daughter Purvi and son-in-law Prafull, who lived with their extended family, were holidaying in Ahmedabad, and were buried alive under the debris.

"Today you are undergoing the same agony. That day you had consoled your brother. You meditate and think of God. It does not solve any purpose that you sink into depression by reliving your nightmares again and again", said Vishakha as the dam of sorrow burst again and tears started overflowing from her eyes.

"Who will console whom?"

Radha entered the flat at that time and on seeing her, Vishakha hugged her and said, "We are both sailing in the same ship. Daughter, we have lost everything."

"Mummy, don't cry any more. By crying your sorrow will manifest itself even more. Won't it affect your heart and mind?" Vinod asked.

Radha went to the kitchen and fetched two glasses of water. Vinod had to plead with his parents to drink a sip of water to wet their dry and parched throats. Soon there was silence and they said nothing for a while.

"Radhabhabhi, while I was in America, I was shattered when I got the news of Tapan's accidental death. It is as if God is giving us a severe test. It seems as if some black magic is being conducted on our family and someone's evil eye is fixed on us. In just one year alone, so many of our family members have gone to God's kingdom. Everyone born here has to die one day, but still this kind of sudden death in youth is beyond imagination and heart-wrenching." Vinod said, looking at Radhabhabhi.

"Vinodbhai, do you know that Sanatan died in a helicopter crash. His father could not withstand the shocking news and suffered a massive stroke. By the irony of cruel destiny, your nephew Tapan, like Sanatan, also died patriotically for the country within a span of a few months. Now I hear that my brother and sister have also perished! How will I be able to bear the loss of five of my loved ones and how am I supposed to carry on with my life?" Radha asked as tears rolled down her cheeks.

"Bhabhi, nobody can alter destiny. We all are mere pawns in the hands of the almighty. But to face this with a strong heart and to learn to accept such challenges with a smile, is what life is all about." said Vinod.

"My son, when you reach our age, only then will you realize our misery. To talk is very easy but to live that way is very difficult. When I think about Radha, it strikes me that Radha's good life came to an end within a short time."

"I now only have my daughter-in-law Rita and my grandson Tapan Jr., whom I call Pappu, to call as family and I have to stay alive until he grows up. My brother, Pulin, who went to meet his friends in Mehmdavad, has also been affected by the bombing. Though his life is saved he has become just a living dead body. Doctors are still unable to diagnose his ailment."

"What has happened to him?"

"He has remained bewildered for days. He has been so deeply affected that he starts screaming like a madman at the slightest noise."

"I have seen the pictures on American TV and I still cannot forget those vivid and horrifying pictures of destruction."

"Manjari collapsed while watching those pictures and ten year old Manish was forbidden from watching those gruesome and horrible pictures," said Vinod giving the details of the bomb blast.

"In Ahmedabad, lacs of innocent lives were lost. More people were killed than in Hiroshima and Nagasaki," detailed Radha. Amid the conversation Rasikbhai and Aunty Manjula from Matunga came in to offer their condolences.

"Poonamchand, we have to live our lives in this darkness and deep sense of loss. There must be no Gujarati family in Bombay who doesn't have a relative living in Ahmedabad. Everybody has lost a member of their family. I have lost my daughter and sonin—law and you have lost your son. Now the radioactive cells will degenerate all over which will damage mankind for generations to come. I hope that God will give strength to all mankind to endure such hardships." Uncle Rasik said,

"When did you come from America?"

"Two days ago."

"How are Manjari and Manish?"

"They are fine. Manjari could not get leave from work, so was unable to come and Manish had to attend school. Even Purvi and Prafull were killed."

"Yes, Vinod, nature has been very cruel to the people of Gujarat. It's as if God has cursed the people of Gujarat. So many people are suffering from unknown diseases caused by the aftereffects of the bomb. Epidemic diseases are spreading like wildfire. This calamity has driven lots of people to poverty and death. In today's world we need scientists like Sanatan, and only then will the world prosper." Uncle Rasik told Radha thoughtfully.

"Sanatan fought for peace until his last breath, but unfortunately he died suddenly and his mission remains incomplete. He had immense knowledge of atomic science and his thoughts were always governed by his principles. Patriotism ran deep in his veins," Vinod paused suddenly and spoke to Radha.

"Can I ask you something, Bhabhi?"

"Yes, please do."

"As I was away in the states for some years, I could not meet Sanatan, but India will always be proud and remain indebted to him for his remarkable contribution towards development in the field of the expansion of nuclear and atomic sciences. But, I wonder whether these energies are for carnage or peace? Why did Sanatan spend all his life experimenting on various nuclear projects?"

"From what I can understand of Sanatan, his principles are for world peace but his research for nuclear weapons was guided by political pressure. Now because of his inventions, we were able to bombard Karachi."

"But the truth is that lots of people were going to die after this. How can world peace be attained after all these deaths and misery?"

"I am saddened to say that even Sanatan would often be exasperated and curse the Government. But, the Government would declare that nuclear devices are necessary for self-defence. So Sanatan would get back to his research projects with more diligence. But his chief motive was to bring about world peace. He strongly believed that nuclear weapons should be abolished from the planet earth and their manufacturing should also be stopped immediately. Nuclear energy can be used in two ways. Peace and carnage."

"It is used in Medicine, Agriculture and Industries for the betterment of mankind. Dr.Bhabha dreamt of a green revolution brought about by using nuclear energy. Various research institutes in India are pursuing this cherished vision of Dr.Bhabha, and many nuclear plants have been installed in various cities for the production of nuclear energy. This would result in bettering the lives of millions and spread peace among the people. Sanatan also shared the same dream, but ironically the dream was nipped in the bud due to his sudden and untimely demise." Radha said with a deep breath.

"Was Tapan following in his father's footsteps?" asked Vinod.

"Yes, I assumed that he would continue this noble work after Sanatan's death. But, tragically, he also had to sacrifice his life for this cause. To fulfill their vision, we will inculcate these values in Pappu so that he can carry on this legacy. I am sure that one day the people of the world will be united and it will become a peaceful place". Radha reiterated.

"How's Rita? Dad was saying that some antisocial criminals killed her father."

"Vinodbhai, luck has turned hostile because something evil keeps occurring at regular intervals. Rita's father died accidentally and she lost Tapan also. The only solace left with us now is Pappu."

"Bhabhi, nobody's life is a bed of roses or like a smooth sailing boat. Life is a cycle of happiness and sorrow. Everybody has to go through their fair share of bad fortune and joy."

"You are right, Vinodbhai. We remember the Almighty only in our times of misery and hardships. We seldom thank the Creator during our happiness and success!"

After a moment of deliberate silence Radha suggested that they would return back home.

"We will give you a lift back to your house." Aunt Manjula told Radha.

"Poonamchand, please look after yourself. Since you are the only caretaker of Vinod and his mother, put your sadness behind you for their sake."

While standing up Rasik said.

"Oh! Though I try to forget and I know that time heals everything, but still the loss is irreparable and unforgettable," said Poonamchand. "God is the only source of my sustenance. This tragedy has battered my life and soul. I do not know how to soothe my bruised heart."

"These survivors will suffer from lots of epidemic diseases. It's better to die than to suffer from these kinds of diseases which have turned people into vegetables." Rasik said chokingly with bleary eyes.

Uncle Rasik drove in silence towards Sion.

"Radha, I understand your misery. Whenever you need us please don't hesitate to ask. We will always be there for you."

"I don't have any other family who can soothe my heart except you," said Radha. "You have given me strength to keep living and given a new meaning to my life."

"It was different when Sanatan was alive. Today you have to face hardships at every step. But please don't be brought down by the troubles of life. When Sanatan was alive he conquered the whole world, and everybody had respect for him." Aunty Manjula said consolingly. "But, today the world will remember him not by his words but by his deeds."

"Aunty, justice will ultimately prevail. It was etched in his heart to evolve world peace and save mankind. I am certain that one day this dream will come true." Radha said.

"Radha, Sanatan has done very rare and unique work in the field of nuclear science, and for this kind of service to mankind, the people of India should be obliged to him. His only aim of life was to destroy all nuclear weapons and in that process help in eliminating all the terrorists from this world."

Soon they reached their destination.

"We would be delighted if you can come in and meet Pappu."

When uncle Rasik and aunt Manjula entered, Rita was attending to a phone call. On seeing Radha she said "Uncle Ivan, Mom has come, speak to her".

Radha talked on the telephone and then she announced, "Uncle Ivan is coming to Bombay tomorrow to attend a meeting and he will have dinner with us."

A ray of hope arose in Radha's afflicted heart which was manifested by a smile on her face.

———◆❈◆———

Chapter 40

At the breakfast table William asked Louis, "How far have we progressed in our inventions?"

"It's a very lengthy process but we will surely succeed"

"When we have the best qualified scientists researching on our projects we are bound to achieve success at an earlier stage."

During their conversation Patrick joined them.

"Dad, I was extremely happy to meet Radha in India."

"Why?"

"I gave Radha the much needed strength and brought a ray of hope back into her mundane and meaningless life. When I left Radha and Rita after four days, their stoic faces had transformed into lovely wide smiling faces."

Louis was delighted to hear this.

"Ivan, please try to keep in touch with them by visiting them almost every six months and by regularly telephoning them. Their wellbeing is of the utmost importance to me", Louis said, on the brink of tears.

"Louis, please don't be disheartened. I realize your pain and feelings. But you have to give priority to our mission. This kind of research perhaps takes many years but to go through this, you need courage", consoled William, "Don't forget that you are not Sanatan anymore but Louis".

A hushed silence fell on the room so William continued,

"Sorry to hurt your feelings, my friend, Louis. I recently sent Ivan to India to meet your family. You can ask Ivan all about them. I have a meeting to attend at 11a.m." said William as he rose to leave.

Louis fired a barrage of questions at Ivan with as William left.

"How's Radha? How's Rita? How's Pappu coping? How are the other relatives?" Louis asked these questions and more of Ivan. Listening to the answers of his questions, Louis was shocked.

He was grieved to hear about the deaths of uncle Poonamchand's children, Ashwin and Prachi and the untimely and tragic deaths of Uncle Rasik's kids Purvi and Prafull by the powerful bomb blasts. Radha's brother Pulin was also living like a dead vegetable in a semi-comatose state.

Hearing this he burst out, "God, what have you attained by all these disasters?"

He stood disoriented for several minutes. On learning of all these tragedies his heart ached. He said a silent prayer.

"I hope that mankind never has to go through such an ordeal again and I shall invent the remedy for this dreaded disease called the atom bomb. Oh! Almighty, the benevolent and the kind, the omnipresent one, please don't let my tears be in vain," he prayed inwardly.

Afterwards, Louis asked Patrick, "Please visit the Mars laboratory. Ask Solomon and Cyprus that by using electro magnetic waves, could they make progress in a new invention or not? Patrick stood up and marched toward the Mars laboratory.

As soon as Patrick left, Louis continued,

"Ivan, Uncle William is right. After undertaking such an important and difficult mission, I shall not delve into my own family matters or keep brooding over my dead relatives forever. He sent you to India to meet Radha and my other family members. When you all are so concerned about my family, I shouldn't disrespect your feelings by contemplating on my misfortune."

Ivan said, patting Louis on the shoulder,

"Friend, you may be a world famous scientist, but after all you are a mere mortal with human feelings and emotions which sometimes supersede your larger academic mind. So don't be too harsh on yourself because it's very natural to react in the manner that you have done."

Louis spent the whole afternoon browsing through various books in the library. In the evening Louis reached the Mars laboratory. Patrick was in his cubicle discussing work with Solomon and Cyprus. Louis joined the debate. "Everybody knows that petroleum, natural gases, minerals and coal are the three main invaluable resources. They are primarily natural resources and cannot be reproduced again. Therefore we must invent such energy, which is everlasting and will never be exhausted."

"Oh, Sir, will these resources be depleted one day?" asked Solomon curiously.

'No they are found inside the earth after a long process of a million years. In this manner, natural ores and resources like energy sources are utilized in the whole world. It seems that one day there will be a scarcity of energy if it is not conserved from now on and used rationally."

"Then we should invent some energy source that can be recycled and renewed", said Cyprus.

"That's what I want to know. What progress has been made in this field by both of you?" Louis questioned them.

"We haven't been fully successful. Converting sunrays primarily into electrical energy and then into mechanical energy, which in turn converts into electro—magnetic waves, is a difficult process. With ample sunlight and the conservation of solar energy, it is possible that there will never be any scarcity of energy. You are absolutely right. But we have to depend only on solar rays to produce solar energy, which could last forever, if only we could invent more machinery to reproduce solar energy!" Cyprus explained his reviews which he had achieved with his other college friends.

"In future we need to find many energy reservoirs. We have to conduct more experiments, hydroelectricity caused by the high tides of the sea waves causes the sea level to be warmed and the water to change into vapour, which in turn generates energy and lightning. If, we are able to tap all these sources of energy in a natural way then there will be no scarcity of electricity. All these sources can be reused again and again," said Louis.

He continued again "Solomon, tell me does light and sound waves travel at the speed of three lakhs kilometres and then changes to electromagnetic waves?"

"Yes, they do".

"Good, this reminds me of an interesting incident which occurred in my college pal Ravindra's dream."

"What interesting incident?" Patrick questioned curiously.

Louis narrated the dream in which his friend was able to prevent the car from sinking by floating it up to the seashore.

They all listened with rapt attention. They knew that whenever Louis spoke there was always a scientific basis to his tales.

"There was a group of learned sages sitting at the shore. A well-built hefty sage was able to pull the sinking car to shore by some force of the electromagnetic waves. After this exhausting and daunting task he was extremely drained and breathless" Louis opined.

"This proves that our body is a powerhouse of stored energy. If this generated energy is used in a spiritual and physical manner, then the problem of the scarcity of energy can easily be solved," interrupted Patrick.

"So Cyprus, to what degree have you progressed in this experiment?"

"Experiments are in progress, Sir," he answered reassuringly.

"With a single remote control we can open a car and its boot. But can we, with these electro-magnetic waves be able to open a million cars and their boots simultaneously with effortless ease?" questioned Louis.

"We are trying our level best to achieve this, but I regret to inform you that we haven't been successful", answered Cyprus.

"Earlier I cited to you the tale of Akbar the great. Once, his court musician and renowned singer Tansen sung the 'Deepak rag', known as 'the tune of light' and was able to light a hundred lamps with some kind of invisible power emitted by his singing. And once again when the '*Malhar rag*', also known as 'the tune of rain' was sung, they were able to bring about the pouring rains. These sound waves might have caused some kind of electromagnetic resonance and waves. I am trying my level best to work on the principles based on this kind of energy. Though initially I progressed somewhat, now I have faltered." Louis said.

"Louis, in our school days we studied science subjects together. I am very hopeful that we can surely generate electro magnetic currents and waves. Only then shall we discover why all scientists have a crazy wavelength in them", joked Patrick.

"Hey Patrick, great minds think alike" and they all laughed.

Soon after the departure of Solomon and Cyprus, Louis informed Patrick, "Today I went into the library and studied more books. We both had the same thoughts running through our minds, after browsing through similar kinds of books. If we could reproduce from one single wave, which could open the doors of lakhs of cars, then we will succeed immediately.

"You are right, Louis. It will be such a noble cause to invent something that will benefit the whole world and mankind. With hard work and sincere dedication we shall surely succeed. We are the lucky ones who have been chosen to fulfill this noble mission", said Patrick.

"Bravo, Patrick, bravo! You are also in favour of world peace just like me. No wonder our wavelengths match. We both have a clear conscience so we can concentrate on this project. It will be a victory of good over evil, a victory of construction over destruction."

He inspected the laboratory thoroughly. Various scientists were at different stages of their work. Each one was trying to outdo the other in this noble cause. They were deeply involved in theories of nuclear physics, and in Einstein's laws of nuclear fission and fusion. The transformation from one form of energy to another wasn't very difficult but it was not easy either. The ambitious and highly qualified scholars were trying their best to accomplish their mission as soon as possible.

Louis was friendly to all the scientists and tried to create a jovial atmosphere by often cracking jokes with them. Patrick saw to it that their work was never interrupted due to any technical failures. They all worked like a big family and Louis knew each one of them personally.

Years passed. William continued sending Ivan to India regularly to meet Radha. News of each and every person was related to Louis via William. Louis's eyes would fill with tears in awe and respect for William who by now was like a father figure to him. He would always remain indebted to William for giving him the honour of fulfilling this noble cause, which would change the future history of mankind.

One day, tired of being immersed in books, Louis walked out of the library to see a thick green forest before him. The beautifully coloured flowers and dancing butterflies enchanted him. He sat there on the bench basking in the glory of beautiful nature and the breathtaking picturesque scenery around him for quite some time. Suddenly a bright idea came into his mind and he slowly sauntered back to the Moon laboratory.

In the laboratory all were immersed in their work with neverending zeal and enthusiasm. The chief, Michael Bob, and his subordinate, Augustine, welcomed him to their cabin.

"Michael Bob, how far have we progressed?"

"Sir, a week ago we were able to generate the resonance and have managed to cross the great hurdle. All our men are likely to finish this project within two to four months."

'Bravo, Michael! Go ahead and keep up the good work," said Louis, patting him on the back, and minutely studying the final file. He met all the technicians and heard their woes and in return inspired them to work better.

The next day William, Ivan, Patrick and Louis all met to discuss the project. Praising the chief of the Moon laboratory Louis said,

"I am very impressed by the work of all our men from the Moon and Mars laboratories. They have succeeded in fulfilling their mission and in just three to four months the final result will be in our hands."

"Does that mean that in Moon laboratory they have discovered the formula which can destroy atom bombs and missiles by electromagnetic resonance and wave?" William shouted in delight.

"Yes uncle, we are in the final stages. I hope you are aware that America has made a bomb based on fission technology by using plutonium and uranium for the first time. This disaster showed its effect in Hiroshima and Nagasaki. Millions of atoms were scattered all over the place, which produced enormous energy and nuclear radiation. In this heat not only human beings but also iron can melt. In the last fifty years, the American bomb is dwarfed by the destructive hydrogen and nitrogen bomb, which causes less heat but spreads immense radiation. Therefore, the whole universe is under the threat of the destructive nuclear bombs." said Louis sorrowfully.

"I have heard there have already been thousands of atom bombs constructed by now." "Yes, it's true. America alone will by now have 1200 bombs of the finest quality. Even Russia might have the same amount of bombs ready. Britain, France and China might have between 500 to 600 bombs by now. Israel, Iran, Iraq, South Korea and Libya also have managed to make successful nuclear bombs. Recently there was a war between India and Pakistan and they may then have obtained 100 atom bombs. All these countries have modern nuclear missiles. You know that one megaton atom bomb has destroyed countries like India and Pakistan. If there is a World War III now and all the modern missiles and atom bombs are used, this beautiful universe will be destroyed. The whole of mankind, all the creatures big and small, the colourful birds and the thick green foliage will be destroyed to the core." Louis sketched a barren imaginary picture of the destruction to his friends.

"We must save this wonderful planet before it is destroyed," said Patrick.

"I am delighted to tell you all this. Last week I visited Moon laboratory. They were already in their final stages of their work. They have been successful in their experiments that have been tried out on animals and plants. Even Mars laboratory has shown similar results in these four days," beamed Louis.

"We should be able to reach a conclusion as soon as possible to save mankind. After a lengthy process of seven years I can conclude that we have almost reached the end. Atom bombs, missiles, electromagnetic waves and resonances have to be destroyed and used in a constructive manner to save the world."

Everybody was mesmerized by Louis's words.

"Do you really think that there will be peace in the world due to this invention?" Ivan asked Louis.

"Why not, after all, the answer must be given by the intelligent scholars. Did our great grand ancestors not live in peace? Though science had not developed much in the olden days, the people still lived in peace and harmony. As science developed it brought with it disasters in life. And people became greedier and developed various kinds of vices within them. The word 'contentment' seems to have disappeared from the dictionary of the modern day world, and I wish that with this great discovery we shall be able to bring a lifetime of happiness, contentment and joy to all of mankind". Louis told William.

"When there is a will there is a way. Your sacrifice of so many years will never go in vain." Saying this, William stood up. They all departed with shining and happy faces.

Chapter 41

After the nuclear attacks on Ahmedabad and Karachi, fierce fighting broke out between India and Pakistan. Guns were blazing on the border dividing the two countries, all the way from Kashmir to Kutch. The fighting broke out in the streets of Kashmir between Indian security forces and the infiltrators from Pakistan. The religious leaders from Pakistan declared this war, between the two nations, as *Jihad*. Hundreds of people on both the sides of the border lost their lives, properties and homes.

The Prime Minister of India went on the television and radio simultaneously to address the nation. He asked the people to get ready for a prolonged war. He ordered the military to destroy all the enemy and terrorist camps in the vicinity of the border.

A no-holds-barred fight broke out in Kashmir as armored vehicles, tanks and infantry were engaged in face-to-face combat on the border. If India was fighting a losing battle in the Kashmirregion, it penetrated deep into Pakistan from the Rajasthan, Punjab and Kutch borders.

The Indian Prime Minister invoked Russian military support. Russia cautioned Pakistan to stop the war and roll back its military forces. Before Pakistan could reply to Russia, China asked Russia to keep away from the skirmishes. The Foreign Minister of India went to the US, the United Kingdom and some of the European countries to explain the position of India. The US Secretary of State Mark MacLaurin visited

Islamabad. He was told in no uncertain terms that, Kashmir was a part of Pakistan. The American President said if Pakistan did not stop the attacks on Kashmir, they would have to stop aiding Pakistan. The military ruler of Pakistan, General Karim Abdullah agreed to stop the war. But the very next day, he announced on PTV that, Pakistan was determined to snatch away Kashmir. He stated that, before advising Pakistan to stop the war, the US should stop aiding Israel against other Arab countries. Similar statements were issued by the governments of Iraq and Afghanistan. The Iraqi President issued a warning to the US to stop supporting Israel in the Mediterranean region or get ready to face the consequences.

On the other side, war was raging between Pakistan and India. The Indian infantry had already crossed over from Haji Pir across the border from Lakhpat and Khavda in Kutch. The infantry forces were moving rapidly under the air cover provided by the IAF jets and the cover fire provided by the heavy artillery batteries. The forces traversed deep into Pakistan, beyond Rahim-ki-Bazar through Badin and Nagar Parkar towards Islamkot. Badin is the last railway station on a railway line beyond Hyderabad. It is one of the most important army and air force bases of Pakistan.

The Pakistan forces were providing effective cover fire to the Mujahideens in Kashmir as they were making some headway in Gilgit, Poonch, Sopur, Baramulla and Akhnur sectors.

From Punjab, the heavy artillery supported the forward march of the Indian infantry advancing towards Sialkot, up in North, beyond Suchetgarh, and beyond

Kasur near Kot Radha Kishan railway station, on the railway line connecting Lahore and Multan in Pakistan.

In the same way, Indian forces made significant advances from Rajasthan towards Hasipur and Khasipur, on the way to Multan and Bahawalpur beyond Harunabad and Fort Abbas.

Meanwhile, a senior IB officer walked fast into the offices of the Ministry of Defence in the South Block. He scarcely glanced at the soldier coming to attention as he stormed into the office of the National Security Advisor. Half a dozen senior ranking military officers and defense ministry secretaries were seated around a large oval shaped conference table. All the faces turned towards him as he leaned over a thin wiry man sitting at the head of the table. He whispered for a full minute in the thin man's ear. He was Pradip Dikshit. As the IB officer straightened, Dikshit surveyed the faces gazing anxiously at him. All of them had been closeted in this room for the last thirteen hours. Belying his wiry frame, Pradip Dikshit spoke in a rich baritone voice.

With a tinge of urgency he uttered, "It is as we had expected, gentlemen. They are preparing for an all round attack on us."

A balding officer in blue blazer asked sharply, "What about Bangladesh and Malaysia? And China?"

This time Dikshit spoke in his characteristic slow yet sharp speech, hardly blinking his eyes. Staffers in the Defense Ministry joked; Dikshit slept with his eyes open.

"Bangladeshi soldiers have opened fire with mortars and light artillery across our Eastern borders from across Dinajpur and Jessore." Dikshit cast a glance towards the Army chief.

General Shaitan Singh, the veteran of 1971 Indo-Pak war, was a mirthless person. He got up from his seat and walked leisurely towards two large maps and moved effortlessly towards the one showing Bangladesh where it joined India. He studied the positions quietly for barely a half minute and turned towards the war room council.

"We will take on the Bangladesh rifles here." He jabbed his finger at a point on the map. "They should not pose any problem with the kind of armaments waiting to be pressed into action at Midnapore and Burdwan."

He was interrupted by the Air Chief Marshal Rahul Bhandari. "A Sukhoi and Jaguar squadron are both on operational standby at Barrackpore and Hashimara. Also, a squadron of Helicopter gunships is in readiness at Shillong."

General Shaitan Singh spoke in a menacingly deliberate and steady tone, "Gentleman, we had expected that this war would take a religious turn. We were not wrong."

He turned to face Admiral Gurusharan Singh, "Before they expect us to move in, we need to prepare for naval operation and bombard on Khulna, Dhaka and Narayanganj. That will be enough to demoralize them."

The Admiral crisply replied, "That's satisfactory."

While the strategic discussion was in progress in the Defense Ministry in Delhi; thousands of kilometers away, Louis and his friends were holed up in Sohali islands near Malaysia. They were discussing the satellite images they had received about half an hour ago. The satellite pictures showed some movements towards

Kahoota and Chaman in western Pakistan.

Patrick said, "It seems they are preparing once again for a nuclear attack."

"Patrick, I don't think they would risk another attack immediately on India. But possibility of the second attack cannot be ruled out altogether." Louis observed quietly.

"Louis, did you observe how the Indian troops are progressing in Pakistan? The phenomena of the 1965 and 1971 wars are being repeated in the regions ranging from Kutch to Punjab. But, the situation seems different beyond Jammu. In Kashmir the Mujahideens and terrorists are supported by Afghan mercenaries and Pakistani rangers. If something is not done, Indian forces will have a tough time containing the invaders." Patrick said at a length.

William who had been listening silently to them said, "Patrick. Perhaps you have overlooked the surface-to-surface missile batteries stationed at Amritsar, Ambala and Pathankot. These missile batteries have laser-controlled highly accurate missiles. I won't be surprised if India opens its missile fire on the terrorist outfits later today. On the part of the Indians, his could be a defensive retreat in Kashmir."

For a while everybody fell silent. They continued to look at the digital map of Kashmir showing the latest Pakistani and Indian military positions.

But, Patrick's attention was not on the map. His entire attention was drawn towards the television, which was giving the latest news. A newsreader of Saudi Arabian TV was reporting that Israel's tourism minister had been shot dead in an ambush near Haifa. A terrorist group stationed in Iraq claimed responsibility for the murderous attack. Israel's prime minister declared the incident as an attack on their sovereignty and vowed to avenge the assassination. The terrorist group from Iraq declared that, such attacks will be carried out by suicide bombers in Israel, the United States and India.

"Louis, don't you think, the World War III could bring about the devastation of the planet Earth?" Patrick asked.

"Yes, you are right. We have been engaged in research to protect our planet. I am confident that, the Almighty always helps us in such noble work."

The following day when Louis went to the library, he found Patrick engrossed in reading a book. When Patrick didn't notice his presence, Louis moved forward slowly and said, "I see that you are deeply engrossed in reading this book."

Patrick gave a start. He said, "I found this book, 'Intelligent', written by I. S. Skylovsky the famous Russian physicist. It's the most fascinating book. Skylovsky writes, *"in our galaxy there exist over a million planets, which are inhabited by some form of life in as much an advanced stage of evolution as ours.* What do you think of this theory, Louis? Do you think that there is life on other planets apart from Earth, for example, on Mars?"

"Patrick, in my opinion some form of life did exist on the Mars thousands or even millions of years ago. Nevertheless, the entire population must have been destroyed due to pollution on the Mars. Mars has a very thin layer of atmosphere consisting mainly of Carbon Dioxide, Nitrogen and other gases. The highest temperature on the Mars remains at around 100 degree Celsius whereas at night it plunges as low as 10 degree

Celsius. This planet is geologically and chemically quite vibrant. Due to highspeed winds blowing on the surface of Mars, clouds of dust have been noticed there. I believe, in millions of years to come, life could once again evolve on Mars, but, planet Earth could be completely devastated due to pollution." On saying this Louis stared at Patrick.

After a while both friends came out of the library. Crossing over the lush green lawns surrounded by tall trees, they entered the secret rooms. Here they viewed the satellite pictures of the earth and switched on a television channel. Skirmishes had broken out in West Bank between Jordanian and Israeli people.Similarly, many Arabs and Israelis were losing their lives in East Jerusalem on southern side of the West Bank.The Iraqi Air Force fighters heavily bombed Israeli positions in the West Bank and East Jerusalem. While Iraq and Syria were governed by the Shias and Sunnis respectively, they joined forces in hitting Israel hard, with the latter engaging bombing missions over Haifa.

Israel owed its existence to a unique set of circumstances—Western sympathy for Jewish suffering; the political influence of American Jews in securing the support of the US President Harry S. Truman; and Britain's loss of determination to continue its rule in Palestine.

On May 14, 1948, at midnight, the British mandate over Palestine ended and the Jews declared their independence in the new state of Israel. Most of the Arab countries didn't like the emergence of Israel, but due to various reasons ranging from religious differences to commercial considerations, they were never be able to unite against it. Besides, the Jewish community's determination and ability to establish and hold on to their own state played a vital role in making Israel a formidable state in Southwest Asia.

Once again, the armies of Egypt, Jordan, Syria, Lebanon and Iraq joined the Palestinian and other Arab guerrillas fighting against Israel since November 1947. America moved its fleets swiftly its fleets in the Mediterranean Sea. Fighters and stealth bombers took off from aircraft carriers as almost the whole of the Arab world revolted against the arrogance of America.

Far away from the turmoil of the Mediterranean region, the Indian capital was relatively peaceful. The American Ambassador had invited diplomats, local political leaders and prominent civilians to the Embassy to celebrate the declaration of the US independence on July 4. Almost all the invitees had assembled. The Ambassador Mark Robinson beckoned his protocol officer Charles McCartney. He sullenly asked, if the Indian Prime Minister had arrived.

McCartney glanced at his watch and said, "He should be here at any moment now."

"And what about the President of Pakistan? I believe he had agreed to be present."

"Sir, he cancelled his visit about half an hour ago and instead sent a message that, Pakistan protests against your support to Israel."

"So, that's it." The Ambassador was lost in thought for a while. As he was about to move towards the French Ambassador who was sipping wine a little distance away, the Indian Foreign Secretary, Balu Raghunathan moved swiftly and fell into step with the Ambassador.

He whispered, "Good evening, Mr. Ambassador."

The Ambassador turned around to look down upon the Indian official. He raised his eyebrows as if he was asking a question. Raghunathan explained he had an urgent message for him.

"All right, come over here," said the Ambassador and ushered his visitor to a room on the wings of the hall.

"Yes, anything important?"

"Yes, Mr. Ambassador; I have an intelligence report that, some terrorist groups have planned to attack your embassy."

"When?"

"At any time or any day from now on."

"Don't you have more accurate information?"

"No, Mr. Ambassador. We will keep you posted with any information that may be useful to you."

"We are awaiting the arrival of your Prime Minister. He seems to have been delayed."

"Mr. Ambassador, he has been in the meeting with the Chief Ministers of Jammu & Kashmir, Assam, West Bengal and the Eastern states. The meeting was convened in view of the fighting on the borders. It seems that the meeting has been prolonged."

"Why don't you check from the Prime Minister's Office, if you can, if the meeting is going to be so protracted that he will be unable to attend?"

"Sure, Mr. Ambassador, I will report back to you promptly."

After a while Raghunathan informed the Chief Protocol Officer of the embassy that the meeting of the Indian prime Minister would be delayed considerably; hence, he has requested to proceed with the celebration without him. The information was promptly conveyed to the Ambassador.

The Ambassador commenced his address, "*Ladies and Gentlemen, it gives me pleasure to welcome you all on this Independence Day of the United States of America. On this day, my nation adopted the declaration of Independence. The United States has always upheld the democratic values. We have beenagainst every kind of oppression of human beings and terrorism.*

In reference to humanity, I propose to urge all the nations to raise your voice against injustice.

The United States of America believes in the principles of . . ."

In the sudden massive blast that shook the embassy building, Ambassador Mark Robinson's words were drowned . . . .

———❖———

Chapter 42

The entire roof came crushing down on the gathering. The whole building collapsed like a building made of playing cards. For a while, the entire hall was filled with frantic cries and shrieks of the bewildered people. Suddenly silence descended. Dead bodies were strewn all over the place. Many organs of dead bodies were scattered in the surrounding buildings. The diesel operated power plant in the building had also caught fire. The fire spread all over the building. There was chaos in all directions. The painful cries were not heard above the cacophonous din. Because of the fire, the sound of burning wood was heard in all directions.

On hearing the news of unforeseen incident of the fire, nearly a dozen fire fighter engines arrived at the spot and tried to get the fire under control.

The intelligence reports later revealed that after taking off from Safdarjung Airport two helicopters had made an unscheduled landing in a farm on the outskirts of Delhi and had stayed there for thirty minutes.

According to the news which appeared in the newspapers the next day, it was reported that two Pavan Hans helicopters had been hired by a film producer for some aerial shots of Connaught Place in Delhi. Perhaps the helicopters that landed at the farm were the same helicopters. One of the helicopters was crashed into the building and the second helicopter crashed onto the terrace of the Embassy building.

It is believed that when the helicopter was crashed into the Embassy Building, at the same time the fuel tanker carrying a large stock of RDX and full of petrol crashed into the Embassy building, killing some security people. According to newspaper reports, the oil tanker had been hijacked from the Delhi-Gurgaon Highway.

The incident not only shook the Americans but left the whole world stunned. It was later revealed that prominent Islamic terrorist group, Jihadi Mijlis, operating in Iraq was responsible for the attack.

Among those killed in the terrorist attack were senior diplomats. The list of the dead read like a 'who is who' of the international political world. The list also included prominent citizens, bureaucrats and senior military officers from various countries. In all, 493 people lost their lives and as many as 113 were injured. Ambassadors of Germany, Spain, France, Belgium, Japan, South Africa and many other countries were among the dead. The Military Attachee, other senior diplomats, many senior foreign office officials and prominent citizens were either dead or grievously wounded.

Prominent among those who were dead were, the 57-year old British High Commissioner to India, James McLean and his wife Dorothy. They were married in 1959. The young couple had spent a fortnight at the Retreat in Simla for their honeymoon. When James McLean was appointed High Commissioner to India in 1977, Dorothy was very happy, because she still cherished the memories of the beginning of their married life. The next day, they were scheduled to leave for Simla for a weeklong holiday. And here their bodies lay mutilated beyond recognition. That was the evening when many dreams were shattered. Naik Gurbachan Singh of the Delhi Armed Constabulary had received a message by telephone that his wife had given birth to their first son at the SRP Police Hospital. He promised Satvinder Kaur, his wife, that he would buy her a pair of gold bangles, if she gave birth to a son. On that fateful day before leaving for his duty, the 30-year old Gurbachan had promised his wife that, when their son was a month old, they would certainly take him to the Gurudwara. Minutes before the choppers crashed on the embassy building, Gurbachan was standing near the side entrance with his batch mate, Harbhajan Singh. Harbhajan had confided to his pal about his love affair with the daughter of Havildar Major Ramsingh Dhillon. Ramsingh was trying get his daughter married into the royal family of Kapurthala. Harbhajan Singh was halfway through confiding his plan to elope with his sweetheart and at that moment, the choppers struck. Both men were blown by the blast. Late that evening, after about two hours, when the fire was doused after fierce efforts by the firemen, the police found a charred headless torso of a policeman near the side gate. Another badly mutilated body of another policeman was found about ten feet away from the side gate. Primary findings revealed that the headless torso belonged to Naik Gurbachan Singh while the other was that of Harbhajan Singh.

The incident caused great anger among the people of many countries. The Pope described the incident as an attack on humanity. Leaders of almost all the countries deplored the attack on the American embassy. The President of Pakistan, while condemning the terrorist attack said that if America had restrained Israel in the West Bank, the Muslims would not have been so angry and such an incident could have been averted. He described Israel as number one enemy of Islam. The US President called upon all the countries to obliterate the Islamic terrorist groups operating all over the world.

Around four thousand miles down in a South-East direction on a nondescript island a few dedicated men, dreaming of ushering in an era of world-peace, were huddled around a large conference table. Their eyes were glued to the massive television screen. Ivan was working somewhere in the Nuclear Research Laboratory. Nearly three months had elapsed following the terrorist attack onthe US Embassy in New Delhi. By this time the political map of the world had undergone great changes.

"Louis, I think the World War III has broken out. I think this is perhaps the murkiest phase in the human history as a World War is perpetrated on humanity primarily for religious reasons." Patrick observed grimly.

"Hmmm . . . , the reasons for the outbreak of the first and World Wars II were more or less economic and politically motivated." Louis observed.

"Yes Louis, you are right; but isn't it uncivilised and barbaric to fight for religious reasons?" Ivan who had just joined them, commented.

"Basically, religion should be a personal or a private affair. It is related to spiritualism." Patrick said.

For a long time nobody uttered a word. Their eyes were fixed intently on the large TV screen. After a while, Ivan came over to Louis. He pulled a chair and sat close to him.

"What do you propose to do now, Louis? The war among the nations is taking a very ugly shape. When are you planning to put your invention to use?" Ivan asked.

Louis looked at him for a long time. Rising to his feet, Louis asked Ivan and Patrick to follow him into a small meeting room. They seated themselves at a round table.

Significantly, their secret laboratory was designed in such a manner that every small room had a computer with access to Communication Access Control. Louis had painstakingly developed a system to monitor the entire telecommunications being exchanged among the nations through satellites. He had his eyes on the developing war scenario.

"Yes, Louis?" Patrick inquired.

Louis silently tapped on the keyboard and selected certain applications on the computer. Both, Ivan and Patrick watched in silence. Within seconds the screen came alive with the World Map and scrolling text. Finally, He broke the silence. "Look here," he pointed his finger at the screen where Europe was shown on the map and said, "Patrick, new equations are taking place this time around. Two opponents during the World War II—America and Japan—have decided to come together to fight the Communists and Islamic religious forces. Moreover, European nations like Britain, Italy, France, Spain, Portugal, Rome and Germany; besides, Australia, South Africa formed an Allied Force."

"What is happening on the Asian front?" Ivan asked.

"Look for yourself." Louis said.

Patrick read out the text appearing beside the map of Asia. He exclaimed, "Oh! The scenario is changing fast in the Far East and in Northern Asia."

He enlarged the satellite images of Northern Asia. All of them could clearly watch troop movements on Karakoram highway slowly moving from Misgar, crossing over from Khunjerab Pass towards Pakistan's Northern frontiers.

Suddenly Patrick bellowed, "Oh no! I can't believe it."

"What is it?" Louis asked.

"Look at this." Patrick pointed at a spot on the map, squinting at the screen.

Louis and Ivan couldn't understand what was wrong. They peered at the screen.

For a long time, Patrick's eyes roved frantically across the map-like image on the screen. He pushed the mouse cursor very deliberately towards a point on the screen. As he clicked the right button of the mouse twice, the image was enlarged 400 times. Immediately, Louis and Ivan realised what it was that had surprised Patrick. They could now clearly see concentrated troop movements at Rakaposhi at over 7700 meters in height in the Gilgit ranges, near Bannu in Pakistan and around the Jalalabad mountains in Afghanistan.

"What do you think is happening?" Ivan asked.

"Well, from the shape of the vehicles, I can tell you that Pakistan and Islamic fundamentalists in Afghanistan are moving nuclear arsenals in these places." Patrick said.

Louis pressed an intercom switch. A female voice replied,

"This is Mary."

"Check the signals in Northern Pakistan and Afghanistan."

"Louis, I am already doing it. I have intercepted several messages exchanged between various installations from the region you have mentioned. It looks like these military units have been assigned to prepare for biological warfare."

"Alright, Mary thanks. Any further information from the Allied forces?"

"A secret meeting is in progress in the UK right now. It is attended by high ranking military officers of all the countries aligned with the US these days."

"Can you switch to Interior Signal Detection Mode?"

"Louis, the meeting is almost getting over now. But I can tell you what they have discussed in a nutshell. Later on, you can review the entire discussion. I have already recorded their entire proceedings."

"Alright, Mary; tell me."

"The United States has advocated the use of nuclear weapons, if there is a real threat to the world from the Islamic fundamentalist forces. Until then, they propose to continue attacks on their military installations." Mary reported.

"Thanks Mary, kindly forward the disk to me." Louis flicked the switch off and turned to his friends. "What do you make out of it, Patrick?"

"I now feel that great pressure will be exerted on Islamic countries everywhere. We will have to keep a watchful eye on their every move." Patrick said.

"For how long?" Ivan asked, worriedly.

"Perhaps a month or even less than that. This war is not going to continue beyond six months unlike the last world wars. It is already three and half months, since the US embassy was attacked in Delhi."

"How prepared are you, Louis? When do you propose to put your research to use?" Ivan once again repeated his question.

"I am waiting for the right opportunity." Louis stoically replied.

Ivan looked at him with perplexed look in his eyes. As Louis turned towards the door, Ivan called to him from behind.

"Would you like to look at this message I have received a few minutes ago?"

A single paper was held in Ivan's extended left hand. Louis sauntered forward and in one quick swiping movement of hand he took the paper and adjusted his glasses to read. It was an excerpt of the President of Pakistan's speech. The statement was datelined at Iraq on the same date. Standing near Louis, Patrick peered over the shoulder of Louis to read the contents of the letter but he could not read it properly.

The note referred to the crucial meeting of All Islamic Nations held at Baghdad that afternoon. After reading, Louis put this note in Patrick's hands.

Chapter 43

While European countries were united in their fight against religious terrorism, certain countries of the Eastern Bloc decided to abstain from joining forces with the US. They were Russia, Azerbaijan, Kazakhstan, Lithuania and many other countries of Central Asia who decided to keep away from taking sides. China while deploring the terrorist attack on the American Embassy in Delhi asked Pakistan and other Islamic countries to exercise restraint in religious proclamations.

India was already in a bloody combat on its two borders with Bangladesh in the East, and Pakistan in the West. After twelve days of fierce fighting, the Indian forces were only seven Kilometres short of Dhaka. The Hindus in Bangladesh provided food and medicines to the Indian soldiers, secretly earlier and openly later. The bordering towns of Dinajpur and Jessore had fallen in the hands of Indian forces within three days of the attack. Narayangunj followed suit on the eighth day.

General Shaitan Singh reporting about the military progress to the Special Operations Group formed in the PMO's office. "The 9th Mahar Regiment is only 2.8 Kilometres away from Khulna. The regiment is provided fire cover by 3rd Armoured Corps. Our first base operations camp at Bashirhat has reported that Bangladesh Rifles are retreating rapidly towards Gopalgunj, beyond Khulna."

"What is the position near Dhaka," Pradip Dixit growled without blinking his eyes.

"One assault helicopter squadron unit is stationed at Faridpur—barely 80 Kilometres from Dhaka and the 9th Mahar Regiment is closing in from Manikganj. We are planning to airdrop commandos at Narsingdih about 35 Kilometres from Dhaka. I believe, Dhaka should fall tomorrow late night."

Far away from the war theatre of Bangladesh, a convoy was moving at steady speed on the Quetta-Kandhar road. The containers didn't bear identification marks on them. Neither the drivers of the tarpaulin covered trailers nor the soldiers guarding the convoy knew of their destination. A marshalling jeep was speeding ahead with Captain Mushtaq Khan of Pukhtoon Regiment at the steering wheel. He looked stoically ahead on the winding road through Kakar Range. Little were they aware that two stealth bombers had taken off from a US aircraft carrier stationed in Arabian Sea. The convoy cleared the treacherous hilly track and emerged in open beyond Chaman a little after four hours drive. Captain Mushtaq Khan signalled the convoy to halt. The temperature was 10 degree Celsius. The weary drivers and the soldiers jumped out of the trucks. Almost in tandem with the movement of the Pakistani soldiers, the two stealth bombers swooped down on the unsuspecting soldiers.

One after the other the two bombers pounced on the soldiers as they looked up with terror-stricken eyes, but that was the last of what they ever saw. The next moment they were a dead lot. Some tried to run and retrieve their weapons, but they were much too late as 30 mm bullets lifted them ten feet high in the air before plunging their dead weights on the ground with a thud. Captain Mushtaq Khan was quick to pullout a sub-machine gun from the rear of the jeep. He jumped behind a small hummock and lay flat. With abated breath, he waited for the bombers to make repeat strafing. He peered over the sand dune and saw two dots getting enlarged with every passing second. The time seemed to fly as swiftly as the sands blowing away over the distant sand dunes. The dots were converted into silently and menacingly advancing F-18 bombers. Captain Mushtaq Khan was a cool soldier. He deliberately lifted his sub-machine gun, pushed the safety catch forward and took careful aim at the bottom of the bomber to his left. He took a deep breath, held it for a long minute and pressed the trigger firmly. The bullets sprayed out as the unsuspecting bomber lowered to merely 45 feet height over the ground to mow down the escaping soldiers. And then, suddenly the fuel tank of the aircraft exploded violently. The pilot had no time either to bail out or lift the aircraft to safety. It quickly turned into a massive fireball, as it went down to meet the earth sweeping fast below it. A bit later, the pilot of the second bomber saw what happened to his mate and instinctively pulled the joystick as the bomber swiftly lifted its long hawk-like nose towards the sky. In no time, it was out of range of Captain Mushtaq Khan's firing sub-machine gun.

Captain Khan was a sharp witted officer. He scampered over the dunes to another 30 feet, before he saw a black dot high up in the horizon pouncing down in his direction. He continued to run as fast as his feet could carry him. Very next, second, ear blasting bullets whizzed past him as he jumped behind another sand dune. The flying bullets nearly missed him. He turned to look up in the sky as the bomber vanished over the hillocks.

Company Havaldar Ismail Mustafa had taken perfect aim with his rocket launcher at the approaching bomber. He had seen the bomber much before Captain Khan could notice it. The pilot of the F-18 cocked his head to his left as he saw an Afghan soldier slowly rising from behind the pointed hillock with a shoulder fired rocket launcher. Instinctively his right hand pulled back the joystick to lift the machine up to the safe emptiness of the sky. He silently congratulated himself for his timely action, but he was grossly wrong. As the massive wings of the bomber swept over Havaldar Mustafa, he turned on his heels and in one swinging motion propelled the rocket up at the escaping aircraft. The pilot felt a thud as the rocket found its target. Still the flier was confident to pull the flying machine out to safety. He soon realised he had erred as he saw red and orange flames spurting out of the starboard engine. Before he could think anything further, the aircraft shuddered violently as it came down like a big rock thrown from the hell.

But heroic acts of both the soldiers were a wasted effort, as the containers carrying armament burst out like an oilrig set ablaze. Shrapnel flew all around. A large metal piece pierced through the neck of Captain Khan before he had time to duck. Red hot blood gushed out of his neck as his windpipe was sheared.

Havaldar Mustafa dashed swiftly away from the container trucks. However, he was much too slow for the lashing tongue of the blaze, as it caught him from behind. His burning body ran forward before it collapsed on the sands. The brave soldier once again fought valiantly with death. But that was his last fight, as he succumbed to his burns after ten minutes of a vicious fight to douse the fire and save his life. There was none alive around to answer his cries for help and a drop of water.

All around, the army convoy ablaze in fire and dead soldiers presented a grotesque scenario. The shells were bursting out every few seconds. A huge mushroom of smoke and dust rose above the place and gradually the sky was overcast with a black cloud of smoke and dust.

After an hour, a Pakistani helicopter hovered over the location of the massacre for about fifteen minutes and then touched ground. A colonel accompanied by an army major and two photographers alighted from the chopper. One of the photographers was from Pakistan TV and the other from Iranian TV. They began recording the macabre slaughter around the location. Shauqat Hussein, a PTV war correspondent and cameraman blurted out,

"Oh! This is perhaps the ugliest scenario, I have seen since the war began."

No one was in mood to respond to his comment. They have been at this job for over three months in various parts of the Indian sub-continent where war was being fought between the armies of the warring nations.

After few days the meeting was called by head of Army. In the meeting there was lot of important discussions were carried out.

Summarising the proceedings of the meet, President General Karim Abdullah was delivering his speech.

"I have no hesitation in declaring that Islam is in grave danger of extinction. The Christians and the Hindus have united to wipe us out from the map of the globe. A systematic campaign is launched against our religion. Our culture is systematically being eroded by Western influence. But we will not let their efforts to obliterate Islam succeed. This time we are out to fight an ultimate battle with anti-Islamic forces. Even if we have to lose thousands of our brethren in this Holy War, we have no qualms whatsoever. Because we know that, those who lay down their lives for the cause of the religion would find refuge in the Heaven and Allah will grant them eternal peace.

The 14th May 1948 will be written as a Black Day in the world history. On this day, Israel was created on the Arab soil. I am very much pleased to note that, forgetting the sectile differences all the Muslims—Shias and Sunnies have come together to fight and defeat the common enemy—Israel. We have suffered immensely at the unjust Western diplomacy. But today, we have the key to the very existence of their economy, industries and military supremacy. We control the largest pool of the crude oil produced in the world.

We, Pakistanis are witness to the unjust attacks of Indian military forces on our international borders. Our Muslim brethren in Kashmir are being killed by the thousand in the Kashmir valley. We support the independence struggle of the people of Kashmir. However, the Indians and other Western nations have termed our Jihad as an act of terrorism. Yes, in order to attain freedom for Kashmir and spreading Islam on the face of the earth we will resort to terrorism. This is our war against the Kafirs. Didn't their Lord Clive say, "All is fair in love and war!" Well, this is our holy war against our enemies.

I especially agree with the honourable presidents of Iraq and Libya that the earth will be a better place to live when only our religion prevails. We already have the power of religion with us. We also possess the economic strength of black gold buried in our soils. We can enjoy the fruits of the natural wealth given to us by the grace of Allah, only if the whole of the earth is left to at our disposal. Yes, that is the fruit of labour of our scientists. I am glad we all have evolved a consensus to use our bacterial and chemical weapons. The warheads of the long-range missiles and ICBMs fitted with these weapons would exterminate everything living within a radius of 2000 kilometres from where they would be dropped. We shall stick to the planned arrangement of dividing the enemy nations within us. I am glad, we all have agreed to explode these deadly weapons at one given moment. There would be innumerable explosions as the enemies will be taken by surprise and within minutes, there shall be nothing left alive worth its name. Within five to six hours, the air will be cleared and after that their buildings, factories, airports, ports, railways and farms will all be left to us. Insa Allah, we shall be able to live peacefully thereafter and there will be only one Islam religion in the world. There shall be no war in the name of religion after that."

Saying the last words, Head of the Army General Karim Abdullah laughed aloud, which was quite unusual for the General. After a momentary pause he surveyed the impact of his speech on his listeners with a faint hint of a smile.

"Our operational committee has chosen 14th August as the strike day. This is the day when our Islamic nation, Pakistan was carved out of that *Kafir* country—India. *Insa Allah*, that will be the last day of the *Kafirs* on this planet and after that Islam will reign over this planet."

Everyone around clapped deliciously and said aloud —"Amen!"

Chapter 44

August 13. It was 23.45 GMT when the US President entered the Operations Room. He wore a grim look, his chin jutting down and the permanent frown between his eyes slightly deepened now. An entourage of the US military and civilian officers followed him. The mission commander Brigadier Thomson came forward and quickly fell in step with the President.

Brigadier Thompson was a tall handsome man who strikingly resembled Sean Connery. He silently muttered, "All the heads of our allies are online, Mr. President."

"Great! Let's have a last minute chat."

"Aye! Ayc! Sir." He beckoned the Signals officer to switch on the teleconference. Suddenly many small screens lit up on the opposite wall. Each screen was designated to a country, which showed up the head of that nation.

The President didn't waste time. He began, "*Gentlemen, I am sure you all have studied the proceedings of the Islamic Conference and the concluding speech made by the President of Pakistan, sent to you today early. It is a matter of concern for all peace-loving nations of the world that the Islamic countries have adopted a destructive stance. It leaves no doubt in our minds about their sinister designs.*

The United States had placed great faith in the Pakistan president to put an end to terrorism in the world and the Indian sub-continent. But our faith has been betrayed. Today, that fanatical idiot has brought the entire humanity of this planet on the brink of extinction. Little he and his fundamentalist cronies are aware that the Chemical and Genetic Weapons they propose to use against us will affect their people too. It seems their scientists have failed to inform him of the fact that explosion of chemical weapons would poison the atmosphere enveloping the planet Earth. Besides, human beings even the animals, plantations, standing crops and orchards will be deliberated from the face of the earth.

There are two fundamental evils—lesser evils and major evils. Since, the President of Pakistan has given a call of the war, we have accepted the inevitable choice of considering war as a 'lesser evil'. The British Prime Minister, Winston Churchill had once said, "There is no middle path in the war." Well, this is the ultimate war. The second evil, the major evil facing the world and posing grave danger for its existence is Islamic fanaticism, and terrorism born out of such mindless fanaticism. It is a matter of pleasure for us that we have come together to eradicate these dual evils from the world.

Now, that we are fully aware of their menacing design to eliminate everything breathing from this earth, it is our duty to stop them from carrying out their devilish plan. The United States counts upon the support of all her allies.

General Karim Abdullah has decided to explode their chemical and genetic armament on 14th August. Once they have their way, no one will not be able to do anything to save our people from massive destruction.

Therefore, it is imperative that we immobilise them before they have time to act. We must act now or never.

I am aware that the nuclear arsenal of nations is on utmost preparedness. Now, I request you to press your readiness switch to enable us to learn about the state of your arsenal."

In an instant green lights flashed on the panel of the Systems Officer. The green flashing lights indicated all round preparedness of the nuclear weaponry system of all the allied countries. The President heaved a long sigh with satisfaction

"Gentlemen, thank you very much." After a pause he continued, "Right now we are at a very crucial moment in the life of humanity. Today, the religious fanatics have posed a grave threat before the world community. However, we did try to dissuade them from carrying out their terrorising techniques and not bring religion in the way of fostering world peace. They have not given any heed to our pleas. What is most alarming is that all the Islamic nations have decided to come together in perpetrating the heinous crime of eliminating humanity from the face of the planet."

He paused to pick up a paper from the table before him, "Well, this is not the time to make speeches. But I cannot help quoting from the letter, I received from the prime minister of India, a verse from the Geeta, *"For a warrior, nothing is higher than a war against evil. The warrior confronted with such a war should be pleased, for it comes as an open gate to heaven. If you do not participate in this battle against evil, you will incur sin."* We have deliberated a lot before arriving at this decision."

He glanced at his watch and went on, "It is right 23.54 GMT. Exactly at 00.00 GMT we will release our nuclear arsenal in unison. We don't propose to kill their innocent people. Our strikes are aimed at their weapon systems—wherever they are located. Nuke strikes from our missiles sites, aircraft carriers and fighters located at various locations will join in united effort to eliminate their striking power."

"Our weaponry system is ready to strike at the appointed time." The prime minister of India proclaimed solemnly.

"We've tested and found our systems in total readiness," affirmed the British prime minister and heads of other nations followed suit.

"Alright, it is right 23.57 GMT now. Only three minutes to freedom for mankind from fanatic terrorism." The frown on the President's furrowed eyebrows quivered a bit. All round in the world ordinary masses were oblivious of the dangerous game plan of their national leaders. All the allied countries had split the enemy countries within them.

Time seemed to be ticking away much rapidly now, as the two black hands on the face of the white dial of the clock moved menacingly ahead. The clock now showed 23.59 hours.

Suddenly a voice echoed, "Reverse count begins— ten . . . nine . . . eight . . ."

Eerie silence descended on the operational rooms spread across the allied nations.

"seven . . . six . . . five . . ."

The prime minister of India stared intently at the red button of the panel that would activate all the nuclear missile batteries on the ground as well as the sea.

"four . . . three . . ."

Chancellor Kohl gingerly caressed the red knob in front of him. He was reminded of the days he had spent in the cold Russian prison during the World War II. The memories of the pain and anguish as he was repeatedly kicked in the stomach by the Russian soldiers, came alive. He had almost forgotten his days of imprisonment. The angry and hateful faces of the Russian soldiers came alive vividly before him as he, now, clutched the red knob tightly as his knuckles grew white.

"Two . . . one . . ."

The British prime minister looked up for a split second and held his breath and as the loudspeakers echoed, "zero" and he pressed the red button.

For a very long time nobody uttered a word. As if their breath were held up by some unknown power. Suddenly as if compressed air from many car tires was released, there was a huge

"Hoooshhhh . . ."

Everyone's eyes were glued on the large TV screen to witness their missiles flying out to destroy the enemy positions. But, nothing happened. Special Operations Rooms in allied nations were abuzz with clamour since they couldn't activate their nuclear arsenal.

The US President mumbled, "It can't be possible. It shouldn't be possible. But there it is."

"Well?" The prime minister of India quizzically looked at the

Army chief, who lifted his shoulder to show his own bewilderment.

He blurted out, "I don't know, Sir. But . . . we can't activate our systems, Mr. Prime Minister."

"Mechanical trouble?" Asked the Indian Prime Minister with doubt in his voice.

"It can't be Sir. The US army faces a similar problem." An air force officer seated at a radar screen shouted. The furrowed eyebrows of the US President further deepened,

"What the hell is happening . . . . Why the hell are the goddamn missiles not fired?"

The military and civilian officers standing around looked at him blankly. The people assembled in the Special Operations Rooms in all the allied nations were watching the bewildering scenario in the US Operations Room.

"I can't tolerate this!" cried the US President. "I can't tolerate it! After so much preparations, so many meticulous tests, is this the state of our nuclear preparedness?"

The Army Chief was looking at him impassively, as if words were not conveying anything any longer. Full one minute passed as the hands of the clock showed 00.01 GMT.

"Ladies and gentlemen," hearing unknown voice from loudspeakers, everybody was shocked. As a dark silhouette of a man appeared on the large TV screen that came flickering alive. It was a calm, impeccable, clear voice. "Dear Mr. President and all the other world leaders, I am addressing you all together. My heart is filled with pain to learn that, you have decided to annihilate the life on this planet. But I won't let you go ahead with your sinister design."

"Certainly you would want to know who I am, where am I speaking to you from. Well, I am Sanatan. I am joined today, by my friend, Iqbal. He hardly needs an introduction to the world. Yes, he is an eminent nuclear scientist from Pakistan. You heard it right. We were declared dead in a helicopter crash off Malaysia seven years ago. No, we weren't killed. The accident was fake." The signals officer ran to the adjoining room and frantically ordered his men to detect the source of the signals. But their direction finding consoles remained blank. Not a needle flickered to indicate the source of the signals. He switched on the 'all station switch', but drew blank. Nothing was operational.

The mysterious voice of Sanatan continued, "You will not be able to harm us. You will not be able to detect the source of our signals. What I want you to do is to just sit calmly and listen to me. Perhaps, that will open up a new vision for you all."

After taking a breath, Sanatan said, "Today, you believe, by cowing down the Islamic nations you will be able to destroy the evil from the world. But no, you are grossly wrong. You want to destroy all that which you hold to be evil and achieve all that which you hold to be good. Yes, I am addressing both the sides of this World War. Both the sides of this Third World War are fanatics about their beliefs. This time, once again the United Nations has been proved ineffective in thwarting large-scale war among the nations. When it was aware of acts of terrorism being perpetrated in various parts of the world, why didn't the UN Security Council take to task the nations engineering such acts in such countries? Why did it choose to turn a blind eye when the US was out to crush Cuba or Vietnam or Korea and even Iraq for that matter? America wanted Pakistan to help them rout Talebans but never gave any heed to India's plea to stop Pakistan supporting terrorist outfits across the borders.

Today very lately, realisation has dawned on the Western countries and especially on America that the Pakistan president is neither a friend of other Islamic countries, nor his own countrymen. He neither respects democratic norms nor does he believe in maintaining good neighbourly relations.

Right now, General Karim Abdullah must be listening to me, I am sure. General, have you, besides, snatching away Kashmir from India, ever thought of making your country self-sufficient in industry or economy? Haven't you learnt a lesson from four wars with India? Today, your country is facing widespread poverty and illiteracy. Your economy is virtually dependent on drugs and weapon trafficking. Since 1947 you have survived on the mercy of America and China.

General, don't you have any self-respect as a head of the nation? Have you ever realized that, today Pakistan is reeling under the debt of over 300 billion dollars? Export of textile from your country is reduced by over 60 percent? Are you not worried about the fact that, certain leading financial institutions have left Pakistan for good? Is it not a concern for you that there are no takers for the Pakistani rice in the international market?

When we traverse the legacy of Pakistan, we realise that all the rulers of Pakistan have given one gift to their countrymen—that is of rampant corruption— more and more corruption. Time and again, they have hoodwinked their fellow citizens by pitting them against India in four wars. What happened? More and more corruption has bred in Pakistan. All rational economists would know, war is the by-product of corruption and again it nurtures further corruption. And after every war, its government has encouraged more corruption.

Iqbal here, and all the decent Muslims of the world would agree with me that, the common people of Pakistan are not the enemies of India. The people of Pakistan and the holy Muslims are our friends, but the worst enemy is President of Pakistan Farooq Azam and head of Army General Karim Adbullah who believe in terrorism. They are the enemies of 16 crores Muslims of India and 12 crores Muslims of Pakistan.

You are all aware that, an average Muslim woman in India is much more happier and prosperous in relation to the women in Pakistan, Afghanistan and other Islamic nations. The war initiated against India is not the war against its Hindus, but that is also against 16 crores Muslims. All the Indian Muslims including the people of Kashmir want to live in the prosperity of democracy and not under the beggared and corrupt military autocrat of Pakistan. The President of Pakistan wants to fight with us and in particular with India in the name of Islam and on the borrowed strength of Arab nations, but that is not only dangerous for World Peace, it is also detrimental for the growth of Islamic culture and humanity. This war is thrust upon the world.

Every ruler of a country must remember that however, war is justifiable in their viewpoint, it is devastating for the man kind. Moreover, when the war fought in the name of religion is never justified even if it is obliquely fought on some other pretext.

But, whether, only General Karim Abdullah and his friends are blameworthy for the threat to the life on this planet? No. I want to emphasize here on the fact that, the violence perpetrated by terrorists do not respect borders. Many innocent civilians have become victims of violence generated by a worldwide political and economical system based on injustice and despair."

The atmosphere of the Pakistani and Indian operations Rooms was surcharged. Everybody waited with abated breath of what Sanatan was to say further. Only the face of Sanatan continued to smile at them mockingly from the massive television screen on the wall.

Chapter 45

Once again, the deep resonant voice of Sanatan broke the reverie of his audience. Hardly anyone moved from his or her seat. Mark McLaurin leaned towards the President to whisper something in his ears, but the President beckoned him to move away.

Sanatan resumed his speech in a serious tone, "If now the US government and other western politicians talk about attacks on the whole civilization; they forget that, this very civilization they are talking about, is responsible for the extinction of hundreds of thousands of lives in non-western parts of this earth. You are also equally responsible for the grim situation facing us today. It is the arrogance of the Western countries and especially America that has been the reason behind economical exploitation and devastation of the economies of the third world countries. You have tilled the grounds where fanatic violence grows. History stands testimony to the fact that the military-industrial complex and the political leadership of the United States has always taken advantage of this tragedy to increase militarism and interventionism in any part of the world.

Is it not true that the United States has always launched campaigns of repression without limit on a worldwide scale?

The Israel is considered Arab attacks on their kinsmen as an act of war; and not to be outdone began their own retaliatory acts of terror. Since then, Israeli retaliation has been in a more military fashion, with excursions into neighbouring countries, seizing land to create buffer zones around them. Today, the Gaza Strip, a contentious holding of the Israelis has been the scene of most of the Middle East violence over the last decade.

The British press has always condemned the most aggressive antagonists of Israeli self-preservation. The standard Zionist position is that they showed up in Palestine in the late 19th century to reclaim their Biblical homeland. Jews bought land and started building up the Jewish community there. They were met with increasingly violent opposition from the Palestinian Arabs, presumably stemming from the Arabs' inherent anti-Semitism. The Zionists were then forced to defend themselves and, in one form or another, this same situation continues up to today.

The British and their Arab friends have to say that, the problem with this explanation is that it is simply not true. They venture to explain that, what really happened was that the Zionist movement, from the beginning, looked forward to a practically complete dispossession of the indigenous Arab population. The Arab community, as it became increasingly aware of the Zionists' intentions, vehemently opposed further Jewish forward march because it posed a real and imminent danger to the very existence of Arab society in Palestine. America wanting to leverage its position in the Middle East and to keep the arrogant Arabs under tight light leash provided total political and logistic support to Israel. This situation was against the great British design to once again rule over the world and exercise control over the oil producing Arab countries. India, Britain and Middle European countries have to suffer attacks of terrorism.

When the Indian Prime Minister was advocating forming a joint platform and working towards removal of widespread poverty, illiteracy and instead developing economy of the third world nations, it was the US who plotted and sabotaged the move.

I know, now the president of the great nation—America would be fidgeting. It is now a well-known fact that, the British and American governments during the Cold War days supported Islamic Fundamentalism. General Karim Abdullah and his likes were CIA and British assets. How can you forget Mr. President, that the United States provided total logistic support to Talibans in their fight against the Russians in Afghanistan?

When Pakistan had turned bankrupt, what was the wisdom of offering them hoards of armaments and liberal financial assistance? That had resulted in spread of further terrorism in the region.

Pakistan government freely encouraged establishment of Madresas in their own country and in PoK. Young children of impressionable age were given training in spreading terrorism in India and elsewhere. Dear Mr. President, you are repeatedly proclaiming that terrorism and the nations supporting it would not be tolerated; then why did you always adopt step-motherly attitude towards India? Is it not true that you are indirectly encouraging Islamic terrorism? Many a time, India pleaded and requested you to declare Pakistan as a terrorist nation, but all that fell on deaf ears. As you went on providing various kinds of assistance to Pakistan, the Pakistan sponsored terrorism grew by leaps and bounds and spread in the Asian Subcontinent, Europe, America and the Mediterranean countries.

Is this not true? Do remember, the terrorism tacitly encouraged by you has become a cause of fear for every peace loving person in the world.

All the western capitalist nations have known—first, a war is always a quick way to peace. I am going to cite examples from the books of history written in blood. You all wanted to form a League of Nations? What did you do? You started World War I. When you wanted a United Nations? You initiated World War II. And now, you all want a New World Order? Hence, you are out to maim and annihilate half the world.

The terrorists do not belong to any religion, caste or country. Till the time the rulers of all the countries would not actively take steps to control the terrorism, the common man will have to suffer and live life in constant terror.

And for that reason, you have given impetus to religious wars in the Middle East. You have decided that, the Arabs must be kicked off the Temple Mount and a new Jewish Temple be built there. In the same way, in India, you the Islamic fanatics are encouraged to build Babri mosque, where the temple of Ram once existed." The American President shook his head in dismay. He leaned his head on right hand perched on the hand rest of his chair.

"At last, we all know of two factors responsible for endangering the existence of all living beings on this planet; they are Nuclear Weapons and Environment. If we cannot restrain these two factors either today or in future days, our entire life would face the danger of extinction. Ask your scientists, astronomers and geologists what caused the obliteration of the life from the Mars. The space research efforts of NASA and other nations have brought to light that, millions of years ago life similar to ours existed on Mars. Scientific evidence points towards gradual decline in the quality of environment suitable for life on the red planet. Traces of existence of water in the form of layers of ice, has been found. Chances of re-evolution of life on the Mars cannot be ruled out. Whereas on the other hand we are fast approaching our own existence by ignoring grave dangers of nuclear arsenals and gradual decline in the quality of environment around us."

Sanatan paused for a moment and resumed,

"Leaving aside the worries of the world environment, I come back to the main issue. Yes, Mr. Prime Minister of England, it is a British design and a very clever one to beat the Americans at their own game and obliterate American status as the only superpower. A very good ally of American cause, eh! It is your desire that America's strong grip on OPEC, through the Saudis, must be diminished. Yes, now don't squirm and hit the table in frustration, as you stand naked on the world stage. This, in fact, is the very idea behind the creation of the European Community. Europe has already made agreements for Russian oil and so the fall of the House of Saudis serves your purpose at the expense of America."

The situation in the US Control Room was one of great confusion. FBI agents were already on the job of detecting the signals. The US Secretary of State Mark MacLaurin asked the Signals Officer to connect him to the British prime minister. To his dismay, the Signals Officer expressed his inability.

Sanatan smiled considerately before he resumed, "You can see and listen to us only when we wish; but you, all the world leaders will neither be able to see each other, nor be able to communicate without our wish.

Let's see what role the United Kingdom has played in creating the present day crisis. At one time it was said, 'The Sun never sets in the kingdom of the Queen'. The physical British Empire declined in the years after World War II, but it seems the United Kingdom has found it difficult to swallow this bitter fact. In the later years, they have turned their attention to creating a brand new global empire. In collusion with their European friends, they have created the European Community with the sole purpose and a continuing part of their march towards controlling the lives of the third world countries.

Today, Britain pledges to be the strongest friend of the US. Have you ever asked how come all the alleged terrorists entered the United States via London? The fact is all the Saudi Arabian dissidents are given shelter in Britain. And the British design to once again dominate this earth can only be realised if the United States stands tattered."

The British Prime Minister's lips were drawn back in an angry snarl. His eyes glowered at the screen. He brushed his hair up looming over his eyes and reached for the Hot Line with the US President. He picked up the phone and listened. The line was silent. He thrust away the receiver in disgust.

Chapter 46

Sanatan kept quiet for sometime. As if he is compiling his thoughts, he continued to speak.

"Perhaps, today I am compelled to bare the vicious designs of world politics. While some countries were perpetrating heinous designs against other countries in order to attain political supremacy, the political leaders of my country, India, have been striving to defeat their rival politicians and amassing financial wealth at the cost of the vital security of the country and the teeming millions of the poor and poverty stricken.

After getting independence, years have been passed away; our leaders are always involved in various misconduct and corruptions. Nobody thinks about the common citizen.

It is wonder that in 1976, our beloved Prime Minister Mrs. Indira Gandhi herself declared that the corruption has been spreaded in all over the world then how India can keep away?

Our leaders have never tried to keep control over the corruption. The corruption is not only limited to deposit crores of rupees in swiss banks, but it has been spreaded to our election system also. Because of this, the Indian public has been divided into various castes and creeds.

At one point of time, an Indian prided in the dictum of 'Unity in diversity'; but over a period of time this has been proved a curse for the nation.

On one hand, we proclaim India as one country, while on the other side one state holds another state to ransom on matters of river-water sharing, inter-state boundaries, industrial locations, backward area benefits, minorities and parochialism.

While the people of the Eastern states were ignored for long, the Kashmiris have been pampered so much that, each chief minister of Kashmir from Sheikh Abdullah to the current day heir of the Sheikhdom have been bleeding Indian economy shamelessly, while contributing little else but bloodshed to the nation."

Sanatan's tone grew harsher as he continued, "I hope, the Sheikh is listening to me at this moment. How can you conveniently ignore the fact that, Kashmir Valley, the hub of terrorist turmoil, is the most prosperous region of the country? Can you deny that the per capita income of a Kashmiri is far too higher than any other Indian living in other parts of India and much more above the national average? On the issue of Kashmiri youth joining terrorist squads, you have chosen to point at the massive unemployment in the state."

Sanatan paused for a short while and took deep breath as he resumed, "Now, let's just see quickly what the reality is. There is hardly any sphere of activity, which the Central Government has not undertaken either by itself or through the State Governments in the Kashmir Valley. Since five-year plan, dissimilar to other states of India, per capita expenditure on development activities in J&K had remained around Rs.962/- as against Rs.270/- in Bihar, Rs.490/- in Gujarat and Rs.822/- in Himachal Pradesh. Per capita consumption of electricity had also remained much higher than other states."

Sanatan intoned, "Statistics does not interest most of the people. However, when we realize how statistics reveal where our governments have bungled, that is the time to wake up from the stupor. My intention here is to let the world know, how India had bled herself in looking after the people of Kashmir Valley who have been provided for many years with subsidized cheap food (perhaps cheapest in the world), subsidized firewood, subsidized salts, subsidized pesticides for orchards, subsidized agricultural inputs and cheaper feeds for animals."

The students of the Kashmir Valley have been provided liberal educational loans training in professional colleges outside the state, which have never been returned. Besides, huge subsidies for establishment of industrial units, liberal loans for housing and what not have also been made available. There is hardly any sphere of life where people of Kashmir did not get preferential treatment. The population of the state is just 0.8% of the country, yet it received 2.7% of the national development outlay. Thus, the per head allocation in case of this state amounted to Rs.1122/- while the allocation in case of other states of the country ranged between Rs.67/- and about Rs.300/- per head. Such huge sums of money have been pumped into the Kashmir Valley to the neglect of other regions during all these years that they have resulted in regional imbalances and regional tensions.

The stark reality is, the insurgency and terrorism in the state has not affected the prosperity of the Muslims of the Kashmir Valley. In fact, their prosperity has increased due to their having taken away immovable assets and agricultural property as also business establishments of the Hindus worth thousands of crores of rupees".

Sadness crept in the voice of Sanatan as he said, "The approach of almost all the Indian governments, since the time of independence to appease the Kashmir rulers, without assessing their patriotic qualifications. It has been misfortune of this country that whenever one correct step was taken, it was subsequently followed by steps, which were all wrong."

General Karim Abdullah of Pakistan clenched his fingers in disgust as his knuckles turned white. He shouted, "Won't anyone stop this monologue." Only the silence replied him blankly. He pushed his chair back and got up and sat down with a thump as the next words fell on his ears.

"The Delhi and Islamabad governments share one key characteristic: both perceive Kashmir's realities and interests as subservient to their own." Sanatan was saying, "This long-festering dispute in Kashmir is the primary cause of hostility between India and Pakistan and a source for endless misery for the people of Kashmir. If the United Kingdom ignited the fire of hatred between India and Pakistan, the United States has done the job of fanning the simmering fire between the two nuclear nations."

Sanatan was saying, "Could we have imagined at some other time that the so-called sane and wise world leaders would be on the verge of using such dangerous weapons that could bring complete elimination of life from this world? But it is true today. Sanity still guides a few people like us who refuse to become puppets in the hands of greedy and foolish political leaders. We will not allow you to cause the devastation of this world that we live in."

"Today, I am joined by my friends Iqbal, Ivan and all peace loving people of the world in addressing all responsible politicians and leaders of the world to put their efforts at ending this proliferation of religious hatred and violence and resultant World War. We call upon all the countries—on both the sides to direct their efforts in extinguishing poverty, discrimination and exploitation, in improving healthcare and education on a worldwide scale. Besides, poverty, malnutrition and illiteracy we need to protect the world environment. If we don't wake up today, future generations will never forgive our folly."

Of this point, General Karim Abdullah beckoned his *aide-decamp* and whispered something in his ears. The ADC saluted and turned away briskly. He went straight to the Chief of Pakistan Army and conveyed the message of the President. A quick frown followed by four lines of creases appeared on the forehead as he lifted his eyebrows in reaction to the President's message. Quickly he bent over the shoulder of the Operations Chief. He extended his hand at the red button to fire a missile carrying a genetic bomb directed on Delhi. He waited patiently to appear for the green light on the panel as a mark of successful launch of the missile.

Suddenly, the voice of Sanatan jolted him. "My dear General Karim Abdullah, can't you stop your cunningness? Won't you ever cease being crafty? No, you cannot fire any weapon today. Not a single weapon that is operated using any kind of electronic transmission system. You can only use your rifles and tanks; but you will not be able to provide them aerial or communication support to your troops. And you must be aware that, the Indian soldiers can outperform your armies in such circumstances. I would advise you not to test their nerves."

General Karim Abdullah cursed and let out a filthy abusive word aloud and suddenly his face turned ashen. He clenched his fists and banged on the table. Again soothing voice of Sanatan filled the operations room.

Sanatan was saying, "History stands testimony to the fact that India doesn't fight or launch offensive in the name of religion. History is full of instances of how innumerable Muslim rulers have crushed minority communities and devastated their religious places. Right from the times of Muhammad of Gizni to the present day rulers of Pakistan, Afghanistan and even Bangladesh have never been kind to the minority communities in their respective countries. Innumerable Hindu temples and statues of Hindu deities have been ransacked and destroyed. Talibans have also destroyed Buddhist historical statues in Afghanistan. These destroyers of cultural symbols forget that, culture lives within the hearts of the people. Cultural ethos strengthens spiritualism and religious sentiments."

"Instead of fighting and destroying the people of other religions we all must divert our attention towards more pressing issues of alleviation of poverty, increasing food production, increasing employment opportunities and finally conservation of environment and natural resources. Besides, we need to tackle the problems of ever-increasing population, health and nutrition. I am sure, in saner moments you would be thinking of these issues." Sanatan paused for a moment.

The Indian Prime Minister nodded with his eyes fixed as if on distant thoughts. Gradually General Karim Abdullah of Pakistan regained his composure. But soon his face clouded with some lurking doubts. But for the present, he shrugged of the bewildering thoughts and looked around him scanning faces of the soldiers.

When he began to speak once again, Sanatan's voice had mellowed. "Ask any mother today—irrespective of her skin colour or religious faith or nationality—would she want her children to die the death perpetrated by you all? Why not ask your wives sitting at home awaiting your safe arrival today for the dinner? Ask your children—would they approve of your inhumane plan to kill lacs of people in your enemy countries? Is not possible to live in peaceful co-existence?" So many questions hung in the air.

Sanatan said in a resonant voice, "We Indians have always affirmed that violence is the most inefficient tool to guarantee the security. We had always accepted the non-violence as a method of action, because we know that this is the best form of relation between persons, peoples and governments. This doctrine is enshrined in the principles embodied in the Panchsheel doctrine. I have reached the end of what I intended you to listen, understand and realize." Sanatan stopped for a moment and smiled, "I am sure you all must have realised, how powerless you are with your so called powerful arsenal. Henceforth, the world community would be free from the dangers of the dirty conspiracies of the fanatics—religious or power hungry rulers. Henceforth, the energies of the scientists would be utilised for facilitating improvement of the quality of life of the people universally. Now, the scientists shall be able to use their talent at harnessing the benefits of the natural resources without depleting them. Perhaps our future generations would be able to tell the visitors from Mars that, their ancestors were much wiser than the ancestors of the Martians." He stopped and looked at his audience grimly.

For a long moment, he stared grimly at them. Suddenly, a bright smile spread over his face. He beckoned to Iqbal, Ivan, William and his team-mates to come in the field of the camera. He introduced each member of his team.

Finally he turned to Iqbal and said, "I think they all deserve some information on how we could immobilise their weaponry system, power plants and communication system."

Iqbal nodded and looked at Ivan. He too shook his head and looked meaningfully at Sanatan. Sanatan's smile widened. He turned his face towards his world audience and said, "My friends have agreed to tell you about our invention very briefly. We assure you that we will give the world the benefit of our invention."

Sanatan continued, "We all know that, billion years ago, a spinning cloud of cosmic dust and gas contracted to form a young star and its retinue of planets. What emerged was the highly ordered structure of the solar system. The influence of the Sun is all-important. As well as controlling the orbital velocities of the planets, it has shaped their characters, so that their chemical composition and mass vary according to their distance from the Sun. The Sun has a strong magnetic field around it and in the same manner every planet has its respective magnetic field. We have made use of the electro-magnetic properties of the solar rays in deactivating your signal-operated weapon system. I won't elaborate on our invention. The only thing I will tell you presently, you all have no alternative but to live and let others live peacefully."

Suddenly the giant video screen went blank. For a long minute in all the operations rooms of all the nations, earthy silence prevailed. Suddenly a new reality dawned on all that they have emerged in a new life, full of promises. Almost in tandem, the world leaders heaved a sigh of relief, as they realised, how close the six billion population of the Earth was from the grave danger of annihilation and now away from it.

At the Vatican, the Pope picked up the gold cross from across the table, touched it to his eyes and lips. Two drops of tears rolled down the pinkish cheeks of the saintly prelate.

On the third day, thousands of miles away, standing at the Indira Gandhi International Airport, tears rolled down the eyes of Radha, who had suffered a seven-year long widowhood. She was watching the crowds thronging at the airport with bewildered eyes. Not an inch of place was left at the airport premises. The security personnel were finding it difficult to manage the milling crowds. For Sanatan, the following day was a golden day, as the President of India was to honour him with the highest Indian award 'Bharat Ratna' in the presence of world leaders. Radha and the members of his family were invited to stay in the Rashtrapati Bhavan.

Large crowds were present to receive the greatest Indian scientist Dr. Sanatan, who had created pandemonium in the International scientist fraternity.

The roads from where the motorcade carrying Sanatan was to pass were decorated with banners, his life-size cut-outs and Indian national flags.

Such honour was perhaps was never given to any world leader before. Arvind uncle, Sanatan's schoolmates—Bansi Patel, Dhimant and Rehman arrived from Umreth to welcome him. Dr. Swaminathan living in Anushaktinagar, Bombay, Dr.Vikram Sarabhai, Dr.Shethna and other scientists, as well as Dr. Mathur, his colleague & the Principal, the Royal Institute of Science, both uncles Rasikbhai and Poonamchand, Maternal Uncle Jeetendraprasad and several relatives arrived in the capital. His old time friend Ravindra Shah flew down from Uganda to be present. From Malaysia his friend Ivan and William also were present. Several relatives were awaiting the arrival of Sanatan for hours.

At last, the great moment arrived and everyone's wait came to an end. The plane carrying Sanatan landed. The new hero emerged from the aircraft. Billions of people all over the world were watching this great historical event glued to their television sets.

A wiry, thin but strong person alighted from the aircraft and as his feet touched the red carpet laid before him, he was given a full throated welcome by a million strong crowd. Men, women and children alike cheered the great scientist who had made the image of India unique and singularly great and elevated the prestige of India worldwide.

The skies reverberated with the cheers—'Long Live Sanatan', 'Long Live India', 'Long Live World Peace' . . .

Shaking hands with the national leaders, Sanatan moved forward. On seeing Radha, he could not restrain himself. Garlanding Sanatan, Radha's throat was choked with emotion and Sanatan immediately took her in his arms. Disregarding the presence of swarming crowds around them the couple stood in each other's arms for several minutes. As if it was impossible to check their pent up emotions as tears welled in their eyes. Gently disengaging clinging Radha, Sanatan moved forward. He saw young Rita, the young widow of his son. Rita found it difficult to control her tears. Sanatan bent and picked up young Pappu, standing between Radha and Rita and hugged the young child to his bosom.

"Rita, now take hold of yourself. Look, I have returned to look after you all again."

The people gathered at the airport were anxious to listen to Sanatan. Sanatan took the microphone in his hand.

"This invention, by which the foundation of world peace is established, is certainly a very significant event. For centuries to follow, the people would remember the history of this invention. Dear fellow citizens, do remember; this is not only my victory. The great scientist of Pakistan and my dearest friend Iqbal, the owner of Sohali Island, an ardent lover of the world peace and my companion of all my moments of happiness and sadness—Mr. William, and his worthy son and a great scientist Ivan too share the honour of this victory with me. Their contribution to this invention was much more significant. I also, express my gratitude towards the other scientists of different countries who assisted me and toiled for seven long years without consideration of the time or tide elements. It fills me with joy to say that, this is not my victory, our victory; but the victory of the love and affection of the entire humanity of this world."

After his short speech, for a while Sanatan remained surrounded by Union ministers, State ministers, diplomats and correspondents from Press, TV and Radio. Gradually, the entire motorcade moved towards Rashtrapati Bhavan. All over the world, the people were swept with emotion after witnessing such a scene as never before was seen. Dr. Iqbal too was greeted at Islamabad airport with the similar pomp and honour. The best and commendable approach Iqbal sacrificed for the world peace was highly appreciated and welcomed. He chose to welcome the great scientist in person in the traditional manner amidst large crowds. Iqbal's wife Mumtaz, daughter Zohra and son Karim found it difficult suppress their feelings of happiness. All over Pakistan, the people were dancing in the street in the joy of finding a new hero of their hearts.

Billions of people all over the world watched in rapt attention the ceremony where Sanatan was honoured with the highest award of the nation—'Bharat Ratna'.

During the Banquet dinner, when the President of India complemented Radha saying, "Behind every successful man, there is a woman," she said emotionally,

"For a little over seven years, I have lived a life of a widow, despite my husband was alive. I have no sorrow, whatsoever, for that today. I am not even sad, today, that my worthy son sacrificed his life for the national cause. I am absolutely not sorry for living a distressful life full of grief for so long. Moreover, you have honoured my husband with Bharat Ratna Award, I am very happy. But I became more happy because my husband, Sanatan has lived a worthy life to achieve good of the humanity. He has protected the lives of the entire humanity by his invention and protected this planet from the greatest devastation."

The President turned towards Sanatan seated beside him and patted him with emotion saying,

"Well done my friend. I heartily congratulate you for spreading in all directions the rays of peace emanating from the Sun. The 'Spatial Echoes' of peace that reverberates from the vacuum will become immortal and will be heard by humanity for centuries to come".

Glossary

Abbajan -	Father
Ammijan -	Mother
Baniyas -	A business community
Bapuji -	Respected Father
Barati -	Group of people accompanying the groom
Beta -	Son
Bhabhi -	Brother's wife
Dalal -	One class of person who does bargaining—Agent
Dargah -	is a sufi shrine built over the grave of a revered religious figure, often a sufi saint.
Deepak rag -	Known as 'the melodious tune of light' and was able to light hundred lamps with some kind of invisible power emitted by his singing.
Diwali -	Is a part of Hindu New Year festival of lamps and fireworks.
Garudpuran -	is an ancient Hindu holy book explains what happens to Bio-Atman after death.
Geeta -	is a Hindu holy book of Hindu philosophy in Hindu scripture in sanskrit
Insa Allah -	with the will of God

Kachhiya Pole - is a name of place where many Kachhiyas who sell vegetables, live.

Kansara - is one of the Hindu castes who are in the business of metallic utensils.

Kanya Viday - is the bride leaving father's house after marriage.

Karma - is the concept of 'action' or 'deed' in Indian religions understood, as that which causes the entire cycle of cause and originating in ancient India and treated in Hindu, Jain, Sikh and Buddhist philosophies.

Kazi - is an Islamic legal scholar and judge

Khadi - is an Indian handspun and hand-woven cloth. The raw material may be cotton, silk or wool which are spun into threads on a spinning wheel called as Charkha.

Lahaul-Bila-Qoowat - Annoyance in Surprise

Malay - is an ancient pond which was built in Umreth by Minaldevi, a queen of Gujarat.

Malhar Rag - is a melodious tune of Indian music known as 'the tone of rains.'

Masala -	Several Indian ingredients mixed and used to make curry tasteful.
Maulvi -	Muslim scholar or Muslim jurist.
Minaldevi -	One famous queen of Solanki dynasty.
Miyan -	is a respectable Muslim gentleman
Muleshwar Mahadev -	A temple of God Shiva
Od Bazar -	is a market place
Panchvati -	is a place where five roads meet and many shops are working in this area
Patra -	is one variety of meal
Puranpoli -	is one kind of sweet wheaten pancake or bread stuffed in with mash of jaggery and pulses.
Razakars -	Those who revolt against the present establishments
Salam Alekum -	Form of Greetings used by Muslim community
Satyagrah -	A fight of civil disobedient developed by Mohandas Karamchand Gandhi
Sherwani -	is a long coat like garment worn in South Asia, very similar to Achkan or doublet.
Siddharaj Jaisingh -	Once upon a time a famous king of Patan, a city of North Gujarat.

Surati Undhiya -	is one kind of mixed vegetable tasty dish famous in Surat, a city of Gujarat.
Tajiya -	is one kind of Muslim religious procession at the time of Moharram
Tonga -	is a means of transport carrier, cart with a horse
Unani -	Alternative therapy used by Muslim communities
Upanishad -	are Hindu scriptures that constitute the core teachings of Vedas
Vada Bazar -	is a market place namely big bazar
Vhorwad -	is a place where many Vhora community stay together.
Ya Allah -	Expression remembering Almighty.
Yaar -	friend

Author's Other Novels

Ordeal Of Innocence

"You know that Sukanya has given birth to a daughter."

"Yes, I know. It's a good thing to happen. You must rejoice on this occasion."

"But what if she is the root cause of my frustration?"

"What are you talking about?"

"That child is not mine."

How could one stormy night lead to a lifetime of tragedy and heartache?

Shashank and Sukanya are a happily married well-to-do Indian couple living in America. Their lives are perfect until the birth of their first child, Laxmi. Due to various misfortunes and misunderstandings, they become estranged and end up worlds apart. Will they ever be able to regain the life and love they shared together?

Jayanti M. Dalal's *Ordeal of Innocence* weaves a yarn of personal relationships with emotional despair and triumph to create a compelling narrative that resonates with Indian culture. Through Shashank and Sukanya, Dalal examines the precariousness of human relationships, whether they are through marriage, friendship, or family, and offers insight into the human spirit.

Follow Shashank and Sukanya as they struggle to survive an ordeal of innocence.

Bleeding Heights Of Kargil

"What is to be done with the dead bodies of these staunch Muslims extremists?"

"Sir, let' practise the policy of 'Tit for Tat'," *suggested one of the soldiers.*

"What do you mean?"

"Just as the extremists killed our soldiers and amputated their limbs and displayed barbaric traits, let's answer them in their own style. We will kill the hostages, too." Said Captain Sharad Sathe revengefully.

"Then, what should we do with the dead bodies of the Pakistani terrorists that are lying here and there?"

"We should give them a respectful burial. In spite of our requests to Pakistan, they are not ready to take the responsibility of the dead bodies of their soldiers." Said Colonel Ravindranath.

The novel 'Bleeding Heights of Kargil' touch upon the issue of cross-border terrorism in the name of religion. Mr. Jayanti M. Dalal impeccably describes how the terrorist outfits recruits young men and systematically become the victims of phoney religious propaganda and allurements wine, women and money.

His characteristic of writing novels on problems affecting the masses today creates an interesting account of how a young Hindu man is converted to Islam and ultimately cast as a hardcore terrorist. The author presents a vivid description of the terrain of Indo-Pak border and the terrorist camps operative in Pakistan occupied Kashmir (PoK). The detailed account of Kargil war brings alive the bloody scenes of war.

No religion including Islam teaches killings of innocents for its spread. The reality is that, the Islam is not in danger, but the world peace is in the gravest danger today. This is the time, when all the democracies of the world must unite to crush such religious fundamentalists from the surface of the earth. If the issue is not tackled immediately, many thousands would lose their lives all over the world.

JACKPOT

Meena begged Malay to quit his racing and drinking habits. It was ruining their marital relationship. The domestic quarrels that were once manageable for both of them to reconcile with each other were now beyond control. Meena's strong protests against his racing habits were tackled by him with the habitual answer,

"Let me win a big jackpot and I will stop going to the races completely."

"Doesn't he understand that he will spend all his life by the time he wins a jackpot? He is obsessed with this vice to such an extent that he is beyond his senses now," she used to mumble in despair.

Meena's demand for money to run the household frequently resulted in ugly abuses and hitting. The domestic matters now became affairs for public discussion with the neighbours having a kick out of it. Often the quarrels took a different turn, more serious and more grim, with Malay taunting Meena of her affair with Manoj.

About the Author

Mr. Jayanti M. Dalal, B.Sc. (Hons), a businessman and writer, was born in Kapadwanj, Gujarat, India, on December 28, 1935. Since his days in school in Umreth of Gujarat State, he took a keen interest in reading a large number of fiction and short stories available in the village library. To date, twenty-five books, including fourteen novels, five collections of short stories, and six compilations, have been published.

He was the first Gujarati writer whose Gujarati novel 'Ankhane Sagpan Ansoona' was translated into English, entitled 'Ordeal of Innocence', and, for the first time, published in the USA in 2005 by Ivy House Publishing Group. To promote his novel, he visited United Kingdom, United States, and Canada in May 2005.

He was honored as "Gaurav of Gujarat" **by the Hon'ble Shri Narendra Modi, the former Chief Minister of Gujarat, India and now Prime Minister**

of India. He complimented to Mr. Jayanti M. Dalal, saying: "It was really heartening to note that a Gujarai Novelist's work is being published in English, and that too in USA. This is 'GAURAV' of Gujarat. Please accept my heartiest congratulations. The subject of your forthcoming novel 'Spatial Echoes' is also very much important, I convey my best wishes to you on publication of the novel."

He was vice president of the All India Plastics Manufacturers' Association (AIPMA) during 1984-85, has been nominated to fellowship in the United Writers Association, and has served on the fourteen-member working committee that prepared the book Introduction to Plastic Furniture in the Country, published by the Ministry of Industry of the government of India in 1988. Dalal has been an honorary editor of a trade publication, Acrylic News (1996), Porwad Bandhu (a quarterly Gujarati community magazine, 1980-2001), and Kala Gurjari (a Gujarati quarterly magazine on art, 1993-1996 and 1999-2001).

He was the pioneer who introduced acrylic furniture to India. In 1997 and in 2013, Dalal was felicitated by a number of prominent people from diverse sections of society in a Diamond Jubilee function organized to celebrate his sixtieth birthday and also in a Platinum Jubilee function organized to celebrate his seventy-fifth birthday. A twenty-minute documentary of his life was presented and was well-appreciated. The life sketch of Mr. Jayanti M. Dalal "Bhavatavini Vate" and "Jindagino Dastavej" was released during the Diamond Jubilee and Platinum Jubilee functions. Frequently, he is invited to appear on the All India Radio and Television network for talk shows and interviews on Gujarati literature and the acrylic industry.

His biography is featured in more than thirty national and international directories. Today, Dalal still writes enthusiastically. *For him, acrylic has been his throbbing heart and literature has remained his oxygen.*